SHADOWS
BEND

SHADOWS BEND

*A Novel of the Fantastic
and Unspeakable*

DAVID BARBOUR and
RICHARD RALEIGH

ACE BOOKS, NEW YORK

SHADOWS BEND

An Ace Book / published by arrangement with
the authors

PRINTING HISTORY:
Ace edition / October 2000

The Penguin Putnam Inc. World Wide Web site address is
http://www.penguinputnam.com

Check out the ACE Science Fiction & Fantasy
newsletter and much more at Club PPI!

ISBN: 0-441-00765-1

ACE®
Ace Books are published by
The Berkley Publishing Group, a division of Penguin Putnam Inc.,
375 Hudson Street, New York, New York 10014.
ACE and the "A" design are trademarks belonging to
Penguin Putnam Inc.

PRINTED IN THE UNITED STATES OF AMERICA

10   9   8   7   6   5   4   3   2   1

For
Howard Phillips Lovecraft
Robert Ervin Howard
&
Clark Ashton Smith
The Three Musketeers of *Weird Tales*

And For
Tori Amos
Singing in the R.A.I.N.N.

With special thanks to
L. Sprague de Camp
without whom this tale would still be lurking in the shadows.

That is not dead which can eternal lie,
And with strange aeons even death may die.

—Abdul Alhazred, *Necronomicon*

Part One

KACHINA

1

IN THE STIFLING CONFINES of the earthbound bus, Lovecraft was dreaming of the stars. Constellations beaming their lucid light through the cavernous blackness of space, and touching, ever so briefly, the eye and the soul of some hapless traveler in the night— their light was ancient, millions and billions of years old. Even in his dream, Lovecraft had the lingering presence of rationality to know that the bright birth of a nova might come from the demise of an ancient star as old as time itself. The old and the new, beaming their brilliant lumens through the absolute cold of space, their rays piercing the dark silence like the birthing cries of an infant.

The baby four rows ahead was crying again, its high-pitched wail cutting through the rumble of the engine. The rattles and squeaks that had become a sort of steady, soothing background drone marking the bus's progress through the desert suddenly seemed to drop away, and the wailing played rhythmically up and down the register; it became an oddly wet sound, with a guttural, almost gurgling quality behind it, as if the infant were slowly drowning in its own fluids, and it was the humanness of this noise—no, not the humanness, but the fleshy, animal quality—that was so disconcerting to Lovecraft. Disconcerting enough to puncture his sleep and wake him into a restless alertness.

He was certain that every one of the passengers was as disturbed as he was, and yet they seemed to ignore the crying. They sat in some dormant state, jostled rhythmically this way and that until they were occasionally bumped in some unexpected way and startled out of their semiconsciousness. The heat felt good to him, but the other passengers all gleamed with a sheen of oily sweat that reminded him of the fat dripping from a capon on a rotisserie; their heads lolled, and even in their torpid faces he could read not so much the lack of consciousness as a lack of intelligence, a stupor.

Lovecraft himself was keenly awake now with anxiety. His discomfort with the infant's crying made him suddenly aware of the movements in his own throat, and he swallowed and swallowed again to clear the dryness from his windpipe. The bus was crossing another patch of bad pavement, and with all the windows open because of the heat, the dust from the front tires rose high enough to waft in.

Lovecraft was uneasy, and he unconsciously fingered the contents of his watch pocket. He had almost tuned out the baby's wailing with the force of his own awareness of it, but now he was convinced that his thoughts had become somehow too palpable. The quiet man who had gotten on at the last stop had been watching him rather too closely, and Lovecraft was certain now that the man could actually sense what he was thinking. He stole another quick glance over his left shoulder. There he was, but was it a row closer now? Had he moved forward since the last time he'd checked? Lovecraft had never looked closely at the man's face, since he had not wanted to meet his eye, but this time he seemed to be staring out the window, and Lovecraft examined his features a bit more attentively. There was something very wrong. Was it his vision, or the rattle of the bus? He couldn't seem to get the man's face in focus. Each time Lovecraft blinked to clear his vision the man seemed to have abruptly tilted his head or made it tremble somehow, leaving an image as uncertain as a reflection on the surface of a rippling pool. Lovecraft turned away, quickly, as the man's eyes suddenly shifted to the front of his face, although he had not seemed at all to move his head.

Sweat flowed with a sudden profusion down from Lovecraft's hairline, and he tasted its acrid salt in the corner of his mouth. The thing in his pocket seemed to become suddenly heavier.

And the wailing—it went on even as the infant's mother gave it a few token maternal thumps. As she lifted the baby so that it faced backwards, and continued to pat its back and its head, the crying infant suddenly saw the odd man at the rear of the bus and abruptly choked into silence. It sounded like a single hiccup, and the quiet that followed was soothing, but then suddenly ominous.

Lovecraft swallowed once again and tried to calm his racing thoughts, but now, as the infant's dark eyes focused on his own, he was suddenly sure that the soul behind the gaze was not the child's but that of the odd man whose reflection, he knew, was that tiny pinpoint in the infant's alarmingly wide orbs.

The infant cried out again, opening its mouth wider than humanly possible—like a serpent, he thought—and Lovecraft suddenly saw that it was not an infant at all. The slimy pinkness of its throat dripping with threads of saliva and mucus, the wet, sucking noise that ran like an undercurrent through its wailing, the gurgly sound like black water in a cavern, the shrill echo ringing beyond the register of human ears—they were all the mark of Cthulhu's spawn.

THEY WERE IN the middle of the town before he even realized it. Lovecraft started awake, jerking bolt upright in his seat. He had been asleep again, though he did not remember nodding off.

The infant and its mother were already outside, and both of them looked up at him through the open window, smiling quite innocently, the infant nearly radiant with the joy of being released from the hot confines of the bus.

Lovecraft stood, feeling the cramp in his lower back, and briefly checked the contents of his pockets under the guise of stretching himself before he stepped into the aisle and took a quick look back. The odd man was gone. Indeed, the bus had cleared out and the only one remaining on board was the ruddy-faced driver, who was slowly stuffing his pipe with tobacco.

"Beg your pardon, old chap," said Lovecraft. "Would this humble town be Cross Plains, perchance?"

"Yessir," the driver said rather smugly, "as plain as the nose on one's face. Next leg is more of the same, so you might get out for a stretch and a drink. Word to the wise, sir."

"Thank you. But I believe I have reached my destination."

"Then I wish you well, sir." The driver managed a successful draw of his pipe and blew his first plume of putrid smoke, his eyes opening wider in what seemed to be surprise. "May God go with you," he said.

Lovecraft turned away and took the three steps down into Cross Plains, Texas, this unwitting way station. It wasn't much of a town, just a place where some roads and power lines seemed to converge for no apparent reason. The few buildings—storefronts and professional addresses—all faced each other, as if to keep the reality of the empty landscape at bay.

A one-horse town if there ever was one, Lovecraft thought. He wouldn't have been surprised to see a hitching post outside the local bar, or a water trough outside a blacksmith and livery stable. He could imagine bowlegged cowboys in leather chaps strutting down the single dusty street, arms akimbo with their fingers twitching just over the handles of their pearl-handled six-guns. Out in the distance, beyond the last building, along the western horizon, there would be the silhouette of a black dust plume—bandits armed with Winchesters and shotguns, riding in to have their last shoot-out with the local sheriff, whose five-pointed star of justice sparkled like a diamond on his vest. The streets would suddenly clear, and in the silence, broken only by the skittering of a tumbleweed, the sheriff would stand alone, squinting toward the horizon to see his death approaching slowly, inevitably, toward Cross Plains, Texas, and he would watch as the riders drew closer and closer—four of them, in black hoods that hid their tiny, animal eyes and the slimy complexions of their inhuman . . .

Lovecraft blinked. What was he thinking? This was Cross Plains, Texas—his stop. There was nothing here but a terminal, a general store, clapboard buildings with paint long flaked away into the desert dust. He shook his head and stepped out of the street into the general store, where the sudden and comforting dimness made him pause momentarily to let his eyes grow calm.

"EXCUSE MY INTRUSION, but might you be the proprietor of this establishment?"

"Eh?" said the old man. He looked up, somewhat startled by the Yankee accent. The man by the entrance was tall and gangly, with a jaw that seemed to have grown ripe, almost to bursting, in the heat. He wore a white suit, rather soiled and rumpled, and a bow tie that was absurd, he thought, mismatched like the old leather suitcase and the cane, which seemed more decorative than necessary. "You ain't from these parts, eh? Waddaya want?"

"I wish to inquire, kind sir, first, about the price of your pork and beans."

"How many cans you want?"

"Three would be adequate."

The old man named an inflated price, and the man in the white suit seemed to think it was fine. A Yankee who thought he was a Redcoat, no less, from that accent. He actually thumped the suitcase on the counter, kicking up a bit of trail dust, and opened it up like a salesman—he didn't look clever enough to be a flimflam man. The old man expected him to produce some newfangled potato peeler or some new brand of axle grease, of which he already had plenty, but the man only put the cans of pork and beans in the case and shut it again.

"I would also appreciate, my dear sir," he said, fastening the buckles, "directions to the abode of one Robert Howard. Robert E. Howard."

"Bobby's place, eh? He's a published writer, you know."

"I am cognizant of that fact, sir."

"Ain't you just?" said the old man, and he proceeded to give a set of directions designed to take the Yankee a few miles out of the way, on foot, through rattlesnake and scorpion country. "Sure you don't need nothin' to drink with them beans?" he asked when he was done. "You might be eatin' them real soon."

"That will not be necessary."

"Maybe some boots? Those city shoes ain't made for hard walkin'."

"I assure you, sir, I have made all the purchases I require."

"Well, good riddance to ya, then."

"And to you, my dear old chap."

DUSK APPROACHED MORE QUICKLY than Lovecraft had expected, and with it a cold wind from the west pushed by a front of dark clouds. Lovecraft had never been in a place so vast, so empty that one could watch the very weather roll across the heavens, a mass of clouds that stretched from horizon to horizon in a slow boil, moving forward in barely perceptible increments, which he knew was actually a fantastic speed; in the far west the sun still flickered a reddish orange and the clouds looked as if they were burning, the flames slowly dying out into maroon, deep purple, purple-gray, and then finally to a shade of not-quite-black as the last of the sun extinguished itself and was gone. If this is how the light should ever die, thought Lovecraft, it is a beauty to which I would not object. If this be the final whimper, at the end, then it redeems us with its beauty. He paused to watch a while longer; by now he had the uneasy and somewhat annoyed realization that the old man had given him an unnecessarily circuitous route to the Howard house. Perhaps it was because the locals were accustomed to driving, or going by horseback, he thought, but more likely it was simply the old man's unpleasant character.

From his long habit of wandering the alleys and back streets of Providence at night, Lovecraft had acquired an acute sense of direction, and now, although he was somewhat disoriented by the very openness of the landscape, he knew he had returned, for the third time, to the same bearing on which he had started. His feet hurt in his narrow shoes, which he had to admit, were not exactly designed for the rocky terrain. For a while he had been thirsty, but now, with his body heat siphoned, nearly torn from him by the wind, it was the cold that was beginning to make him truly uncomfortable. He scanned the sky, shivering involuntarily, watching the mass of clouds grow darker and approach like a mobile, alien landscape.

The wind grew fiercer, in gusts that had begun to pick up the sandy soil and fling it at him. Lovecraft squinted. There was the house as Howard had described it in his letters, in the confines of a picket fence. Lovecraft smiled and hunched his shoulders into the wind just as the first jags of lightning flashed across the distant western sky. He counted, automatically—one, two, three, four—past fifteen before he heard the dull rumble of thunder, and then, shortly afterward, the closer hissing of approaching rain. He walked more quickly, squinting into the wind as the last grayish gap in the western clouds was blotted out and darkness fell so abruptly it seemed a curtain had suddenly fallen from the heavens.

There was something disquieting about the approaching storm, some lingering unease Lovecraft couldn't help but associate with the odd man on the bus. The lightning skittered along the bottom of the cloud bank as if it were stones of flint skipping an inverted lake; not one flash seemed directed at the earth. And the wind, the clouds—they seemed to be coming from all directions, converging upon him. He thought it must surely be some optical illusion, since weather, he knew, always moved in colossal swirls about the globe. But was it mere coincidence or some preternatural force that made him the very epi-center of this mounting tempest?

The air was suddenly loud with the crackle of hail. White dots jit-tered madly, just barely visible in the distance before him. Lovecraft had scarcely the time to lift his suitcase over his head before the hail-storm reached him, so fierce that its buffeting of marble-sized ice balls nearly tore the case from his hands. He ran, as quickly as he could, through the open gate in the fence and up the steps of the porch as another flash of lightning, this one nearby, finally made its explosive connection with the earth.

THE THUMPING ON the door was barely audible after the explosion of lightning and the deafening thunder that followed. Howard was still blinking back the purple afterimages he saw projected on the page in the typewriter, his ears still numb and ringing, when he heard the banging, which was neither random nor regular enough to be the work of the wind. The electric lights flickered momentarily, and when they came on again, one of the bulbs remained dark.

"Poppa!" he called. "I think I hear someone at the door!"

Dr. Howard was already at the door, somewhat surprised to have a visitor at that hour in that weather. "I've got it, Bobby," he said. He turned the knob, and suddenly the door was wrenched from his hand and pushed inward by a fierce gust of wind; it pivoted all the way around on its hinges and slammed violently into the wall just as another bolt of lightning cast a strange silhouette through the flimsy screen door. Dr. Howard took an involuntary step backwards. The figure in the door was at least seven feet tall, with a wide, rectangular thing where its head should have been. Some odd appendage or proboscis hung from the left side of its head, angled toward the ground in the middle of a pendulous swinging motion.

"Bobby!" Dr. Howard grabbed the door, which had knocked chips out of the wall, and was about to slam it shut again when the figure in the doorway removed its rectangular head and revealed itself to be a tall man in a white suit carrying a suitcase and a cane.

"How do you do?" said the stranger. "Howard Phillips Lovecraft. And you must be Dr. Isaac Howard."

"W-what did you say, Mister?"

"I am a friend of your son, though I'm afraid only in epistolary fashion. I am here to see Robert E. Howard, if I may."

"Why, come in," said Dr. Howard, gathering his wits.

"My sincerest apologies for my uncivilized appearance," said Love-craft as he opened the screen door and stepped inside, scattering tiny beads of melting hail around him. "I'm afraid I've had the misfor-tune..." He dropped his suitcase and walking stick and, as they thumped to the floor, very slowly raised his hands.

"Who are you?"

Dr. Howard turned to see his son in the doorway of the study, cock-ing the hammer of the old single-action .45 he kept for occasions like this one. "Bobby, this stranger here says he's a friend of yours," said Dr. Howard.

"I asked you who you were," said Howard. "I suggest you answer while you can, Mister."

The man's flesh seemed nearly blue against his soiled white clothes, and he seemed to have been out in the storm for quite a while, or perhaps he was terrified of the gun, because he was shiver-ing so violently it seemed unlikely he could keep his hands up. He had an odd expression on his face, but Howard couldn't tell if it was terror or some weird and maniacal amusement. His lips moved hesi-tantly for a split second, and then, in an entirely unconvincing attempt at a Southern drawl, he said, "Howdy there, Two-Gun Bob."

Howard and his father looked at each other. The Doctor's expres-sion suggested he thought they had an escapee from some asylum, but Howard's eyes suddenly went wide, and his jaw swung open. "Love-craft!" he said. "How did—What in the Sam Hill are you doin' out here?"

"I must speak with you immediately, Bob. It is a matter of the utmost importance, whose ramifications may be far more profound than we can guess."

Howard motioned for him to put his hands down with a wave of the pistol, then thought better of it and carefully uncocked it. "You're dyin' of consumption, man, come in! Father, this is my good friend, Howard Phillips Lovecraft. HP for short."

"Well, pleased to meet you," said Dr. Howard, taking Lovecraft's hand to give it a firm and rather quick shake. "My God, you're cold as a snake in February! Get comfortable inside, and I'll fetch you some hot coffee and a towel to dry off."

Lovecraft joined Howard in the dim interior of the living room, where, despite the storm still rumbling outside, the air had retained a musty quality. Howard put his .45 down on the coffee table and took a captain's chair, motioning for his friend to sit on the davenport. Lovecraft removed his hat, tapping off the small beads of hail still trapped on the brim, and placed it on the cushion to his left. He could see, immediately, that Mrs. Howard had been incapacitated for a long time. The room was obviously in need of a woman's touch; it was littered with the evidence of men making do without the requisite feminine supervision: medical journals, general magazines, and even a few issues of recent pulp journals lay haphazardly in piles at the sides of the chairs in which Howard and his father habitually read them. Every surface needed dusting, the curtains hung subtly askew, telltale traces of ash lingered where an ashtray had been hastily moved, a pair of boots stood at attention under a chair.

"I apologize for the rude welcome, HP, but you can see for yourself that we weren't exactly expectin' guests."

"I quite understand."

"So what brings you to my neck of the woods? You say it's important."

"I've journeyed here, Bob, because I believe you are the only mortal alive whom I can trust to assist me without condemning me as a madman. The most horrific events have transpired, and I do sincerely believe that even more evil things are in store." Lovecraft hugged himself and shivered.

"Take off that wet coat, HP."

Lovecraft removed his jacket just as Dr. Howard returned with a towel draped over one arm, carrying a tray with a pot of coffee and a few mismatched pieces of a service. The aroma of fresh coffee made Lovecraft suddenly weak, and he slumped back on the davenport.

"It was already brewin'," said Dr. Howard. "I say you'll need plenty of it. You've got the look of hypothermia about you, HP."

"Thank you, Doctor." Lovecraft dried himself with the towel and hunched over the steaming cup of coffee the Doctor poured for him.

"Sugar? I'm afraid we're fresh outta cream."

"Thank you," Lovecraft said again, and while the Doctor poured for himself and his son, Lovecraft spooned one, two, three, four, five spoonfuls of sugar into his cup as the two men watched, spellbound.

"Like a little coffee with your sugar there, HP?"

"I admit I do like it rather on the sweet side."

"You'll have to excuse us makin' do like this," said Dr. Howard. "But I'm afraid . . ."

"Father," said Howard, "I already told HP about Ma's condition. I don't mean to be rude, but could you leave us alone for a while?"

"GO ON, GO ON, then," Dr. Howard said, getting to his feet. "I'll step upstairs and check on your mother. Lightnin' musta woke her up anyhow."

"How is she faring?" Lovecraft asked when the Doctor had left the room. "Your last report was laden with rather pessimistic sentiments."

"She hasn't gotten any better, HP, but I'm still hopin' to God that she'll pull through in the end."

"I'm sorry," said Lovecraft.

They sat in silence for a moment, sipping their coffee. It suddenly grew quiet outside, and Lovecraft realized that he had grown so accustomed to the roar of the hailstorm that it was only now, as the hard sounds of the icefall turned to the more soothing hiss of rain, that he noticed it again. Outside, the storm seemed to lull, though the rain was a hard one and lightning continued to flash periodically, farther and farther away.

"Flash floods," said Howard. "There'll be hell to pay when this freak storm's over."

"Indeed." The heat of the syrupy coffee made Lovecraft sigh with relief.

"What is it, HP? You look like a harried man."

"I'm afraid my mental faculties have been diminished," said Lovecraft, at length. "I've had the most unpredictable and irregular flights of paranoiac fancy of late. I daresay I might have begun to believe the fantastic contents of my own fiction, so do bear with me if my imagination seems to have gotten rather out of hand."

"All right," said Howard. "Why don't you start from the beginnin'?"

"Well," said Lovecraft, "my current plight originated in my abode in Providence." He poured himself more coffee and added another surprising quantity of sugar before he took a preliminary sip and, satisfied, began his long narrative.

2

"As you know from our long correspondence, I am a man of semi-invalid constitution and therefore while away the vast majority of my time in the confines of my humble domicile. I am nocturnal by habit, though I will occasionally compromise my odd daily routines to fit the needs of my visitors or hosts.

"A fortnight ago I received a package from my friend Samuel Loveman, whom I have mentioned to you on occasion. Periodically, he has presented me with various curios and artifacts for which he knows I will have some proclivity or fascination. Over the years he has given me such things as a Mayan statuette, an *ushabti* figurine from an ancient Egyptian tomb, and a wooden monkey from Bali. So it was with no surprise—indeed, it was with great delight—that I opened his most recent package to find, within, an item which I immediately recognized as a Kachina doll, a small rendition of one of the strange gods of the Hopi or the Navajo, I believe. I must confess that this particular type of Kachina was novel to me, but its stylized headdress and the features which had been depicted thereupon were startlingly familiar to my eye and would have been to anyone even passingly cognizant of my Cthulhuvian scribblings. This particular Kachina had the unmistakable squidlike face and the distinct peripheral tentacles of one of the Old Ones of whom I write.

"I was not alarmed at first. Indeed, my initial reaction was of amplified delight because I took the evidence before me to signify an unusually thoughtful gift. I believed Loveman had conspired with some regional Indian artist to mold the features of this particular Kachina to his specifications thereby to provide me with an amusing distraction in the guise of a folk artifact.

"You can imagine, then, that it was with genuine eagerness that I unfolded the accompanying missive and began devouring its contents. Loveman is a pleasant and lively correspondent, always full of news and good cheer, so it was with profound alarm that I read the terse and tense lines of his letter. I cannot quote them to you, for I had occasion only to glance at them once with a haste born of urgency, but the gist of Loveman's note was that the Kachina had, in fact, been delivered to him by a mysterious messenger who had mistaken him to be me. There was some confusion at first, owing to the fact that the messenger had mangled my surname into Loveman's. But there was no mistaking the first two initials, HP, or the messenger's particular knowledge of my weird writings, although he seemed to have read them in some other ghastly language.

"Loveman wrote that this messenger's master, a man even more mysterious, had possessed the artifact for decades, suffering tragedy upon tragedy owing to its evil influence. The unholy thing had plagued him so with misfortune and otherworldly nightmares that now, suspecting that some creature from one of those very nightmare realms had manifested itself in the flesh to stalk him from the shadows, and thus threaten not only his sanity but his very life, he had forwarded it to me, knowing that I, of all mortals, would know the proper means of its disposal. Moreover, this master wanted dearly to meet the author of the weird Cthulhuvian fantasies in the flesh to discuss some arcane lore about the Kachina's miraculous healing properties, about which he hoped I would be able to illuminate him.

"Of course, Loveman took this man to be another of the many crackpots who mistakenly believe my tales to be true, but there was something sinister about the messenger that made Loveman take the man more seriously. Loveman did not divulge to him my whereabouts, he said, for concern over my safety or at least to protect me from unwanted annoyance. But, he said, the messenger told him that his master was intent upon visiting me in the wee hours of August 8. Why this particular date was a mystery to him, but Loveman thought I should be made aware, just in case some lunatic took it upon himself to make good on the promise. He believed the man who portrayed himself as the messenger was, in fact, the master of whom he spoke—since this style of disingenuousness is common among irrational admirers of the weird bards—so he believed the man's need for direct intercourse with me had been met through association, through him, and yet the lingering unease had compelled him to write to me. That was all.

"Of the Kachina, I must tell you something else. It was a mere foot in height, depicting a figure in the midst of some unholy dancelike contortion, and its head, or its headdress, was cylindrical, with a smaller cylindrical protrusion that served as a nose, holes for eyes or perhaps only the sockets of eyes, and a stylized collar of jagged scalloping. The painting on its face had been meticulously handled in red, black, and white.

"I was, by turns, amused, repelled, and troubled by Loveman's letter, but in the end I must say the amusement won out, leaving me to believe it all the melodramatic product, and perhaps the twisted generosity, of some obviously deluded reader. I placed the Kachina upon the mantel, betwixt a few like artifacts, some of them being the ones I mentioned, and returned again to one of my tedious revising chores for my pestilent and inarticulate client, de Castro, whose bad writing, I'm afraid, haunts me more annoyingly than any ghost. Even the troubling date of August 8 eventually dissolved from my consciousness by the end of the evening.

"In the following three days I endured most vivid nightmares, far more disturbing than any I have ever suffered before—and as you well know, I have both enjoyed and suffered the most unearthly of dreams.

These were singularly unique in that they seemed to correlate directly with the arrival of the Kachina, which now rested in a sinister light above my fireplace. I need not belabor a description of these nightmares, because you already know them well from my Cthuluvian tales.

"Near twilight of the third day, as I was taking my customary stroll in the lengthening shadows of the trees that line the streets of my neighborhood, the subtle but persistent intuition came upon me that I was being watched by the unseen eyes of strangers. Several times I quickly turned my head and managed a half glimpse of some persons or some sinister beings peering at me from around the corners of buildings or around the trunks of the more ancient trees. I retreated in haste back to my home, and later, as I peeked nervously from behind the drapes of my bedroom window, I found my anxiety quickly overshadowing my rationality. I was certain, dead certain, beyond the palest shadow of a doubt, that the entities stalking me were connected to the presence of that blasphemous Kachina doll. I decided that even if it was a mere paranoiac fancy guiding me, I had endured more than enough. Quickly, I approached the Kachina and lifted its unnatural weight with the intention of banishing it from my house. I learned, soon enough, that the material of the Kachina's head was terra-cotta because, in my anxious state, I fumbled and dropped the unlucky thing upon the floor. It cracked neatly in two, almost as if it had had a seam, and when I bent to pick up the pieces, I perceived the raw coloring and texture of the inner surface.

"But it was not the Kachina, ultimately, that drove me here, Bob. When I picked up the doll to make an attempt at reassembly, I noticed it was markedly lighter, as if something were missing. The balance of the missing weight might have been made up if the doll's head had been filled with fine sand of the type the Hopi use in their ritual sand paintings—or perhaps something even weightier, like pellets of buckshot. I curiously surveyed the floor to see if anything had fallen out, looking hither and thither, and just on the point of giving up, I let out a gasp of horror at the obscene thing I saw before me. It was nearly invisible upon the floor, for the light in my room was dim, but also because it was remarkably small and seemed, additionally, to have taken on both the coloring and the contours of the floor itself. At first, I pried at it with my thumbnail, thinking it had adhered to the wood, but then I quickly realized it was its deadweight that made it so. The Artifact, as I will call it, was a rounded triangle, exceptionally flat and only the diameter of a shirt button, but for its dimensions it was more massive than anything in this world has a right to be. As I weighed it in my palm, the thing became the color of my flesh and even mimicked the fine filaments of the lines on my skin. It was slightly warm to the touch. I lifted it closer to my eyes to examine its surface, and that is when I realized, with dire certainty, that dark and dangerous things were ahead.

"For the image on the artifact was the face of Cthulhu, exactly as I have described it.

"In my anxiety and apprehension, I do not know how it was possible for me to fall asleep that dawn, but later, shortly after the sky had just blued with the rising sun, I awoke, dripping in a gelid sweat, from a singularly horrific night terror.

"In my childhood, as you know, I was constantly tormented by recurrent nightmares in which a monstrous race of entities I called Night Gaunts would clutch me by the stomach and bear me up through the black air over towers of the most horrible, dead cities. They would drop me through a gray void, down onto the needlelike pinnacles of mountains miles below, and in the midst of my relentless plunge to those jagged and toothlike peaks, I would start awake and have no desire ever to sleep again.

"This night I had a similar dream—it was the lean, black Night Gaunts, with their rubbery bat wings and barbed tails that visited me again. The flock of Night Gaunts tormented me like Harpies, and then, after their ritual tickling of my belly, the minions lifted me in their claws and flew with me high, following their master and his two captains, who flapped their way before us in a pointed V, toward some nameless range of precipices in the remote distance. But this time, unlike the other occasions, the dream ended differently—they did not drop me upon the jagged peaks below. The minions deposited me atop a bleak, oblong plateau, and then scattered to reconfigure themselves, flapping madly until they formed a black vulturous circle in the steely gray sky overhead. And the master of the Night Gaunts, with his two captains, alighted before my prostrate form, hideously folding their leathery wings and proceeding to approach me upon their scratchy claws.

"The Night Gaunts are entirely faceless—indeed, that is one of the qualities that makes them so terrifying to me—but on this occasion, as the trinity loomed before me, they thrust forward the obscene blankness where their faces should have been, and though they were as featureless as ever, I had the sudden, disturbing intuition that I knew who they were. Some instinctual part of me recognized their faceless faces, and the clutching terror of that realization was what woke me.

"Two nights running, I had had this dream, each night the realization growing stronger and somehow more desperate. But on this third occasion, as the unholy trinity stood before me, their featureless faces took actual shape. I say the master of the Night Gaunts was a he, but in actually, as it loomed over me, leering at my helplessness, readying itself to utter its blasphemous words, its face was that of my *deceased mother*. And its two captains—they wore the guises of *my aunts*.

"The terror those faces invoked within me was truly unendurable. There was something so uncannily *accurate* about their features, something so palpably *evil*, that I found myself teetering precariously on the very brink of madness. I was at the verge of a profound and unholy realization, the very thought of which would drive me forever into the other side of sanity as, simultaneously, it would drive me over the precipice to my death. I looked at this black trinity for that final clue, and the master opened his mouth and silently formed the syllables of the words that would be my final undoing. The lips moved, drawing closer to me until they filled my vision, and as the first wet syllable formed itself, I bolted upright in my bed, too terrified even to scream.

"When I had gotten my wits about me, I realized I had been awakened by a rustling noise emanating from the sitting room. I rose qui-

etly, and with my fire poker clenched in my trembling hands, I cautiously stepped into the shadowy chamber, peering fearfully about.
There, in the shadows, lurked three dark figures with glowing eyes.
The instant I perceived them, two of them blurred blackly inward to
the left and right, vanishing without a trace. The one in the center
seemed to take on a darker visage, as if it had absorbed the other two,
and its eyes glowed a brighter, nacreous green. I confess to you that
my legs were trembling, and like so many of my own weak heroes, I
was on the verge of swooning; but I somehow drew up the courage to
lift the poker over my head and take an aggressive step forward. Then
the black, hooded thing leaped at me, engulfing me, and I bolted
upright in my bed, once again, covered in a cold sweat.

"I had been dreaming. I had dreamt that first awakening, for when I
paused, this time for a longer duration, to let my racing pulse grow
reasonably calm, I heard once again the rustling noises from the sitting room. Now I did not know if I was still trapped in the world of
dream, whether this waking was, itself, a false one. This time, I chose
not the heroic course, but quickly dressed and packed my suitcase and
travel bag.

"The remainder of my time in Providence is difficult for me to
recall. I know I wandered the length and breadth of the deserted city
with lurking shadows constantly on my heels. I cannot clearly distinguish between dream and memory and fancy here, for I was uncertain,
that entire duration, of my psychic state. On the one hand I felt the
constant possibility of yet another false waking, relegating my experience to yet another layer of dream. On the other hand I believed none
of it had been a dream, but merely brief lapses of memory, and that the
Night Gaunts and the bleak, black world of my nightmare was entirely
real. I half recall passing the Halsey mansion on Prospect Street
because I heard an alien gibbering issuing from within. I recall haunt-
ing the cemetery of the Episcopal Cathedral of St. John for a time,
winding my way among the fog-enshrouded headstones and the mau-
solea as I heard, and perhaps even saw, sinister half-things flittering at
the periphery of my overtaxed senses.

"Toward daybreak I found myself at the bus station with a ticket in my hand, boarding a westbound bus, and it was not until we had been under way for several hours that I realized I had eluded the monsters, whether they were of the dream world or of this one. And I realized, too, that I had purchased a ticket with my meager funds to come petition you for your assistance.

"For the duration of my trip, I have been lapsing in and out of states which I cannot clearly distinguish as contemplation, daydreaming, sleep, or hallucination. In Oklahoma, a mysterious man boarded the bus, a man whose face I could never make out, a faceless man. If he is an intruder from the world of the faceless Night Gaunts, I must still be dreaming, Bob, but I believe this mysterious odd man has been following me ever since, and that he is somewhere in Cross Plains, biding his time, even as I narrate this fantastic tale."

3

THERE WAS A LONG SILENCE punctuated sporadically by the sounds of the storm, which was gathering strength once again. The two men did not look at each other. Lovecraft sat on the edge of the davenport, hunched forward over his empty cup of coffee; Howard seemed to be looking somewhere into the distance, considering how to respond to the wild tale he had just heard.

"Have ya had supper?" Howard spoke so suddenly that Lovecraft started and jerked upright at the unexpected question.

"Why, no, I have not."

"Look," said Howard, "you dig through your stuff and fish out that Kachina of yours while I make us a fresh pot of coffee and rustle up some grub. I get the feelin' we're goin' to be talkin' for a long stretch here."

Howard rose stiffly to his feet and bent down to lift the coffee tray. "Know how to shoot?" he asked.

"In my opinion, the ability to pull a trigger is innate to all humans."

"Well," said Howard, "if that odd fellow should barge in while I'm in the kitchen, just ventilate him with that." He motioned, with his eyes, to the .45 on the coffee table.

"That was my intention, quite independent of your suggestion."

They both laughed uneasily, but the release of tension allowed Lovecraft to sit back at ease for a moment while his friend was absent in the kitchen. Now that he had told his story, he wondered again if he might be asleep at that very moment, dreaming the entire episode. He casually gave himself a pinch, smiling tiredly at his half joke.

In a little while, Howard's voice called him out to the dining room, and Lovecraft carried his travel bag over and joined him at the oak table for sandwiches and more coffee.

"Bob, let me tell you now that if you had recounted this very same tale to me, I would at this very moment be doubting your sanity. I know that you are more inclined to believe in things mystical and supernatural, but I fear my behavior, even in that light, may seem highly irrational."

"Show me the Kachina," said Howard. "I'd say your tale seems a tad tall, but we Texicans can smell the real thing."

Lovecraft opened the black-oilcloth satchel and produced the Kachina with the broken headpiece. Howard turned it back and forth, then upside down, in his hands, examining it from every angle before he put it down on its stand.

"Nothing remarkable about the handiwork," he said. "I've seen dozens just like it in curio shops. But you're right about the face, though it takes a little stretch to see your squid-faced Cthulhu in it."

"You don't seem inclined to believe me at this point." Lovecraft's tone held a hint of injury, although his face showed nothing. "Have you no confidence in me, even after our long correspondence?"

"I trust ya, HP. Now show me the Artifact. I think that'll prove your point for sure if anything will."

The act of reaching into his watch pocket sent a sudden jolt of pain through Lovecraft's side. He winced and paused momentarily.

"What's the matter?

"No. Nothing to be alarmed about. It's just a cramp." Lovecraft first placed the Artifact flat on his left palm, then turned it so that they could both watch the object slowly mimic the slightly bluish color of his flesh. Then he put it on the tabletop, and Howard gasped as it seemed to vanish into the grain of the wood. Both men felt the hair rising on their arms.

"It's like a damned chameleon!"

"Pick it up," said Lovecraft.

Howard leaned forward, getting partially out of his chair to reach for the Artifact, but before he could close his hand over it the whole world seemed to vanish in an incredible blue-white flash, and in the deafening roar that followed a window exploded inward, showering them both with fragments of glass and wood.

Lovecraft thought he was blind at first, but through the purple afterimages that ringed his vision, he could make out the faint glow of the Artifact on the tabletop. The house was dark, the electricity out, and he could hear a weak voice calling for Howard.

"Stay where you are," said Howard's voice. "That was a damned close one. Hit the cedar by the porch. I'll see to my mother and bring some light."

"Bobby! Bobby!" Mrs. Howard's voice called out again in the dark, and Lovecraft heard the burly man stumble off toward it.

But that was not all he heard. Lovecraft turned his head left and right to pinpoint the source of the other sound, but it did not vary. At first he thought it was simply a hallucination produced by the ringing in his ears after the thunderclap, but it was too irregular to be a ringing, and too low, too husky, like a whispered voice. He concentrated. He located the coffee cup in the dark and took a sip.

In a moment, as the shrill tone died down in his ears, he could almost make out the words—*Cthulhu fhtagn Cthulhu fhtagn Cthulhu fhtagn*. He had to laugh, even in his uneasiness—the words were from his own stories—it was clearly his overactive imagination unbridled by the stresses of the past several days. *Cthulhu fhtagn Cthulhu fhtagn Cthulhu fhtagn*. The demonic whisper was joined by another voice, then another, until their overlapping sounded like leaves rustling in the wind. Lovecraft pressed his palms flat over his ears, and still he could hear the murmuring. He looked around the room, or tried to in the pitch-blackness, but all he could see was the faint, greenish glow of the Artifact pulsing subtly brighter and brighter, growing more intense in unison with the sound. It was the source of the voices.

IN THE KITCHEN, Howard opened the utility drawer and picked out the flashlight by feel. When he switched it on nothing happened until he banged it once on the counter and jostled the batteries into place. The flashlight cast a distorted circle of dim light against the ceiling. Howard turned the beam to the floor and followed the patch of weak illumination into his mother's room, where Hester Howard was alone, propped up in her bed by a mass of pillows and bolsters; her face was turned away, toward the window, and if it hadn't been for the wheezing sound of her breathing, just barely audible over the rain, Howard would have thought her dead. With the flicker of distant lightning strobing constantly, Howard found he hardly needed the flashlight.

"Ma?" he said. "I'm here. Are ya all right?"

"Bobby, my baby," Mrs. Howard said, still facing the window. "Did the lightning give you a fright?"

"I'm fine, Ma. I think it hit one of the trees outside. We just lost our lights is all."

"Daddy says your good friend's come . . ." Her voice grew thick and phlegmatic for a moment and then cleared again. ". . . for a visit."

"Yes, Ma. It's Howard Phillips Lovecraft. The Yankee writer from Providence."

"He seems like a nice boy."

"He's older than me, Ma."

"Tell him I'm sorry I can't be a proper hostess."

"All right, Ma."

"Make him something to eat. A sandwich."

"I did, Ma."

"Daddy's got no sense about how to treat guests"—she coughed—
"so you got to do your best to show the proper hospitality." Mrs.
Howard turned her head, and the harsh, sporadic illumination of the
lightning made the lines of her face seem deeper and darker, like fis-
sures that cut all the way into her skull. "Don't let Daddy hog all the
talk, and tell him to watch his language."

"I will, Ma."

Mrs. Howard closed her eyes and seemed to lean farther back into
the pillows. Her health had been deteriorating since the complications
following her gallbladder surgery. Although the abcess along her inci-
sion had finally healed, even the trips out to Lubbock and to Amarillo
for the dry Panhandle air hadn't improved her lungs. In the damp of
the storm, she was sounding more congested than ever.

"Where's Father?" Howard asked, but in the next flash, he saw that
his mother had fallen asleep. He listened to her troubled breathing for
a moment before he tucked the blankets more securely around her and
gave her a light kiss on the forehead.

As Howard turned to leave the room, another strobe of lightning
illuminated the room, but this one cast an odd shadow across the far
wall. He froze momentarily and waited until the next flash revealed
the black silhouette of a man outside the window. Without hesitation,
Howard ran into the bathroom, where he threw open the wall cabinet
and picked up his .38 automatic, which he kept loaded for emergen-
cies. Flashlight in one hand and the pistol in the other, he walked
quickly out of the house, securing the door behind him so it would not
blow open in the wind.

The tree by the porch had been blasted into black slivers by a direct
strike. Portions were still smoldering, even in the heavy downpour,
and he could smell the pleasant odor of burnt cedar. Howard carefully
circled the porch, squinting to keep the rain out of his eyes. As he
edged around each corner, he swiveled into a firing stance, scanning in
front of him with the beam of the flashlight, which was almost useless.
In the black gaps between the lightning flashes, he could see nothing
at all.

Howard circled the house until he was sure no one was lurking outside, then he proceeded to the garage and directed the beam of the flashlight in through the loose door that creaked shrilly each time it swung back and forth. Something inside seemed to catch the light. He raised his pistol, taking aim at the patch of light. The next time the door swung open he saw them clearly—two glowing orbs at eye level, glaring out at him. Whatever it was let out a low, moaning sound and moved with surprising speed toward him. Howard stumbled backwards, his shout cut short by the dark figure that hurtled out at him. He pulled the trigger more out of instinct than intention, and the .38 coughed twice in his hand, the bullets tearing splinters through the weathered wood of the garage door. When he gathered his wits again he realized it must have been some trick of the light as the door swung at him. Nothing had emerged from the blackness of the garage.

With more caution, Howard crept up to the loose door. He paused, gathering courage, telling himself that what he had seen was more than just a reflection of the flashlight off some fragments of broken glass. He wanted to go back indoors and come back with help, but then what if it *was* only a trick of the light? He didn't want to be humiliated in front of his friend and his father. Taking a deep breath, then two, to calm himself, he crept up to the door and yanked it open, stepping aside to get a clear shot at whatever lay in waiting for him.

Nothing.

Howard lowered the gun, and it was then that the thing flew out of shadows, knocking him off his feet in a flurry of feathers. In his panic, he cried out, shooting off another round before, with a sudden acuity in his senses, he realized he had been bowled over by a barn owl even more frightened than himself.

Still on his back, Howard felt with his left hand for the flashlight he had dropped, but before he found it some other light appeared from above him, and he squinted.

He looked up to see a lantern swaying in the grip of a large, rugged hand. He heard laughter.

"Quite a hero," said his father's voice, finally. "Almost shot yerself a lil' ole hoot owl."

"Where were you?" Howard said, struggling to get to his feet without slipping. "You left Ma all by herself."

"Why, she had her best little boy to protect her," said Dr. Howard. "I don't like the mess of candles, so I just borrowed this here hurricane lamp from Mrs. Butler. What're you doin' outside?"

"I thought I saw someone."

"Yer always seein' things, boy."

"Outside Ma's window."

"A minute ago?"

"Yes."

"That was *me*, boy, just checkin' the property. We damn near got blasted to hell by that lightnin'. Why don't you just go back inside and see to yer delicate-lookin' Yankee friend, eh? Heat him up some *tea* or somethin'." The wind seemed to twist Dr. Howard's expression into one of disgust.

WHEN HE HAD DRIED OFF and returned to the kitchen, Howard was surprised to find Lovecraft illuminated by a flickering candle stub attached, with a drip of wax, to the lid of a tin can. He was sitting at the table, still sipping his coffee, his shoulders hunched together and his right foot shaking with anxiety.

"I see you found a candle," said Howard.

"My travel bag is equipped for such eventualities. I believe I heard shots outside."

"It was nothin'," said Howard. "Thought it might be the fellow you mentioned, but it was just my father prowlin' around. Everythin's fine." He went back into the kitchen for a moment and returned with two new candles on their holders. As he lit them from Lovecraft's candle stub, he saw the black-oilcloth satchel open on the table and couldn't help but notice the ivory handle of a knife protruding from a compartment.

"It's a flint knife of African origin," Lovecraft said, noticing his glance. "Another present from my friend, Loveman."

"Just what we need to cut the still-beating heart out of a lovely nubile virgin, eh, Lovecraft?"

"It's best to be prepared for the widest possible range of eventualities, Bob, although I'd be forced to defer the honors to you."

Howard's friendly slap on the back nearly knocked the more slender man out of his seat. "Sorry there," said Howard. "Didn't know my own strength."

"I shall take that as evidence of your past pugilism," Lovecraft said, coughing to clear the coffee that had gone down the wrong way. Now that they had other candles, he pinched his out, filling the room with the odor of burnt wax.

"Where's the Artifact?"

"On the table, where it was when you left."

Howard followed Lovecraft's gaze to the tabletop and saw the Artifact, nearly indistinguishable from the wood grain except for its faint contours, which seemed to be absorbing the light from the candle flames. The first time he tried to pick it up, his fingers could not grip it. As Lovecraft had done before him, he had to use his nails to pry its unexpected weight off the table.

"My God," said Howard. "This thing's got no right to weigh this much." He held it closer to his face, turning it to catch the light as its color changed to match his flesh. At the instant when its transformation was complete, it glowed momentarily, revealing the lines of its hideous face. "I've never seen anything like it."

"Nor have I."

"Let's go back out to the livin' room, HP. I'll light the heater to kill some of this damp. We got a lot more to discuss."

They left the dining room, leaving one candle behind. Howard discovered that when he held the other candle close to the Artifact its flame dimmed and grew smaller, as if the thing were robbing it of air, but when he drew the flashlight closer, its beam grew more intense.

"Exceedingly curious," said Lovecraft. "Those phenomena were ones I had not noticed."

"There's somethin' electrical about it." Howard put the candle down on the coffee table and walked into the shadows to ignite the heater. He heard a sharp exhalation from Lovecraft, and he swung the beam of light around to illuminate his face.

"My leg!" cried Lovecraft.

Confused, Howard moved the light over the contours of Lovecraft's body until the beam highlighted his outstretched leg. At first the white fabric of the pants looked mottled with shadows, but the shadows moved oddly, as if their two dimensions were rising into a third, and as they seemed to take on a tangible shape, Howard suddenly realized they were alive—insects—crawling spiders. Lovecraft cried out again, more shrilly, and frantically brushed them off until they were all scattered somewhere in the darkness of the room.

"Shine the light this way! Crush them!" said Lovecraft.

"They're only spiders, HP. Might as well leave 'em be." Howard tracked one with the flashlight until it disappeared under Lovecraft's hat. "I'll be God damned," he said, very quietly.

There was something very wrong with the hat.

The white pellets of hail on the hat should have melted long ago, but they were still there; the crown of the hat and its rim seemed to be trembling. Howard moved the light closer, then arced it from side to side, swearing under his breath. Tiny spiders, hundreds of them, thousands of them, had just hatched from the white pellets and were swarming all over the hat and around it, spreading across the table, covering everything in their path. Howard picked up a copy of *Weird Tales* and swatted at them, crushing dozens with each blow. "Gimme a hand, Lovecraft!"

"I—I—" Lovecraft's words changed abruptly into a cry of alarm, then shrill sounds of disgust as he swatted at his legs once again, brushing the tiny spiders off.

The insects were easy to see against his white suit, so when Howard could see no more, when it became futile to look for their tiny, skittering shapes in the inadequate light, he helped his panicked friend until Lovecraft finally sat down, shivering from both cold and repulsion. On the cover of his *Weird Tales*, the curvaceous body of the scantily clad maiden in distress was covered in the sticky gore of crushed spiders, plastered with still-trembling legs. Howard dropped the magazines, faceup, onto the coffee table. "Damn shame," he said. "That nice art-work ruint."

Lovecraft thought it no loss to have defaced the lurid covers, but he kept silent as he examined himself carefully in the dim candlelight.

"You're right," Howard said. "There's somethin' mighty strange goin' on here. It can't be just coincidence that all of this happened just after you walked in."

"You believe me now?"

"I believe what I see, Lovecraft. But that don't mean I can help ya with any of it."

"On the bus, I had more than ample time to review a wide range of possible strategies." He held himself, hunching his shoulders, and shivered involuntarily before he continued. "My conclusion was that I would ask you to be my ally and join me on a trip to visit Klarkash-Ton in California. I believe he would know how to dispose of this unholy thing."

"Clark Ashton Smith is a good choice, HP. He's smarter than the both of us. But I'm afraid I can't join you on this adventure." Howard went back to the interrupted task of lighting the heater.

"Bob, you must," said Lovecraft.

"I can't."

"I would not have come here if I thought any other option were available to me, Bob. I'm afraid you're my only resource."

"It's out of the question. I have to stay here to look after my mother." He handed the Artifact back without giving it another look, and Lovecraft quickly placed it back in his watch pocket.

"I understand your profound devotion and concern, Bob. I lost my mother not too long ago, and so I can empathize. But there's nothing you can do, nothing anyone can do for advanced tuberculosis."

"It ain't TB!"

They both stood momentarily in silence, equally stunned by what Howard had just said. Lovecraft looked down, hanging his head, like someone defeated, while Howard tried to compose himself.

A light glowed in the hall, and Dr. Howard entered, carrying the hurricane lamp, which illuminated the entire living room, though dimly. The darker shadows retreated.

"I'm sorry, HP," said Howard.

"You best be sorry your dear mother's dyin'," said Dr. Howard. "What the *hell* do you think you're doin' raising your voices like that and stompin' all about like a coupl'a flamenco dancers? Your mother's rest is hard enough to come by with the heavens blazin' down on us."

"My apologies, Doctor. It was my irrational fear of insects that caused the commotion."

"You get used to 'em out here mighty fast," said Dr. Howard, taking his place at his favorite leather chair. He sank in with a sigh, adjusting his glasses as he put the lamp down on the coffee table. "Heck's—that's Mrs. Howard's—gallbladder operation didn't go quite right. Scar got infected, and we had to go outta' town a couple times. Her lungs ain't doin' much better, probably on account of the anesthesia in her weak condition. Lotsa folk get pneumonia, as you know.

"Now, I do that *pranayama* bit, myself, for clearing out the lungs and brain, but Heck ain't one for Hindoo mumbo jumbo and such. Her lungs been getting steadily worse, even with my magnetic-healin' treatments I give her when she's asleep."

"Father," said Howard, "I don't think my friend needs to hear—"

"Just hold your hoss there. I heard everythin' you two been sayin' all evening and now Mr. Lovecraft here can listen to my voice for a kindly moment or two." He turned to Lovecraft, his blue eyes flashing even in the dim light. "You don't mind, do you?"

"I suppose it is only polite to reciprocate your hospitality by lending an ear."

"Couldn'ta said it better myself." Dr. Howard exchanged glances with his son before he went on. "Now, from what I heard, Mr. Lovecraft here said this Artifact of his might have some healin' powers. Just now I heard the two of you sayin somethin' about electricity. The way I reckon it from my perusal of that Artifact, I would say it's got somethin' to do with that force the Hindoo call *fohat*. Some kinda magnetic thing that could be healthful for you or detrimental."

"He saw the Artifact?" said Howard, turning to Lovecraft.

"While you were out."

"Why didn't ya tell me?"

"There was no occasion, and I didn't think it entirely relevant."

"So I seen it!" said Dr. Howard. "And let me tell you, boy, it's some infernal machine. Take the likes of Edison or the madman Tesla to figure it out scientifically. But your friend here seems to know something about it already, if those whoppers he tells in that magazine of yours are even half-true. So what's the harm in humorin' him a little while, eh? Ain't nothin' you can do here for your mother's health. Yer taxin' her with all that attention she pays ya."

"I don't appreciate you meddling in business that's not yours, Father." Howard held his face in one hand; Lovecraft could see his jaw tensing and relaxing.

"Bobby," said Dr. Howard, "it's about time we admitted what was what around here. You ain't no doctor, son. Only God's good graces is gonna make any difference now. Dammit, help your friend while you got a chance and do two good deeds insteada one."

"You're gangin' up on me! You're tryin' to get me away from Ma!"

"I've a mind to flay your ornery ass and hang it out to dry!" said Dr. Howard. "Stop bein' Heck's little pansy boy and act like the man you should be, son!"

Lovecraft saw Howard's eyes flash with a rage pent up for years, and although they shifted for only the barest instant to the .45 on the table, he knew that Howard could have murdered his father at that moment. He saw Howard's right hand flex open, as if in a spasm, before he clutched it into a white-knuckled fist and smashed it so hard on the table that the oak split from end to end and the pistol fell to the floor, its hammer clicking hard on an empty chamber. When Howard looked from the gun to his father again, the rage was gone from his eyes, and the elder Howard grimaced, half in relief and half in contempt, before he turned his back and walked away into his wife's bedroom.

"I'm terribly sorry," said Lovecraft.

"The hell you are."

"I was most earnest with you, Bob." Lovecraft saw there were tears in Howard's eyes, but out of respect for his friend, he pretended not to notice.

4

THE LATE NIGHT drew on without excitement; even the weather lost its strange fury. Dr. Howard said his good nights and retired, leaving his son and Lovecraft in the living room, where they talked of less-charged matters for a while, reminiscing about past issues of *Weird Tales*, planning overlapping stories, and dreaming of their great future works as if the evening had been a long-anticipated social engagement and not the inauspicious beginnings of a troubled adventure.

It was near sunrise by the time they were done chatting, and the faintest touch of sun was beginning to burn away the gray false dawn in the east. The odd incidents of the night seemed now to be a mere series of coincidences, though the artifact remained to remind them of more dire things.

"I'll go with you," Howard said, finally. It had been clear that he would come around to agreeing, but for him, forcing the words out of himself was another matter.

"I am delighted, relieved, and honored," said Lovecraft. "You do not realize the great favor you are doing me."

"It ain't no favor," said Howard. "Come on, we gotta pack up and hit the road before it gets too hot." He excused himself momentarily and went back to his mother's room.

Lovecraft could hear the muted inflections of an argument, or at least a sad leave-taking. Howard did not come directly back out to the living room, but went outside, where he seemed to be loading his car. In his twilight state of consciousness, Lovecraft closed his eyes and listened to the thumping of the car doors, the creak of the garage, the muffled sounds of Howard swearing. He heard the heavy sound of Howard's footsteps on the porch, the scrape of the front door, more footsteps, silence.

"HP?"

Lovecraft opened his eyes to see Howard standing over him, his expression tired and concerned. In the light he looked dead tired and rather forlorn. "Yes?"

"I was worried for a moment. You looked like you were in some kinda trance."

"I'm sorry. I didn't realize I had closed my eyes."

"Are ya ready?"

"As always."

"Then let's go," said Howard. "I've explained everythin' to Ma, and I don't exactly want to be wakin' my father, if ya know what I mean."

"I believe I do," said Lovecraft. He followed Howard outside and got into the passenger's side of the dark green '31 Chevy two-door, putting his cane and his satchel in the back. He had to try twice before his door would catch.

"I packed some supplies and I'm bringin my pistols, just in case. We gotta get some gas and some grub," said Howard. He pulled out onto the deserted road and headed toward town just as the sun raised itself fully over the eastern horizon, over the silver angel on the radiator cap, illuminating a landscape still fresh with the scars of the night's storm.

• • •

AFTER GASSING UP the Chevy, Howard forced the reluctant Lovecraft into the local diner for breakfast, but only after assuring him that the coffee would be free. The regulars were already there, heads bowed over their steaming black Texas joe, chewing thoughtfully in silence or holding sideways conversations about the same tired old topics with the same tired people. They paid Howard little heed, but all eyes watched the Yankee newcomer as he tucked up his soiled white pants before scooting into the booth. The waitress approached them immediately from behind the counter, ignoring the beefy man who held out his cup for more coffee.

"Mornin', Sally," said Howard. "I'll have a stack of hotcakes."

"Sausage, eggs, bacon?"

"Yeah, I'm feelin' a little hungry."

"And for you, sir?" Sally looked down at Lovecraft as if she were about to scold him about something—probably for his strange attire.

"I've brought my own repast, if you don't mind," said Lovecraft.

" 'Scuse me, sir?"

"I've brought my own food," said Lovecraft, somewhat annoyed. "And if you don't mind, I shall enjoy it with some of your free coffee."

Sally gave Howard a quick glance, about to say something, but the look on Howard's face quickly changed her mind. "Well . . ." she said. "I s'pose I don't mind, Mister." She went off mumbling.

"May I borrow your spoon?" said Lovecraft. "They seem to have neglected a full setting for me." He produced a can of pork and beans from under the table and proceeded to open it with a small can opener, being careful to go only seven-eighths of the way around so that the top stayed on when he folded back the jagged circle of tin.

"Look, HP, I'll buy ya some breakfast if ya can't affort it. Ya ain't really eatin' *that* at this hour of the mornin', are ya?"

"My diet is quite suitable for my constitution, thank you." He poured an inordinately long stream of sugar into his coffee and stirred briskly before licking the spoon and dipping it into the open can. "Do you mind if I begin without you?"

"No, not at all," said Howard, rolling his eyes. He sipped his coffee loudly, glaring, while Lovecraft ate his pork and beans with his tea-spoon—the man seemed to have no clue about his eccentric behavior. When his own food arrived Howard dug into it like a starved man. The smell of beans had been rather unappetizing at first, but it had made his stomach rumble with hunger nevertheless.

They ate quickly. Each time Lovecraft tried to make conversation, Howard snubbed him and went back to his food until he had mopped up his egg yolks with his toast. When Lovecraft was on his third cup of coffee, much to Sally's annoyance, he began to glance around at the other customers in the diner. "Are you acquainted with everyone here?" he asked Howard, looking from person to person.

"Yeah. More or less."

"No strangers?"

"No. Look, they ain't likely to accost us in no diner at breakfast time."

"The minions of Cthulhu can be most subtle," said Lovecraft. "As you are well aware from my writings," he added as an afterthought.

"Let's go, HP." Howard fished some change out of his pocket and left it on the table. "How about you leave the tip?" he said.

"What you've left is more than generous." Lovecraft carefully folded the lid of the can back down and slid out of the booth, taking the empty container with him. He followed Howard to the door of the diner and scanned up and down the street although there was absolutely no traffic.

"What're ya lookin' for?" said Howard.

"Just attempting to confirm my intuitions," said Lovecraft. "I have the oddest feeling that we are being followed. Can't you sense it your-self with those barbarian instincts of yours?"

"I know what it feels like to be watched, HP, and it don't feel that way to me now. Don't let your imaginin's get the best of you now. Things are weird enough."

"Then I shall beg your pardon." Lovecraft glanced once more over his shoulder and shrugged. "Perhaps they are watching from some other realm or though some arcane sorcerer's contrivance."

"Or maybe just binoculars," said Howard, opening the door to his car and pausing to let out the blast of hot air. He wiped his brow, though he hadn't broken into a sweat quite yet. "It's gonna be a hot one."

Lovecraft got into the passenger's side and settled comfortably against the hot leather, closing his eyes and stretching his neck backwards as the engine labored and then roared to life. "Yoik," he said, placing his can between them on the seat.

"What?"

"An enthusiastic expression."

"I'll be enthusiastic when this is all over and done with." Howard slammed the gearshift and lurched forward into the road, not bothering to look behind him or check the rearview mirror. While Lovecraft was looking the other way he quickly grabbed the empty can and flung it out of his window.

THE BLACK SEDAN glided silently out of the side street, muffling the crunch of gravel under its tires, consuming the sound. The car was large and hearselike in its proportions, and its outward design was in no way remarkable; and yet where its black finish and polished chrome should have gleamed or sparkled, its surfaces had an oddly flat quality. One would have imagined the entire sedan to be covered in a coat of dust, but it was remarkably clean, indeed, strangely clean for having driven through the dusty roads of north Texas.

The window of the sedan opened very slowly, and an oddly indistinguishable face emerged to take a momentary look at the discarded can. And suddenly, in a motion so swift it would have been no more than a blur to anyone watching, the figure inside leaned out and snatched up the can, returning to its pose in the car window as if it had not moved at all. The face sniffed at the can, its nostrils quivering like those of a famished wolf; a black, serpentine tongue emerged from between tight lips and pushed its way past the jagged metal lid into the cylinder, emerging slowly, covered in the syrupy bean gravy, a single wet bean clinging to its split tip; and now the indeterminate face turned to the air and took a quick draught of it before it was swallowed up once again in the flat darkness inside the car.

The black sedan pulled out onto the road and turned silently eastward. In a moment the can flew out of the passenger-side window and landed at the roadside, crumpled and punctured as if it had been chewed by some large predator. The can lay in the roadside dust, glistening and wet, but not even a starving coyote would dare approach it.

AFTER A FULL TWENTY MINUTES on the road, Lovecraft finally broke the silence. "May I inquire," he asked, "as to what finally prompted you to change your mind?"

A series of expressions formed and unformed across Howard's face, as if he were trying simultaneously to reveal and yet mask his true feelings. "You said somethin' about that damned thing maybe having healin' powers, didn't you?"

"I didn't mean to involve your father in what is your affair."

"Never mind it now."

"Loveman was never able to unlock the Artifact's secrets, Bob. And there is no guarantee that Klarkash-Ton will have any better luck with it. But I must assure you that it was no desperate stratagem on my part, knowing how both you and your father are devoted to your mother's welfare."

"I said never mind it, HP." Howard grasped the wheel with more force, so tightly that the car actually swerved toward the right.

Lovecraft took this as a clear indication that it was time to change the subject, but even at the risk of his friend's wrath, he had to finish what he had begun. "I sincerely beg your pardon, Bob. But there is one last thing I must mention regarding the Artifact and its possible healing powers."

Howard's glowering profile grew hunched, like the mass of muscle and gristle on a bull's back, and a trickle of perspiration began to descend from where it had already beaded around his right temple.

"All right. You have your say, but make it quick. And that best be the end of it or by Sam Hill . . ."

"I understand." Lovecraft worried the Artifact in his vest pocket, reminding himself, by light of day, that it did, indeed, exist outside his imagination. Now, choosing his words carefully, he cautioned Howard about the potential dangers of using the Artifact on his mother even if they were successful in learning how to tap into its powers. There was no way of knowing, except in retrospect, whether the Artifact was even made to be used by humans. It could just as well be some hellish machine whose purpose was to transform unwitting people into monsters. Lovecraft went on for a while—longer than he thought prudent, in fact—but Howard's expression did not change at all, and he realized that he was not listening. He might as well have been some wooden Indian figurehead mounted over the wheel of his car.

This friend, he thought. This ally. He would not hesitate to unhinge the gates of Hell if only to add a single extra moment to his mother's earthly sojourn. In their years of correspondence, he had never imagined Howard quite like this. A massive barbarian, a savage freeloader, even a naive but bullishly determined historian of his home state, but never a filial son. During his long bus ride, as he drifted in and out of the paranoid dreams, which shifted with the landscape outside the window, he had hoped against hope that someone would help him, and now that that ally was at his side, driving with reckless speed over the just-warming blacktop, he felt at last a measure of confidence.

"You figurin' to bake somethin', HP?"

"Eh?"

"It's hot as Hell's kitchen in here, man! Roll down your damn window."

Lovecraft complied, but only halfheartedly. He had been enjoying the mounting warmth.

"Don't ya sweat?"

"I rather like the heat," said Lovecraft. "Perhaps I have some atavistic trait lingering from our reptile ancestors."

"I figure you're cold-blooded as a gila monster, though your color don't match. No rattler's gonna sidle up in your bag at night."

"I fancy not," said Lovecraft. "Would you mind maneuvering *away* from the obstructions and not *toward* them?"

"Uh-huh."

They drove on for a while in silence, Howard intent on the road, Lovecraft watching the landscape as it changed from minute to minute as the dew burned off the patchy grasses and the air grew parched. He could smell the tang of the land as it hovered in the air like a living vapor, the subtle bite of sage, grass, and dust. He wondered if it was possible to become so accustomed to this air that it faded into the dull regularity, the mundane familiarity, of a city's atmosphere. But then he remembered the pleasant surprises of Providence, how rounding the block he would suddenly taste the salt of a sea breeze, or how a blast of cold through a patch of pine would wake him from a winter stupor. He scanned the horizon to the right of the car, playing with the disparity in apparent motion as the things nearer to his eye blurred by while the distance remained fixed and solid. There were few landmarks out here, he was thinking, when Howard let out a grunt.

"Breckenridge comin' up. And it looks like nasty storm brewin'."

Lovecraft cast his gaze out across the horizon, following the span of the huge, billowing black cloud that stretched as far as he could see. It was no cloud, he realized, but a layer of black smoke not quite conjoined with the grayer overcast above it. He could smell the burning now as the dark plume enveloped the faint reddish glow of the sun.

"That's no storm, Bob."

"The smoke's smoke, but that's one hell of a storm above it. I don't like the looks of it." A shadow passed over Howard's features as the sedan entered the darkness that now reached beyond them across the arid landscape.

"Nor do I like the looks of it myself," Lovecraft mumbled under his breath. He looked toward the north, where the smoke seemed to be more lively, swirling very slowly in a current of wind and mixing rather unexpectedly with the cloud cover. It reminded him of the confluence of two rivers carrying different shades of sediment, or, more likely, he thought, the whorling patterns in the bands of Jupiter. Swirls within swirls, signifying the dance of storms that could go on for centuries like the fury of the great crimson eye, the Red Spot.

Howard drove on, oblivious, in his own thoughts, but Lovecraft's eyes suddenly went wide. There were faces in the chaos of clouds and smoke, indistinct at first, but more and more defined as he focused on them. They were palpitating with a force that seemed to push at them from some unearthly dimension, their features shifting ever so subtly across a spectrum of different visages that Lovecraft immediately recognized from his own descriptions in his dark fantasies. These were shoggoths, he knew, and they were mouthing soundless words, taunting him, trying to frighten him with warnings of death. He felt an electrical buzzing in the air, bitter with the tang of ozone, which he knew was more than the charge of lightning in the storm ahead; it was the very speech of the Old Ones' minions, enfolding them like a cloud of angry hornets, pricking them with tiny injuries of the flesh as they seeped into their minds. *You will die a death of ten thousand agonies. Your friend will die a death of a thousand fragments. Be warned now and bring unto us what is rightfully ours.*

"No," said Lovecraft. He did not realize he had said it out loud.

"What's the matter?" Howard asked, glancing at him sidewise. "You look like you seen a ghost."

Lovecraft knew that what he saw was invisible to his friend. He was thankful for that, though he knew that those forces would open Howard's eyes soon enough. It would do no good to try to explain himself at the moment, he realized. They had to drive headlong into the monstrosities he saw before him and hope that they were mere portents or a flamboyant show to scare them off. "I have seen a ghost," whispered Lovecraft, his throat dry with fear. "I am seeing the most horrific ghosts even as I speak, Bob, but you will reply that it is only my overactive imagination further complicated by the fatigue of a sleepless night and an overindulgence in coffee, which I could not help but watch you notice. So let us explain this away, for the moment, as a case of mild heatstroke, and continue on our way."

"What the hell's comin' over you?" Howard turned to him momentarily, then fixed his eyes back on the road, where he saw what appeared to be two police cars in the distance, forming a roadblock. "You just hush up for a while, you hear?"

"Certainly, I shall."

In a moment Howard eased the car to a stop in front of the two Texas Rangers who manned the roadblock. He leaned out of his window, mopping his brow and squinting toward the horizon, though he hardly needed to.

"Howdy," said one of the Rangers. "Sorry to be corralin' y'all like this, but we got one heckuva brush fire on our hands."

"Never seen nothin' like it hereabouts," said Howard.

"Ya don't say. Had us a freak lightnin' storm last night musta started it, and it's been burnin' ever since. You boys best take a little detour now. Where y'all headed anyways?"

"Well, we were aimin' for Route 66 westbound."

The Ranger consulted briefly with his partner, then came back and explained how to get to Vernon and Highway 5, which would take them on to Amarillo and Route 66. "Ain't what you want to hear, I know, but beats the heck outta burnin' in hell out here, if you know what I mean."

"Figure I do," said Howard.

"Y'all drive safe, now."

"Appreciate it." Howard backed up a short way, made a Y-turn, and returned the way they had come, much to Lovecraft's displeasure.

"YA SEE THAT fella in the passenger seat?" said the Ranger.

His partner pulled a long face in imitation of the Yankee. "What necka the woods you s'pose he's from, huh?" He laughed.

"It's the weird shit always comes in threes," said the Ranger. "Damnedest thing, ain't it? Nothin' out there but some post oak and mesquite. And I ain't never seen a fire burn so long or hot across the desert without no wind to stoke it. And now I don't like the looks of that Yankee we just seen."

"That's only two," said the other Ranger. "What's the third weird thing?'

"I s'pose we'll just have to wait an see, huh?" He opened the flap pocket of his shirt and pulled out a pouch of tobacco. "Gimme some paper, why doncha, and we'll have ourselves a little smoke. I don't see a damned thing comin' for quite a while."

Above and behind the Texas Rangers, the boiling clouds and smoke began to flatten out, dispersing slowly into an anticipatory calm through which something moved—something that looked like the shadow of a car.

5

No words passed between the two men for the next ninety minutes as the Chevy rumbled along the detour kicking up dust, rattling and squeaking. Occasionally there would be a jarring thump as the suspension failed to compensate for a pothole or a loud knock as a stone was thrown up into a wheel well. The noises punctuated the silence more than adequately, and Howard felt comfortable, though hot, as he jockeyed the wheel. Occasionally, he glanced over toward Lovecraft to see him gently patting at his sweating brow with a folded handkerchief.

Lovecraft's upper lip seemed to perspire more heavily than the rest of his face, but oddly, Howard had never noticed him wipe it. It wasn't until he was mopping his own forehead that he saw Lovecraft out of the corner of his eye; he was resting his handkerchief daintily against his brow, looking still, but he had stuck his tongue out, and with a long deliberate stroke, he expertly lapped up the sweat that dewed his upper lip as if it were a sweet nectar.

Howard winced in disgust and turned his eyes back to the road.

They were approaching a small town called Thalia. In a few minutes, Howard pulled into the first gas station, a tiny one-pump operation across the street from a cafe.

The grease monkey who approached the car had crooked yellow teeth and an expression that looked like a wince frozen permanently on his face. "What'll it be, mister?"

"Fill'er up. Ethyl," said Howard. "And check the radiator for me, would ya?"

"Shuure."

Howard headed for the bathroom. "Why don't you go over to the cafe and get yourself a Dr Pepper or somethin'?" he said to Lovecraft. "I'll join you in a minute."

Lovecraft stumbled as he stepped from the car. One of his legs had fallen asleep from the knee down. He leaned back in to grope for his satchel, and while the grease monkey pumped the gas, tossing curious glances his way, he went to the trunk and retrieved a can of pork and beans from his suitcase.

When the man sidled over to try to get a look into his open suitcase, Lovecraft hastily shut it and slammed the trunk with a little more force than necessary. Now the grease monkey grinned in embarrassment, exposing his yellow teeth, but Lovecraft took it as a look of rustic suspicion, like the misleading smile of a chimpanzee. He gave the man an annoyed stare and headed across the street toward the cafe.

When Howard emerged from the bathroom, wiping his wet hands on the legs of his pants, he noticed a flash of red. It was a young woman standing alone at the bus stop across the street, her arms folded primly in front of her, a single cheap suitcase at her feet. Her red hair waved like a warning flag in the breeze, its motion at odds with how still she stood, as if she were frozen in that posture. She was out of place here, obviously; he could see it from the cut of her dress, a city girl's dress that accentuated her figure.

Howard heard a loud hiss and turned toward the car to see the cloud of steam billowing from under the hood. He stepped up to the grease monkey, who was leaning away from the radiator, where he had draped a grimy rag over the cap now bubbling with hot water. "Shoulda waited a bit longer," he said. "What do I owe ya?"

"That'll be a buck fifty-five."

Howard took his thick wallet out of his back pocket and unfolded it. He glanced across the street again. The redheaded woman hadn't moved; she faced west, squinting a bit, and now a gust of wind blew the fabric of her dress against her body, outlining her full figure.

"She's a right pretty one, ain't she?" said the grease monkey.

Howard turned to him and saw his repulsive, smarmy smile. "How much did you say?"

The man held out his tobacco-stained hands. "A buck fifty-five'll do it."

Howard paid him. "Yeah," he said. "She's all right, I guess."

"Much better-lookin' than the ones we usually get driftin' through this part of the belt."

Across the street, the woman turned, impatient now, and the wind gusted again, throwing her hair across her face. She wiped it away like water.

"Want to know how much?" asked the grease monkey.

"Exactly what in the hell are you talkin' about?" Howard said, his indignity a bit forced.

"I'm saying . . . ahem . . . her bus ain't due for say . . . another hour?"

Without a word, Howard got into the car and slammed the door. He was glad to be obscured by the open hood, because he was both offended and interested by the lewd innuendo. He mopped a trickle of sweat from his brow, and was just about to call out to the attendant when the hood came down with a slam, startling him. He looked up into the grease monkey's leering yellow grin.

"Oh, by the way . . ." the man said through the windshield.

"What?" Howard snapped.

"Radiator's fine. Just watch the temperature, if you know what I mean." He winked.

Howard fired up the engine and pulled out in reverse as the man broke into laughter. Then, on second thought, he shifted and barreled back into the station, directly at him. The grease monkey threw up his palms, as if he could stop the car. "Hey!" he shouted. "Hey!" Howard screeched to a stop with the bumper so close that the man involuntarily slumped forward onto the hood. Before the man could recover, Howard spun the wheel sharply and pulled out, leaving him to tumble onto the black dirt. He heard the cursing behind him as he crossed the street and parked outside the cafe.

LOVECRAFT SAT AT a window booth, fastidiously sipping from his glass of water while carefully observing everyone on the street outside. He had not failed to notice the redhead at the bus stop, nor Howard's obvious interest in her. When Howard, still angry, joined him at the table, Lovecraft set his glass down and resumed scribbling in his open journal.

"Have you ordered yet?" asked Howard.

"Yes, I have. To my satisfaction."

Howard snorted and took a quick glance at the tattered menu lying before him. He flipped it over, examined the other side just as quickly, and craned his neck toward the kitchen door, looking for the waitress.

She appeared from the other end of the cafe, obviously annoyed. The place was otherwise empty—perhaps she wanted to keep it that way, Howard thought as she approached the table. "Afternoon, mister. Today's special is the meat loaf sandwich"—she glanced at Lovecraft with a gleam of contempt in her eye—"or are you having what your friend here is having?"

"I don't know. What'd you get, HP?"

Lovecraft did not immediately respond, but in his pause, the waitress reached into the pocket of her soiled apron and pulled out a can opener, which she placed deliberately and somewhat loudly on the table between them. Lovecraft winced more at her displeasure than at the sound. Howard frowned in confusion for a second, then his face grew red with embarrassment as Lovecraft sheepishly lifted his can of pork and beans up from his seat onto the table.

Howard tried to give the waitress his friendliest smile, but she would have none of it. "Uh, ma'am," he said, "I'll have the special and a Dr Pepper, thanks. Oh, and some Tabasco sauce?"

"Coming up."

"Where's your can opener?" Howard asked when she had gone.

"In my haste to enter this fine establishment, I left it in my suitcase. And since you were preoccupied with your own automotive antics . . ."

"Damn it, HP. A man can't live on nothing but pork and beans." Howard tapped the top of the can with three fingers, looking somewhat preoccupied.

"Actually," said Lovecraft, "I once spent ten days traveling through Virginia and ate nothing but—"

"Look, I'll spring for your damn meals from now on if for nothin' but to save me the embarrassment," said Howard.

Lovecraft picked up the rusty can opener and wiped it on his napkin. He eyed the can in front of him and then looked sullenly at Howard, who seemed to be waiting for an answer. Howard gave in. "For Christ's sake, go ahead and eat your damn beans. But this is the last time in public."

"Since you insist." Lovecraft jabbed the blade of the can opener into the top of the can and began cutting with expert jerks of his wrist, being careful not to go more than seven-eighths of the way around, as was his habit. When he was done he peeled the lid back and involuntarily wet his lips.

"I got an important question," said Howard. "So, what is it exactly makes you think Smith's gonna be able to help us figure out that Kachina and that hunk of metal?"

Lovecraft spooned some beans into his mouth and chewed slowly, almost as if to annoy Howard before he answered. "Two months ago, I received a missive from him." He wiped his lips with the other side of his napkin. "He described in it a trip to San Francisco from which he had just returned. Whilst browsing in his favorite antiquarian bookshop on Powell Street, he had come across a tattered volume, which he guessed to be at least two centuries old." He spooned more beans into his mouth.

"So what's an old book gotta do with us?"

"The book was in a Latin cipher, of which he could read precious little, but he did not need to be a philologist or a cryptographer to read the strange occult symbols of which it was full."

Howard shrugged indifferently and drummed his fingers on the table. "Let me guess—it reminded him of that black book he uses in his stories."

Lovecraft put his spoon down and leaned forward as if he were afraid of being overheard. "Not exactly. Not *his* book. Until recently, it is a tome which I believed to be a fiction born of *my* fevered dreams." There was a moment of silence as the two men searched each other's faces for their next words.

Howard grinned, breaking the tension. "Oh, come on, HP. You don't really think Smith found the *Necro*—"

"—*nomicon*. No, not precisely. The original is long lost, as you know. But this is surely a translation of the mad Arab's text. I am absolutely convinced of it after the events I've experienced over the past several days."

"Okay," said Howard. "So let's suppose it is the *Necronomicon* or some other book for castin' spells and raisin' demons from Hell. How's that goin' to help us?"

Lovecraft reopened his journal and pulled a folded slip of paper out from the inside back cover. He slid it across the table to Howard, as if it were some secret bid.

Unfolding it, Howard saw dozens of small, crude reproductions of various occult symbols spaced out in rows of three. Some of them he recognized as Hermetic symbols, astrological symbols, and Masonic symbols. Others seemed to be Teutonic runes and Egyptian hieroglyphs, and some looked like a distorted Chinese script to him. "What's this?"

"Klarkash-Ton copied these from the tome and posted them to me along with his letter. Examine the symbol on the far left, second from the bottom, if you will."

As Howard oriented his eye on the paper and picked out the now-familiar symbol, Lovecraft took the Artifact out of his watch pocket and placed it next to the symbol on the paper, juxtaposing the two to show that they were the same. In fact, when the Artifact had taken on the color and texture of the paper, it seemed to have been penned there all along.

"Holy Christ!" said Howard.

"I can assure you, Bob, the Christian savior has nothing to do with what lies before us." Seeing the waitress approaching with Howard's order, Lovecraft quickly replaced the Artifact in his pocket and slipped the sheet of paper back into the pages of his journal.

The waitress placed Howard's sandwich and soda in front of him.

"Thank you, ma'am."

"You're welcome," she answered, glancing with barely reserved contempt at Lovecraft and his can of beans.

Lovecraft, oblivious to her attitude, stopped her just as she began to leave. "Pardon me, good woman, but I believe you failed to bring my companion the Tabasco sauce he requested with his meal."

The waitress stepped back to the table and looked down at Howard's plate, her hands on her hips in mock drama. "Why, sir, I do believe you are right," she said in a bad imitation of Lovecraft's accent. "I most humbly apologize." From where she stood, she turned, leaned over to the counter, and grabbed a bottle of Tabasco sauce. She placed it squarely on the table in front of Lovecraft. Howard looked on, uncomfortable with the tension, but Lovecraft remained unflappable.

"Anything else, my good man?" said the waitress.

Lovecraft looked at her, somewhat puzzled, as he had not yet gotten her joke.

The waitress picked up the can opener. "If you are quite through with the can-opening apparatus, I will return it to the chef. I believe it is nearly time to feed the stray cat out back."

Howard covered his mouth and chuckled under his breath as the waitress stalked off, and it was only then that Lovecraft understood. He was not amused. "Bob, I sincerely hope that any gratuity you were planning to leave for that scullery maid will be adjusted accordingly to reflect her insolent manner toward me."

Howard couldn't hold back any longer. He laughed out loud. "Admit it, HP. You had that comin'."

"I will admit nothing of the sort."

"Bringin' your own food into a diner is a damned insult to the folks who run the joint. Goes against common decency."

"The only 'damned insult' I'm currently aware of is this dubious eatery charging you twenty-five cents for that rather anemic portion of meat loaf and calling it a 'special.' "

With a chuckle, Howard lifted the top slice of dry bread and sprinkled his meat loaf sandwich with a liberal portion of Tabasco sauce. As he took his first big bite, even Lovecraft was forced to give in; he broke into a wan smile, if only for a brief moment.

THEY EXITED THE CAFE arguing about the generous tip Howard had left. As they stepped toward the car, Howard looked down the street to see if the redhead was still waiting for her bus. She was there, sitting on her suitcase in a pose Howard thought was decidedly masculine, her elbow propped on one knee, her chin on her palm. For the first time, Howard noticed that she wore a pair of men's cowboy boots with her dress, and that perked his interest even more strongly.

Three young men were coming down the street toward the redhead—as purposefully as they could manage in their obviously drunken state. They were probably oil-field roughnecks wasting their salaries at the local bar. Howard hoped they would not bother the woman, although he could not say why he was so concerned for her.

"Bob?" said Lovecraft, his door poised open.

"Hold on a minute."

Lovecraft turned to see what had captured Howard's attention. The three drunks had surrounded the young woman and stood in menacing attitudes. One of them, sporting a battered homburg cocked at a ridiculous angle, stood just in front of her, practically between her knees. "Where ya think you're goin', bitch?" he said.

The woman rose defiantly to her feet. "You just stay the hell away from me! All of you!"

"You didn't think we was gonna let you just up and run off on us like that, did you!" The man in the homburg pointed at her, then thrust his index finger into her collarbone, leaving a spot of grease on her pale skin.

The woman swatted his hand away. "Don't touch me!"

The second man, who stood behind her, snatched the woman's suitcase and spilled its meager contents—mostly undergarments—out into the dusty gutter. "We want our money back," he said as he poked at her clothes with the tip of his grimy boot.

The third man, a mustached fellow, tried to pull the woman's purse from her shoulder. She struggled to hold on to it. "God damn you, bastards! I said leave me alone!"

Howard was agitated. He shifted his weight from foot to foot, not quite knowing what he should do. At that moment a burly man with a shaggy mane of hair arrived to interrupt the fracas; he jerked the mustached fellow backwards, forcing him to let go of the purse strap.

"You boys heard what the lady said. Leave her alone!" roared the burly man.

The three roughnecks now formed a circle around the intruder.

"Sam," said the man in the homburg, "why're you stickin' up for this lowlife thievin' little bitch?"

Sam positioned himself as best he could to defend himself and the fearful woman. "Can't rightly say I believe that, knowin' you boys the way I do," he said. "Get along now! Go on back to your wells! I don't like beatin' a man who ain't sober, but I'll whup all three of ya if I have to!" To illustrate his threat, he raised his fists and assumed an old-fashioned boxing stance. It merely caused all three of the muscle-bound roughnecks to laugh.

"Think ya can lick all three of us, do you, Sam?" said the man in the homburg.

"Hell, boy, the way you all stink of whiskey, I think your mama could take the three of you with one hand tied behind her back."

"This ain't none of your affair, Sam. Mind your own damn business 'fore you get hurt!"

From across the street, Howard watched the scene slowly unfold, adrenaline starting to pump through his veins—but Lovecraft was indifferent.

"Come along, Bob. We should be on our way."

It was a matter of conscience and proper conduct for Howard; he scuffed his feet nervously against the dirt, muttering under his breath. "That ain't right. Three men gangin' up on one."

Unable to discern Howard's whispers, Lovecraft got into the car. "Bob, the petty squabblings of those dim-witted roustabouts is really beneath our concern."

It was too late. Howard had made up his mind. "Wait here," he said with an odd authority in his voice. He strode down the street toward the commotion, walking in a way Lovecraft had never seen before.

Lovecraft shut the door to put a barrier between himself and the unpleasant events he was sure were about to ensue. "What do you think you are doing?" he called after his friend, but Howard ignored him and increased his pace just as fists began to fly. "This isn't one of your barbarian tales, you know!" Lovecraft called. He quickly glanced up and down the deserted main street for a stray police vehicle; and seeing none, he nervously watched his friend leap into the middle of the brawl, issuing a loud, dramatic battle cry. "Or perhaps it is," Lovecraft said to himself.

Howard dived between two of the roughnecks with his arms outstretched, hitting them squarely on the backs of their thick necks; and then, as his weight bore down upon them, he folded his arms, trapping them in headlocks as he tumbled to the pavement. They were so surprised they had no clue what had hit them, and in their drunkenness, they must have thought the earth itself had heaved. Sam was caught off guard by Howard's sudden appearance; he took a clumsy right to the chin from the man with the homburg, and he stumbled momentarily backwards into the arms of the redheaded woman. She caught him and helped him right himself as the man in the homburg turned to see what had happened to his friends. "What the hell?" he said. With the strength and persistence of a pit bull, Howard furiously gripped the two in the headlocks, a low growl of exertion involuntarily escaping his throat. Sam was somewhat embarrassed to be the victim of a sucker punch, even if it was poorly aimed; he pounced back toward the man in the homburg and tapped him on the shoulder, and, as he turned, Sam slammed a solid left hook into his jaw. A glass jaw. The man in the homburg wobbled for a second, then collapsed straight down, unconscious even before he hit the ground.

Howard was now on his knees, still vigorously choking the two men. To Sam it looked like a cowboy had jumped down onto a pair of frightened horses on a stagecoach to wrestle them to a stop. Howard had lost his grip on the mustached man, who slipped out from underneath him and stood up to kick him wildly in the back with his work boots.

"Let go of 'im, you son of a bitch!"

Howard yelled out in pain, but like a badger that has sunk its curved teeth into its tormentor, he refused to yield his choke hold. The face wrapped in his arms was beginning to turn blue.

Sam pounced onto the man with the mustache, knocking him into the gutter with the redhead's scattered clothes. The woman gave him a fast kick in the ribs, and he curled up in pain. The man in Howard's unrelenting grip had gone limp; Howard let him drop to the ground, where he gradually regained consciousness, wheezing for air.

The mustached man got back to his feet in a rage. He tried to rush Sam, who deftly stepped out of his way with a feline grace rather unexpected from a man of his age and build. The mustached man ran square into Howard, who swiveled his entire upper body into a right cross that nearly skewered the man through the gut. He fell in a fetal position, in too much pain even to make a sound. Howard glanced around wild-eyed, then he turned back to the mustached man and kicked him in the back. "Kick me, you son of a bitch?" he shouted. "You kicked me? You God damn kicked me!" The man coughed and made a feeble motion to protect himself. Howard slammed his foot into his back once again, causing a sickening sound in the man's flesh. "Kick me?" Howard shouted again. He pulled his foot back, this time to kick the man in the head, but before he could, Sam grabbed him and swung him up against a wall. Howard was in such a blind rage he didn't even seem to notice what had happened to him.

"Son, that's enough!"

Still overwhelmed by his rage against his attacker, Howard struggled momentarily to free himself from Sam's grip.

"These boys are licked," said Sam. "We done knocked the fight out of 'em." His sincere, calming tone soothed Howard back toward regaining his composure. Sam patted him gently on the shoulder and released him. "Son, you okay now?"

Howard wiped the sweat from his brow. "Yeah. I guess so."

Sam smiled and extended his hand. "Name's Sam. What's yours?"

"Bob. Bob Howard." He shook Sam's hand.

"Much obliged, Bob."

Howard's mood was immediately softened by the genuine friendliness and sincerity that radiated from Sam. Howard smiled sheepishly back at him like a second grader who'd just been praised for his penmanship.

Leaving a small crowd of onlookers who had gathered to watch the fight, Lovecraft approached, watching the shaggy-maned Sam dutifully helping the three injured roughnecks to their feet. Sam lined the three men up side by side and pointed them at the cafe down the street, where the waitress and the cook were standing outside the door.

"You boys go on over and get some coffee, hear?" Sam yelled down at the waitress, "Penny, give these boys some coffee on the house!"

"Sure, Sam!"

"And give 'em some aspirin, too!" He firmly nudged each of the roughnecks to start them staggering toward the cafe.

Howard bent down to help the redheaded woman, who was kneeling to gather up her scattered belongings. It was mostly underclothing, and Howard didn't realize it until the thing he picked up unfolded and fell open into a brassiere. As his eyes went wide with embarrassment, his gaze met the redhead's. His face immediately flushed red, and he handed her the bra so hastily he nearly dropped it. The woman smiled warmly, with just a touch of amusement at the corners of her full lips. Howard quickly turned his attention to Lovecraft.

"Bob, are you all right?" asked Lovecraft, casting a furtive glance over at the kneeling woman .

"Yeah, I'm fine," Howard said, rubbing his elbows. "A little banged up is all." When he turned back, Sam had helped the redhead to her feet.

" 'Scuse me son, I've got someone who'd like to thank you," said Sam. "Bob Howard, this here's Miss Glory McKenna."

She smiled and extended her hand rather formally. "Thank you, Mr. Howard. It was very brave of you to step in and help Sam like that. I hate to think what would have happened if you two hadn't . . ."

Howard hunched his shoulders and shifted from foot to foot, his head hanging like a little boy both proud and uncomfortable with praise. "Wasn't nothin', Miss," he said.

"Nothin's about what anybody else would've done for the likes of me in this town."

Now Lovecraft stepped up to join them, his eyebrow raised with puzzlement at Glory's remark.

"Bob," said Sam, "aren't you gonna introduce us to your friend here?"

"Oh, this is HP. Uh, Mister Howard Phillips Lovecraft." He gestured to Sam and Glory. "HP, this is Sam and, and—"

"Miss McKenna, if I recall." Lovecraft, ever the gentleman, tipped his hat in deference to the lady. "I am delighted to meet you both. I wish the circumstances could have been more pleasant ones."

Sam extended a huge paw of a hand and shook with Lovecraft, who winced at the pressure of the man's grip until he realized his error and quickly relented. "Pleasure's ours," said Sam. "Don't see many strangers the likes of you in town."

After the episode with the waitress in the cafe, Lovecraft couldn't fail to see the double meaning in Sam's words, even if they were not intended that way. He thought it best to leave quickly. "Well, Bob," he said, "I suppose we really should be on our way."

"You two headed up toward Vernon by any chance?" said Sam.

"Yeah," said Howard. "We'll be passing through on our way up to 66."

"Bob, Howard, I hate to impose on you like this seeing as how I just met the both of you an' all, but do you think it would be too much trouble to give Glory a lift up that way?"

Glory was embarrassed. She could see that the two men were obviously reluctant. "Oh, Sam, that's really not necessary."

Sam ignored her protest. "See, way things stand, I really think it'd be best to get her out of town right away. The bus ain't due here for another hour an' a half yet."

Howard and Lovecraft remained silent.

Sam turned to Glory. "When those fellas start to sober up, and they've had a chance to lick their wounds, they're liable to be lookin' for you."

"I'll be long gone, Sam."

"The bus ain't exactly famous for bein' on time, Glory." Sam turned to the men. "Hell," he said, "I'd take her myself, but my damn truck just busted a clutch this mornin'." He waited for a reply.

Lovecraft, giving in to the stalwart gentlemanly air he'd cultivated for years, was about to say yes, but Howard stopped him with a tap on the shoulder.

"Excuse us for just a moment," said Howard. He drew Lovecraft a few paces away, out of earshot, and whispered, "We can't do it."

"I don't relish the idea either, but I pride myself on being a proper gentleman, Bob. Besides, it's only twenty or thirty miles to Vernon, isn't it? We'd only have to be inconvenienced by her company for an hour at most."

"That ain't the point." Howard seemed hesitant to speak his mind about what was really bothering him.

"Then what, may I ask, is the point? You have rescued this woman from ruffians, but you are now loath to offer her a lift?"

Howard finally summoned his resolve. "She's a harlot, HP."

Lovecraft wasn't able to contain his surprise. He looked over at

Glory to see if there were any telltale signs in her appearance that would corroborate what he had just heard, but he saw none. She was hardly dressed like a saloon girl, which is how he imagined a prostitute out in the West; nor was she garishly made up in rouge and lipstick. Indeed, in his perception, she was not dressed the least bit provocatively and looked very ladylike, except for the men's boots she wore under her dress. And that, in Lovecraft's mind, seemed a perfectly rational bit of expediency. "And how did you come upon this lurid revelation?" he asked.

"The fella at the gas station told me as much."

Lovecraft frowned dramatically. "You mean to tell me that the fine upstanding fellow there, covered in automobile grease, the fellow with the delightfully yellow dentition which points to the four quarters of the compass?"

Howard had no quick reply to offer in defense of his accusation.

Lovecraft took the silence as victory and stepped back toward Sam and Glory; Howard followed grudgingly, close behind.

"Bob and I would be glad to provide Miss McKenna with transportation to Vernon if she so desires," Lovecraft said to Sam.

Sam gave a broad, toothy smile. "That's just dandy. Thank you both."

"Yes, I really appreciate it," said Glory. "I can pay you for your trouble."

"Nonsense. That will not be necessary. We would not endeavor to assist you for pecuniary gain." When he turned to gesture politely toward the car, he saw that Howard had already popped the trunk to load the suitcase.

A few quick good-byes, and they were ready to leave. Glory sat somewhat forlornly in the backseat and gave Thalia one last look. It was hardly a place to feel nostalgic about, but the sight of Sam's cafe still touched something in her. Just as she turned away, as Howard put the car into gear and started out onto the road, Sam leaped out of the cafe.

"Hold on up there a minute!" Sam roared.

Glory smiled.

Sam stalked up to the car with a large jar of beef jerky and several cold bottles of Coca-Cola in his hands. He leaned through the passenger window and droppred the items into Lovecraft's lap. "Something for the road."

"Thanks, Sam," said Howard.

"Yes . . ." said Lovecraft, trying to figure out what was in the jar. "You are much too kind."

"You fellas have a safe trip." Sam looked back at Glory. An unspoken communication passed between them.

"Good-bye, Sam," Glory said with a smile. "I want to thank you again for being a true friend."

"Good luck in Las Vegas. Be sure to send me a postcard, now. Let me know how you're doin'. I'd be lyin' if I said I won't worry about you."

"I will." .

As the Chevy pulled away and Thalia disappeared behind them in a cloud of dust, Glory's last vision was of Sam's face, the wind blowing his shaggy mane of hair across his eyes.

6

GLORY MCKENNA SQUINTED in the backseat where the wind from both front windows buffeted her already-unruly hair against her eyes, tangling it into a mass she knew would be agony to comb through. The two men seemed to be holding their annoyance behind a silence so thick she could almost see it—sealing her off in the back behind a layer of soundproof emotional glass as if she were some dignitary in a posh limousine. She pushed her hair out of her eyes and leaned against the seat back, between Howard's and Lovecraft's heads, placing her chin over the interlaced fingers of her hands.

"So," she said, "where are you fellas going, anyway?"

Lovecraft continued to stare out of the window. Howard, his neck slick with sweat, swiveled his head to give her a quick sideswipe of a glance.

"What's it to ya, anyway? If I was you, I'd be happy to have this ride, Miss."

"That was a very chivalrous thing you did back there. What's your name again? I'm terrible with names."

"Robert. Robert E. Howard, the greatest pulp writer that ever lived or will live," he said, glancing sideways again, but this time at his pale companion.

"Indeed," said Lovecraft.

"Why, I'm sure you are," said Glory. "What have you written that I might have read?"

"I doubt you've read any of my work," said Howard. "It ain't exactly written to the tastes of womenfolk."

"I see."

"Indeed, some would say that the pulp genre is hardly written even for the tastes of *men*folk," said Lovecraft, "but we who labor in the genre are part of a heroic and mythic tradition that hearkens back to the earliest epic narratives."

"And what's your name again, honey?"

"Ahem—" During his momentary pause, Glory could see the back of his left ear begin to turn a bright red. "My name is Howard Phillips Lovecraft. At your service, ma'am."

"I can't believe it," said Glory. "You boys are *writers*? Do you make it a habit of driving around the country picking fights and rescuing damsels in distress?"

"Beggin' your pardon," said Howard. "But you hardly look like a damsel to me, Miss."

"I believe she was being figurative," said Lovecraft. "It's hardly appropriate to demean her after our expenditure of energy in her aid."

"Well, ain't you a donkey," said Howard.

Lovecraft was silent for a moment, obviously puzzled. "Donkey?" he said.

"Donkey Oatey."

"Donkey Oatey?"

"That's right," said Howard. "Or ain't you as literate as you say?"

"Donkey Oatey," Lovecraft repeated.

Glory laughed as much at the two peevish men as at the wit. "You know, that's what I thought it was the first time I heard it, too."

"Excuse me, but what?" said Lovecraft.

"Slow," said Howard. "That's how lizards get when they're cold. She means Don Quixote, HP. When I was a kid that's how I heard his name."

"This has become a rather circuitous insult," said Lovecraft.

"And I don't need you defending my honor or chastity—or whatever it is you think you're defending," said Glory. "And you, Robert E. Howard, greatest living pulp writer, just watch what you insinuate."

"Well, Glory be," said Howard. His foot seemed to grow suddenly heavy on the accelerator pedal, and the brief lurch threw Glory backward into her seat.

"Insinuate. Sinuous. Sssss. Snake," said Lovecraft.

"What did you say, HP?"

Lovecraft was silent.

"Robert E. Howard Phillips Lovecraft," said Glory, looking out of the side window at the dusty landscape blurring by. "You boys are joined at the hip, aren't you?"

"What?" they said in unison.

"Nothing," said Glory. "Nothing." It was hardly an auspicious start, even if the ride was only to Vernon. Glory remained silent, and the interior of the car lapsed into the dull, surging roar of the wind. When Lovecraft opened the bottles of cold Coca-Cola and passed them around, he did it without a word.

LOVECRAFT ROTATED THE stub of his pencil to keep the point from wearing down on one side. He told himself, mentally, that he must remember to buy another pencil at their next stop. A fresh pencil smelling of cedar, the wood resistant to rot and insects. In his cramped script, he was jotting down his most current thoughts, and though he was still on edge from his recent adventure, he felt a calm satisfaction of knowing he had done a good deed. "On detour with Howard," he wrote. "He continues to steal surreptitious glances at our not-unattractive, or perhaps she is better described as most subtly voluptuous and sensuous, temporary companion. Howard does not believe I notice him, and he continues this transparent charade, though our companion, G, herself, can hardly fail to notice. Perhaps she is encouraging him with her sidelong attentions."

"What you writin' there, HP?"

"I beg your pardon, but it is none of your concern," said Lovecraft.

"You writin' about me?"

"It is my journal. An account of my day's thoughts and activities. You are part of such activity, as you must surely know."

"You writin' about her?"

Lovecraft closed the pages of his journal quickly over the pencil stub and looked over his shoulder at Glory's smile.

"What are you writing about me, HP?" she asked, batting her eyelashes and coyly shrugging her shoulders.

"Yeah, HP, what are you writin' about her? Anythin' you'd care to share with us?"

"Certainly nothing you'd like to hear," Lovecraft replied, his voice even more nasal than its usual pitch. He turned back to his journal and, perching on his seat, trying like some peevish child to put himself into the farthest possible front and right corner of the car, he absorbed himself once again in his writing until, after nearly half an hour of silence, he found his eyes growing tired.

They must be approaching Vernon by now. Perhaps he should take a nap until they arrived. He saw the sign blur by outside the half-open window—VERNON—too fast to make out the number of miles. We must be getting close to Vernon, he thought again; his attention was lapsing with drowsiness, and he found himself reviewing that same thought yet again as if he were trying to make sense of an abstruse passage in some philosophy text. Vernon, he said to himself. Vernon. No-Vern. Ca-vern. Cave. He closed his eyes to think more clearly and was suddenly enfolded into the warm comfort of sleep.

RED STREAMERS OF finest Cathay silk billowing in the wind. A banshee howl over the vast desert, the breath of a god so fierce the flying sand could flay a camel down to its bones in no time. What is this unholy place? Red streamers quieting in the muting breath and now they are no longer silk but hair, human hair, passionately red—glorious. Glory's hair. She is facing the wind with her arms outstretched, and in her hands she holds the Artifact as if she were offering it to a lover. The wind is still fierce, and yet some irresistible attraction draws her forward, something like the power of scent over an animal in must. Her nostrils flared, her expression intense, her radiant green eyes even more beautiful in their squint, she sniffs at the air and strides forward, her mouth slightly open, her full lips warm with the force of her breath. There is a romantic, almost ethereal, quality to the tableau, and Glory recalls, though it hardly seems possible, the delicate, smooth-skinned models of the pre-Raphaelites, their soft, creamy innocence, the willowy curve of their naked shoulders, the youthful budding of their half-clothed breasts. But all that innocence waiting to be stripped. Dark potential longing, with full, red lips, to be bared, exposed. Calumnious emotions ready to slip out of their civilized pretenses. Unseemly underbelly, slick and wet with a prurient perspiration. Naked, corpulent pink flesh burning to be touched. Touched by infernal heat.

Lovecraft's consciousness could not penetrate this tableau. He tried to push his way into Glory's thoughts, to insert his own mind into hers, to somehow push her uncontrolled impulses aside with the force of his own will; but it was for naught. Round and round went his consciousness, in and out of touch with Glory's. He pressed against her, his will rigid with power, until he felt her begin to yield. She let out a yelp of surprise, a cry of pain, and then, suddenly, Lovecraft felt a stab of agony shooting down the ridgepole of his spine, a clawing pain like the sensation of nails raking across his flesh, and the pain moved up and down, faster and faster, pulsing ever more rapidly until it grew white-hot and exploded through his head, leaving him hollow and powerless, full of shame at his failure to stop her. Glory continued to walk forward to that unseen thing, her arms reaching out, beckoning, it seemed, and Lovecraft watched with disgust, though avidly, as she advanced, step by step, toward that unclean and unholy thing just beyond the range of his imagination. To give it the Artifact would be the most unpardonable sin. To surrender to its will would be to demean all of humankind, a sin no one could repent. A sin with no penance, for there would no longer be a God of man to make penance to.

Her body was wet with perspiration. He could feel its slick, sticky texture in his mind. Unpleasant. Pungent. He felt the odor seep into his olfactory canals, into the caverns of his sinuses, where it clung to the vulnerable tissues, which he knew, with an odd certainty, were a small fragment of his brain making direct contact with the outside world. Suddenly he was preoccupied with this idea—that it was only in smelling something that his brain actually touched the world. Odors, infinitesimal molecular fragments of the thing itself, filling the air like an aura, and the brain poking itself tentatively forth inside the protection of the sinus cavity, most cautiously touching the world. And here, the world, most unpleasant and horrific, and the thought caused his head to fill, rapidly, with a protective mucus. He must eject this intrusion out of his brain, out of his mind, out of his thoughts. The mucus began to flow copiously from his nose, and then, in the fringes of his consciousness, Lovecraft heard Howard's distant voice say something about Vernon, and he felt himself convulse with a violent sneeze.

"Why, bless you," said Glory.

Lovecraft opened his eyes wide and drew back in alarm. The off-white of his jacket was covered with a large yellowish white glob of mucus which he had just ejected from his nose. It was still dripping, but moving as if it were stretching a hesitant tendril down his jacket. He fished for his handkerchief to clean himself, but then he sniffed the air in the car. He was more alert now, the last webs of sleep wiped aside, and it was not dust as he expected. It was something else—the unspeakable fishy odor of Dagon's degenerate spawn.

• • •

EVEN BY THE TIME they reached Vernon, Lovecraft was ill at ease, and the Artifact felt like a bruise on his side. The images from his dream still lingered with him. He knew they were strong portents to be ignored at his own peril, and yet he was loath to say anything to Glory and Howard because he knew that now, especially with the presence of the woman, Howard would merely ridicule him. He would wait until she was gone to tell him, but then what about her role in the dream? Was it merely symbolic? He wished he had been more attentive in his reading of the dream book by Dr. Freud—it had contained useful insights into the dreaming mind—but he had found the old Jew's fixation on sex and genitals and bodily functions so distasteful he had put the book aside.

VERNON. VERNAL. VENEREAL. Veneration. They were there, just past the outskirts of town, and Howard, after Glory's offer to ask directions for him, had grudgingly pulled over to the curb. Through the open back window, Glory was talking to a passing man, reviewing the turns they would have to make to get to the bus station.

"Ain't it a shame," said Howard, his voice low.

"And what is this shame?" Lovecraft asked.

"We're done with her so soon, HP. She's a purty woman as you can see."

"What are we done with, Bob? Are you imagining what your Conan would do with her? Or perhaps one of your two-fisted Texian roughnecks? Are you so close to confusing fantasy and reality that you're unable to control your own baser instincts?" Howard widened his eyes at this, and Lovecraft drew back, shocked by his own vehemence.

"Just pullin' your leg there, but now I'd say you're a jealous man, HP. Jealous and righteous like many a red-blooded minister, huh?"

"I beg to differ."

Glory pulled her head back into the car, waving a friendly good-bye to the pedestrian. "A left, a right, a left, and a right," she said. "I'll call out the turns when I see the streets. You just drive, okay?"

Howard tipped his hat and lurched forward, pushing her against the backseat. He followed Glory's directions without a word, and within a few minutes they had made their way down Juniper Street and Eleventh Street, over the railroad tracks and through the dilapidated part of town to the bus terminal.

"Well," said Glory, "I'm so very glad you boys came to my rescue. I don't know what I would have done without you."

"We coulda got here with just one turn," said Howard, not meeting her eyes. "That bum gave you a runaround."

"Well, we're here, aren't we?"

"Yeah, I reckon so."

"Thank you, boys." Glory leaned forward and planted a quick kiss on each of their cheeks, and before Lovecraft could offer to unload her bag, she was out, the door shut. And before he could say even a cursory good-bye, Howard gunned the engine and pulled a violent U-turn and accelerated away. Lovecraft craned his neck to look out of the back window. He could sense Howard's dark mood, and he was loath to say anything at the moment, but something caught his attention, and he waved his left arm at his companion to slow down.

"Why you flailin' like a chicken, HP? I can't hardly see the road."

"Slow down or stop."

"We're losin' time. Gotta get back to the highway."

"Stop!"

Perhaps it was the shrill note in his voice—Howard pulled over and smoothed the car into a halt at the end of a block. "What's got your goat now, huh?"

"Look, Bob. See that sedan?"

Howard could see many sedans, all black, but the one Lovecraft indicated was unmistakable. At first he thought it might be his eyes, and yet any amount of squinting or blinking made no difference— there was something about the blackness of the car that made it seem to be devouring the light around it, leaving a subtle aura in its periphery where all colors collided into that unnatural blackness.

"You see it," said Lovecraft.

"Yeah. And you don't have to say nothin'."

In the black sedan sat two figures. Howard found it impossible to think of them as men although they had human silhouettes. The figure in the driver's seat was more visible than the other; it wore a black suit with tight lapels and, underneath, a white shirt with a black tie. Its face, by all measures, should have been visible, but what Howard saw there was a mask of strangely unfocused features; the only things that stood out, with an ominous clarity, were the two eyes. Odd, Howard thought. He wouldn't have been surprised if there had been several. Even without corroboration from Lovecraft, he knew that this was the odd man on the bus. There was no mistaking it, no way to confuse these creatures with people, even if they had precisely the same outward appearance.

The second figure in the car seemed more human for some reason. Howard intuitively knew this was because it had been among people for a longer time, gathering experience, doing the bidding of some ungodly power. The thing sat in the passenger seat exuding a palpable authority, and as Howard's gaze touched it, it turned its head without seeming to move. Suddenly the shifting features were where the back of its head had been, and it was staring at him through those ghastly clear eyes. Why hadn't Lovecraft mentioned the eyes?

"Lovecraft . . ." Howard began.

"It's the odd man from the bus," said Lovecraft, unconsciously fingering the Artifact in his pocket, "and now he has an accomplice."

"I wouldn'ta believed it about the face. Thought it was your imagination."

"The detail is far too strange to be fiction, Bob."

"Well, whataya aim on doin' now? They've been on our trail, obviously."

"I hate to interrupt your brooding, but I am at a loss at the moment. I believe they were already at the station when we arrived." He winced in pain as the Artifact throbbed.

"What?" said Howard.

The black sedan pulled slowly forward, and now it was alongside

Glory, who still stood at the entrance of the terminal. Through the open passenger-side window, the odd man from the bus had angled his head to speak and his intention, even from that distance, had the force of an intimate whisper. Glory walked innocently up to the open window and leaned forward.

"We've got to go back," said Howard. "They know she was with us."

Glory must not have noticed the man's strange appearance, because she stood in rapt dialogue with him, smiling, then looking oddly placid as he said something to her. She motioned back toward her suitcase, but then her arm seemed to fall limp, and she straightened to move toward the back of the car.

"Bob!" said Lovecraft, to voice his alarm, but Howard had already put the Chevy in reverse and stepped on the gas. The car kicked up two gouts of dust and pebbles and careened backward, causing passersby to curse and shield their eyes. Howard steered expertly in reverse, his eyes on the street, his right arm draped across the seat back. Two approaching cars veered out of the way, sounding their annoyance on their Klaxons, but Howard was too intent to notice. Just as it seemed he would collide with the dead black sedan, he slammed on the brakes and skidded to a stop, the Chevy's bumper a scant inch from the other car, and as Lovecraft trembled in his seat, trying to regain his wits, Howard leaped out and grabbed Glory just as her limp hand closed on the handle of the door.

"No!" cried Howard. He wheeled her around and saw the blankness in her eyes flare suddenly into a wide expression of rage. She snarled at him and brought her other hand around, fingers curled, to claw at his face. Howard ducked like an expert boxer and brought his shoulder into her midriff, lifting her up in a fireman's carry as he rose again, and while she kicked and flailed at him, he picked up her suitcase and strode back to his car.

Several people had gathered by now to watch the excitement. Lovecraft, in his calmest tones, announced to them that it was merely a lover's quarrel, but his appearance didn't seem to lend him much credibility.

"Let me go, you bastard!" said Glory. "Put me down!"

"We'll take you to Vegas, okay? We're going that way anyways."

"I said put me down!"

Past Howard and his uncooperative load, Lovecraft saw the front door of the black sedan open. The odd man seemed to flow out of the car like a dark cloud and re-form himself on the sidewalk. He straightened his elegant, timeless clothes and stepped forward. "Bob!" he called.

"What?" said Howard, turning around, puzzled to hear Lovecraft's voice from behind him.

The odd man's face did a strange thing. Part of it solidified momentarily into a mouth and a smile. The lips moved very deliberately, as if forming sounds alien to its speaker. "Give. Us. The. Woman." As he spoke the odd man drew open one side of his jacket and revealed a long, serpentine blade hanging where an inner pocket would normally have been. He drew the blade, very calmly, as if he did not care if the gathered people could see it. "Give. Her. To. Us. And. We. Shall. Kill. You."

Howard paused, trying to understand the logic of the threat. Some hypnotic quality in the voice overlay its imitation of Lovecraft's tones. He felt himself becoming relaxed even when part of his mind had begun to feel an instinctive terror and repulsion.

The odd man drew closer, so close that the arcane symbols on the blade became distinct. They were not serpentine, but something else, something more tentacle-like, something that despite the abstractness of the etching exuded a feeling of disgusting wetness like a slug's mucus trail.

"The hell with you," said Howard, reaching toward his belt with his free hand. He paused and looked alarmed not to find his pistol there.

The odd man didn't quite move the blade; it simply seemed to appear elsewhere, his arm attached to it. As he stepped forward, the aura around his body didn't quite keep pace, and the air around him rippled as if it were distorted by waves of heat. Howard stepped backwards, clenching his free fist. He was frightened at the thought of what that blade could do—materialize suddenly in his gut or fly with imperceptible speed across his throat—but he was willing to make a fight of it. He prepared to put Glory and her bag down, wondering why she was suddenly so limp. "Lovecraft!" he called. "Where the blue blazes are you?"

"Bob!" The voice came from behind him, but Howard didn't dare turn his head to see.

"Bob!" echoed the odd man, drawing closer.

"Bob! I have officers of the law here!"

"Officers," echoed the odd man, pausing where he stood. The blade made one of its odd movements again and was gone. The odd man stood casually and yet with an inappropriate formality, as if he were posing for a portrait.

"What the Dickens is going on here?" said a voice.

Howard turned and saw the two police officers approaching. Lovecraft stood slightly behind them and followed as if he were pushing them along in front of him. Like hand puppets, thought Howard.

The other officer tapped a billy club absentmindedly against his thigh. "What's the commotion, folks?"

"They were takin' her against her will," said Howard, gesturing toward the odd man and the sedan. "He has a knife under his jacket."

"And what do you say to that, Mister?" the policeman said to the odd man.

"Knife. Under. His. Jacket," said the odd man, still in Lovecraft's voice.

"You makin' fun?"

"He was about to stab me, Officer."

The odd man said nothing.

The policeman stepped forward and directed the tip of the billy club at him. To Howard's eyes, the black wood seemed to distort the aura around the odd man without piercing it, but the officer was oblivious.

"Open the jacket, Mister."

The odd man complied, almost graciously, with a smooth sweep of his arms. Both flaps of his jacket flared back in the breeze like black, silk-lined wings; they shimmered luxuriously in the sunlight, rippling subtly like vertical pools of black water. There was no blade to be seen.

"What did you say he had under his jacket, eh?"

"I swear, Officer, he had a knife. A ceremonial dagger."

"You been drinkin'?"

"Drinking," said the odd man.

"Shut up," said the policeman. "You ain't done nothin' wrong I can think of at the moment, but I don't like the looks of you, Mister."

The odd man closed the wings of his jacket, furling them around him like the fleshy black wings of a bat. Howard could see the inhuman quality permeate the air around him, the aura expanding, but again the policeman didn't seem to notice anything unusual.

"Maybe I'm mistaken," said Howard. "But they were harrasin' the lady, like I said."

"Miss, was this man bothering you? Miss?"

Howard jostled Glory, then he thumped her on the back as if he were burping an infant before he swung her down to her feet, where she blinked her eyes in confusion. The two policemen exchanged glances before the first one asked again, "Was this man botherin' you?"

"Why, no," Glory said, rubbing her eyes like someone just awakened from sleep.

"Were you botherin' him?"

She looked suddenly alert. "Just what are you insinuating?"

"We don't like the looks of you, neither, in our town. I suggest you take the first bus out of here."

"Why, you son of—"

Howard put a hand on Glory's mouth before she could finish the sentence and get herself into trouble. "Sorry, Officer. I suppose we got this all under control now, if you don't mind."

"Well, this ain't no kidnappin' by my reckoning, though I can't say I'd be all that concerned either way."

Lovecraft saw Howard's response. Before his friend could do something foolishly chivalrous, he stepped up between them and thanked the officers for their help. "I am most grateful for your assistance in this small matter of law enforcement," he said. "My friend and I shall escort the lady now to her destination."

"Yeah, yeah," said the policeman. "You folks just get outta town, if you get my drift."

"Before sundown, certainly," Lovecraft said, amused by his own wit.

"I'd say before I have a mind to put you in the damn slammer," said the policeman.

"I beg your pardon."

Lovecraft rejoined Howard and Glory at the car. He paused momentarily to look over his shoulder at the odd man, who had been standing in the same posture during the past few minutes. He could feel the ill intention radiating from him, so strongly, perhaps, that the small crowd of babbling passersby left a distinct space around him.

"Jake," called the other officer from where he stood by the odd man's black sedan.

"Yeah?"

"This car here's parked in a police zone. That's illegal, far as I know."

"Why, ain't it just?" He turned to the odd man. "Well, Mister, I think we got some legal matters to discuss. Now, what do you say to that?"

The odd man showed absolutely no change of demeanor. "Discuss," he said.

Lovecraft turned away, determined that they should escape during the distraction. Howard was having words with Glory. They each had a hand on the handle of her suitcase, though Glory had only been able to slip one finger past Howard's beefy paw.

"Look, Miss," said Howard, "we're takin' you to Vegas, and there ain't no more arguin' about it."

"I could say you boys were kidnapping me."

"And I have a notion to tap your jaw after we saved you back there."

"Saved me? From what? The gentleman in the car was perfectly nice. He said he was headed to Vegas, and his car is a hell of a lot nicer than yours!"

Lovecraft cleared his throat. "I am rather loath to interrupt such a lively quarrel," he said, "but consider for a moment the unlikelihood of such a coincidence. Two vehicles with a destination that happens to be identical to yours."

"And what's so odd about that?" said Glory. "He was very nice, and he offered to take me all the way to my sister's front door."

"And was this at your prompting?" Lovecraft asked.

"No. He volunteered, as a gentleman should."

"And you explained to him that you were on your way to see your sister?"

"Why, of . . ." She trailed off.

"How was he cognizant of the fact that you were on your way to visit your sister if you did not divulge such information?"

"So what're you sayin', HP? Now you're gonna tell us they read minds?"

Lovecraft nodded, and to Glory's puzzled and confused look, he replied, "Those creatures that pass for men are minions of Cthulhu. Their intentions, I must say, are evil, and you are unfortunately associated with the current focus of their unholy attentions."

Glory's expression didn't change noticeably, so Howard added, "They woulda kidnapped you and who knows what the Sam Hell they woulda done to you."

"Why?"

"They are Cthulhu's minions," said Lovecraft, as if that explained everything.

"They're after HP," Howard said. "And now that they've seen you with us, you're in danger, Miss."

"What would they want from me? Call the police." She seemed to be emerging from her daze now. Howard and Lovecraft ushered her into the Chevy while she was still compliant. They tossed her suitcase in after her, got in, and drove off before she could fully regain her wits and perhaps call the policemen herself.

As they pulled away, Lovecraft couldn't help but glance back once more at the black sedan. The odd man was still speaking to the police officer, and the small crowd had now encircled them and the car, blocking traffic in front of the bus station. The officer had his pad open and jotted something in it while his partner absently slapped the tip of his billy club against his palm. Lovecraft felt a sudden sense of relief wash over him, but just then the odd man turned his way, and in his eyes Lovecraft could see the message as clearly as if it had been written in the pages of a book: "Die." Lovecraft turned away, his heart pounding, before he could see more. He looked out of the windshield, westward, at the sun hanging ominously over the horizon.

7

DRIVING ON INTO THE RED GLARE of the westward sun toward Amarillo, Howard tried to blink away the weight of sleep. The episode at the bus station had left him enervated and full of a strange languor. He had accused Lovecraft of being like a lizard, but now it was he who wanted, more than anything, to stretch out on a warm rock and drowse in some interminable torpor. In the backseat, Glory was unconscious, having drifted off into a fitful sleep within moments of leaving the outskirts of Vernon.

"I'm gettin' mighty hungry," Howard said. "I could use a bite to eat and a pot fulla coffee. Whataya say, HP?"

Lovecraft stopped his scritching and folded his pencil stump into his journal for the umpteenth time. "I concur with your sentiments, particularly regarding the hot coffee."

"What you writin' there this time?"

"Some notes. I wanted not to forget the specifics of my dream. The Artifact has pained me since we were in the proximity of the odd men, Bob. I believe their influence is what precipitated my dream about our hapless passenger."

"You dreamt about Glory? Why don't ya tell me about it? Keep me awake, for God's sake. I'm feelin' a bit like a cat in the sun."

"It was a dream of unusual vividness, much like the night terrors that haunted my childhood," Lovecraft began. He recounted, as much as he remembered, the details of his dream, but out of his own shame he could not mention the erotic charge he had felt, or the sheer vividness of the sensory details. Instead he emphasized the direness of his feelings, the sense of urgency, and the psychic connection he seemed to have with Glory. "Perhaps it is irrational for me to draw such a conclusion, but I believe this was more of a vision than a dream. It had a certain numinous quality to it. It was foreshadowing something I dare not imagine."

Howard quietly chewed it over before he answered. "You know," he said, "I wouldn't have believed you before I saw that odd fellow. When you told me about that man on the bus I figured you added a shot or two from your tall tales. Even with the bugs in my house. But when I saw that face, I had to give it to ya, HP."

"I don't know whether to be honored or insulted," Lovecraft replied with a smile.

Howard reached over and thumped him on the chest with the back of his hand, and Lovecraft doubled over, an involuntary puff of air escaping his lungs. The two men laughed as both recovered from the shock.

"We got good imaginations," said Howard. "How do ya explain those faces? I never even read about such a thing."

"I suppose we could explain that phenomenon just as well by pretending to fictionalize it. Perhaps those creatures are only partially in this dimension and what we are perceiving is some oscillation between our dimensions. I dare not even imagine what must be on the other side."

"You do enough of it in your Cthulhu yarns."

"No, I do not. I go only as far as to insinuate those unspeakable details to allow them resonance in the reader's mind."

"Well, there you go," said Howard, motioning with his head to a roadside diner. "Let's fill this tank and our bellies, eh? Won't be another outpost for a while."

"For your heroic role today, I shall purchase you a cup of coffee," Lovecraft declared.

"Mighty generous of ya, buddy." Howard slowed down to pull off the highway, checking his rearview mirror to make sure they weren't being followed. Even at this distance from Vernon, he had the nagging feeling that the dead black sedan was nearby.

THE GAS STATION attendant was a half-blood, bronzed and angular, and his gray-black coveralls appeared to be more grease than fabric. He wiped his oil-blackened hands on the startlingly clean rag that protruded from his back pocket and approached the Chevy, in which he saw the unlikely trio of disheveled travelers. The driver's face was stained with dust washed into pale rivulet patterns by the sweat that dripped from under the brim of his hat, and in the passenger seat, the pale, gourd-jawed man in his dingy white suit glanced about with the bulging eyes of a fish. In the backseat, as he approached, he saw what he thought was a fiery red animal pelt—perhaps the fur of an exotic fox—but it was a white woman, puffy and unconscious with sleep. "A hatted bear, a pale fish, and a sleeping red horse will come your way," the old shaman had said to him. "You must let me know when they arrive, for those who come after will be witches." He recalled the old man's words as if they were being whispered to him now, with the force of urgency and dread.

"Check the oil, sir?" the attendant asked the hatted bear man.

"Suppose so," said Howard.

The attendant gave the pale fish man a lingering once-over as he got out of the passenger seat, and Lovecraft returned the favor, equally fascinated.

"What're you gawkin' at, Chief?" said Howard.

"Ah, nothing, sir. Check your tires?"

"Yeah, why don'tcha."

Howard motioned Lovecraft over to the diner and leaned into the back, where Glory was still asleep, looking feverish and uncomfortable in the heat. It took a long time to wake her out of her thick slumber, and when she finally opened her eyes, she burst into tears.

"What's the matter?" Howard asked. "How are ya feeling, Miss?"

"Oh, God," she said. "I feel like shit. I must look like shit."

"I'd have to disagree with ya there," Howard said with a smile. "I doubt you could ever look like shit."

Glory rubbed her face, quickly felt her hair, and checked her breath against her palm. "I had the most terrible nightmares," she said. "I dreamt those gentlemen back there were murdering my baby."

"You have a baby?"

Glory was silent for a moment, as if she were considering what to say. "No. I lost my baby a while back."

"I'm sorry to hear that," Howard said.

It was a reply Glory had heard too many times; it surprised her now to hear the sincerity in his voice. She followed Howard to the diner and excused herself to go to the ladies' room to freshen up. She still felt disoriented; though she could remember everything that had happened since she had gotten out at Vernon, she still had an odd dislocated feeling as if she were waking in an unfamiliar room.

His fingers curled around the trigger handle of the gas pump, the attendant watched the red horse woman disappear into the ladies' room, her mane so red it seemed to burn the air. Under his breath he repeated the names of the figures to himself: hatted bear man, pale fish man, red horse woman. They had come from the east and they were pursuing the sun across the land, into the house of night. He would report this to the old shaman, he thought, repeating the story to himself until it became a soft chant. Unconsciously, with his free hand, he fingered the beaded medicine pouch he wore around his neck. Evil times were coming. The time of the gourd of ashes was nearly upon the earth.

• • •

"I'M TELLIN' YA I didn't like the way he was lookin' at you," Howard said, glancing in the rearview mirror at the lights of the diner receding in the darkness. "Put a little firewater into a half-breed like him and he can't control his animal lust for white women."

"The man is likely the product of such an unfortunate coupling," Lovecraft added.

"What are you two saying?" Glory said incredulously from the back. "His father raped his mother? Where do you boys get ideas like that?"

"I assure you it is not due to our overabundance of imagination," said Lovecraft. "The inferior races and classes have a proclivity for hypergamy, and when that is not a legitimate possibility, they may resort to force."

"When they can get away with it," Howard added. "It's the duty of the Aryan frontiersman to protect his womenfolk from that sort."

The two men looked approvingly at each other. Rather smugly, Glory thought from their silhouettes. "I can't believe you boys," she said. "What makes an Indian any different from you except the color of his skin?"

Lovecraft gave a sort of snort. "Shall I endeavor to enlighten the lady?" he said to Howard, as if Glory were not even there.

"Yeah, HP. What's that book you told me about—the one about the evolution of races? Tell her some of that."

"At your service."

Glory settled back against the door and stretched out in the seat. "Look, Lovey," she said, "I'm glad to hear you've done a lot of reading on the subject, but I'm not in the mood to hear about all this Aryan race rubbish at the moment."

"The Aryan race is irrefutably the one destined to be dominant on this planet, during this very epoch," said Lovecraft, lapsing into his pedantic tone.

"The Aryans aren't even a race."

"And upon what authority do you base that assertion?"

"I said I didn't want to discuss this rubbish."

"But I am curious," Lovecraft insisted. "How would a woman of your background have the intellectual resources to ponder coherently the complex subject of the races of man and their evolutionary hierarchy?"

"I—"

"What are you sayin' about her background?" Howard interjected. "Don't insult the lady, HP. She's dog tired, on account of your odd men, and she's been havin' bad dreams. Let's put a cork in the lecture till later."

"I beg your pardon," said Lovecraft.

A long silence ensued, and Glory noticed Howard adjusting the rearview mirror so that he could look at her occasionally when he thought she wouldn't notice. She felt awkward and yet girlishly comfortable to have this man of simple passions wanting to be her protector.

She sighed and nestled into the folds of the jacket she had taken from her suitcase to ward off the desert chill. There hadn't been any other traffic for nearly half an hour, and the night outside seemed to be darker than it should be. Out of the rear window, she could see the stars in the distant east slowly blotted out by an approaching cloud. Odd, she thought. The wind had been blowing from the west all day, or was she confused by the wind rushing by the car? Or perhaps it was another layer of air, higher up in the atmosphere, that carried the dust. She recalled that in the early 1880s an island called Krakatoa had exploded, and the ash from the volcanic eruption, lingering in the upper atmosphere, had darkened the whole earth for months. Her grandmother had been in Java at the time and witnessed the aftermath of the giant tidal wave that had crashed into the neighboring islands, crushing and drowning nearly fifty thousand people. "We heard an explosion like the end of the world," she'd said. "Then we felt it in our flesh and our bones, and out on the coast it was as if the ocean had spat its guts out onto the earth. It reeked for months of rotting fish and death, but I must say the sunsets were spectacular for years after."

Why am I remembering Grandmother? Glory thought, Why am I

thinking of volcanoes and tidal waves when I'm out in the middle of the desert at night with two eccentric strangers who might as well be kidnapping me? Kidnapping, she thought again, and the word, with the memory of her grandmother, took her suddenly back into the nightmare she had had earlier.

It was Christmas, and she was sitting under the tree, which was a Douglas fir, a giant tree that seemed to go up and up and up forever, though it stood in the living room across from the fireplace. Her father was in his comfortable chair smoking his pipe, his legs crossed, his feet in his favorite slippers; and her mother was there, sitting on the floor with her, ready to admire the presents. Her grandmother stood by the fireplace, looking somewhat disapprovingly at the sheer number of presents in their fancy red-and-green wrappings. "Go ahead and open it," said Father. Usually they didn't open their presents until Christmas morning, but Father was in a good mood tonight, and it was past midnight. They had stayed up drinking eggnog and eating chocolate cake, and she had been eager to open just one present, the one wrapped in the blue cord and not the ribbon. "Go on," said Father, "you can open that one. Just that one." So she looked anxiously at Mother, who nodded with a smile, and she tore the package open with a cry of delight. The inside of the paper was wet, for some strange reason—water leaked out when she took the layer off—but Glory knew it was supposed to be that way. She pulled the wrapping away, and Mother gave her a paring knife to cut the cord so she could get the present out of the red box. She was so excited she was all out of breath, and by the time she had the box open she was covered in sweat, so excited it was painful, and when she reached inside, she felt something soft and round, and she shrieked in delight. It was a doll! A beautiful, perfect little doll. And she pulled it out and hugged it and wrapped it in the swaddling cloth that Mother gave her, and she looked into its perfect blue infant eyes and cuddled it so tight she thought she might crush the life out of it. Then she looked down at it and saw that the eyes were closed. They were the sort of eyes that closed when you laid the doll down and opened again when you picked it up. Sometimes they stuck a little and you had to jostle the baby a bit, but they always worked eventually, so she wasn't worried. But when she picked the doll up the eyes stayed shut. She laid it back down again and then picked it up again and then laid it down and picked it up and then she jostled it and thumped its little back and shook it and shook it, but the eyes never opened again and the baby never woke up. And then she looked at Mother for help, but Mother was gone. She was just a ghost, and Father was a dark-eyed hollow man, and the only person who could do anything was her grandmother, and Grandmother hated her because she was going to miss school because she had been spoiled by the doll. She started to cry, and then she heard an odd voice that couldn't really speak English. "It. Belongs. To. Us," said the voice. "We. Will. Take. It. Now," and Glory looked through her tears to see the two lawyers in black suits standing over her, both reaching toward the doll in her arms, which had suddenly become limp and heavy like the infant it was supposed to be. Her tears suddenly became hysterical, nearly choking her, and she had woken up in the backseat of the Chevy.

"Are ya okay, Miss?" It was Howard's voice.

"Yes," Glory replied, wiping her eyes. "I was just thinking."

"You never told me about that nightmare," he said, as if he had just read her mind.

"Oh, it's nothing you'd want to hear about. Just a silly dream with an obvious meaning. I must have had it because I'm going to visit my sister so I can see her little boy."

"Why don't ya tell me about it? I'm getting set to nod off here behind the wheel. And my partner ain't doin' much of a job keepin' awake, neither." He jerked his head a couple of times to indicate Lovecraft, and Glory noticed suddenly that the man must have been snoring for a while by now.

"I'd rather not talk about it," said Glory.

"Fair enough," said Howard, glancing at her in the mirror. "You said you lost a baby. What was his name?"

"Huh? Oh, it's Gabriel."

"The angel?"

"Yes, he was an angel. And now he's with them, I suppose."

"Beggin' your pardon, but ya don't sound convinced about that. You sound like a woman without much faith."

"I only have faith in what I can touch. And that nightmare really touched a wound in me." She sat up and leaned against the back of the front seat again, her mouth only inches from Howard's ear. "Tell me what's really going on, Bob. I'm tired of hearing you and your friend be short with each other. I need to know what I'm in for, though I do appreciate the ride."

"You'll have to ask HP when he wakes up, Miss."

"Please call me Glory."

"Glory. There's some things about what we're doin' that I don't rightly believe myself. I'd hardly expect you to believe them now, would I?"

"I guess I'll just have to hear it from the horse lover's mouth?"

"Horse lover?"

"That's what 'Phillip' means."

"And where did you learn that?"

"I know what you take me for," said Glory, "but things aren't always the way the appear, are they?"

"I s'pose you could say the same about me and HP here. Sorry for misreadin' your character, but there ain't much more than appearances to go on now, is there?"

"I suppose I could say the same thing."

Howard nodded and was quiet for a long time. Outside, the night grew progressively darker as the cloud that followed them overtook the car and slowly blotted out the stars in the distance. The twin beams of the headlights, slightly askew, became sharply visible as a dark mist enveloped them. There was no sound other than the car, whose noises grew muffled in the descending dust. Howard found it lulling, like driving in a soft snowfall on an empty road. "Dust storm," he whispered. "But I ain't never seen one like this. Don't really seem to be blowin' from nowhere."

"It fits my mood," said Glory.

• • •

HOWARD COULD NO LONGER SEE where he was going, and he knew the car was in danger of overheating from the dust clogging the air filter. For the past several miles the signs themselves had been obscured by the dust, and he realized he had no idea where they were on their route. Lovecraft startled awake when he hit a pothole; he offered to check the map and even managed to unfold it to approximately the right place, but Howard found the rustling and the darting beam of the flashlight so annoying he told his friend to stop.

"Look, HP, we're comin' up on a road sign. I'll just get out and see if I can read it."

"Why don't we stop for a while?" Glory said from the back. "I could really use a smoke and a little stretch."

Howard let off on the gas, stepped on the clutch, and coasted slowly to a stop just far enough from the sign to illuminate its gray-black face with the headlights. With the engine idling, he stepped out onto the deserted stretch of road and wiped his palm across the sign in a wide arc. He had to do it several more times before he revealed enough fragments of lettering through the fine dust to guess at what it said. "Welcome to The Exham Priory," Howard read. He wiped his brow with the back of his dirty hand and walked back up to the car, frowning. "This don't help us a whole hell of a lot," he said to Lovecraft. "I was hopin' we were near some town."

"I think it wise that you get some rest now," Lovecraft replied. "Even a few minutes, Bob. You've been drowsing at the wheel. I'd gladly relieve you of the tedium, but this is hardly the time for you to instruct me in the intricacies of operating your automobile."

"Yeah, yeah," said Howard. "Where's Glory?"

"She stepped out to 'stretch,' as it were."

"Why's her suitcase gone?'

Lovecraft turned the beam of the flashlight into the back and saw that it was, indeed, gone. "I was not aware of that fact," he said.

"Glory!" Howard called into the darkness. "Glory! Where are you?"

There was no reply. Not even a cricket interrupted the black silence, which was punctuated only by the throbbing of the Chevy's exhaust and the slightly irregular rumble of the engine. Howard took the flashlight from his friend and shined it into the blackness. "Glory!" he called again. "Glory!" The darkness seemed to stifle the sound, killing its resonance the instant it left Howard's lips.

"Which way did she go, HP?"

"I'm afraid my back was to her. I was perusing the map to determine our position."

"You lost her!" Something cracked in Howard's voice. "I oughta—"

"Can't a lady have a moment of privacy?" came Glory's voice, out of the darkness.

Howard turned toward the sound, almost suspiciously. "Why didn't ya answer?"

"I was preoccupied."

"Why couldn't you just say where you were?"

"Because," Glory replied, losing her patience, "I was taking a piss. Can't a girl have a little piss in peace around here?"

"Just a word woulda been enough."

"Well, I was smoking, too," said Glory.

"Why did you take your suitcase? Where is it?" Howard illuminated her with the flashlight, moving the beam up and down to examine her. Lovecraft, though he was perturbed about what Howard might have said to him without the interruption, looked carefully on.

"It's back there," said Glory.

"Why did ya leave it?"

"Because! It sounded like you were about to pop your cork. Now get the light out of my face!" She shielded her eyes with her forearm, grimacing.

"Do not allow her to approach any closer," Lovecraft said suddenly.

"Hold it right there, Glory."

"What the hell's gotten into you two?"

"Just stay right there," said Howard. "Why did ya take the suitcase in the first place?"

"My cigarettes were in there."

"Why couldn't ya just take them out? HP, take the other flashlight and find the suitcase. Make sure you only see one set of footprints, and check for unusual tracks. Glory, you stay right there where I can see ya." While Lovecraft fumbled for the other flashlight, Howard eased back to the car and, almost incredulous at himself, pulled his .45 from under the driver's seat and cocked the hammer back.

"Bob, will you stop this nonsense and let me back in the car? It's cold out here, and I'm a little scared, to tell the truth." Glory lowered her arm and squinted at him, confused, the light glinting in her eyes. Howard was sure there was an odd quality to her voice.

"Glory, I'm tellin' ya to stand right there. I've got my gun aimed at you."

There was no mistaking the tone of his voice, and Glory stood in place, her arms hanging limp at her sides though she had claimed to be cold. Howard saw the other pool of light jitter and jump as Lovecraft walked around her into the desert.

"I think you boys need to stop reading your fantasy stories," Glory said rather flatly.

After a few long moments, Lovecraft's voice called out of the darkness: "Bob, I've located the suitcase. Everything appears normal. Wait . . ." Silence. "There appears to be . . ." Silence. The sound of sagebrush crunching. "Bob, it's blood!"

Howard nearly pulled the trigger at that instant, but stopped when he saw the expression on Glory's face. It was a complex expression, one he couldn't exactly read, though it seemed to reflect frustration, disgust, humiliation, and anger all in combination. It was certainly not the workings of a woman hypnotized, or a zombie, or some inhuman impostor. It flashed rapidly across her face, and then she said in a low but clearly audible voice, "I'm having my period, Bob. I carry my pads in my suitcase if you must know."

"Blood!" came Lovecraft's shrill cry once again, and this time Howard broke into loud guffaws that shook his frame so hard he dropped his flashlight. In the darkness, Glory's musical laughter joined in.

When Lovecraft, still trembling with terror, had made his way back to the car, they decided to drive a few miles farther before making camp—in case the bloody menstrual rags attracted animals. They found a flat, empty patch of desert and pulled over again after making sure they were not in a dry streambed. The tension had certainly broken. Even the air had cleared to some degree, but they were all still on edge at the thought of what might so easily have happened.

Howard made quick work of setting up camp. He scoured the area nearby for sagebrush to burn, checked for suspicious rocks and animal burrows, made sure they were far enough from the road not to be seen. He set up around the car as if it were a covered wagon during the days of the pioneer trails—Glory was to sleep in the backseat, where she would have the comfort of the cushion and could protect herself from the elements by simply closing the door. Lovecraft and he would stretch out on their bedrolls on either side of a small fire.

At first they had decided against a fire, but then they succumbed to their instinctive fear of the dark and lit one, even at the risk of being spotted from a distance by anyone who might be following them. The night was too sinister to spend without relief. With the small campfire burning, Howard immediately fell on his bedroll and balanced his hat over his eyes. Within a few breaths he was snoring away in a deep sleep.

"I'm sorry if I frightened you back there," Glory called to Lovecraft from the backseat of the Chevy. "But a girl's got a certain sense of modesty, you know."

"I understand perfectly well," Lovecraft replied. He made his way over and sat in the front seat with the door open. "I believe you are also correct about the nature of our imaginations, though certain license is clearly warranted given the events of the day."

"I still have no idea what's going on. Will you explain it to me?"

"Certainly," Lovecraft said, "but I would prefer not to speak of such things tonight."

"I understand."

"But do feel free to discuss other topics."

Glory stifled a yawn and tapped a cigarette out its pack. She lit it with a quick flick of a match and drew a small puff. "When I was younger," she said, "I used to wish the sky would rain ink or snow ashes. Do you mind my smoking? I know it's unladylike and all."

"It's hardly my place to enforce social conventions upon you. Please do as you wish."

"I always wanted to take astronomy. My school had an observatory, and Professor Mitchell was always encouraging the girls to explore the vastness of the universe. It's too bad I never got around to it, because sometimes I just like to sit alone at night and look up at the stars. It would be nice if I knew them better."

"From the reference to a professor, I take it you attended a college? Though I must admit your appearance certainly belies such a conclusion."

"I went to a girls' school back East for a while. Three years. Never finished."

"But surely, even if you did not complete your education, you must know some of the constellations and their stories?"

"Yeah, I know a couple. The Big Dipper, the Little Dipper. And I know how to find the North Star." She pointed with the glowing tip of her cigarette. "That's about all."

"Those are otherwise known as Ursa Major, Ursa Minor, and Polaris," said Lovecraft. "I once wrote the astronomy column for a local publication."

"Oh, that's wonderful!" It was genuine pleasure in her tired voice. "So tell me, what's that over there?" She moved the tip of her cigarette again, and it bobbed up and down like the tail of a glowworm.

"That would be the Pleiades."

"And that?"

"That is Canis Major, the Dog Star."

"When I was little my mother told me that every star was an angel. But they've had names all along."

Glory pointed off to the southeast at a string of stars. "And that?"

"Ah," said Lovecraft, following the tip of her cigarette with his finger. "There, in fierce gorgeousness crawls the Scorpion, with its brilliant fire red star Antares. A fitting portent of the flaming scenes which await our warriors on the Hun-infested plains of France."

"Why, you sound just like a professor, Lovey."

"I was merely quoting from a piece I wrote some years in the past," Lovecraft replied, rather abashed.

"The Hun-infested plains of France?" said Glory.

"Well, *many* years in the past, if you'll forgive me."

"And what are those?" Glory asked, pointing north now, toward three bright stars in a line. "Those look like they should add up to something."

"Ah, that would be the belt of Orion, the great hunter—Osiris, as the ancient Egyptians, the builders of the mysterious pyramids, knew him. With his consort, sister, and wife, who was known as Isis, his was the most revered constellation."

"Osiris—he married his sister?"

"Yes," said Lovecraft. "That was not at all strange for royal families in those times."

"Why, that's incest," said Glory in mock surprise. "Must have had some ugly kids."

"Actually, they did have progeny," said Lovecraft. "He became the new god of the sun, but the tale of Osiris and Isis is a tragic one. In some sense, they are literally the star-crossed lovers."

"How romantic. Tell me the story. I always liked bedtime stories."

Lovecraft could hardly resist the invitation, nor could he have asked for a better audience. He began with a flourish, his fishy eyes sparkling in the firelight.

"The most enduring tale from the Egyptian mythos is that of Osiris and Isis. Osiris, the god of the sun and the father of agriculture and Isis his sister, wife, queen, and consort, his helpmeet, the moon. They were the ideal couple, who represented man's primary connections to terrestrial cosmology, but alas their happy reign was not to last.

"Osiris had a brother named Seth, who was god of the desert and of dry things. Where Osiris was benevolent and kind, Seth was harsh and parsimonious. He was terribly jealous of Osiris, and he was terribly cunning; he wanted to do away with his brother and take his place as god of things fertile. He invited Osiris to a great feast and presented him with a wonderful and elaborately engraved sarcophagus with inlaid bands of gold and silver. 'I have made this magnificent gift for you, my brother,' Seth said to Osiris. 'Won't you honor me by confirming that I have made it the right size?' Osiris could not refuse. Indeed, he was honored and flattered, and so he lay down in the sarcophagus, which Seth's servants immediately sealed with bands of steel and threw into the Nile, down which it floated until it reached the sea.

"At the conclusion of the feast, Osiris was nowhere to be found. Isis began a quest, seeking her vanished husband to the ends of the earth until, after long labor, she found him at last in the land of Mesopotamia, the place between two rivers. This is the fertile crescent, the place which we now call the birthplace of civilization. She found Osiris's sarcophagus entangled in the roots of a tree that had grown over it. She released him from the roots and brought him back to life with her healing arts and magic, which she had learned from the great Thoth.

"Upon hearing of Osiris's return to the land of the living, Seth once again plotted his brother's undoing, and this time he committed outright murder. He ambushed Osiris, killed him, dismembered the body, and scattered its parts across the four corners of the world. And once again Isis set out on a quest, this time to find all the parts of her dead husband's body and to reassemble him.

"When she found him, with the help of her sister Nephthys, she sang this lament, which comes to us from the Coffin Texts." Lovecraft looked over at Glory and noticed she had already fallen asleep. He sighed, and concluded his tale only for himself.

Oh, helpless one, sleeping one!
Oh, helpless one, lying here
In a place which you do not know.
But I have found you, alas,

Lying listlessly on your side.
Oh, sister Nephthys, behold our brother.
Come, let us lift his head;
Come, let us assemble his bones;
Come, let us join his limbs;
Come, let us end his woe!

Lovecraft found himself getting teary-eyed as he went on. "And once again, after long labor, she found his every part excepting one, for which she created a substitute with her magic. She revived her reassembled husband with a kiss that taxed nearly all of her depleted strength. The vitality which she bestowed upon her husband nearly spent, they had only a short time to conceive their child, Horus, the winged one, the new sun, the avenger of his father and conqueror of Seth."

"Hmm?" said Glory, apparently in her sleep.

"Osiris became ruler of the underworld," said Lovecraft, "and to this day he is honored in the great monument whose shaft is aimed directly at his star in the constellation Orion."

"Thanks, Lovey," Glory mumbled.

"Good night," said Lovecraft.

8

LOVECRAFT TOUCHED HOWARD'S SHOULDER. "Bob," he whispered.

Howard mumbled something in his sleep, but then he was instantly awake, his hand automatically reaching under his improvised pillow for his pistol.

"It's no emergency," said Lovecraft. "I've been ruminating over the day's events, and I merely wanted to tell you a few things. Important things to discuss before the night is any older."

"What is it, HP?"

"I feel calm at the moment, but must confess to you that my trepidations grow ever more severe," said Lovecraft. "Consider the peculiarity of this atmospheric phenomenon. It is consistent with the turns of weather that have followed us since yesterday."

"Ain't much we can do but wait it out now," said Howard, rubbing his red eyes as he lay back on his bedroll. "We drive much farther and we're bound to overheat. I ain't got but a little spare water in the trunk, and we might need that to drink if we get stranded out here."

"Well, perhaps your attitude is the best. Please sleep, Bob. My apologies for waking you unnecessarily. I shall keep vigil for wayward reptiles."

"Mighty good of ya, HP. 'Night," he said, and he was snoring again within moments.

Lovecraft sat with his back against the front bumper and tilted his head back to look directly up into the night. The stars were out again, though they were enshrouded, in every direction, by the black dust. He realized it had settled over them like a tulle fog, like a cloud displaced from the heavens onto the earth. He wished he could sleep, but he was too agitated now in the quiet and he had promised to take the first watch. Earlier he had pretended to drift off to allow Howard and Glory a span of privacy together, and now he wished he could sleep as well as he had during that pretense.

He unscrewed the lid of the Thermos, then the top, and poured himself some coffee. He couldn't smell it in the dry air until he had lifted it halfway to his face, but then it washed over him, and he felt suddenly at ease. A cautious sip. A frown at the bitterness. He reached into his pocket for the paper napkin in which he had folded away a few handfuls of sugar just for this purpose and very carefully trickled some into the Thermos lid. There was nothing to stir it with—he would have to retrieve his spoon from the car for that—so he stirred with his pencil, smelling the odd mix of cedar and sweet coffee, and took another sip. He smiled involuntarily, added a little more sugar, and leaned back once more to savor the night and the stars.

"Someday they will all be dissipated into feeble and uniform waves of radiant heat," he whispered to himself, paraphrasing something else he had written years ago. "Too feeble to provide any perceptible warmth. It will be a terrible desolation, a vast and tomblike universe of midnight gloom and perpetual Arctic cold. And through this sepulchral universe will roll dark, frozen suns with their hordes of dead planets covered in the dust of those unfortunate mortals who will have perished as their stars faded from the skies."

He took another sweet sip of coffee and smiled again, though his own words had made his sense of foreboding grow stronger. From his watch pocket, he removed the Artifact, which had been paining him all day, and he wasn't surprised at all to see its eerie pulsing glow illuminate the darkness with its cold, nacreous light. Lovecraft felt strangely at ease now, not at all like the fearful man he really was; he felt like the protagonist in a story with a predictable and heroic outcome, confident that despite the trials ahead all would turn out well. Part of himself was alarmed by this lulling of his usual anxiety; he suspected that this confidence was a ploy by his pursuers designed to put him at ease, to make him vulnerable.

Lovecraft noticed the Artifact's glow seem to diminish while the background light seemed to increase. He jerked his head around in alarm, then looked up to see that the moon had just emerged from a patch of dark clouds, its cold silver light washing out the glow of the Artifact. Compelled by some whim, he held the thing up, juxtaposing it with the orb of the moon, to compare the nature of the light. In front of his face, the Artifact was the same size as the moon, and its aura blended uncannily with the halo around the lunar disk until it appeared that they were emitting the same light. Lovecraft didn't even have to shift his eyes back and forth to notice that the man in the moon was changing; its expression, usually a sort of tranquil melancholy, was distorting into a hideous grimace. Then the face lost its anthropomorphic qualities altogether. Squidlike tendrils crawled across the surface, forming a hideous chaos that slowly coagulated into the face represented on the Artifact clutched in his hand.

Lovecraft lurched to his feet and nearly stepped into the dying fire as he stumbled over to Howard and shook him. "Bob!" he said in a loud whisper. "Bob!"

Howard grunted, and then sat bolt upright, his pistol magically in his hand. "Where is he?" he said.

Lovecraft waited momentarily while Howard got his bearings, then he showed him the Artifact and directed his attention up at the moon.

Neither man could believe his eyes. It had changed again. They both stared, mesmerized by the bizarre and amorphous shapes that seemed to emanate from the very surface of the pockmarked satellite.

"Do you see them?" asked Howard.

"Yes. They are the children of Dagon, the elder god of the deep."

"They're coming out of the craters."

"The *mare*. They are called seas in Latin. Now I understand the appropriateness of that appellation. The old astronomers must have known the truth."

"I say we hightail it outta here, HP."

"Where shall we go to hide from the moon?" Just then the moon vanished once more behind a bank of swift clouds, leaving the desert suddenly smothered in blackness illuminated only by the last red glow of dying embers and the cold pulse of the Artifact.

WHEN THEY HEARD the scream, Lovecraft and Howard were momentarily confused. They had all but forgotten that they had a woman with them; they thought, for an instant, that what they heard was the cry of some desert animal in the jaws of a predator. The sound lingered in the upper part of the register, part of it lost in a range beyond hearing; it cut through their spines like slivers of glass, and in the split second it took them to place its origin, they were on their feet, turning toward the car. But once again, they were disoriented, petrified now by what they saw.

Howard could make out tiny points of light, like distant fireflies, moving quietly across the darkness; when he turned his head he saw that they extended everywhere, from horizon to horizon, in small, moving clusters. He blinked, trying to adjust his vision, which had been blinded by the bright light of the moon. Lovecraft put the Artifact quickly back into his pocket, and to his eyes, which were naturally more acclimated to the night, the lights were far more numerous; they stretched into the distance, and what appeared as dispersed blobs to Howard resolved themselves into groups of glowing specks, large and small, slowly approaching. Some of the lights blinked on and off; others remained steady and grew as they approached.

"Glory!" Howard shouted.

"Oh, God, I'm glad you're alive," came Glory's voice. "I thought . . . Oh, my God!"

"Glory, turn the headlamps on," Howard instructed in a steady voice.

As the specks of light rapidly closed on them, they heard a click and the headlights switched on, lancing through the darkness like a flash of lightning. In the twin beams, which shone blindingly bright to Howard and Lovecraft, they saw what lay behind the multitude of tiny lights: animals—large and small, predator and prey—all moving like automatons slowly toward the car. They were unnaturally silent; not a squeak or a hiss or a growl issued from them; the only sound, like the dry scratching of leaves, was the noise they made stalking, scrabbling, slithering across the dry earth. It seemed to echo in the distance, growing subtly louder each second.

The two men moved slowly, lest they trigger something in the animals, and they eased toward the car. "Roll the windows up," Howard said to Glory. "Make sure the doors are shut. Do you know how to drive?"

"Yes," came the reply.

"Crawl into the front and—" Suddenly the distant sounds were upon them—not at all the echoes of the terrestrial beasts, but the fleshy fluttering of wings. The thunderous chaos descended upon them first, and then, before they could respond, the air was full of black shadows darting madly, changing direction in mid-flight; and now they could hear the occasional cricketlike shriek of the bats as they sounded out their targets and swooped to attack. Howard, in his hat, swatted more in annoyance than fear at the bats, but Lovecraft shrieked in almost the same pitch as he flailed his arms, not knowing whether to protect his face or the top of his head. As they clawed at the doors, the Chevy's engine fired up, and in the momentary reprieve as the vibrations frightened the bats, Lovecraft and Howard leaped in.

"Drive!" said Howard, contorted in the front seat, feeling the top of his head to confirm it was his hat and not an animal there.

Glory threw the gearshift into first and turned the car toward the road, the headlights swinging in a wide arc that illuminated an unbelievable array of desert animals in their circumference. Just as they began to gain speed there was a sudden lurch, then a strong jolt as the rear of the car tilted at an odd angle and the headlights shone up, askew, into the dusty night. Howard began to curse their luck, but his voice was drowned out almost immediately by all manner of bumps and scratches against the car as the first wave of animals reached them *en masse*. They could hardly see through the front windshield, now obscured by the fleshy, membranous wings of bats that pressed themselves there, drooling, their thick saliva dripping down the glass.

The larger animals began hurling themselves against the windows. Coyotes leaped against the glass so hard they could see it bend almost imperceptibly against their weight. At the rear right window, in the corner where Lovecraft cowered with his hands over his ears, some small rodent had managed to gnaw through the rubber seal and now tried to claw its way in. When Lovecraft saw it he took the only weapon he had readily at hand—his pencil—and poked at the animal until he felt it stop moving. He drew the pencil stub back in and nearly retched when he saw it dripping red, but then he screwed up his courage and used it to jab again and again until it broke. He fumbled through his satchel, trying to find the stone dagger he knew was in it, but in his haste he resorted next to his pen.

Howard had once been inside a tin shack during a hailstorm, in a rattling, thunderous chaos of echoing collisions; he felt the same way now with the animals hurling themselves at the car. In the hailstorm he had merely waited until the stones had stopped falling and the echoes had quieted in his ears before walking out into the fresh-smelling desert. He wondered how long this attack could last. It was a mere annoyance, after all. What could these small desert animals do to them in the safety of the car? Whatever force was causing their strange behavior had also dulled their natural instincts, and they seemed to have lost their animal quickness. In the worst case, Howard expected he would be trapped until the heat of day made the beasts retreat into the shade or back under the rocks from which they had crawled, and then he would have to save the car. "HP," he said, "don't use your flashlight unless you really got to. Don't want to run out of juice. I think we should shut the engine off to save our gas, too."

Lovecraft shined the beam against the windshield again at the thickening ooze of bat saliva dripping there. The sounds had diminished now, probably because the entire car was covered in animals, which muffled the assault of others. Lovecraft shut the beam off. "What shall we do?" he asked, his voice cracking.

"Please," said Glory, "you can't shut the headlights off. I'll go mad in the dark. How will we know if anything gets in?"

"A rat or lizard ain't gonna kill us," said Howard. "Just gotta be careful of snakes, though I don't know how they'd get in."

Glory closed her eyes and began to pray silently. She tried to control her breath to avoid breathing the rank air in the car. It would only get fouler as the night drew on. "Please," she said again, "you have to get us out of here."

"What is it, HP? You think all they want's the doohickey of yours?"

"Undoubtedly. But even if we surrendered it, they would surely devour us. Cthulhu has no regard for men."

"That's what I woulda guessed. Get ready for a long and sweaty night, folks. It's gonna get mighty hot and sticky in here with all them varmints outside." He reached past Glory and shut the ignition off, and then the headlights, suddenly leaving them in a thick gloom.

"Oh, God," Glory said out loud. "I feel like I'm in a cheese box with rats gnawing their way through."

"Look, Glory, if it gets desperate, I'll step out and get us out of the hole. It just ain't a very pleasant thought at the moment." Howard leaned back against the passenger-side door, unfazed by the vermin pressed against the glass. He could hear the muffled wheezing and rustling sounds, the occasional tap of a claw against glass, the annoying vibration of rodent teeth gnawing at metal.

Lovecraft shivered in revulsion as he occasionally poked his pen at the space in the window, each time meeting fleshy resistance, sometimes hearing a tiny squeal of pain. He did not know if he could last the night without losing his mind.

There was a loud thump on the hood—something so heavy they felt it throughout the car. They heard scrabbling noises, as if the smaller animals were getting out of the way, and then a bloodcurdling scream. The thing that had jumped on the hood was so heavy that it tilted the vehicle back to its horizontal position.

"What was that?" said Glory. Lovecraft was silent.

"I got a bad feelin' about this one," Howard mumbled, flicking on his flashlight. He pointed the beam at the windshield, and through the distortion of the bat saliva, he saw an earth-colored feline form. A cougar, he thought. The only desert animal that might have the strength to smash the glass of the car. "I gotta shoot this one," Howard announced. "I'm openin' the window here a crack, so you two get ready to block anything that tries to come in. Ready?"

There was another loud shriek, and they saw the cougar batting smaller animals aside as it stalked up to the windshield, attracted by the light. Its eyes flashed like red embers in its skull, and its fangs, even in the dim light, looked like stalactites in its cavernous mouth.

Howard rolled down his right sleeve and buttoned it, then he turned the window down, just far enough to allow for the thickness of his beefy arm, and stuck his .45 outside, his flashlight still pointed at the windshield. Lovecraft shined his own beam at Howard's arm; he saw shapes moving outside, but nothing seemed intent on entering at the moment.

With the first deafening explosion of the .45, everything went deadly quiet. They could see the giant cat twitch. It stumbled, seeming momentarily confused, and then the pain of its injury enraged it and it let out another bloodcurdling scream and leaped at the windshield, its front paws hitting so hard the glass visibly moved.

"Shit!" said Howard. He quickly adjusted his awkward aim and fired again. In the explosion of light from the muzzle, they saw the cougar lurch again, hit somewhere in the shoulder. This time it growled and swatted with one paw at the window with a loud thump, leaving hair-line cracks radiating from the impact. "Well damn you ta Hell!" Howard fired again, with a holler of pain this time, and the bullet caught the giant cat squarely in the head. Blood and brain tissue splashed against the windshield, and the animal fell on its side, its staring eyes still reflecting its evil intent.

Howard quickly jerked his arm back inside and rolled up the window, cursing under his breath. There were tiny tears and one lone rip on his shirtsleeve; he was oozing blood from several scratches, but one particular wound was bleeding freely. "God damn bats!" he said. "Wish I had a damn Gatlin' gun and I'd show 'em." He put his pistol on the seat next to him and examined his wounds.

"Thanks," said Glory.

"Don't mention it. You got somethin' for this, maybe?"

"I have a few items for first aid in my satchel," Lovecraft offered. He opened it quickly, and Glory leaned over to tend to the cuts.

Outside, the animals had grown quiet. When Lovecraft shifted his light to investigate, what he saw made his stomach turn. Dozens of small rodents and even a coyote had climbed onto the hood to pick at the carcass of the dead cougar. The coyote had already ripped the cat's belly open, and hordes of tiny eyes were swarming up to gnaw at the innards. He turned away before he retched.

"Bob," said Lovecraft.

"Yeah?"

"I've noticed that our vehicle is now once again in a horizontal orientation due to the weight of the animals. May I suggest we attempt forward movement?"

"Good idea. But I ain't drivin' but a few yards on account of we might have a broken wheel or axle or somethin'."

"I find that quite suitable."

With his wounds dressed, Howard awkwardly scooted to the left while Glory raised herself up, arching so that he could slide under her to get to the driver's side. It was a tricky maneuver in the dark, and Glory couldn't help sitting on his lap, ever so briefly, as they changed position.

"All right," said Howard. "HP, you get yourself as far left as you can. Glory, you slide back this way. We gotta get all the weight off the rear right tire."

They rearranged themselves, and Howard fired up the engine. In a moment he eased out the clutch in first and the car began to move tentatively forward. Howard eased up a little more, simultaneously gunning the engine, and they heard the right rear tire spinning freely, throwing gouts of sand into the wheel well, but in a second it seemed to catch and they jerked forward. They heard the cougar's body shift on the hood and the sound of small animals scrabbling to keep their footing. From the roof came scratching noises—the sound of hundreds of rodents' claws.

Howard cut the engine again and wiped the sweat from under the brim of his hat. "Well," he said, "we're free for the moment. But I ain't riskin nothin' else till I can have a look. I say we take a breather."

To save the flashlight, Lovecraft lit his candle stump. He shared the remaining coffee with Glory, though it was hard to drink in the stench that now enveloped the car. Howard leaned back once again to catch a nap. "Don't worry till another cougar shows up," he mumbled. "And that ain't likely in these parts."

Things were quiet again for a time. Glory and Lovecraft hardly exchanged a word, but Howard could hear their breathing and their sipping at the still-hot coffee. He touched his injured arm, where the bat bite was throbbing with an uncomfortable heat under the improvised dressing Glory had made out of one of her slips. He couldn't help a smile at the thought of that—just like the Westerns where the kindhearted saloon girl comes to the Marshal's assistance and rips the hem of her poofy French skirts to stop the blood from his flesh wound. The stories never change, he thought as he nodded off. They just get closer to home.

He was home again when he opened his eyes. The house was lit in a weird blue light, and there was a strange buzzing sensation in the air, as if everything were charged with electricity. He took a tentative step forward from the living room into the hall and was surprised to feel his feet slipping on something. No, not slipping. His feet were gliding just an inch off the floor and he was floating forward, but because he wasn't used to it, he felt like he was sliding on ice without skates. "Ma?" he called. "Ma? Are you home?" He continued to move forward like that, sliding one foot after the other, though somewhere in the back of his mind he was certain he could just fly to his mother's room. "Poppa?" he called, and this time there was a muted answer. "Bobby," came his father's voice. "Bobby, what the Dickens are you doin' here? Get the hell outta this place at once!" Howard kept moving, past the framed pictures of his grandparents and his parents in their younger, happier days in Dark Valley, past the odd, hanging souvenirs, until he stood at the door to his mother's bedroom. The light in there was different— warm and reddish. It clashed with the blue light in the hallway so that where the two colors met everything was tinged in a terrible violet aura. Howard slid into the aura and winced in pain—pins and needles seemed to jab at his body, and when he looked down at himself he suddenly realized he was just a little boy. His knees were all scabby and he was wearing those uncomfortable tight boots his father had bought for him. "Poppa," he said again. "Poppa, how come I can't see Ma?" He was past the violet fringe now, and he stood just inside the doorway looking at his father's back. His mother's bed had been moved, or perhaps the room had taken on some other shape, because he couldn't see her; she was obstructed by his father's broad back. "Poppa?" Dr. Howard turned, revealing his face, which was spattered with black fluid. He was moving something up and down with his right arm, as if he were pumping something. "Bobby, I told you to get the hell outta here. Now listen to me, boy!" "But, Poppa, I wanna see my Ma! I wanna see Ma!" "You want to see her? You really want to see her?" said Dr. Howard, his eyes widening into frightful circles. "Then look at her, damn you! Look!" He stepped aside, and suddenly Howard saw what he had been obscuring with his body. His mother lay propped up on the bed, all naked, shriveled, and deflated. Protruding from under her right breast was a giant needle attached to a length of black rubber hose, and that led into a large hand pump the size of a bicycle pump. His father slowly pulled the lever, and there was a nauseating sucking sound; his mother's body deflated a bit more, shriveling more tightly around her bones. Already her cheeks had the sunken look of a mummy; the flesh had pulled back from her eyes until they were no more than glaring white balls that couldn't close. "No!" Howard shouted. He suddenly leaped at his father with clenched fists, but his father merely swatted him away. When he tried to attack again, Dr. Howard pulled the giant needle out of his wife's chest and pointed it at his son. Howard drew back, afraid his father would impale him with it, but instead, he pushed on the handle and sprayed him with a fountain of bloody tubercular phlegm, laughing all the while. On the bed, his mother began slowly to collapse in upon herself, the black hole in her chest leaking out her vital fluids. "Ma!" Howard shouted. "Ma!" He reached out for her, but she was behind a barrier of glass. "Ma!" he shouted again, but he was helpless. Her body was slowly dissolving, bubbling, leaving a disgusting skeleton covered in clots of foul meat and pus-laced blood. He pounded and pounded against the glass, but it only thudded hollowly under his helpless fists.

"Ma!" Howard screamed. "Ma!" There was a thud against the inside of the windshield.

Lovecraft and Glory bolted upright, spilling what was left of the coffee. Lovecraft switched the light on, revealing Howard slamming his injured hand against the glass. Just beyond that were the remains of the dead cougar, barely visible behind the dried blood and saliva that caked the windshield.

Howard pounded the glass again, just in front of the cougar's skull, a discolored white mass with black eye sockets. "Ma!" he called again, then, "I'll kill you, you son of a bitch! I'll kill you!" He reached for the window.

"Stop him!" cried Lovecraft.

Glory leaned forward and tried to restrain Howard, but he was too strong for her. He grabbed his pistol in his left hand and started to roll the window down with his right.

"He's having a nightmare! Wake him up!"

Glory pulled at Howard. "Bob! Wake up! Wake up! You're okay!"

Howard merely swatted her away, stuck the pistol out of the window, and pulled the trigger. Light and sound exploded just outside the window, and the recoil, in his loose grasp, snapped the metal barrel against the window, leaving a long crack in it. Howard suddenly froze. He looked around him, quickly, then drew the gun inside and rolled the damaged window back up before anything could get inside. "I'll be God damned," he whispered.

"Bob, are you lucid again?"

"Where the hell are we?" Howard asked.

"We're in New Mexico. You were having a nightmare," said Glory. She reached over to feel his forehead. "You're feverish. Take your hat off."

Howard brushed her hand away. "He killed Ma," he said.

"Who?"

"That bastard killed her."

"It was a nightmare, Bob. It is the doing of Cthulhu. Wake up."

Howard blinked at the flashlight beam in his face. He frowned. Then his face relaxed, and he appeared wide-awake. He looked at Glory, then at Lovecraft, in the dim light reflecting from the inside of the windows. "I ain't lettin' no wild animals kill me," he said very soberly. "They can eat my dead carcass for all I care, but they ain't killin' me. No, sir." He lifted his pistol again, this time pointed at his head.

"Put it down!" said Lovecraft. "Put the gun down, damn it!"

"Look," Howard replied with a deadly calm, "I saved three bullets. One for each of us. I say we use 'em while we can. I'll be glad to do the honors before I shoot myself. Glory?"

"You're a raving maniac!" said Glory. "Shoot the damned animals, not us!"

"You're sure?"

"You're out of your mind!"

Howard rolled the window down again, this time just a crack, and fired; a coyote fell dead, punctured through the eye.

"HP?"

Lovecraft wasn't as quick to reply. He could see the cold logic of it. Indeed, it was heroic logic, to be sure, and he wished he could participate in it like a man, but some primal instinct for self-preservation, even with the knowledge of imminent doom, prevented him. "No, Bob."

Howard fired again, and something screeched in the near distance. He rolled the window back up, and when Glory reached for the gun, he slapped her away with the side of the barrel. "Keep on your side," he warned, pointing it at her. Glory scooted back to the passenger's side and waited. Howard put the pistol barrel just above his right ear and, without a moment of hesitation, he squeezed the trigger. Glory closed her eyes involuntarily at the explosion, the flash, the sharp smell of cordite. When she opened her eyes again she saw Howard and Lovecraft looking at each other over the seat back in a stunned silence. There was a thud on the roof, and blood began to ooze down through the bullet hole—animal blood.

"You stupid son of a bitch, look what you done!" Howard shouted. "That was my last bullet!"

"You're a coward!" Lovecraft shouted back hysterically. "You're just a big coward! I'm not letting you kill yourself!"

"Now how am I gonna—" Howard stopped abruptly and seemed to get his bearings once again. "Oh, sweet Jesus," he whispered.

Glory looked at the expression on his face. "Bob?" she said. "Are you awake?"

"I'll be God damned," said Howard. "Did I just do what I think I did, or was I just sleepwalkin'?"

"You weren't exactly walking," Lovecraft replied, unable to stop a smile at seeing his old friend back to himself.

As Howard loudly berated Lovecraft for causing the hole in the roof of his car, the tearful Glory closed her eyes and prayed for God's help. In all the excitement inside the car, they had forgotten to pay attention to the animals outside, and when Glory opened her eyes again, she noticed she could see outside without the help of a flashlight. At first she thought the sun had risen, but the light was the cold light of the moon. "Look," she said.

The animals had begun to disperse. The loud din of fluttering bats had faded, and in the quiet moonlight the desert creatures had come to their senses once again. In a few moments only the few shadowed lumps of dead carcasses were visible, and the landscape was once again cold and clear.

STILL, IT TOOK a while for them to gather the courage to get out and examine the car. Howard pulled the dripping remains of the cougar off the hood and flung it as hard as he could; it broke into two pieces and landed several yards away. He opened the hood with hands trembling with fatigue; the first hose he touched hissed and fell to the ground, where it quickly slithered away, but otherwise, there was nothing seriously amiss, just some easily remedied dust clogs and patches of fur.

Lovecraft, on the other side of the car, dragged a dead coyote off the roof. Under the dimming beam of his flashlight, he cataloged the dents and scratches on the chassis, some unexpectedly deep but none detrimental to the car's mobility. Even the tires had escaped any significant harm.

And later, while Howard and Lovecraft compared notes and argued about how best to wash the car in the middle of the desert, Glory stood against a back fender, slowly puffing on a cigarette to relax herself. Her legs would not stop shaking, and her head was still abuzz with images of the feral animals. The first cigarette did not last long; she finished it and ground it out under her heel before she realized she wanted another. With jittery fingers she fished one more out of the pack and snapped a match against the box. The small, sulfurous flame exploded with momentary light and pungency before it settled into a steady glow in the windless night. Glory put the tip of her cigarette to it, puffed until the tobacco glowed, then blew the flame out of the corner of her mouth, extinguishing it. Odd. She could still see something past the glow of her cigarette. She thought it must be the afterimage of the match flame, but when she turned and blinked her eyes, there was no afterimage. She cupped the cigarette in her palms and looked once again out into the darkness and saw a single steady light, like a lantern, approaching from the distance. In front of it bobbed two other lights, glowing orbs she was now more than familiar with—the glowing eyes of a nocturnal animal.

Glory cried out in alarm.

9

HOWARD WAS ALREADY in position to fire, his .45 in one hand, his flashlight in the other, illuminating the figure that had come out of the desert. It was no glowing-eyed monster, just a gray-haired old Indian man in a headband, carrying a lantern, a very wolflike German shepherd at his side.

"Hold it right there!" called Howard. "What do ya want?"

"I am here to help you," said the old man.

"Help us?" Howard replied. "What the hell can you do that we can't?"

"Bob," Glory whispered in a chastising tone. "Be civil, at least."

The old man seemed entirely unfazed by the gun, as if he knew it was empty. He smiled, and said, almost in a chant, "The hatted bear has a temper. The pale fish is sensitive. The red horse is full of passion and nurturing." He swept his arm, indicating the desert. "Tonight the animals were walking in their sleep, and I came out to wake them up."

"To which animals are you referring?" asked Lovecraft. "The three you've just mentioned or those that kept us hostage?"

"Tonight all the animals were sleepwalking. I have been waiting for you. Come to my home, and we shall talk about why you are here."

"I say you just go back the way you came," said Howard, jerking his pistol. "We had enough trouble as it is. How do we know it wasn't you, huh? With that Injun mumbo jumbo. Keep that wolf of yours away from us."

"The pale fish man," said the old man, his voice very patient. "He carries a thing that brings evil. He carries a thing that was hidden in the mind of a holy Kachina, and now it has no protection. He comes from the seashore to the desert to ask the bear for help, and the two friends have found the red horse woman at the home of the lion man. I have known this for many years. And I have known that you will come with me. So come to my home and we shall talk." He said something under his breath, and the dog bounded off into the darkness.

"Who are you?" said Lovecraft.

"I am Imanito Shakes-the-Gourd."

"You a witch doctor?" asked Howard. "A medicine man?"

"Yes. I am a healer of those who are sick."

"We ain't sick."

"You are injured. You are having evil dreams. You are sick."

"You gonna heal us?"

"No," said Imanito. "I can only tell you a story that will help you heal yourselves."

"Figures," said Howard.

"Please, I have been waiting many years to help you. I have prepared my role. I can even help you repair your automobile."

"It ain't broke, so it don't need fixin'," said Howard. "The car's fine. Just needs a good washin' to get all the blood and guts off. You got water out there?"

"I will gladly help you wash your car."

That seemed to please Howard, and now, although Lovecraft and Glory expressed their misgivings, he was agreeable to following the old man. "How can you just accept his story?" Glory whispered. "Especially after what you've been through today?"

While the old man waited with his lantern, Howard made his way to the front of the Chevy to close the hood. "Everything bad's given me a bad feelin'," Howard replied. "This old Injun gives me a good feelin'."

"That's hardly enough to base an important decision on."

"God damn!" Howard exclaimed, leaning into the engine compartment, one hand still holding up the hood.

"Bob?" Lovecraft appeared with his flashlight.

"Shine it down here, HP."

When Lovecraft turned the beam of his flashlight down to the earth, Glory saw that the ground was dark with water. Drops were still falling from somewhere under the hood.

Howard twisted off the radiator cap and cursed again. "Must have been the snake," he said. "We got a punctured hose, and I ain't carryin' enough spare water to make up for this."

"Mr. Imanito said he had water," Glory offered.

"You would almost conclude he had sent the animals himself," said Lovecraft. "But you're right, Bob. He gives me a good feeling also."

"More likely it was that bucktoothed bastard back at the gas pump in Thalia that did it," said Howard. "But it don't matter. We need water now." He turned to the old man. "We ain't walkin' in the dark and gettin' bushwhacked, so climb in. There's enough water to get to your teepee."

"I think the proper term is 'hogan,' " said Glory. "Mr. Imanito is a Navajo. Mr. Imanito?"

"Yes, I happen to live in a hogan. But my people are closer to the Hopi." He climbed into the backseat with Glory, balancing his lantern carefully between them.

Howard started up the Chevy and eased it forward. "I thought all the Hopis lived in Arizona," he said. "Ain't never heard of any in New Mexico. This is Navajo country."

"That is true," said Imanito. "I do not live among my people at the moment because I have been awaiting you."

"Stop the bullshit, old man."

Imanito smiled. "Come to my home, and the bull will give you many more droppings."

Howard looked momentarily puzzled at this unexpected response, but then he broke into a grin. "Well," he said, "what are we waitin' for then? Which way?"

Imanito gave directions from the back. There were no real turns to make after he looked once out the window and established their bearing by the stars. From the front seat, Lovecraft confirmed the old man's sense of direction based on his own long experience as an amateur astronomer, something he pointed out to Imanito. Once Howard got accustomed to steering around the few shrubs and cacti in their way, it was slow but steady going.

"So who are your people?" Lovecraft asked. "I am especially intrigued by the existence of an ancient elder race of Indians in this region."

"I dwell among the people whose name comes from '*Hopitu*,' which means 'the peaceful people,' " said Imanito. "They have remained peaceful, and they have kept the old ways because they are keepers of the old stories."

"The Hopi are the only tribe that kept to the pueblos," said Glory. "They hold to the purest form of pre-Columbian life in North America."

"You're sounding rather like a professor," said Lovecraft. "Is primitive societies a topic you studied in college?"

"No. I met an anthropologist once while I was working one of the oil towns. He talked a lot. Studying for his Ph.D. exams."

Imanito's eyes glinted with amusement. "Most of my people live on three mesas north of what you call Winslow in Arizona. We have only a dozen villages left, and the old ways are dying."

"My impression was that sagacious old men of the Indian tribes were rather taciturn," said Lovecraft. "And they usually refer to their own people as 'we.' "

"There is little time and there is much I must tell you," Imanito said, avoiding the implied question.

"Why didn't you write it down for us if you've been waiting all these years?"

They had little sense of distance in the dark without landmarks, and they reached their destination before they knew it. Imanito's home loomed ahead of them so suddenly it seemed to have sprouted out of the earth. What the headlights illuminated in the middle of nowhere was a hogan, but a decidedly odd one, constructed of adobe brick, mud, twigs, wood scraps, and what appeared, against all logic, to be driftwood. They climbed out of the car. Howard left the engine running and went with Imanito immediately to fetch water.

"Now that is decidedly odd," Lovecraft said to Glory. "Shouldn't they shut the motor off if it is in imminent danger of overheating?"

"You'd think so, wouldn't you?"

When Imanito and Howard returned with water, Lovecraft posed the question once again, and Howard answered rather arrogantly, happy, it seemed, to play professor to his friend for once. "You gotta keep the water circulatin', HP. If you shut the engine off and pour cold water into the radiator, it all hits the engine in one jolt and it could make the cylinders crack from the sudden temperature change. You pour a little at a time and it cools down slower and safer."

"Remarkable," said Lovecraft. "One would never expect that a backwoods pulp writer could so concisely explain the thermodynamics of an internal combustion engine."

When the radiator stopped steaming and the chugging of the Chevy sounded oddly contentented, Howard shut the engine off. "Now we gotta fix this hose," he declared. "Where are we gonna get a hose out here in the middle of nowhere?"

"I have such a hose for you," said Imanito. "But I know you are all hungry from your ordeal, so please eat first."

"And you wouldn't happen to have a tool box handy, would ya?"

"I have also kept the tools you will need to fix the hose."

"You don't say. I'm likin' you more every minute, old man."

As they entered Imanito's home, Glory paused to give the old man something small in a packet, and he said a gracious thanks. They retired into the hogan, where they sat on low stools around the fire. The interior of Imanito's home was dim in the unsteady light of the fire, and not much was fully visible, but there were tantalizing glimpses of a vast array of traditional artifacts and modern junk. Howard was especially struck by the poster of the shapely young diving woman in the red swimsuit advertising Jantzen swimwear. In the flickering firelight, she seemed to be swimming through warm ripples of water.

Lovecraft found his stomach immediately rumbling, and he fixated his gleaming eyes on the pot of stew on the flame, the source of the delicious, hearty aroma that filled the hogan.

"It would be improper to perform a ritual on a full stomach, but you are not of my people, and therefore you need not be bound to our ways." Imanito ladled out bowls of the thick stew and served it in stoneware bowls with hunks of puffy fry bread.

The travelers hadn't realized how hungry they were; they ate ravenously, stopping only to let Imanito refill their empty bowls.

"This is delicious," said Howard. "What is it?"

"It is made from corn and lamb," said Imanito.

"What do ya call it in Hopi?"

"*Nokquivi*," said Imanito.

"Knock-quee-vee," Howard repeated. "Mighty satisfyin'."

"Now," said Imanito, "I will tell you why you are here."

"Well, give it your best shot," Howard replied, slouching forward on his stool with his elbows propped on his knees.

"Many years ago when I was still a boy, I was told a story by my father, who was a medicine man. At that time it was just a story to me, because it did not fit with the sacred stories he told. I thought that it might be something he had made up just for me to entertain me because I was just a boy and found the ways of the healer difficult." Imanito passed around a pack of cigarettes as he spoke, and Howard and Glory each took one. The old man produced a small pipe, which he filled from a pouch of tobacco. "This is the story he told me," he said. "A long time from now, in the future, when you are an old man older than me, you are visited by three travelers who are of the white people. They are riding in the belly of a black horse made of iron. It is a horse without legs, and it rolls like a cart which is drawn by horses. On its head sits a hummingbird woman, who protects it from afar. It is in the desert, and many animals have come to eat it, but they cannot eat it because its flesh is iron and they themselves are asleep in a sleep made for them by an evil sorcerer.

"The three travelers are tired and hungry and scared. Their horse has eyes that light up the darkness, but it cannot find its way because it is thirsty. Its intestines are leaking, for they have been bitten by a snake, and its water has fallen to the thirsty earth. The horse growls like a mountain lion. It breathes hot steam like the bowels of the earth. Inside it, the three travelers grow hot and afraid.

"These are the three travelers: the black-hatted bear man, the pale fish man, the red horse woman. The two men are tellers of tales and keepers of secrets they themselves do not know. The woman is a mother, who is not a mother, who wishes to visit a mother. Her hair is the color of fire and her death is cold and clear as the air. The death of the black-hatted bear man is the color of caked clay; it is hot and full of thunder and the smell of sulfur that fills the belly of his black horse. The death of the pale fish man is quiet and white, and it is like the pain that a boy feels in his side when he has run too fast and too hard and he pants like a fish that has been taken from the river." Imanito paused. "These were all riddles, as you can see. It was a good story whose meaning I did not know truly until tonight."

"I don't like the sound of all that death," said Howard. "You tellin' us you brought us here to fortune-tell how we're gonna die?"

"No. That is only part of the story. My father's instructions were different."

"You wanna hear more of this mumbo jumbo, HP?"

"I find it rich and fascinating," said Lovecraft. "Please continue, Mr. Imanito. But we haven't all night, so perhaps you should summarize the gist of things."

"My father told me that I must go out into the desert on a certain night to help the three of you. He said I had to wake up the sleeping animals, and he gave me the song that would do it. He said I should bring you back to my home and feed you and give you a new piece of intestine for your horse. And I was to tell you how to go to the place where shadows bend, for that was the place of his first battle, and the pale fish man carried a thing that must be buried there to keep the world safe until the time of the gourd of ashes." Imanito stopped again. "Now I must tell you what you must do, but the woman cannot see the things I must show you."

"Why not?" said Howard.

Glory was momentarily flattered and pleased that he would want to include her, but then Imanito stated that the knowledge was for men only, that women's eyes would pollute it, and that seemed more than satisfactory as an answer.

"What'll we do about her then?" Howard asked. "Can't exactly put her out in the car now, can we?"

"Not to worry," said Imanito. "I have prepared a place for her." He indicated a corner, or rather, an area in the round interior that he had set off behind a partition of hanging blankets. "Red horse woman may rest in there where I have prepared blankets."

"I'm dead tired anyway," said Glory, unable to mask the disappointment in her voice. "What are you going to show them, anyway? A sand painting? I've seen those before."

"Yes," said Imanito. "There are instructions I must show them. It would not do to have them seen by your eyes."

"All right. Good night, fellas." She parted the hanging blankets and entered a dark enclave surrounded by stacks of junk. When she let the blankets fall back into place, a little light from the fire still managed to shine in underneath, between the blankets and the floor.

Imanito had laid out a couple of clean horse blankets and a thinner one, an army blanket, for her. While the others muttered on the other side of the partition, Glory lay back in the soft bedding and relaxed. She looked around as her eyes adjusted to the dark and was amazed by the junk the old shaman had collected over the years. There were stacks and stacks of popular magazines piled from the dirt floor to the roof; she recognized some of the stray volumes of *Life* and even an issue of *Weird Tales*, with its usual cover depicting a scantily clad

woman in dire terror. At one side of the small enclave were open
wooden boxes stacked with mason jars whose contents were either
mysterious or absurd—unidentifiable colored pastes or tiny toy cars;
there was a Frigidaire with its door permanently open, filled with
books and crinkled contour maps of the U.S. Geological Survey; a
scattering of postcards—used ones—from odd parts of the world;
dried herbs and flowers hung from the rafters; several dozen identical
black men's shoes—all for the right foot—were stacked in a corner;
and there was an open box just next to her filled with fabric and rug
scraps, old wooden Christmas ornaments, part of a Confederate flag,
and a teddy bear with one eye. It was as if Imanito had worked at a post
office and kept random parcels for himself; his hogan was like a personal dead-letter office accumulating a mass of things that were truly
odds and ends. Glory pulled her blanket more snugly over her shoulder and, with the dim images still in her mind, she was asleep before
she realized it.

As HOWARD AND LOVECRAFT sat hunched over on their low
stools, sipping bitter black coffee, Imanito sat with legs crossed on the
floor of the hogan and began his tale. As he spoke, he reached for a
series of small containers at his side; he dipped his hands into these
and began trickling colored sand onto the flat part of the earthen floor
by the fire. He was speaking some of the lore of the Old Ones,
recounting the meanings behind various Kachina figures, reading
their stories in a series of small sand sketches as he went on. Soon the
square contours of the painting took shape, and then the outlines were
elaborated with a key of designs in contrasting colors. Red, white,
blue, green, yellow. Lovecraft and Howard were both amazed at how
concisely the old man could draw with the sand that trickled from the
crease in his palm. If they had been told that it was magic, they would
not have hesitated to dismiss it as some trick, but Imanito went on
matter-of-factly, the complex lines and shapes appearing under his
palm so quickly it seemed he was following patterns already there on
the floor. But the floor was bare.

Now Imanito told the great myth of the Emergence, the origin of the Southwest Indian peoples, and part of the story was a long litany of names: Navajo, Zuni, Lipan, Jicarilla, Laguna, Tiwa, Keresan, and Hopi; part a cataloging of living communities like Walpi, Sichomovi, and Oraibi, which had come down from ancient times.

"Long ago when the world was still new the old ones and the old creatures lived under the earth. Everything was dark because there was no light there. Even above the earth, there was no light.

"It was the time of four worlds. This world, where we live, and the three cave worlds below, one on top of the other. The old ones and the old creatures multiplied so fast that they filled the lower cave world and overcrowded it. It became so crowded that they jostled each other when they tried to move, and the cave was filled with their filth and their shit. The people complained and groaned, and said it was not good to live that way, but no one knew what to do about it.

"Then the Two Brothers came forth from among the people, and they broke holes in the roofs of the cave and climbed down into the lowest cave world where other people were living. The Two Brothers planted many plants, one after the other, until finally one of them grew tall and strong and jointed like the plant we know as a cane plant. It grew so high it went through the hole in the roof of the cave. It was strong enough for the people and creatures to climb, and the joints were like the rungs of a ladder, and that is how they got to the second cave world.

"When some of the people had climbed out, they realized it was dark and there was no way to tell how large it was, and so they were afraid it would be too small. They shook the ladder and made the slow ones fall back down.

"It took a long time, but the second cave world also grew full and as crowded as the first, and so once again they used the cane ladder to go through the ceiling into another world. And once again they shook down the ones who took too long.

"The third world was as dark as the second world, but it was larger, and in this one the Two Brothers discovered fire. That changed every-thing, because now the people could light torches and carry them around. They could travel, and they could build their houses and kivas, but the easiness of life with fire also made the people change.

"It was while the people and creatures lived in the third cave world that the times of evil came. Women grew crazed and behaved like men, dancing and neglecting their babies, and men behaved like women, taking care of the babies. Still, there was no day, only the blackest night lit by the people's torches.

"To get away from their troubles, the people climbed up into the fourth world, which is the one we live in now. But at that time, this world, too, was in total darkness. In the light of their torches, the people found tracks. They were the tracks of Death, the Corpse Demon, the one we call Masawu. They followed the tracks to the east, but the world was wet, and the tracks led out into the black waters.

"The people tried to make light in order to illuminate this world. They had the help of the five beings who had come up with them, and one after the other, they tried. It was the five beings that made the lights that became the sun, the moon, and the stars.

"And now that they had light, the people could see the tracks of Masawu and follow them to new lands in the east. Masawu was the only one who awaited us in this world when it was the world of water. When the waters dried, it left the earth damp and fertile, and it was Death that taught people how to plant and grow things.

"Now let me tell you the important thing, the thing that you came here to listen to. When the world dried, it became hard like stone, and many strange tracks were left in it. From men, and animals, and the strange creatures that no man knows anymore. These tracks could be seen stretching westward from where the people came out of the cave worlds into this one, and among them were certain tracks that had been left there by the Old Ones who had been in the world of water.

"Long, slithery tracks that looked like giant things had been dragged. These Old Ones were the beings that had dwelled in the dark world of water before the coming of men, and when the world dried, they had to escape into the deepest and darkest waters or be trapped in the drying stone. Most of the Old Ones escaped away from the land, but a few of them were too slow, like the slow people from the lower cave worlds, and they were trapped in the stone caves that formed when the waters bubbled out and went to the oceans.

"There is an Old One still trapped nearby. It has been calling for a long, long time, and the Corpse Demon, Masawu, told the ancestors of the Hopi to look out for the three who would answer that call. We were to tell them this story so that they would know if their duty was to men or to the Old Ones, because if the Old Ones return to the dry land, then they will bring the black waters with them once again, and this world will end in water and not in flames, as it should.

"This is the story. It is finished. And now I must tell you the tale of how to rid the world of monsters like the Old Ones, the ones who had no voices because they lived in water. The ones with names like K'thul'hu." He recounted the stories of the Monster-ridding cycle and explained that it is not just they, the North American Indians, who told this, but that it originated with the older, more advanced civilizations that built the Mayan and Aztec pyramids, the civilizations that traced their roots to the now sunken Azatlan or Ixtlan, or—as Lovecraft and Howard well knew its myth—Atlantis.

In the sand paintings that accompanied the stories, Howard and Lovecraft recognized angular icons that were vaguely reminiscent of the figure on the Artifact. Though they had not shown it to him, the shaman painted an uncanny representation of the Kachina in its dancelike pose with its cylindrical headdress, which, in the flat painting, was rectangular. Then, next to the Kachina, in a line connected from one of the zigzag lines of scalloping around its neck, Imanito drew the Artifact itself. He explained how it was an unholy power that was supposed to be left behind in the lowermost Black World, but which promised, again and again, to break through to the surface and rule those who had formerly escaped its power.

Lovecraft took this to be his cue, and he finally did what he had been impatiently waiting to do. He produced the Artifact and held it rather proudly in his palm for Imanito to see, for him to confirm that it was, indeed, just like the one he had drawn in sand.

But Imanito averted his eyes. "Put the terrible thing away!" he commanded. "Too look at it is to let its evil enter your spirit."

Lovecraft quickly put the Artifact back into his watch pocket.

"When it comes time to rid yourself of it, you will find that you cannot let go," said Imanito. He turned to Howard, and said, solemnly, "You, black-hatted bear man, must help take it from him."

"Sure," said Howard. "Whatever you say."

Imanito now laid out a surface of black sand, and on it, in lighter colors, he began to trace an oddly disorganized pattern of lines and shapes that looked nothing at all like the other sand painting, which was beautifully structured and symmetrical. As he created a shape with the sand in one palm, he would connect it to another shape with the sand in the other, and with each shape he pronounced what sounded like the name of a place: "where the earth is chalky, where the water is clear as air, where the upper teeth are large, where the foul breath comes."

Lovecraft suddenly realized that the old man must be diagramming an underground labyrinth. It was a map he had drawn. He pointed this out to Howard.

"Looks like it could just as well be an animal's guts," said Howard.

Imanito finished and wiped his palms. "You must remember this map," he said. "This is where you will enter the lower world." He moved his finger across the intricate network of joined shapes passing a symbol that looked like a stylized letter H. "And here is where you will lock the gate with the evil thing."

Howard and Lovecraft both looked closely at the map, but they hardly bothered to memorize it. Imanito solemnly continued, giving them instructions about what dangers to avoid, finally explaining how to place the Artifact in a certain receptacle. "Now I am done," he said. "All this I can speak but once."

"And what if we don't know what the hell you've been talkin' about?" Howard asked rhetorically.

"You will."

"You've provided us with more information than can reasonably be absorbed in such a short span of time," said Lovecraft. "Why not allow me to make a sketch of these rather elaborate patterns?"

Imanito smiled. He parted his arms, palms up, to indicate the two very different paintings, then he looked up toward the smoke hole in the center of the ceiling and began to chant something the others could not understand. He closed his eyes, leaned forward, and passed his hands back and forth in front of him, smearing the sand so thoroughly that the paintings were irreparably destroyed. And at that moment, outside, the wind began to moan with an ominous force, its sound climbing up and down the register until it was so loud they could hear the sand particles it carried beating against the outside wall of the hogan.

As the sandstorm began to build, they heard whip-cracking bursts of dry heat lightning, and through the smoke hole in the center of the roof, they could see veins of blue-white light jagging across the sky. In moments the air was filled with the smell of brimstone; their hair stood on end, and they heard the wind's volume grow to the roar of ten thousand voices in the darkness. When Imanito finished sweeping the grains of colored sand and reached over for his pipe, electric sparks crackled between his fingertips and the stem.

"You will remember," said Imanito. "I know you do not believe this thing I have told you, but you will in time. And when you need the map I have shown you, you will simply return here, to this time, now, to see it once again."

"Do I infer correctly that what you mean to say, in this figurative fashion, is that we will attempt to remember the map?" Lovecraft asked.

"No," said Imanito. "I do not speak figuratively."

Lovecraft shook his head—sadly, Howard thought.

"And now the dawn is coming, and you must go," said Imanito, and as if on cue, the wind abated outside. There was a scratching sound at the door of the hogan, and when Imanito opened it, his dog entered with a whimper. He dropped what appeared to be a piece of black fabric at Imanito's feet and curled up in front of the fire.

"The creatures of blackness are near," said Imanito. He knelt and picked up the material. He rubbed it between thumb and forefinger, as if testing its texture, then handed it to Howard.

It was not fabric. Howard could not determine what kind of material it was. Obviously, it was the cloth that the odd men's suits were made of, but it was a material with no threads. The texture of the black substance reminded Howard of the fleshy surface of a wet mushroom; it smelled faintly of mold or mildew. Howard gave the black patch to Lovecraft and absently wiped his hand on his pants.

"Remarkable," said Lovecraft. "One would never guess from the appearance."

Suddenly a shrill scream came from behind the partition. Howard instantly leaped up and yanked the blankets away, expecting something dire and horrible, but it was just Glory, sitting up, wide-eyed and covered in sweat.

"I'm sorry," she said. "It was just a bad dream."

"At least you've awakened at an opportune time," said Lovecraft. "We are making preparations to leave."

Howard helped Glory to her feet.

THEY WERE SPEECHLESS when they saw the car. The wind had sandblasted it so thoroughly that there was hardly a sign of the dried blood and gore and scraps of fur that had made the Chevy appear to be not so much a black horse as Imanito's father had said, but the huge, skinned carcass of one. Only a few spots in the leeward side of the car still showed a few dark stains and threads of animal hair. The other side had been buffeted so violently that patches of paint had eroded away, revealing the raw metal underneath. Small areas of the glass were pockmarked with tiny craters.

"I suppose we shan't need to be washing the automobile," said Lovecraft. "But I hazard the guess that perhaps the windshield will need replacing instead."

Glory walked up to the Chevy and ran the tips of her fingers along the rear fender. "It's amazing," she said. "I'm glad we were inside."

Now Imanito came out of the hogan carrying what looked like a dead black snake in one hand and a pair of crescent wrenches in the other. "Let us repair your car," he said to Howard.

"Well, I'll be damned," said Howard. "The guts of my iron horse! How in the hell did you know what kinda hose to get?"

"I'm a medicine man. Magic." Imanito laughed and Howard joined him. They preoccupied themselves at the front of the car, replacing the damaged water hose, and afterward, Imanito re-dressed the wound on Howard's arm with a foul-smelling herbal salve.

In the last layer of the dressing, he placed what looked like a poker chip. When Howard looked puzzled, Imanito merely waved his hand as if to assure him that it had some sort of healing property. Howard rolled his eyes and humored him.

"Remember these words sung by the man who was helped by the eagle people," Imanito told the travelers as they got into the car. When Howard pulled away, the old shaman chanted a few lines from a version of the Bird Nester's song:

> *I rise up*
> *to the black mirage*
> *that flies*
> *in the center of the sky,*
> *and in the shadow*
> *of his black wings*
> *I come.*

"I shall await you on the island of birds, pale fish man," he said quietly. The old Indian and his dog stood silhouetted in the red dawn light of the vermilion desert, and soon they were lost in a fog of dust.

AS THE MORNING drew on and the temperature in the car grew to a comfortable level of nearly oppressive heat, Lovecraft halfheartedly attempted to dismiss the old shaman's intimations of death. He held forth about savage superstitions and parlor tricks; he brought up

Harry Houdini's campaign to expose spiritualists and charlatans who performed such deceptions, then drifted off into a digression about ghost-writing a story for him set in the pyramids of the Giza plateau. "I find myself unable to take seriously anyone, even a man who appears to be a reputable noble savage like Imanito, who believes in the existence of Atlantis," Lovecraft said finally. "I must confess I was impressed at first by his seeming keen knowledge about us, but upon reflection I am inclined to think the way Houdini thinks about such deceptions." But much to his surprise, he could get no corroboration from Howard, whom he knew to have similar sentiments. At least they'd had occasion in the past to argue rationally about the existence of lost continents like Atlantis and Mu. But now his friend seemed too seriously disturbed by recent events to support his criticisms of Imanito. Lovecraft was much relieved when Howard finally made light of things.

"I have a joke for you," said Howard. "What does Santa Claus say in the Southwest desert?"

"What?"

"Nava-ho ho ho!"

"Shouldn't that be 'Nava-ho ho Hopi' in order to be more inclusive?" Lovecraft said.

"Well, ain't you suddenly an Injun expert. I have another joke for you, then," said Howard. "What leaks out of a Southwest desert Injun after he's drunk too much?"

"What?" Lovecraft asked.

"Nava-Ho-pee," said Howard, bursting into giggles at his own wit. Lovecraft gave a high-pitched titter of approval.

"I have a joke, too," Glory said after a few moments.

"What is it?" asked Howard.

"What do you call a Texan who makes a damned fool of himself?"

"What?"

"A Tex-anus." Glory and Lovecraft laughed this time, and Howard glowered at them from under his thick brows.

Soon Lovecraft had dozed off while scribbling in his journal, and in the moments of uncomfortable privacy it offered, Howard tried awkwardly to break the silence.

"What do you suppose he meant about you?" Howard asked. " 'A mother who ain't a mother, who wants to visit a mother.' That's a pretty riddle, ain't it? And right on the button as far as I reckon, at least the first half of it. But then that thing about your dyin' in cold air—that seemed pretty peculiar."

"I am visiting a mother," Glory replied. "My sister lives in Vegas, and she has a little boy. I've wanted to see them for a long time."

"You believe the old Injun?"

"How could he have known?"

"Anyone who reads *Weird Tales* could find out about me and HP easy enough," said Howard. "There was an Injun at the last gas station who could've brought him the hose—and put a hole in the old one, come to think of it. He coulda told him the three of us were comin'. The rest is just mumbo jumbo."

"Why would he bother?"

"Huh?"

"What would the old man have to gain by feeding us and repairing your car? Why would he go through such an elaborate charade just to do that?"

Howard scratched his hat. "I don't know. Maybe he's workin' with those fellas in black who tried to kidnap you."

"He certainly didn't seem to want to harm us in any way."

"Well, who the hell knows?" Howard said, losing his patience. "Maybe they got some custom among the Hopi to help people of the Master Race."

"You've got to be kidding," said Glory.

"Well, I can't figure it. Everything that's happened in the past couple of days has been spooky as hell, and I'd just as well it all stop. I like to write this sort of thing, but livin' it ain't exactly my idea of fun. We'll see what Klarkash-Ton has to say about it when we see him."

"Klarkash-Ton? That sounds like some Moorish prince."

"Sorry," said Howard. "It's Clark Ashton. Clark Ashton Smith."

"The poet?"

"You heard of him?"

Glory's voice suddenly grew soft. "Hasn't everyone? I love his work."

"Figures." Howard sped up and passed a slow-moving truck loaded with empty chicken cages. Feathers flew outside the window. "I been meanin' to ask ya," said Howard. "Why did you scream back there? Another nightmare?"

"Yes," said Glory. "It was bad. The same dream I had before about those men in the black suits taking my baby. There really was something uncanny about that hogan."

"Could you tell it to me?"

Glory was quiet for a moment, ruminating. "I'll tell you why it was so terrible," she said finally, "but I can't bear to repeat the dream."

"Fair enough," said Howard, glancing at her in the mirror.

"I was away at college back East when my mother passed away."

"I'm sorry to hear that, Miss."

"Thanks for your sympathy, but it was a while ago. I was a junior when I heard the news. It was in the spring, and losing her that time of year was terrible for me. My mother was the most important person in my life. When I got the telegram I couldn't stop crying for days. I hate telegrams now. I cried my eyes out, and then I had to get away from everything. My roommate and I ran off down to New York City with our clothes packed in typewriter cases to fool our professors. We hitched a ride on the Old Post Road with two men who were going down from upstate to work on a skyscraper. They were just workers, you know, the coarse and rough type, though they were really nicer than any real gentlemen or the West Point boys we knew. We stopped along the way by a beautiful lake for a picnic, and then one thing led to another, as they say. My friend was fine, but by the time the school year was over, I knew I was pregnant." She saw Howard's grip tighten on the steering wheel at the mention of the men. She knew what he was thinking. "And you're right," she said to him, "the boys were probably Indians, though we never asked. You must be wondering why a college girl would sleep with an Indian. You must think it's demeaning, don't you? But then you never would have imagined me at a women's college until I told you, right? You boys have been thinking of me as a common oil-town whore. You boys really don't know all

that much about the world, though you seem to pretend an awful lot."
She saw Howard's grip relax, perhaps out of embarrassment, perhaps
because he was just sleepy after having stayed up through the night.

"You got me there, Miss."

"Please call me Glory."

"Glory. You're right. I never woulda pegged you as a college girl. So
you never finished school?"

"My father's plan was to have me graduate and find me a West Point
man. They used to come up from the Academy by bus for our dances
almost every weekend. I was able to hide the pregnancy all summer,
and I had to do some real soul-searching to decide if I wanted to keep
the child. You know what I decided?"

"Well, I woulda kept the baby. God's gift, even if his father was an
Injun . . ."

"You're right. I decided to keep him. Halfway into the fall semester
I couldn't hide it anymore. There's only so much you can do with
baggy sweaters, especially in a school full of women. They found out
and sent me back home to have the baby, and then everything went to
shit." She saw Howard visibly wince at the word. "I decided to keep
him, but it wasn't because of God or anything like that. It was because
my mother was gone, and I had to balance things. I owed it to her. My
father knew plenty of good doctors and even some shady quacks who
would have done the job, but I wouldn't hear of it. He said it was too
much of a shame on our family, and Grandmother agreed, and I was
supposed to disappear for a while, as if I were still away at school, until
they could find some story to deal with the baby. I don't know what
they had in mind—probably something laughable like finding the
poor infant on their doorstep in a basket—something like that. Well,
they sent me off to a sanitarium, and I heard the rumor there that
Grandmother had found a family to take the baby, so after he was born
I took him and ran away."

"You just up and ran off? Did you have money or some relations to
take you in?"

"I didn't have anything. And I didn't want to become a Salvation

Army charity case, either. That's why I ended up in an oil town making ends meet by being friendly to men and letting them be nice to me in return. It wasn't all that bad, you know, and the kind of finishing education I got made it easy to talk about lots of different things. That kind of education is just to make a wife good for upper-crust cocktail parties, anyway." She paused for a while, listening to the wind outside, the growl of the tires on the road, the occasional rattle and thump from the trunk. "I didn't do bad with my baby, you know. He was the sweetest thing. I got marriage proposals all the time from boys who wanted to take care of us—wanted to have a wife and a son all in one package. I had a little oak crib in my place, and he was quiet most of the time. It was hard, of course, trying to take care of my baby and those boys at the same time, but I managed. I used to keep him in the crib on his tummy, like the doctor told me after he had the croup, and one day, just after I was done with one of my customers, he just didn't wake up again. He just went to sleep and didn't wake up again. He looked just like he was asleep, for a couple of hours. I left him like that. I might have checked for his breathing if he'd been a few weeks littler, but I didn't because he was sleeping so nicely, and he just didn't wake up. He was sleeping . . ." And now, as if the desert air had dried up her tears, she couldn't even get a proper cry out of herself.

10

NEW MEXICO. HIGH BLUFFS, mesas in the distance, clapboard shacks, adobe trading posts with Indian head logos, abandoned hulks—all westbound—on the roadside. They passed within a dozen miles of the ancient pueblo of Acoma, then the old trading town of Santa Maria de Acoma, where they saw the new mission church, which seemed to grow out of the side of the rocky mesa just above the settlement. For the next twenty miles they found themselves in the badlands, where they wove through the *malpais*, a bizarre landscape of hardened black lava flows, millions of years old, that encroached upon them from either side of the road. Had they known that the Navajo said these knife-sharp jags of volcanic rock were the clotted blood of ancient monsters slain by the great Twins, they would have found it easy to believe after Imanito's story. In the distance they were tracked by the snowcap of Mt. Taylor, the highest peak in the San Mateo range. A few miles west of Thoreau they finally reached the Continental Divide.

"Well, here we are," said Howard, pulling over as if he were at the end of their trip. "We're sittin' smack on the backbone of America. If it was rainin' and a drop hit some sharp rock and split in two, half of it would go down to the Gulf and the other half would go down to the Pacific. What do ya say we celebrate with a drink of somethin'?"

Lovecraft gave in to Howard's enthusiasm, and they stopped at the Great Divide Trading Post, where they bought three ice-cold sodas and ritually downed them with Glory. To amuse Howard, Lovecraft and Glory each sprinkled drops both east and west before getting back in the car. They continued downhill now, passing Fort Wingate and a sign for Kit Carson Cave, which Howard was loath to miss; they passed red-sandstone cliffs, and then they could see the lights of Gallup in the near distance across the flat land before they climbed into the Arizona high country.

Howard pulled over for gas at a Phillips 66 in Kingman; he parked, and while the gas jockey filled the tank, he did his best to wash and wipe the cracked and pockmarked windshield himself, griping under his breath about the broken suspension, which had made for quite a rough ride since they had left Imanito's hogan. "Hey, y'all," he said through the window, "how about some food? That Injun stew ain't holdin' me much longer."

They stopped to eat breakfast at a nearby diner, a wood-framed building with a false adobe facade. Howard, ever the Texas loyalist, once again ordered his native soft drink. "I'll have a cold Dr Pepper," he called to the waitress. "Got some trail dust that needs washin' down."

Glory lit a cigarette despite Lovecraft's disapproving look. "What a good idea," she said. "I'll have an omelet, Miss, and a Dr Pepper—hot." The waitress raised her eyebrows. "That's right," said Glory. "Hot. Nice and hot, but make sure you don't bring it to a boil or you'll kill the flavor. And add a wedge of lemon if you've got any."

Howard screwed up his face in a look of disgust. "What possessed you to do that? Dr Pepper ain't meant to be drunk hot. That's just damn stupid."

Glory was getting fed up with Howard's holier than thou attitudes;

she decided to provoke him. "Well, Bob, there's a lot of things I've done that 'ain't' meant to be done. You know, sleeping with men I'm not married to . . ."

Lovecraft was looking around at the neighboring tables; he visibly winced when he saw the disapproving look of the elderly couple sitting just behind them. He gave them a sheepish smile before he turned back to his company.

". . . getting knocked up in the middle of a fancy college education I was supposed to have so I wouldn't have to spend my life cleaning up after some man . . ." Glory took a long, manly drag of her cigarette and playfully blew a plume of smoke out of the corner of her mouth. ". . . and smoking." She pulled the cigarette out of her mouth and held it in front of Lovecraft's face. "Twenty years ago, a woman would have been thrown in jail for this." She put the cigarette back in the corner of her mouth and went on in a purposely stilted mumble. "Kind of stupid when you really think about it, *ain't* it, Bob?"

Howard was momentarily speechless at Glory's tirade. Lovecraft made a note to himself not to raise her ire.

"Besides," she said, "maybe drinking it hot will catch on one day."

Howard shrugged. "The hell it will," he said under his breath.

Glory looked at him, trying to figure out what it was he had just said.

Howard repeated himself more loudly for her benefit. "I said the hell it will. No soda pop invented in Texas is ever gonna be drunk hot."

Glory gave a melodious laugh at Howard's misguided bullish Texan patriotism. "Hey, why don't we make a short detour and go up to get a look at Boulder Dam?"

"What for?" said Howard.

"I've always wanted to see it. It's supposed to be one of the most spectacular pieces of engineering of all time. How about it, boys?"

Howard couldn't agree, probably out of principle. "I say we keep our pace. We can't afford to diddle around out here. Whattya say, HP?"

Lovecraft looked thoughtful, as if he were weighing options. He was eager to get to Smith's place, to be sure, but he had always had the tourist's itch in him. "Well, my understanding is that the project is nearly finished. And the stop is actually right along our route, isn't it?"

"Yeah. So what?" said Howard.

"It is also my understanding that Texans enjoy things that are large, or vast, or massive, given all the jokes I've heard. Let's go, Bob."

Howard just grumbled contemptuously and blew bubbles in his Dr Pepper when it came, watching Glory take dainty sips from hers.

THEY TOOK HIGHWAY 466, turning north off of Route 66. Just before noon they pulled over to look down at the nearly completed dam and the partially inundated valley that would soon be called Lake Mead.

"Don't look like no wonder of the world from up here," said Howard. "Looks like something a schoolkid would make in a shoe box."

Glory had to admit that the scene wasn't quite as awesome as she had expected. Driving through the desert landscape did something to your sense of scale—you couldn't tell after a while in that flatness if something was massive and distant or modest and close; you had no sense of how far away the mountains were because they always seemed the same distance away on the horizon. "Come on," she said. "Let's go down and see what it's like from up close. I bet it's different."

"Uh-huh." But Howard was pleasant about it. He parked on top of the dam and they got out to look over the edge, and this time it was an entirely new place.

"Incredible," said Lovecraft, the wind from below blowing back his short hair and causing him to squint involuntarily. "Incredible indeed."

Even Howard couldn't hide his awe. He leaned forward as far as he could, holding one hand over his hat to keep it from blowing off, and gazed down into the slope of concrete that arched downward like a half parabola that seemed to go on for miles. "This must be bigger than the pyramids," he said. "All these trucks fulla concrete are like ants dragging crumbs to build a mountain. Makes you proud to be a man, huh, HP?"

Lovecraft gave Howard a sideways look and smiled.

But Glory was more interested in the water—so many millions of gallons it would be measured in acre feet—trapped behind the monolith of concrete, inundating the features of the valley in which it was trapped. She wondered what was there. Animals? Vegetation? People and their homes? All of it would be drowned in the clear water of the Colorado River as it came out of the Grand Canyon. It would sit there, those millions and millions of gallons, seeping slowly into the rock faces of the valley walls, pushing at the single smooth barrier of man-made stone except where it would be channeled out in the spillways. She imagined what it might be like to live in that valley, where the air would be water; if she didn't breathe, if no bubbles came from her nose and mouth, the clear water would be indistinguishable from air, only colder and thicker, more shimmery and beautiful the way the light rippled in it.

Howard looked at the information on the roadside billboard. "I can see why it was man that conquered the planet," said Howard. "Sorry, Glory, for bein' so difficult."

"Don't mention it."

"Seven hundred twenty-six feet high when it's finished. Wow, that's higher than the tallest pyramid, ain't it?"

"The Great Pyramid of Khufu is only four hundred eighty-one feet tall, if I remember correctly from my research for Houdini," said Lovecraft. "The dam will be thirty feet shorter than the pyramid is wide when it is complete."

"Well, that makes this a hell of a lot more magnificent, don't it? A nation like this could conquer the world, huh?"

"Do not forget," said Lovecraft. "The Mesoamericans built an even greater pyramid. The old druidic races built Stonehenge, the Romans built their Coliseum, their roads, and their aqueducts. This makes me think less of conquest than of the wonders of the ancient world."

"Please," said Howard, but he was too late.

"The great Colossus over the harbor of Rhodes, the Lighthouse of Alexandria, the Hanging Gardens of Babylon, the Temple of Artemis at Ephesus, the—"

"Great Eye Pyramid of Atlantis," said Howard, knowing that it would annoy him.

Lovecraft drew his eyebrows together to mark his displeasure. "Well, and now what are they all but ruins or myths? This rampart of stone is impressive for the moment, but it will not stand the test of centuries. Nor will the nation that built it. As for Atlantis, perhaps it has left not even a ruin of its great pyramid because it was all a figment of some man's imagination."

"Well, thank you very much for such an uplifting lecture," said Glory.

"I'm sorry, I didn't mean to damp your high spirits," said Lovecraft. "It's just that I have little regard for such myths as Atlantis, Mu, and Lemuria. It has always disappointed me that Bob and Klarkash-Ton would write of such places when their own imaginations could have provided ample rich settings."

"Like what?" Howard asked. "Some inbred New England backwater where you wouldn't know if you were diddlin' your cousin or a cow?"

Lovecraft turned away and didn't reply.

"Bob," Glory said, "don't you think . . ." He had already stalked off to the car. She joined him there and sat for a while until Lovecraft had cooled down enough to return, and they drove the rest of the way to Boulder City in a stony silence.

WHEN THEY REACHED the fringes of the burgeoning town of Las Vegas, Glory was filled with the relief of knowing her trip was over. "Take the next right on Fremont Street," she said.

"Where did you say your sister was employed?" Lovecraft inquired as if he were about to note the fact in his journal.

"The Boulder Club."

Lovecraft couldn't help the sarcasm that tinged his voice. "Ah, I should have guessed," he said. "It seems to be a running theme in this barren province."

As they entered the dim interior of the Boulder Club, Lovecraft was suddenly struck by the cold. He pulled his jacket around himself and looked around through the smoke that tinged the air. The smell of spilt beer and liquor, stale smoke, bad cooking from the kitchen; a tinge of anxiety, excitement, and dejection in the air in the scent of human sweat; the murmur of voices, mumbles under the breath, the occasional loud curse or shout of joy. This was not the place for him; this was the gateway of a doomed city, the fringe of Gomorrah waiting for its harbinger of destruction. Lovecraft followed Howard and Glory past the clatter and click of one-armed bandits spinning out their symbols and spitting out their change, the rustle and shuffle of dealers flicking cards onto green-velvet tabletops. And in the periphery, men pretending to look nonchalant as they kept vigil over each and every customer.

Glory's sister, Beatrice, appeared to be about five years her elder. Her station was behind the ornate wrought-iron grillwork of the cashier's booth, and when Glory surprised her and they embraced through the bars it looked as if she were in a baroque jail cell. Glory made introductions, Beatrice eyeing the men, particularly Lovecraft, with a hint of suspicion. But she was pleasant, and after she signaled for someone to cover for her, she motioned the men over. "Here, please accept a complimentary chip on the house." She gave Lovecraft and Howard each a fifty-cent chip. "You can only spend it here. Good luck." Taking the hint, Lovecraft and Howard excused themselves to wander about the casino while the sisters absorbed themselves in their sisterly talk.

The casino was hardly full. As they walked about, obviously at a loss for what to do, a dealer motioned them over to an empty blackjack table.

"Afternoon, gents. Care to try a hand of blackjack?"

Howard looked down at the chip in his hand as if he had never seen one before. "Well, I'll be damned," he said.

"I beg your pardon?"

Howard pulled at the dressing on his arm and produced the chip Imanito had wrapped there. It bore the symbol of a rock—exactly like the chips Beatrice had given them. "Now how do ya suppose he knew, huh?"

"Once again, I must beg your pardon, Bob. I have no clue regarding your allusion."

"Imanito gave me this chip from this club." When Lovecraft didn't share his wonder, Howard simply shrugged. "Whaddaya say, HP? We've both got a chip, and now there's this extra. How' bout some blackjack?"

"No thank you, Bob. I believe I've experienced enough cheap parlor tricks for one trip with our Indian companion last night." He handed his chip to Howard. "By all means though, you go right ahead and give this fine establishment its money back."

"Since you're insistin'."

Howard placed both chips on the table and on his first hand he hit blackjack: a queen of spades and an ace of clubs. The dealer stopped with eighteen, and Howard had doubled his money. He grinned with pleasure and let the money ride, winning again. "Hey," he said. "This could get to be fun."

The dealer lost the next four hands in a row, busting each time after a sixteen or seventeen and Howard was up to sixteen dollars. Lovecraft was suspicious, but was not sure why until he realized that Howard had never been dealt a red card. Lovecraft paid close attention to the dealer now, but there was nothing amiss about his dealing except for the occasional twitch in his neck—probably just a nervous tic from working in such a stressful establishment. Now Lovecraft turned his attention to Howard, watching from behind as he flipped his facedown cards over to examine them. There was also nothing amiss, but once, as Howard was in the process of turning the card over and it still faced the table at an oblique angle so that its suit was still hidden to Howard, Lovecraft was sure he saw a seven of hearts. He was certain of it—it flashed a brilliant red, but then as the card angled up between Howard's thumb and forefinger, it seemed to shimmer for a split second, and what Howard saw was a nine of spades. Lovecraft rubbed his eyes and shook his head. He tried to follow the turning of other cards, but Howard never again flipped one at just the right angle.

Finally, Lovecraft pulled Howard aside. "Doesn't this seem to be the least bit strange to you?"

"What? I'm up to thirty-two bucks already."

"I do not profess to know much about games of chance, but this dealer seems suspiciously inept. And have you noticed that you haven't held a single red card? That flies against the laws of probability."

"Look, I know you see Cthulhu and your Great Old Ones in every dark corner, but I don't think he hangs out in a damned casino. Leave me be, okay?"

The dealer was looking off toward the dining area where a pair of well-dressed gentlemen were nursing their drinks. He turned back to Howard and nervously interrupted his conversation to challenge him to go double or nothing on one last hand.

"What—am I winnin' too much for ya?"

"No, sir. I'm going off duty in a minute. You're more than welcome to continue with the new dealer, but I thought I should do you the honor."

Lovecraft could not fail to notice where the dealer's eyes kept looking. Howard accepted the challenge and won again. "That was fast," said Howard. "How about another hand before you're off?"

"Sir, ah . . ."

Lovecraft pulled Howard aside and whispered, sternly, "Bob, listen to me very carefully. I would strongly suggest that you heed the old maxim 'quit while you're ahead.'"

Howard took a deep breath, ready to argue his point, but the genuine concern in Lovecraft's eyes sobered him, and in a moment he regained control of his senses. "You—you're right, HP. Hell, I've got more than enough to get my car fixed up."

"Yes, you do. Now, shall we see if Miss McKenna has returned?"

Howard swept up his winnings with a flourish and thanked the dealer while Lovecraft eyed the man warily and cast a furtive glance back toward the dark corner booth. There was something familiar about that palpably thick darkness, and a sense of dread made Lovecraft hasten his steps to follow Howard out of the room.

They found that Beatrice was back in the cashier's booth and Glory was loitering just in front of the bars, talking to her. Howard proudly scattered his winnings on the speckled marble counter in front of a rather surprised Beatrice and announced jubilantly, "Miss McKenna, I just won fifty dollars at the blackjack table thanks to the chips you gave me an' HP."

Beatrice was incredulous. "In ten minutes? With only a dollar to start with? Why you must be a regular card shark, Mr. Howard."

Howard beamed with misplaced pride; Lovecraft rolled his eyes as Beatrice exchanged the chips for cash and counted it out. "Glory," said Howard, "now we can get that damn suspension fixed so ya won't be bangin' your head on the roof no more."

"I need to talk to you boys for a minute," said Glory, her voice almost grave. She led the puzzled men away from the counter and her sister. She hesitated before she said, "I—I'm staying here."

"What?" Howard suddenly realized how much he wanted her to come with them. It was some unconscious assumption he had made, but now the thought of her staying in Vegas made him feel an unexpected desperation. "But you can't—" He stopped himself as he realized that she had no way of knowing all the things the old shaman had told him and Lovecraft the night before.

Lovecraft quickly interjected to cover his companion's gaping question mark. "Miss McKenna, Bob and I think that owing to the strangeness of the situations we've encountered recently, it might perhaps be in everyone's best interests for you to accompany us on the remainder of our journey. Or at least until we can get things sorted out."

Howard glanced over at Lovecraft, impressed by the subtle way he had just pleaded with Glory, but when he looked at her to see if she had bought any of it, she was frowning.

"What does that mean?" she asked. "Whose best interests? Yours or mine?"

For once, Lovecraft found himself at a complete loss for words.

"Look, I appreciate the ride and all—" Glory stopped in mid-sentence and laughed at what she had just said. "No, actually I don't appreciate the ride at all, it's been pretty goddamn hellish for the most part!" The men were forced to acknowledge her candor with subdued, nervous chuckles, but she didn't let that disarm her. "To tell you the truth, I'm just plain scared of whatever it is you two are mixed up in, and I've got a terrible feeling in the pit of my stomach that it's going to get worse if I don't get out of it right now."

They knew she was right. And yet, even with what Imanito had told them about her still ringing in their ears, they had to admit that they did not fully believe him. They looked at each other, both thinking that they must tell her what the old shaman had said. Howard began: "Look, Glory—ah, I don't even know what the hell's really happening here, but there's something we've gotta tell ya—somethin' the Indian told us about—"

Glory interrupted forcefully, "You both thought he was a crazy old man, right?"

"For the most part, yes," Lovecraft reluctantly agreed.

"Right, so I couldn't care less whatever it is he said when you all had that little powwow I couldn't see. Look, I'm sorry, but I'm staying here with my sister and my little nephew—and that's that." Glory stood with her arms folded defiantly at her stomach, but her tone was soft now. "I wish you both the best on this quest or whatever it is you're on."

They had lost the argument.

"Thank you," said Lovecraft. He saw that Howard's posture was sagging, and yet tense, as if he had not decided whether to accept defeat or explode in anger.

"Thanks," Howard said, shoving his hands into his pockets.

Glory stepped up to them, lowering her arms, and then she suddenly hugged them both at the same time, much to their astonishment and embarrassment. "Good-bye," she said. "Say hello to your friend Smith for me when you get to California and tell him that I loved 'The Litany of the Seven Kisses.' I think it's the best poem he ever wrote."

Lovecraft pretended to straighten his already too-wrinkled suit. "Ah—I will gladly pass along your compliments to our dear friend, although I believe 'The Hashish Eater' to be his finest achievement myself."

Glory smiled at Lovecraft's maddening habit of always having to have the last word. As she walked away from the two men she turned. "Never thought I'd say this, but I'm thinking I might actually miss you, HP." She gave a tiny wave and went on her way.

Lovecraft was puzzled but secretly flattered; he turned to Howard to say something, clearly unable to hide the pleasure on his face.

"Now what the hell does that mean?" said Howard. " 'I think I might actually miss you, HP.' " He did a coy imitation of Glory's voice. "There somethin' you ain't tellin' me?"

"Not a thing," Lovecraft replied. "Not a thing."

IN THE SHADOWED corner booth across the large game room, two dark figures sat watching. It appeared that they were playing five-card draw, but it was either a laughable imitation or some perverse variation of their own making. The men held their five-card hands splayed out, faces directed at the other player. They did not draw from the pile in front of them, and they did not discard. At first glance they seemed merely to be showing each other their hands, holding the cards still as if the other had difficulty reading them; but on closer examination one would have seen subtle changes—the red ink on the two of hearts bleeding into a six of diamonds, the face of a one-eyed jack contorting into that of a suicide king. To fix your gaze on a single card would have been like trying to hold down a bead of quicksilver under a finger only to have it scatter and re-form elsewhere. What the shadow men played at was a test of wills, each holding his hand while trying to change his opponent's into something inferior, and when they were done they scattered the rectangular cuts of paper across the tabletop, entirely blank.

THE CHEVY CLANKED and clattered especially loudly as if it were on its proverbial last legs, and Howard could have sworn he felt potholes in the immaculately paved Vegas street. At the garage he ordered the cracked windshield and suspension to be repaired, slipping the elderly mechanic an extra five to have it done by nightfall instead of having to wait overnight.

"I can give you a deal on some new paint," the mechanic said, running his fingers over a patch that had been sandblasted in the storm.

"I ain't concerned about the looks of her," said Howard. "She can look like a nag as long as she runs like a mustang."

"There's fine-looking mustangs and there's ugly ones, if you know what I mean."

"Look, I don't need no paint, old-timer." Howard walked back to the car and told Lovecraft they should split up while he took care of some business.

"What business would you have in Las Vegas?" Lovecraft asked, rather puzzled.

"Man like me's got business in lotsa places, HP. Why don't ya take in the scenery and we can meet later at that restaurant down the street. You remember what it was called?"

"The Grand Gallery? It hardly seems auspicious to dine at a place named for a tomb."

"What?"

"A certain interior feature of the Great Pyramid is called The Grand Gallery."

"Well, what do I care? It ain't like we're gonna get beaned by some fallin' bricks, right?"

"I suppose not. Very well, I shall meet you there, although I find this business of yours highly unlikely."

"You go on and think whatever ya like. Two hours. Just don't be late, hear?"

"I understand." Lovecraft stood for a moment and looked around, scanning north to south and east to west as if getting his bearings. He really had no place in mind, but the thought of wandering through this just-established town had a certain appeal. He gave Howard a nod and headed up the street toward what seemed to be the denser part of town.

Lovecraft found himself oddly out of sorts as he walked along the streets. He didn't understand what it was at first—he enjoyed wandering through towns and cities without any real destination—but then he realized that it was a sense of unrealness he felt. The buildings were all new, so freshly constructed that they seemed almost to have sharp edges, and the streets were all too wide and too orderly, the paved streets too neat and clean. Under the big sky with nothing on the near horizon, the buildings seemed two-dimensional. He wouldn't have been surprised to discover that they were mere facades like those Hollywood towns propped up on wood braces with nothing more than empty lots behind them.

On one of the side streets he found a low stucco building that announced itself as the public library. Inside, he found it impossibly dim until his eyes adjusted, and then he was disappointed to see how pitifully inadequate it was. He had seen reading rooms better stocked. For a moment he entertained the notion of staying and browsing through their selection of magazines, but when he saw their pathetic selection he approached the librarian's counter. "I beg your pardon," he said, "but might you have a title called *Weird Tales* among your periodicals?"

The librarian was in the back room, and when she emerged, Lovecraft immediately knew the answer. She had her spectacles dangling from a chain around her neck, and if it weren't for the heat, she would surely have worn a cardigan sweater with index cards protruding from the pockets. "*Weird Tales?*" she said. "I can assure you we carry only wholesome periodicals, sir. You'll have to check the tobacco shop for that."

"I beg your pardon," said Lovecraft. "But if you would bother to look beyond the covers of that journal, you would find some fine examples of popular writing."

"I beg *your* pardon," replied the woman.

"And are these all your books? Or perhaps I've stumbled unwittingly across the Las Vegas branch library?"

The woman gave a wry smile at this. "This is Las Vegas, sir. Strangers don't usually come here searching for reading material. Unless maybe they've lost all their money and are waiting for their companions to do the same."

Lovecraft left with a terse "good day" and walked out again into the red glare of the early-evening sun. A steady wind blew from the east—it would have been cold blowing so hard if not for the desert heat it carried. All along the eastward horizon, from one end to the other, a vast pall of ominous clouds hung so low the sky underneath was no more than a ribbon. Jags of lightning flashed in the distance, and yet no sound carried in the quiet roar of the wind. Lovecraft turned west to put his back to the wind; he wandered, meandering through the still-forming idea of a town until the first neon signs lit up the semi-darkness, and then he walked back to the Grand Gallery. By then the wind was strong enough to carry an abrasive cloud of Nevada sand, and as Lovecraft squinted to keep it from his eyes and hunched his shoulders to keep it from his neck, he remembered how, years ago, he had dreamed of visiting the great Giza pyramids across the Nile from the ancient city of Cairo.

At the restaurant, the waitress placed Lovecraft by a window away from the other tables. He sat there, fiddling with his pen, trying to get ink out of its recalcitrant tip. He shook it vigorously, and tapped it, and nearly dug through three layers of paper with its clogged point, but all he got was a few blackish clots. "Confounded pen!" he exclaimed before he suddenly realized that the clots were dried animal blood from their siege in the desert. He had just given up on the idea of writing when Howard appeared over him, laughing at his misfortune much to his annoyance.

"It appears you are late for our appointment," declared Lovecraft. "And it is no laughing matter for a writer to be without a reliable pen."

"Wouldn't know about that, HP. I'm a confirmed typewriter myself." Howard scooted into the seat opposite and pointed out the window, where Lovecraft could see the Chevy looking somehow refreshed—though he knew nothing had been done to improve its outward appearance.

"I don't know how anyone can compose on those loathsome clattering machines. To my dying day, longhand will always be my preferred method." Lovecraft lifted his pen again, then decided against another futile attempt and let it drop to the table with a clatter.

Howard smiled, reached into his pants pocket, and pulled out a small gift-wrapped package, which he placed ceremoniously on the table. "In that case, HP, happy forty-fifth birthday, ya old coot!"

Lovecraft was visibly stunned, but he quickly resumed his usual aloofness. "So," he said, "this is the reason for the painfully transparent subterfuge this afternoon."

"Yep."

Lovecraft picked up the thin package and turned it back and forth in his hand. "I did not even recall it was my birthday until I opened up my journal a few minutes ago."

"Go ahead and see what's inside already!"

Lovecraft carefully unwrapped the paper and opened the box. It was a state-of-the-art black fountain pen monogrammed in silver with the initials "HPL" on its shaft. He turned the black pen in his fingers, feeling its balance, watching the light glint off its glossy black finish, and he felt his throat go tight. It took a great effort to conceal the fact that his eyes were on the verge of tearing, and it was a moment before he was finally able to summon words to his lips. "This is most . . . fortuitous," he said, ". . . particularly in light of the fact that I was about to discard this . . . poor excuse of a writing tool."

Howard smiled at his friend's struggle to find the right words. He knew he'd succeeded with the gift and didn't mind the palpable awkwardness that lasted the next few moments.

Finally, Lovecraft rose. "Bob, I was about to go to the Western Union office next door to send Klarkash-Ton a telegram to let him know when we expect to arrive. I shall return momentarily."

"Good idea." Howard buried his face in the menu in front of him. "I'll go ahead and order for the both of us while you're gone. What'd ya want?"

"Actually, I was just going to have a bowl of vanilla ice cream."

"Go on, I'll take care of it."

Lovecraft stood momentarily with his new pen in one hand and his old pen in the other. As he left, the turned back to Howard.

"Oh, Bob."

Howard looked up. "Yeah?"

"Thank you."

Howard said nothing. He smiled and returned to the menu.

Outside the restaurant, Lovecraft held his old pen the way he might have held a dagger. He looked up at the ominous banks of dark clouds, the distant flashes of lightning. "It is . . . finished," he declared, and he did something so uncharacteristic he surprised himself. He flung the old pen as hard as he could into the night, and felt great relief tinged with foreboding when he heard its distant clatter. It reminded him of how he would drop pebbles into the well when he was a boy, how that hollow, wet echo would haunt him afterward.

THE DISCARDED PEN lay on the pavement not far from the gutter. From around the corner, at the end of the block, a flat black sedan approached, gliding quietly over the dark tarmac. Through the windshield, on the driver's side, one could see the silhouette of a man—so much a silhouette, in fact, that it seemed to be cut from black paper. In the passenger seat the other man seemed to be having some sort of seizure. His head and neck jittered as if the car were rattling over a cobblestone street, and he made clawing gestures with his thin, black fingers, making them appear even more slender. There was no noise from the car, but what happened next should have sounded like an explosion or the shattering of glass; the man's figure scattered into a million pieces and then solidified again, with an unbelievable sudden-ness, into the form of a gargoylelike creature whose black wings were so wide they seemed to fill the interior of the car. The driver contin-ued, nonchalantly, and the car stopped, without a sound, its front left tire exactly parallel to the pen. The driver's side door of the car seemed to slide open—though by all rights it should have swung open—and from the shadow inside emerged another shadow, the tendril of a shadow, and it quietly looped itself, tentacle-like, around the shaft of the pen. And though the shadow did not move in any way, it seemed to leech away at the light that illuminated the writing instrument, turn-ing it dim, and then dark, and then into nothing.

LOVECRAFT STEPPED INTO the Western Union office and paused before he approached the counter. Seeing his confusion, the clerk pointed soundlessly to a stack of forms on a shelf along the far wall; he made writing gestures, indicating that Lovecraft should fill one out.

"Thank you." Lovecraft produced his new pen and began filling out one of the forms, relishing the texture of the point against the paper. It must have been an expensive pen, because it moved smoothly, without a scratch, across the cheap paper fibers. He filled out one form, then tore it neatly in two and wrote the same thing on a fresh one, just to practice his penmanship. When he slid the finished telegram across the counter to the clerk, the young man merely glanced at it out of the corner of his eye.

"Probl'y won't get it till tomorrow dusk."

"That's an awfully long time, isn't it, old chap?"

The clerk made a dismissive gesture, tossing his head. Lovecraft noticed what was preoccupying all his attention: he was practicing one-handed cuts on a fresh deck of cards.

"Well then, how much will it be?" asked Lovecraft.

The clerk shuffled the deck, making a crisp fluttering noise, and he flipped over the first three cards to indicate the amount. A veritable cardsharp.

Lovecraft frowned as he drew some coins from his breast pocket to pay. When he opened his palm, his eyes locked on to the image of the Indian head on a nickel. A single feather, pointed forward; an angular, aquiline profile. Aquiline—that was to be eaglelike, and the coin next to it was a quarter, tails up to reveal the eagle with its wings spread wide. Spread eagle. Lovecraft blinked, as if to clear his vision, but then suddenly he was jolted as if he had been struck in the face.

The first image was simply the face of the old shaman framed in firelight. It was comforting, like the face of his dear grandfather Whipple Phillips. Imanito wore a serious but tranquil expression, as if he were thinking of something dire and yet remaining calm. The fire behind him flickered, and then it suddenly all surged in one direction and Lovecraft heard a voice—not Imanito's voice, but also somehow certainly his: "Red horse woman is in danger. Go to her." Lovecraft felt his eyes tremble in their sockets. The image went black, and then with every twitch of his eyes the same thing flashed again and again: Imanito's face disintegrating, turning, in jagged steps, into the black silhouette of the Night Gaunt from his childhood nightmares. Lovecraft shuddered and lurched back in the face of his childhood terror. Involuntarily, he tore at the air in front of his face and turned his head to the side, craning his neck so suddenly he felt a sharp pain in the back of his head.

"Hey, Mister, you okay?"

The clerk's question brought Lovecraft slowly back to the mundane world. He shook his head to snap himself out of the trancelike state he had lapsed into. "Fine," he said. "I'm absolutely, perfectly fine." He flung the offending nickel onto the counter and rushed from the office. He could hear the clerk cursing behind him.

HOWARD WAS IMPATIENTLY DRUMMING his fingers on the tabletop, hungry and anticipating the arrival of his dinner. Lovecraft didn't even bother to sit down. "Bob, we must find Glory immediately!"

"What is it, HP?"

"Now!" cried Lovecraft, his voice breaking.

"Calm down, HP. We got time to eat, ain't we?"

"There is not a moment to lose!" Lovecraft grabbed Howard's arm and, with surprising strength, yanked him out of the booth.

11

ENSHROUDED IN TWILIGHT, dust devils swirled and twisted about the hastily constructed homes that dotted the periphery of the unpaved road like the white negatives of shadows. The wind had picked up again—from all quarters, it seemed—and where they conjoined here and there the miniature twisters coiled, briefly, like living things, and vanished in a scattering of debris.

The houses had spouted up here like those puffy, substanceless mushrooms one often finds after a rain; but in this case, the rain was a shower of cash from nearby Vegas. In time the homes would become more solid, to be sure, but now even in their flimsiness, they served their purpose well enough. At the tip of the cul-de-sac at the end of a row of such houses lurked a dead black sedan, clearly out of place though there were black sedans in several driveways farther up the street. This car was parked askew, as if the driver were drunk, but its windshield was pointed directly at the living-room window of the house across the street—the house of Glory's sister, Beatrice.

• • •

THE LIVING ROOM was lit by one large imitation Tiffany lamp on an Art Deco end table at the end of a plush, poorly reupholstered sofa. Nothing in the house quite matched, and Glory wondered how and where her sister had gathered the odd assortment of furniture. It certainly couldn't have been a matter of taste.

Beatrice was on her seventh cigarette of the evening, sitting just out of reach of the overflowing ashtray so that she constantly had to scoot over to flick off her ashes and then scoot back into her easy chair. She was still prattling on about her no-good husband, who had run out on her that February and forced her to get the job at the club. Glory was playing Snakes and Ladders with her seven-year-old nephew, Archie, who sat on the floor next to her, rolling the die with a clatter onto the game board. "Six," he announced. He clomped his playing piece over the squares and landed on a ladder. "Aw," he said.

"What's the matter?"

"Now I gotta go back."

"No, Archie, you go *up* a ladder. Remember, the ladder is up and the snake is down." She had had to explain this several times throughout the evening. Archie would remember for a while, and then, for no apparent reason, he would want to go down a ladder or go up a snake. Glory figured it was the same sort of confusion children had when they learned left from right, but it still puzzled her. Snakes and ladders were so entirely different, after all.

Across the room, the illuminated dial of the radio flickered. Beatrice paused in her monologue for a moment and bent her head to listen to the ominous weather report—the impending dust storm was going to be more severe than originally anticipated.

"Damn it," said Beatrice. "The last big one about took half the shingles off the roof, and I still haven't had those replaced."

"Well," Glory said, "we'll take care of that as soon as I can find a job." Archie impatiently tugged at the hem of her dress. "Auntie Glory, it's your turn."

Glory dutifully rolled the die and moved her game piece three spaces. Ladder. A long one. She rolled her eyes and slid her piece four levels down the board.

"Auntie!"

"What?"

"Ladder is UP! SNAKE is down!"

Glory laughed at her mistake. "See," she said, "you did it so many times now you've got *me* doing it, too." She mussed Archie's hair and put her piece back. It didn't make sense—the ladder was clearly at the bottom of her space. She should have known not to take it down, especially after explaining to Archie. She frowned.

Beatrice gazed at her sister's features for a long moment and smiled at the familiarity. "Glory, you don't know how good it is to see you again. After Daddy ran you out of the house, I cried for a month of Sundays. You know Auntie and me begged him to let you come home."

"I couldn't have—even if he apologized," said Glory. "You can't take back words like that. Not when you say them to your own daughter."

"He was angry. He was afraid of what the neighbors—the church— would say. He hated himself for what he said up until the day he died."

"Who told you that? Auntie?"

"Yes."

"She's a bigger goddamned liar than he was," Glory said bitterly. "At least Daddy wasn't afraid to say what he thought—" She noticed Beatrice looking at Archie at her feet, probably checking to see if he had caught the harsh tones. She reddened a bit, embarrassed that she allowed her anger to overcome her better judgment.

Beatrice glowered. "Kindly watch your language around my son," she said in a low voice. "He heard plenty enough gutter talk from his no-account father."

"I'm sorry, Beatrice."

Beatrice put out her cigarette and took a drink from her glass of lemonade. "So, did you ever go back and finish at Vassar?"

Glory gave a deliberately curt response. "No."

Beatrice knew from her sister's tone that there was no point in pressing for more. "That's too bad. You would have been the first girl in the family to—"

"I know, I know."

An awkward moment of silence lingered over them until Archie broke the spell again. "Aunt Glory?"

Glory moved her game piece, thumping it down space by space on the board. "Sorry, Archie. Your mother keeps pestering me."

"Yeah, Daddy use to say so all the time."

"You watch that tongue, boy, or you'll be out picking a switch off the weeping willow!" Beatrice's tone made it clear that she was only half-kidding. Archie feigned a wide-eyed expression of mock fear and opened his mouth into a big O. It forced a smile out of Beatrice. Glory laughed.

"And now that song you've been waiting to hear yet again," said the voice on the radio. "Be nice to your shoe salesman. It's The Inkblots! 'Christmas in June'!"

Archie jumped up from the floor, nearly knocking over the game board. "Momma, my song's on! My song's on!" He ran over to the radio and turned up the volume.

Glory looked a question at her sister.

"Yeah, he loves to sing along with it," said Beatrice. "Must have giggled for a week the first time he heard it."

Outside the wind howled with increasing intensity. They could hear the clatter of shingles on the roof, and Glory was reminded of the night before, the sounds of the dazed desert animals on the roof of Howard's car assaulting her senses.

Archie listened intently to the chorus on the radio, and when it came again he clumsily sang along:

> *Christmas in June,*
> *What a happy pause.*
> *Sing a Yuletide tune,*
> *Hello, Santa Claus.*
> *Oh, it's Christmas in June,*
> *And it's just beCAUSE!*

Glory smiled at Archie's determination. She was about to offer him some encouragement and praise when she was distracted by a loud flapping noise, an odd sound, that rose steadily in volume, as if some giant canvas sail were approaching.

Glory looked up, concerned. "Beatrice, do you hear that?"

"What?"

They both heard a loud thud on the roof.

"Oh, hell! If that's another broken branch off Mrs. Appleton's tree, I swear—" Beatrice stubbed out her cigarette and got up to go to the front door.

Glory sensed something was very wrong. "Bea, wait!" She ran up to her sister and put a hand on her shoulder. "Don't go out there."

"Why not? I've got to see if there's a hole or not." She brushed Glory's hand away, annoyed, but then she saw the genuine fear in her sister's eyes. "Glory, what is it? What's wrong?"

Glory hesitated. She didn't know where to begin, or whether she should even recount the weird things that had befallen her since her path had crossed with the odd couple of pulp writers back in Thalia. "Beatrice, I—"

The radio suddenly went dead, and Archie's voice awkwardly trailed off into silence. He turned to give Beatrice a questioning look, but before she could reply, all the lights went out in the house, without even a flicker, and everything was pitch-black. And now, through the moaning wind, their ears more sensitive in the dark, they all heard the skittering sound on the roof—like giant clawed footsteps racing across the shingles.

"Momma, where are you?"

Beatrice took a few disoriented steps and bumped into the coffee table, knocking an ashtray halfway across the living room. "Damn!" She fumbled for her lighter and flicked it; sparks flew from the flint, but nothing happened. She flicked the wheel twice more before the wick lit and gave off a reddish yellow flame—barely enough to see by. "I'm over here, Archie." Guided by the faint light, Archie ran for the safety of his mother's arms. Beatrice craned her neck to look up at the ceiling. "What in God's name is that?"

Glory quickly locked the front door. "Beatrice, where are your candles?"

"In the kitchen."

"Quick, let's go there. It'll be safer."

"Safer?" Beatrice said, guiding them through the dark hall with her lighter. "What do you mean?"

The strange sounds on the roof seemed to follow them into the kitchen, somehow tracking their movement from above. Suddenly, they ceased.

Beatrice found a few candles in a kitchen drawer as Glory picked up the phone. "I'm calling the police. Is the back door locked?"

Beatrice lit one candle and set it on the kitchen table. She lit another for herself before shutting her lighter. "No, I'll get it." Candle in hand, she hurried over and locked the back door, which had a small curtained window in its upper panel. The swaying shadows of tree branches jittered and rippled against the fabric as distant lightning flashed outside. Beatrice thought she heard something other than the trees creaking outside, but the roll of thunder obscured the other sounds.

Glory slammed the phone down. "The line's dead."

"Phone's always getting disconnected," Beatrice said absently as she drew the curtain back to see if the Appletons' power was also out. For a fraction of a second, the flickering candle illuminated something outside the window. Still blinded by the afterimages of the lightning, Beatrice couldn't be sure what she had seen. She pressed her face closer, against her better judgment, and squinted to see past the glare of the candle flame on the glass. "Hello?" she said. "Is anyone out there?"

Something moved. Beatrice thought it must be something blown by the wind, something like a textured piece of wet leather, but when it turned and she could make out its unmistakable shape, she let out a shrill scream. It was a featureless head, a head that looked as if its face had been removed, and it was directly behind the glass. Beatrice recoiled, screaming again in revulsion as much as fear, and the candle fell from her hand to snuff itself out on the floor.

"Beatrice?" Glory ran forward with Archie and pulled her sister back. They quickly moved back into the living room.

"Oh, God," said Beatrice. "What—who was that?" She was trembling violently.

Glory had an idea, but didn't say anything.

"Momma, I'm scared."

"I know, darling. Momma is, too."

"We've got to get out of here," said Glory. "Make a run for one of the neighbors' houses."

"But there's someone out there!"

"I know, but—" Glory stopped in mid-sentence when she saw the dark shadow on the cheap white living room curtains. It was the silhouette of a large winged creature.

"What is it?" said Beatrice. She turned, and she and Archie could see what Glory saw. "Oh, my G—"

Just then another flash of lightning cast the black shadow starkly against the curtains, and in the deafening peal of thunder that followed, the living-room window exploded into a million pieces, scattering splinters of glass and wood. They all shielded their eyes and turned away, so it was only in the afterimages, at first, that they saw the thing that leaped in through the yawning hole in the wall. The wind dashed the curtains left and right, obscuring the thing's face, and it ripped the fabric away from itself with a black claw, revealing not a face, but the eerie absence of one.

Glory stood there wide-eyed, like a stunned animal. No, she thought, no, never, could such a thing exist. If the earth had ended by some calamity that had produced the most horrid abominations, if the gods had played a game of chance to see which of them could most cruelly insult nature, then perhaps this thing could be. He stood there, looking like some huge, freshly killed thing, his coloring an odd, flat, lamp black, and yet his fur gleamed with the sheen of the best-groomed Angus cattle. There was something oddly noble about him; she could not explain it, but he exuded authority. His bloodred tongue lolled down as he noticed her, undulating like an eel. He hissed at her and slowly approached.

The thing towered over Glory, even at that distance, and he radiated a cloud of foul odor—his hiss, as he stepped closer, sounded like a snake with the throaty undertone of a lion. The sound and the odor overwhelmed her, and Glory felt as if she were falling—she did fall. Down on her knees, she grabbed for the edge of an end table to raise herself and knocked over another one of Beatrice's overflowing ashtrays. She knew, with an odd certainty, that she was going to die, and the tranquility of this knowledge soothed her. Death awaited her like a safe refuge that the creature could not enter, and a flood of memories from her past began to flash before her as if she were drowning. When she was ten, still a little girl, she'd had nightmares of standing on a high precipice. She would stand there and consider, too rationally, the cost of living versus the cost of dying. She must have been a philosophically minded girl, rather high-minded for a ten-year-old. She knew this to be true, even through the fog of confusion that overwhelmed her at the moment. On that precipice, she had decided to jump because, after all, there was no God, and if she were dead, she would simply cease to be conscious, and she would feel no pain and know no regret—know, in fact, absolutely nothing, as if she had never existed. But just before she stretched her arms out like wings of flesh, she had looked out into the distance—it was the east, and the faint rosy colors of the dawn were touching the horizon. And it was so breathtakingly beautiful, like nothing that could have come from the mind or the hand of man, and she had suddenly felt the kindness of some creative force. Suddenly she had remembered the beauty of the total eclipse of the sun she had seen in Nova Scotia, the calm quiet of the craters of the moon, the myriad colors of the stars that come out at night. She had decided to live then, if only to experience such beauty in order to divine whether some extrahuman power must have created it all. And she had awakened in a cold sweat in her bed, shaking with the lingering terror—not of having nearly leaped to her death, but of having compromised her faith in the absence of God. And now she was on this weird quest with two men who were little more than strangers to her; she had nearly been devoured, in the night, by desert animals that had surrounded their laughable one-wagon train. How the mighty are fallen, she thought. If she hadn't fallen into hard times, she might have been someone like her sister, but after she lost Gabriel her heart had solidified into rock.

Glory snapped back into herself, too frightened even to scream, the fear frozen like something caught in her throat. She thought she must have drifted off for a while, but the creature had hardly moved. She heard a whimpering sound beside her—Archie. She grabbed him, pulling so hard he lost his balance and tore the candle from her hand as he tried to right himself.

Glory ignored the candle sputtering on the floor and raced blindly down the hallway. Beatrice followed just behind them, the fear moving her though she had no volition of her own.

They crowded into the small bathroom and locked the door behind them. In the flickering darkness, Beatrice finally began sobbing—great gulps of air and loud exhalations that made it impossible to hear anything else. She moved the candle away from her face before she blew it out inadvertently, and she shoved a hamper up under the doorknob and pushed it, jamming it there to barricade them in. Glory glanced around, left and right, undecided, and then she put Archie in the bathtub and began frantically rifling through the drawers. She yelped in pain and quickly drew back her hand—blood was welling up in the long cut along the palm, just beginning to drip. She saw a half-open straight razor in the drawer; she grabbed it with her other hand, unfolded the blade all the way, and turned toward the door.

Everything was dead silent outside. Not a rustle, not a scrape. Glory suddenly felt compelled to open the door to peek out. It was quiet, after all. The thing they saw couldn't possibly be what she remembered—it was probably some wild dog or something, and it had probably run out of the house by now. She took a tentative step forward and reached for the hamper to pull it away.

Beatrice pulled her back. "Glory!"

As Glory turned to look behind her, a huge, gnarled fist smashed though the bathroom door as if the wood were mere veneer. A long scaly arm thrust through the jagged hole in the door, grabbing for Beatrice as if it could see her. Beatrice pressed herself as far back as she could go, shielding Archie in the bathtub with her back.

Through the hole and just behind the silhouetted creature, Glory saw flames crawling along the wall in the corridor. The candle, she thought. The house is burning down. She had to wrench her eyes away from the flames with an act of will, just in time to see the creature dig its talons into Beatrice's shoulder and jerk her forward. Beatrice was too frightened even to make a sound; her mouth merely twisted open in a horrible expression. Glory scrambled to her, but there was nothing she could do. Beatrice was pulled up against the door, and the black talons were so forceful there was a sickening sound, and then her clothing and flesh tore away from her shoulder and the pain made her scream.

Glory wedged herself in between her sister and the battered door, and she brought the razor down hard on the creature's forearm, cutting a deep gash into its reptilian flesh. There was an earsplitting shriek that drowned out Beatrice's own cries of pain, and the claws opened, letting her fall to the floor in a trail of blood.

Beatrice was already in shock. Glory tried to help her up, but she was a deadweight, and Glory had to struggle with all her might to lift her sister enough to push her into the tub with Archie.

With the flames growing in intensity behind it, the enraged demon began pounding at the door with its other hand, splintering what wood remained. Glory pushed at the tiny window above the shower-head—it would only swing out partway. "Archie, listen to me. I'm going to put you out the window, and I want you to run as fast as you can to the neighbors and get help, okay?"

Archie sobbed a barely intelligible, "Okay."

Glory lifted him up and tried to shove him headfirst through the crack just as the creature reduced the last of the door into splinters with one final blow from its uninjured arm. It was all going to end momentarily. Glory struggled in vain, and she realized that Archie was stuck halfway through the window. Exhausted and in tears, she let his legs go and turned defiantly, razor extended, to face the creature one last time. But to her surprise, it was gone.

She heard a window shattering in the bedroom. Already she could feel the blast of heat coming from the burning house. If they couldn't get through the bathroom window, they'd have to run down the hallway now, before the flames grew any worse. How was she going to drag Beatrice and make it through the fire? She turned to pull Archie back in, but even as she touched him, he was suddenly yanked out of the window by an unseen force on the outside.

"Archie!" Glory dropped the razor and lifted herself up to the tiny window, expecting to see the hellish, winged creature spiriting her nephew away, but what she saw instead, against the windswept night sky, was Lovecraft awkwardly holding the sobbing boy in his arms. Glory screamed again, this time in relief. She saw Lovecraft cringe.

"Calm yourself, boy," said Lovecraft, and then to Glory in the matter-of-fact tone she had grown to love, "The cavalry has arrived."

Still braced in the window frame, Glory turned her head and saw Howard's form silhouetted heroically in the bathroom doorway, gun in hand, his back to the flames. At that moment he could have been one of his own swashbuckling heroes.

"Come on, Glory. We've got to go," said Howard.

"My sister's hurt." Glory gave a quick wave to comfort Archie outside and dropped from the window into the tub.

Howard tucked his pistol in his belt, lifted Beatrice, and threw her over his shoulder. "Follow me now." He led Glory into the bedroom and out the shattered window into the night, illuminated by the rippling light of the flames that consumed the house.

12

BEATRICE LAY SEDATED and bandaged in a metal-frame bed, her breath heaving regularly, a little wheeze issuing from her nose with each exhalation. Her face appeared drawn, tired, and relaxed the way faces look after a long ordeal. In the cushioned seat at the side of the bed her neighbor, old Mrs. Appleton, sat drowsing, with Archie asleep in her arms.

Glory had just had her cuts and scrapes bandaged downstairs. As she handed Mrs. Appleton the envelope containing the note she had written to Beatrice, she noticed, for some reason, that the paper she had thought white at first was actually a subtle cream color when juxtaposed next to the bleached white bandages on her hand. "Please give this to Beatrice when she wakes up," she said. "It explains why I had to leave so suddenly."

"You really should stay, you know."

"I know, Mrs. Appleton. I'm very sorry to have appeared out of nowhere like this just to leave her life in a shambles. But I don't have much choice at the moment, especially if I want her and Archie to be safe."

"You called the police?"

"It's better this way, Mrs. Appleton."

"If you say so, dear." She took the envelope and slipped it between the two flower vases on the bedside table. "If you say so."

Glory gently kissed her sleeping sister and her nephew. At the door she paused to look back. White on white on white. Everything white, but no shade was the same as another. A cacophony of white. She turned away and walked slowly down the hall to where Lovecraft and Howard were waiting for her. "Let's go," she said. "I'll be less ready if we wait any longer."

They took the stairs down to the parking lot in silence and got into the car.

"This may sound rather unfeeling," Lovecraft said, as Howard pulled out into the street, "but I have been wondering why the Night Gaunt only toyed with you instead of simply killing you outright when it had the opportunity."

"I don't know," Glory answered flatly. "And you're right—it's an unfeeling question, you bastard."

"Then I beg your pardon."

"You've got a lot of pardon to beg. You're the one who's gotten all of us into this."

Lovecraft was silent.

"But I wanted to know, anyway," Glory said in a moment. "How did you know I was in danger?"

Lovecraft didn't reply, so it was Howard who answered. "HP had one of them weird visions. I wouldn't have believed him, but he insisted."

"Thank you," said Glory. "You have my pardon." She leaned forward and kissed Lovecraft on the cheek as Howard watched in the rearview mirror.

Lovecraft quickly turned red, simultaneously embarrassed and touched by Glory's sincere and natural display of affection and gratitude. He mumbled a reply and turned his face toward the window. "Bob," he said finally, "it is absolutely urgent that we reach Klarkash-Ton as soon as possible. I have the terrible presentiment that things will go very ill otherwise."

"Yeah, HP. You and Glory just keep me awake, even if ya have to take turns pinchin' me. I think we can hit his place in one long shot."

"Thank you, Bob."

THE TRAFFIC WAS LIGHT that evening, and by the time they had left the outskirts of Vegas and entered the empty desert, hardly a car was to be seen on the road. They drove on, making small talk, each of them not wanting to bring up the topics that would cause them to remember their fear or dwell on things unpleasant. Hours passed, and they began to climb the foothills of the range that separated the desert from the California Central Valley.

Howard checked the rearview mirror frequently, anxious that they were being followed. He was relieved not to see the telltale headlights behind them, but then again, he knew that the odd men would hardly need to use headlights at night. For all he knew, their automobile was as weirdly constructed as the fabric of their suits. Did it even have an engine? Did it roll? Or was it some sort of organic monster that slithered its tirelike belly across the pavement in mockery of a car?

Each time he thought of the black-clad men—and they appeared to him unbidden now—what came to Howard's mind was the image of undertakers in a hearse. But these undertakers did not deal with the mortal bodily remains of a man; they had some greater sinister purpose behind them; they were probably the stealers of the human soul, waiting within a breath's reach to snatch away a man's spirit with a puff of air from his lungs. What was the word? The one that meant a sound with a puff of breath? The one that connected the air with speech and the soul? Lovecraft would know it—probably used it in a story recently.

Howard began tapping rhythmically at the wheel, blinking hard to keep awake. Soul, he thought. That's a synonym for spirit. His father had told him again and again that what Ma needed was to keep her spirits up. The clogging in her lungs wasn't getting any better, all that fluid and mucus building up. She could hardly breathe at night, and she had to sleep sitting up so high he didn't see how she could get any rest. She had to stay happy, keep her spirits up, not give up her spirit. His mind was beginning to wander. A spirit was like a soul. A spirit. Aspirate. Aspiration—that was it! What a great word, full of lots of meanings. He had aspirations; he talked with aspirated sounds about his aspirations. He aspired to being the greatest writer of pulp fiction ever to live. A spire, like a tower. A tall, dark, spiral tower reaching up into the stars; a needle-thin minaret scraping the belly of heaven. That was an image worth remembering for a Moorish story. A needle-thin . . . and the image of the tower dissolved into a quick glimpse of a long, steel needle protruding from the shaft of what looked like a bicycle pump. An aspirator. That's what it was—the horrible thing his father was using in his nightmare. His mother lying in bed with that needle jammed through her breast, shriveling as the stuff got sucked out of her clogged lung.

Howard coughed involuntarily and brought himself back to his senses, jerking the wheel quickly back before he swerved. The car was drifting and Lovecraft—damn him—wasn't doing his job. Howard looked at his companion, who had his head turned outward to gaze out the window at the dim landscape under the moon. He saw the bald dome of a mountain in the distance. "Hey, HP," he said.

Lovecraft turned, surprised, blinking those fishy eyes of his.

Howard's momentary anger dissolved. "Now here's a bit of cheery place-naming," he said. "We're passin' through the Specter Range at the moment, and that hill over there is called Skull Mountain."

Out in the distance, under patchy clouds through which the blue-white light of the moon shone down, Skull Mountain glowed like a bald dome on a thinly haired head. The light above the mountain had an eerie quality to it; it was palpable, hanging over the dome like a mist or a pall of pale smoke. Glory and Lovecraft were both watching the mountain when they heard a dull explosion from the back of the car.

"Bob?"

"Shit!" said Howard, grabbing the wheel more firmly to keep control of the steering. "We just blew out a back tire."

"Do you have a spare?" said Glory.

"You kiddin' me?"

"Well, do you?"

" 'Course I do. What idiot would go on a road trip without a spare?" Howard eased the car off to the shoulder and came to a slow stop where the road was at a shallow grade.

"One might have expected Mr. Imanito to have anticipated this and prepared us for it, as well as for other things," Lovecraft said with mild sarcasm. "I find myself disillusioned with his acute auguries of the future."

"Pipe down, HP. This ain't gonna be no fun." He opened the door and stepped out into the cold night air. "Hey, you two get out. Can't jack up a car with a passenger inside."

While Howard popped the trunk and got the spare and the jack out, Lovecraft occupied himself with the other flashlight, making a journal entry with his new pen. "Skull Mountain in the Spectre Range," he wrote, enjoying the way the nib of his new pen glided over the surface of the paper.

What an appropriate appellation for a domed patch of barren rock in a forsaken landscape! Had I seen this region in the stylized shadings of a relief map, I wager the shapes of the parallel ridges in this range would take on the appearance of ribs jutting out under the wasted flesh of an emaciated body; and Skull Mt., most naturally, would take its position above. The remnants of ancient lakes, long dry, for eye sockets, perhaps. Exposed granite faces for teeth. A roughly triangular gorge to represent the sunken remains of a nose, and the picture would be complete. Now, I wager, we are parked somewhere on a spinal protrusion roughly halfway between the rib cage and the pelvic girdle.

Lovecraft quickly reread what he had written. These were images familiar to him—the stock of his writerly trade—but suddenly this anthropomorphized landscape, this lingering on death, seemed repulsively morbid to him. He quickly drew a large X through the paragraph and closed the journal.

Glory was smoking again, cigarette in one hand and flashlight in the other, illuminating the back fender well of the car for Howard. She stood in a tired pose, one hip thrust out, her head hanging slightly, her hair in her eyes. She seemed hardly to have the energy to hold the cigarette between her two fingers, let alone the heavy electric torch.

Howard propped the spare against the running board. He loosened the lug nuts with his long-handled lug wrench before he jacked up the back wheel to change the flat. The rear end went up with annoyingly loud clicks and shrieks of fatigued metal that resonated through the night. As he was kneeling, loosening the lug nuts one by one, then turning them by hand because it was faster, Howard was preoccupied; in the poor illumination of the flashlight beam, he didn't notice that the flat tire was slowly swelling along the bottom.

Pulling her hair away from her eyes, Glory leaned slightly forward to watch what Howard was doing. "Can you see?" she said, leaning even closer.

Howard turned his head to face her. Under her flannel shirt, which she wore loose and unbuttoned like a jacket, Glory wore only the T-shirt she had taken from her sister's house; it was a little small for her, and it pressed revealingly against her breasts. Howard didn't fail to notice that, or the scent of her hair, or the warmth of her body so close.

Glory smoothed her hair away from her face, revealing the pale flesh of her neck, the dark hollow of her collarbone. She smiled and watched Howard frown and turn away. Over his shoulder, she thought she saw something odd about the tire, so she leaned even closer, touching his shoulder as she angled the beam of the flashlight. Several large bumps were beginning to form along the bottom edge of the tire. "You should have a look at the tire," she said.

Cocking his head around, Howard answered, annoyed. "Oh, I'm havin' a look all right," he said. He wondered what his mother would say about this—a harlot sidling up to him at night in the middle of nowhere, making such a flagrant pass at him. He felt the blood still hot in his face, so he turned his attention elsewhere; careful not to lose track of them, he began laying the lug nuts down in the dirt. "*Kaput*," he said.

"What did you say?"

"*Kaput*. It's German for broke."

"There's something very strange about the tire. Should it be—" Glory screamed, grabbing Howard with her free hand and yanking him backwards.

From his awkward kneeling position, Howard instinctively turned away from the tire and fell on his back. Utterly confused, he looked up at Glory, only to be blinded by the flashlight as he heard the strange double sound of the tire exploding. *Crack! Kraak!*

The black rubber had burst from the internal force that had engorged it, spewing a mass of bright red skittering things that made a hideous crackling noise as they fell in the dirt. Howard scrabbled back in shock, his limbs all contorted. "Scorpions!" he cried. "Glory, get back!"

Standing there still disoriented from her own scream, Glory hesitated until she turned the beam of the flashlight down between her legs. There were hundreds of them, some longer and thicker than her fingers, their hard, segmented bodies scattered in the dirt, their tails arched and rigid, and the poison tips of their needle-sharp stingers probing the air, quivering with anticipation for something to pierce. One scorpion had already found her boot, and it jabbed its armored tail into the side, hardly puncturing the thick leather but squirting a tiny drop of venom from its hypodermic tip. Glory jerked her foot away, parting her legs wider, only to hear a sickening crunch as she stepped on another scorpion.

Lovecraft stepped around the front of the car, his journal fluttering. "Glory?" he called.

"Stay back!" Howard shouted, scrabbling to his feet and stomping wherever he could, crunching the hard arachnids under his bootheels. It was difficult to see exactly how many there were; they had scattered everywhere from the exploding tire. Glory aimed the beam of her light at her own feet, and with involuntary shudders at the sight of the creatures coming at her, she gritted her teeth in concentration and stepped hard, pushing with her hips for force. The things under her boots cracked and splintered, only to make room for others to crawl at her with their sharp stings upraised and twitching.

From the front of the car Lovecraft contributed his own flashlight beam, aiming at Howard's feet. With the help of the light, Howard flicked several of the remaining scorpions off his pant legs and casually stomped them into the ground before striding over to Glory. He lifted her into his arms and walked back past the car, grunting with the surprise of her weight. As he put her on top of a rock, he noticed a movement in her hair—yet another scorpion, tangled there, almost invisible in the waves of red. He pinched it by the tail and jerked it away from her, flicking it into the darkness even before she was able to protest with a loud "ouch" of pain.

"What did you do that for?" said Glory, smoothing her hair.

"Sorry. My watchband musta got caught."

"Well, thank you, kind knight." Glory planted a quick kiss on his cheek and Howard turned away, his face fiercely red, only to catch a glance from Lovecraft.

Howard wondered if his blush had been visible in the moonlight. He checked the surface of his boots, which he had been fortunate enough to wear. The stingers had left droplets of venom, which had discolored the leather to a darker hue, but none had penetrated the thick leather. Howard checked Glory's boots, helping her wipe away some of the wet dripping gore on their soles, and then he went back to attend to the tire. He cautiously finished with the spare, cursing when he realized he had lost a lug nut in the excitement. He had to pause at least a dozen times to squash an errant scorpion that had gotten too close for his comfort.

Lovecraft and Glory sat together on the rock like people stranded on the roof of a flooded house. Glory pointed her light at Howard as he finished changing the spare; Lovecraft used his like a floodlight to scan the dirt in front of the rock. The scorpions seemed to have scattered or wandered off into the night.

"All right," Howard called when he was done. "Let's pack back in." Howard started the car and switched on the headlight. Glory got cautiously into the backseat and Lovecraft stretched out in the front after checking inside with his flashlight. "Just a moment," said Lovecraft, sounding somewhat annoyed. "If you don't mind, I must . . . ahem."

"Go ahead," said Howard. "Just watch where ya step."

Lovecraft opened the door and stepped out again. A pale creature was skittering toward him in the dirt—a ghastly albino scorpion. Lovecraft lifted his foot with a sneer of disgust and brought it down, hard, on the thing, crushing its erect tail down onto its own body until its smashed appendages oozed out from under his shoe sole. He shook his foot to clear it of the splintered shell and the sticky gore, but it clung there until he scraped his foot again and again on a rock, smearing its surface with the sickening mess. He averted his face and stepped back into the car. "Never mind, Bob," he said. "Let's go. I shall never endeavor to eat lobster again. Well, not that I did in the first place."

13

THEY HAD JOINED Highway 40 at Reno, and now they were in the Sierras, passing clusters of beat-up old cars and homemade trucks that had pulled off the road to form campsites. Through the back window Glory could see a rusted old Model A that had been rigged with a wooden platform to look almost like a covered wagon; an entire family's possessions—pots, pans, farm tools—were roped to the sides or hanging from hooks; beyond the truck she could see the haggard faces of the poor farmers and their families gathered around makeshift fires sharing what little food they had with their fellow travelers. Even in her current circumstances, Glory knew she was far happier than they—she hadn't lost a farm to the sun; she hadn't seen her life and her land literally burned away and dried into dust that blew for hundreds of miles across the barren prairie.

"Lots of them must have broke down or overheated on the grades," said Howard, noticing her expression in the rearview mirror. "Thank God I ain't a farmer. Just look at 'em."

"At least it's not winter," said Glory.

From the front seat, Lovecraft began his own musings. "Winter," he said. "Ah, if this were winter, then those wretched souls would be in the same predicament in which the Donner Party found themselves. Imagine eating the flesh of your own fellow travelers in the madness of hunger."

"I'd rather not," said Glory.

"They ate their two Injun guides first," said Howard. "Started low on the totem pole, if ya know what I mean. Makes me wonder if they tasted any different since they eat different food and all."

"One might infer that human meat tastes like pork," Lovecraft replied thoughtfully. "This, I would gather from the similarity of diet one finds among humans and members of the porcine persuasion." He snorted at his own sarcasm.

Glory saw the sign for Donner Pass and immediately lost patience with the men. "I don't like what I've gotten myself into," she said. "You boys had better give me a full explanation of what's going on, or I'll ask you to drop me off at the next town. Or at one of these campsites."

"I wouldn't recommend ya congregate with a buncha Oakies," said Howard.

"And why not? They're not making fun of your circumstances. They don't get showered with scorpions or attacked by desert animals. Or kidnapped by strange men."

"Sorry."

"You boys were doing me a kindness, if I recall. Is that still the case, or what?"

"HP, you tell her," said Howard. "We owe her an explanation at least." Howard braked momentarily to slow down for a group of ragged farmers crossing the road ahead with a deer carcass slung between two of them.

"I hardly know where to begin," said Lovecraft.

"How about at the beginning?"

Lovecraft turned around to look at Glory. "I'm afraid the beginning may be untold millions of years in the past, so I shall begin with the present. Is that agreeable to you, Bob?"

"Yeah. We might as well tell her why we're goin' to see Smith."

"Very well," said Lovecraft. "As I have explained earlier, we are going to Auburn to visit a mutual friend, who, I believe, has obtained a translation of the *Necronomicon*. Each of our adventures—or misadventures—since we took you on as a passenger has been the attempt, by the forces of Cthulhu, to prevent said visit."

"That's not much of an explanation," said Glory. "Visiting Clark Ashton Smith is one thing, but you think naming some ancient lost book explains all the weirdness? I feel like I must be in one of those god-awful stories you two write."

"I assure you, the two of us have begun to feel the same way," said Lovecraft. "And as for the ancient lost book—that explains things in a way more complicated than you would at first imagine. You see, the *Necronomicon* is a fiction. Or so I believed until this translation was found. And now this fictional book become real seems to be the key to explaining the other mystery, which is the true reason for this journey."

"You said the *Necronomicon*," said Glory. "That *is* a real book. I've read about it—back in college, I think. And wasn't there even a biography or something about the insane Arab author—Abdul Alkazar or something?"

"Alhazred. The mad Arab Abdul Alhazred—it all flows from the tongue together with his unmentionable work, *Al Azif*. It is all purely fabrication, tongue-in-cheek. Abdul Alhazred has a basis in reality, of course, but not in the way people imagine."

"Oh?"

"I was given that name when I was five. By some relative who was taken with the fact that I had declared myself a follower of the prophet Mohammed. I had begun to gather artifacts even at that tender young age, I suppose, after reading *The Arabian Nights*."

"So *Al Azif* would be another joke—'all as if'?"

"Exactly. You catch on quickly. I would have assumed you read of the book in one of Klarkash-Ton's stories since you seem to know his poetry."

"I never read his stories. But I'm sure I read about that book and the Arab in a reputable source. It wasn't in some cheap magazine."

"It all goes to show how cleverly and effectively we perpetrated our little hoax. And it certainly doesn't speak to the intellectual credit of the stodgy old scholars who presume to know fact from fiction. They are all tantalized and seduced by the mere hint of something of which they might not know."

Lovecraft gave Glory a brief summary of what had happened to him since he had received the Kachina doll. It was interesting for Howard to hear his friend tell the same story to someone else, because this time, even as Lovecraft emphasized the rationality of his actions, Howard found that the story seemed much less credible. If not for the series of bizarre and life-threatening things that had occurred since Lovecraft had appeared at his door, he would almost certainly have dismissed this man as an eccentric who had lost control of his imagination. Glory listened patiently—the way a doctor might hear out a madman's tale before committing him, thought Howard—but when Lovecraft was done, she asked particular questions.

"So you think those horrid men are actually creatures from your childhood nightmares?" she said. "It doesn't make sense to me. If these men are after you because you somehow exposed Cthulhu in your writing, what does your having the Kachina have anything to do with things? And why are they nightmares from before you even made up Cthulhu?"

It had not occurred to Howard to pursue this line of questioning himself, but he realized Glory had an excellent point. He himself had begun to accept Lovecraft's story on the face of it—there certainly was enough to go on even on the surface—but the underlying logic was a bit shaky.

At first Lovecraft seemed a bit put off by the cross-examination, but he, too, was patient. "It is not merely Cthulhu of whom we speak," he said. "The list is long: Cthulhu, Azathoth, Nyarlathotep, Shub-Niggurath."

"And don't forget Yeb and Nug," said Howard.

"The ones with the less exotic names," said Lovecraft. "Of course there is also Bob's own Friedrich von Juntz and his Unaussprechlichen Kulten with the hideous *Black Book* and Klarkash-Ton's Tsathoggua and *The Book of Eibon.*"

"But those hardly sound as real," said Glory. "Where did you get the name for the *Necronomicon*?"

"It came to me in a dream," Lovecraft replied. He added an "of course," but by then his voice had taken on the tone of dark realization. There was a thick silence. They looked at each other, each recalling the horror and reality of their recent dreams.

"If I remember my Latin, it means something like 'The Book of the Names of the Dead,' " said Glory. "I can't help but think it's the opposite of the book that Christ is supposed to have in His second coming, the book with the names of the saved."

"To pose it as an unholy mockery of such a book was not my intention," said Lovecraft. "But if it takes on that resonance, then all the more credit to my dreaming mind." He paused. "Not that I had the sort of dreams I am wont to experience these days, thank God."

"You haven't answered my original question," said Glory. "If you didn't make up these demons until you were an adult, then what business do monsters from your childhood have in this story?"

"I have pondered that myself," Lovecraft replied finally. "The conclusion at which I arrived after much thought is that my childhood imaginings were foreshadowings. I was a sensitive child, much isolated and taken to long bouts of vivid imagination. I am the first to admit that I do not believe in premonitions and the like, but that is the only conclusion that makes rational sense."

"You're forgetting another one," said Glory.

A thin smile touched Lovecraft's lips. "Yes. That I am mad. But then I must remind you that you and Bob are then participants in my vivid mania."

Howard had been paying attention to the mountainous road, but he finally interjected himself. "You remember Jules Verne?" he said to Glory.

"Of course. I must have read all his books when I was a girl."

"Well, think of him. He was just a fantasy writer back then, but he wrote about submarines and airships and airplanes, all before those things came true. Now a rational man would say that what he wrote helped those things come true. Or if you're inclined to believe in the supernatural, then maybe you'd say he predicted those things."

"You have a point there," Glory replied. "I guess plenty of people believe in predictions and prophecies. The Bible's full of it, after all."

Lovecraft looked pleased to be compared, even indirectly, to a classic writer and the biblical prophets. "We are all in agreement that many weird phenomena have been following us. Correct?"

"Yes," said Glory.

"Then even though I am inclined to be skeptical, let us view these things the way Charles Fort views such things as rains of fishes or strange lights in the sky—with an open mind. And let us proceed pragmatically from there. I myself have adopted the outlook of Sherlock Holmes: Once the impossible has been ruled out, then what remains, however improbable, must be the truth." He sounded very pleased with himself.

"Fine," said Glory. "But I would still rather not be with you two. You can consider me a hostage of circumstances beyond my control. The ride to Vegas was plenty for me."

That ended conversation for a while. Howard attended to the road, and Lovecraft scribbled furiously in his journal. Glory gazed out of the window at the soothingly real landscape.

SHORTLY AFTER NOON, having driven through the night, they passed through the old part of Auburn, still hanging on from the days of the Gold Rush. A mile or so farther on, they crossed the railroad tracks that Smith had identified as the best landmark for finding the road to his house.

"Here," said Lovecraft. "Turn here."

"You sure this is the right road?" said Howard. "It don't look like more than a trail."

"This is it, Bob. There's no other turn. Klarkash-Ton was very clear."

Howard turned onto the rutted trail, up the forested hill, driving very slowly to avoid the loose rocks and pits. It was pleasant and quiet, the air punctuated only occasionally by the sound of a bird. "I'm glad we fixed the damned suspension," he mumbled as he was jostled up and down. The forest on either side of the road seemed to converge as they continued uphill around a blind curve, and as they came around, the trees approached almost into the road itself, looming up on either side; where there were large branches, they laced together to form a tunnel of shade. Howard stopped momentarily, looking down the dark green throat under the trees. "I don't see no road ahead," he said.

Lovecraft and Glory squinted forward. They, too, were suddenly suspicious and uncomfortable. "I believe the road bends," Lovecraft concluded after a moment's hesitation. "It only appears to come to an end."

Howard eased slowly forward. "Well, we either go all the way forward, or we back outta this place. Ain't no room to turn around."

They had all expected a house on some side street of town, and after their recent misadventures, they found it difficult to relax despite the idyllic surroundings. The air was dry, having already taken on the afternoon heat, and there was a thick, somnolent silence everywhere, almost eerie.

Just before Howard's patience had expired, they saw the weathered old sign, lettered rather roughly in faded paint: *Timeus Smith*. Howard recognized the name, and for an instant he thought they had come upon the grave of Clark's father. He was still slightly disoriented when they came through the weave of trees into a dry, grassy clearing, where they could see an old cabin.

Howard honked the horn after they got out, and Smith appeared at the door, looking weary. He was neatly though casually dressed, probably because he was expecting them; his dark hair combed wide over his broad forehead gave him an especially intellectual air, and his heavy brows and slightly sunken eyes added a touch of the suffering artist. To Howard, Smith looked too feminine—like a lady's man, but to Glory his asymmetrical features conveyed empathy, sensitivity, and soulfulness. She found him instantly attractive.

Smith gave a broad, crooked smile and walked down the slope to greet them. "Welcome to my humble abode!" he called. "Always refuge for weary travelers here."

Howard and Lovecraft staggered up to the house, finally realizing how exhausted they were. Glory, feeling bloated and wretched from having slept in the heat, grudgingly followed them up the pathway.

Smith said his manly hellos to his friends with much shaking of hands and patting of shoulders. At first Glory thought it had been a long while since they had all seen each other, but there was a strange awkwardness about the way they looked at each other, as if they were comparing the man before them to some former image. It was almost a kind of suspicion, or disbelief, or maybe just simple disillusionment. She realized that this was the first time they had actually seen each other; though they had been corresponding for years, this was their first meeting in the flesh.

"And who might this be?" Smith asked Lovecraft. "Aren't you going to introduce us?"

"Ah," said Lovecraft. "Clark Ashton Smith, this is Miss Glory McKenna. And vice versa if you please."

"Delighted to make your acquaintance, Miss McKenna," said Smith. He took her hand and planted a mock chivalric kiss on its back. "I hope Bob's wild driving wasn't too taxing on your nerves?"

"Pleased to meet you, Mr. Smith," Glory replied. "I've enjoyed your poetry for years. And no, the driving wasn't as wretched as you'd expect."

"Please call me Clark," said Smith. "If HP had told me he'd be bringing a lady friend, I would have made better preparations."

"She ain't no lady friend," said Howard. "We were givin' her a ride to Vegas, but now she's in over her head."

Smith gave Howard a sidelong glance, then turned back to Glory. "Please, let's go inside. You may want to freshen up before you join us for"—he pulled a watch out of his pocket—"ah, lunch. Miss McKenna?" Smith held the door open and motioned her in.

"Thank you. Call me Glory." She stepped into the cool shade of the cabin. "Clark?" she said.

"Yes?"

"Would you mind terribly if I called my sister first? She's in the hospital and . . ."

"Ah, I'm terribly sorry, but as you can see, we're rather isolated and rustic out here. I'm afraid we have no telephone. Or electricity or running water for that matter."

"Goodness, how do you get by?"

"We do fine. How did people get by before all the cluttered inventions of the modern age?" While Glory went into the kitchen, Smith ushered the others back outside to unload the car. He was surprised by how little they were carrying.

"You're hittin' it off purty quick," observed Howard. "I didn't know you were such a skirt chaser."

Smith smiled. "Who is she? And do you mind my asking?"

"She ain't neither of our girlfriends, if that's what you're askin'," said Howard. "I'll leave it at that."

"It slipped my mind," said Lovecraft.

"Eh?" said Smith.

"I forgot to mention that she was accompanying us. But let me assure you, she is now an important member of our party."

"Well, then, I'll not compromise your professional relationship," Smith said with a smile. "And by the way, you boys look like the cat dragged you in. And speaking of cats, perhaps you'd like a nap after lunch?"

"Tell ya the truth, I wouldn't mind hittin' the sack right now," said Howard. "You, HP?"

"My energies are a bit more flexible, but I, too, would welcome a chance to visit the Land of Nod."

"Nod is where Cain went when he was banished," said Smith. "East of Eden, into the Land of Nod."

"I have hardly committed fratricide," Lovecraft replied quickly. "I was alluding to Winkin and Blinkin."

Smith smiled and didn't bother to argue.

"Just one thing," said Lovecraft. "Since we have come this far in a state of high anxiety, let us at least confirm the existence of the book before we retire."

"This way," said Smith.

Howard didn't look pleased, but he nodded his assent. He followed Smith and Lovecraft up the walk into the house, lagging slightly behind to hide his .45 strategically in his bag.

Smith took the two men inside, where they laid their things down in the living room before proceeding into the kitchen. Glory was standing near the back door, smoking a cigarette. On the table lay an oblong shape over which Smith had draped a red-silk scarf. For some reason the arrangement reminded Howard of a body laid out for cleaning before a wake. Smith pulled the scarf away with a flourish. Howard and Lovecraft expected to see the cover, but what they got instead was a thick rectangle of black velvet.

Smith noticed their puzzled expressions. He had wrapped the book in the velvet first out of respect and now, more recently, out of uneasiness. He did not exactly fear the book yet, but lately his dreams had begun to take on a sinister quality infected by the scraps of ciphered Latin he had been able to decode: obscenities, incoherent rants, wholly illogical assertions. He did not know whether it was his translations that gave them their weirdness, but he was wont to suspect that the cause lay in the original Arabic of the mad Abdul Alhazred. "My apologies for the false drama," he said as he unwrapped the bundle, and there it was, the mythic book come to life. The binding was a lightly tanned vellumlike material, but clearly not vellum. It was stamped in a weathered crimson color, the letters embossed so long ago their depth was nearly gone: *NECRONOMICON* and *Abdvl Alhazred*. On the spine of the book were yellowed slivers of something that must have been ivory, and bound into the spine itself was a long, coarse-woven ribbon of bleached white. Howard and Lovecraft stared at the book, mouths nearly agape, as if they had witnessed the unveiling of a holy relic.

"I recognized it immediately," said Smith. "It wasn't by sight, but by intuition. I swear to you it gave off a black aura that I could feel from across the store. When I saw the cover and the contents, that only confirmed my first impression."

Lovecraft ran his fingers over the book, tentatively stroking the cracked cover. "I still find its authenticity rather dubious. What did the dealer say?"

"It's bound in human skin. Slivers of bone in the spine, and the bookmark is made of bleached human hair."

Lovecraft quickly drew his hand away. "And how would an anti-quarian bookseller establish all this?"

"He happens to be the son of a prominent mortician, HP."

"Isn't there some law against this sort of thing?" asked Glory.

Smith shook his head. "The book is a relic. And the seller was happy to get rid of it while doing me a favor at the same time. He's a great fan of *Weird Tales* and the like."

"So this is the big deal?" said Glory. "I thought you had a fancy pan of brownies under the cloth."

"I beg your pardon," said Lovecraft.

Smith smiled. "Glory, if only a fraction of what HP imagined about this book is as real as this seems to be, then what we have here is one of the most gruesome products of human history."

"I'm sorry," said Glory. "I guess I'm punchy from the trip."

"Thank you, Clark," said Lovecraft. "But now that I've confirmed its existence, I find myself drained of all physical and mental energies. I now second Bob's suggestion that we rest before proceeding."

"Come on," said Smith, "I'll show you where you boys can both get some sleep. My parents may be back by tonight, so that leaves only two rooms. We can all shack up in the living room together, or I have a better plan. It's a bit hot for it now, but tonight we can sleep outside in my study, which is what I usually do unless it rains. I'm assuming that you boys will do the gentlemanly thing and let your lady friend have my room?"

"She ain't our lady friend," Howard said again, looking at Glory out of the corners of his eyes.

"Shall we proceed to the living room for now, where it's cooler, while the lady finishes her cigarette?"

Howard found both of the sofas much too soft to sleep on, so he let Lovecraft take the comfortable one and went back out to the car to get his bedroll. When he came back up, he found Smith standing awkwardly in the center of the living room with an armload of linen and pillows. Lovecraft was stretched out, still in his clothes, having only removed his shoes for comfort. Smith put his load down and gingerly covered Lovecraft as if he were a child.

"Help yourself to the sheets and whatnot," said Smith. He lifted Lovecraft's foul-smelling shoes by the tips so as not to touch their sweat-soaked insides. "I'll put these out to get some air."

"Here's mine," said Howard, sitting on the empty sofa to remove his boots. "I figure we're gonna need a couple hours at least. Then we'll wanna wash up and eat."

"I should be able to whip something up in the kitchen while you boys are out."

"That would be mighty hospitable of ya, Clark." Howard said it with a touch of sarcasm, but Smith replied with a genuine smile.

"It's really good to see you after all these years, Bob. You're not what I expected, actually, but it's always like that when you meet the man behind the letters."

"You ain't exactly what I expected, neither," said Howard. "But then, neither was HP." He chuckled at the memory of Lovecraft's appearance as he knelt on the floor and spread out his bedroll. Smith tossed him a pillow, and he puffed it before placing it at the top. "I'll be seein' ya, then."

"Sleep well." Smith turned and went to the kitchen; he could hear Howard snoring before he even reached the door.

In the kitchen, Smith found Glory sitting silently at the table, smoking a fresh cigarette. She seemed both relieved and unhappy. There was an interesting plasticity about her features, slightly puffy and yet remarkably expressive, with the subtlest shifts of nuance. Smith found her face fascinating, and he paused at the door to observe her with a sculptor's eye.

Glory looked up. "Excuse me," she said. "But I haven't been able to shake this bad habit of mine."

"Then I'm both happy and sorry to hear that," Smith replied. "Bob and HP are sleeping. Would you like to go freshen up? It must have been pretty unpleasant driving in that heat."

"It was."

"You also look like you could use a change of clothes. Shall I see what I can dig up?"

Glory blew a plume of smoke. "You keep women's clothes buried in your root cellar?"

Smith laughed. "Not exactly. But clothes have a certain way of accumulating. My mother has things she hasn't worn in most of my living memory, and she'd be more than happy to see them be useful."

"That's very nice of her."

"You'll have to make do with our primitive facilities. But there's a tub out back, and in this weather, I think you won't mind the cold water. When you're done look on the other side of the partition. I'll have some clothes laid out for you."

"Thanks."

Smith went out with Glory, and after showing her the outdoor bathroom and the water buckets, he went back into the cabin, where he looked through his mother's wardrobe, sorting through the stray pieces of clothing that she hadn't worn in decades. He found a silk blouse and a pair of jodhpurs that would fit Glory. He had a keen eye for the sizes and shapes of things—he could see her in those clothes, her curls of red hair wet and slicked back from her face. Yes, she would be lovely in those clothes. He went back out and laid them out on a stool in front of the partition to the tub; he heard Glory pouring water from a bucket, humming under her breath, and he paused for a moment, to listen to that quiet intimacy.

Smith went back into the kitchen. He rewrapped the book and took it into his study, which was still in shade when he went there, the light gentle through the west-facing windows. He laid the bundle on his massive mahogany desk, intending to leave it alone, but some impulse made him want to look inside. How had this book entered Lovecraft's mind, he thought, hefting the heavy tome in his hands and throwing back the black cloth. He said he had fabricated the whole thing, and yet some of the snippets Lovecraft had made up bore an uncanny similarity to the phrases he had managed to translate. Perhaps Lovecraft had run across this very volume or its counterpart at some time in the past and had forgotten. Perhaps his reference to the book was merely another example of the fantastic power of unconscious memory. Smith ran his fingers over the embossed cover, which always had a simultaneously dry and clammy quality to it. He sat down in his swivel chair and opened the volume to some random point in the middle and looked down at the neatly hand-printed text and the accompanying diagram, a line drawing that could have been taken from Bosch's Hell panel in his "Garden of Delights" triptych.

Here was something that looked like an octopus with its tangle of limbs and its gruesome parrot beak, and yet this was no octopus. The appendages flowed in a chaotic pattern reminiscent of something he had once seen on a Minoan vase, and yet within that chaos there was hidden some message his brain could not quite decipher. He felt it only as a kind of obscenity. Severed human limbs around the octopus-thing's beak, torsos in its tentacles. Instead of suction cups, it had barbed hooks on its limbs, and several of these had punctured the body of a naked girl, whose mouth was obviously open in the shriek that would end her life. In the background, a pit, its great depth represented in a wash of solid black ink. Sprinkles and smears of red ink to represent blood and gore. On the recto page the text commented upon this image, and repeated several times in red, in the way Christ's words were often highlighted in deluxe editions of the Bible, were the words *CTHVLHV* and *FHTAGN*. He could make out a few other words, but their meaning was unclear to him.

There was a light tapping sound at his door. Smith looked up and smiled. " 'Tis some visitor, I muttered, tapping at my chamber door," he said.

"Only this, and nothing more," Glory finished. She was as beautiful as he'd imagined in the silk blouse and jodhpurs, both of which clung to her form as if they had been tailored for her. Her men's cowboy boots didn't quite match, but that added an exotic charm. "I hope you don't mind," she said.

"I'll have to compliment my mother for her good taste."

"I mean for interrupting your reading."

"No—by all means do come in and have a seat."

Glory walked in, her eyes lingering on the objects in the room, scanning the bookshelves for titles. She ran her finger across the spines of books as if she were rattling a stick across a white picket fence, but her attention was most keen on the group of grotesque sculptures Smith had laid out on one side of his desk. One unfinished piece, of what looked like an Easter Island head, lay on its side, an open jackknife next to it covered in white dust from the soft stone.

"This is quite a collection. I didn't realize you did carvings."

"Oh, I dabble in illustration and sculpture," said Smith. "Something to idle away the time and make use of the rocks I get from my uncle's mine."

"You know, I never imagined you living in a place like this."

"Oh?"

"From your writing, I imagined you living in some bleak stone mansion like Rochester's Thornfield. Dank corridors, studies with high ceilings, sealed-off rooms."

"Not very homey, those accommodations."

"No," said Glory. "I'm pleasantly surprised, actually."

"So what do you think?" asked Smith, feeling slightly uncomfortable despite himself. "Do you know that you happen to be in the same house as the Three Musketeers of *Weird Tales*? Three of the finest writers of the pulp genre ever to live? I'm only being partially facetious."

"I've seen the magazine, but I could never get past the lurid covers," said Glory.

"Then how do you know my work?" He rose and poured two glasses of sherry from the decanter he had left on his desk that morning and handed one to Glory, who took it gracefully between her fingertips.

"English 300," said Glory. "My Romantic and Lake Poets course junior year. Professor Brismann had us read Coleridge, De Quincey, and then you."

" 'Kubla Khan,' *Confessions of an English Opium Eater*, and obviously my 'Hashish Eater'? That's quite an honor to be placed in such fine company. I'll have to thank your Professor Brismann."

"She didn't like 'The Hashish Eater' all that much. She called it an enjambment of Keats and Coleridge. Her point was that the tradition was getting watered down, but I disagreed. Always thought De Quincey was a windbag and Coleridge . . . well, I guess 'Kubla Khan' was his best mostly because he never finished it."

"Or so the story goes."

"You're not an opium addict, are you?"

In answer to that, Smith took a gulp of sherry. "Should I be taken aback? Or should I explain the long trajectory of poetry dedicated to the idea of dreams and hallucinations? I see myself as growing out of the British influence on Americans like Hawthorne and Poe. I've had my sips of absinthe and laudanum, but they could never rule my life the way imagination has."

"I envy you." She quoted a few lines from "The Hashish Eater," but then recalled something more immediate. "I kiss thy mouth, which has the savour and perfume of fruit made moist with spray from a magic fountain," she recited, "in the secret paradise that we alone shall find; a paradise whence they that come shall nevermore depart, for the waters thereof are Lethe, and the fruit is the fruit of the tree of Life." She paused. "That's how the world seems to me sometimes on the brighter days."

"For me, at all times. Here's to the milk of paradise." He threw back the rest of his sherry, spilling a little on his collar, where it stained the fabric like lipstick. "Tell me," he said. "How is it that you joined this party?"

Glory swirled her sherry around in her glass before taking another sip. "Bob rescued me from some ruffians, and then the two of them offered me a ride to Vegas to my sister's place," she began. It took a while and a few more glasses of sherry to give Smith all the details of the trip and answer his sometimes pointed questions. "And what are you doing out here in the middle of nowhere?" she asked when she was done. "I would have expected someone like you to be living in San Francisco or Chicago or New York."

"This is where I belong," said Smith. "I find the seclusion does me good, and I would never think of leaving my parents in their old age. The quiet and the physical work suit me, and it allows me to enjoy company like yours."

"Oh, you are so shameless."

"And you?"

"I lost my shame a long time ago," said Glory. When she turned to give him her *femme fatale* look, Smith was standing behind her on her right side. All she had to do was lean her head back and open her lips to his warm, sherry-soaked kiss.

The *Necronomicon* still lay open on the desk.

IT WASN'T UNTIL nearly dinnertime that Howard and Lovecraft woke from their thick sleep. Each had had restless nightmares, and their rise into consciousness seemed instant and simultaneous, accompanied by an odd thumping sound like the slamming of a door. Fortunately, they recalled nothing of their dreams, their senses overwhelmed by the smell of cooking from Smith's rustic woodstove.

By the time they had taken their turns outside in the bathroom and managed, as well as they could, to make themselves presentable, Glory and Smith had prepared dinner in the kitchen. They all sat down to a meal that was unexpectedly formal. Lovecraft couldn't help but notice the truly awful condition of his rumpled suit, and Howard, accustomed to eating his own improvised meals with his father, felt distinctly awkward. But there were no complaints. The dinner was a simple fare of steak and mashed potatoes with vegetables and garnish, and both Lovecraft and Howard ate ravenously, hardly pausing to make conversation through their full mouths.

It was after he had eaten that Lovecraft realized that if it were not for him and Howard, the meal might have been a romantic candlelit dinner between Smith and Glory. He had not commented on her change of clothes, but he had hardly failed to notice. Howard was a little less observant, but he, too, could feel the chemistry between Glory and Smith in the air, and he often glowered at Smith from under his brooding brow.

They all complimented Glory for the meal, and while she prepared coffee, they got down to the business at hand. Lovecraft and Howard took turns relating the details of their journey, interrupting each other to add details, embellishments, insights. Often they did not fully agree with each other, arguing a point of fact or adding something the other should have noticed. Smith found it a little confusing, particularly because Howard's style was to narrate the gist of the action while Lovecraft had a tendency to take his time laying the background for the events, often not getting to the point until Howard expressed his impatience. It was altogether unbelievable.

"If the both of you didn't look so wretched, I'd believe you were out to hoax me," said Smith. "I know you're both storytellers, and I know you have no reason to be making all this up, but it all exceeds the realm of plausibility."

"I can corroborate some of what they said," Glory replied for them. "Half the things I've seen I wouldn't believe, either."

Lovecraft added more sugar to his coffee—so much that Smith wondered why his spoon didn't simply stand upright in the cup. "Since you are suddenly such a skeptic, Clark, let me reveal to you a piece of physical evidence that might sway your opinion in our favor." He produced his satchel and opened it on the table, and from one of its compartments, he withdrew the Kachina doll.

Smith held the doll and turned it back and forth in his hands before he passed it to Glory. "Quite interesting," he said. "I don't know much about Southwestern Indian lore, so I can't say much about this doll. Wait a moment." He left them for a few moments and returned from his study with a small carving, which he placed on the table. It was one that Glory had not seen with the others; she put the Kachina next to it for comparison and heard a sharp intake of breath from both Lovecraft and Howard.

"My God," said Howard. "Did HP describe it to you before we came?"

"No. The image came to me in a dream." Smith's carving was only half the size of the Kachina—it was only a bust—but the face bore a startling resemblance to the odd features of the doll. "It's been my experience that coincidences like this one are meaningful," he said.

Lovecraft gulped his coffee. "Bring the book, Clark. I want to see that page you copied for me earlier."

Smith excused himself again, and this time he returned with the black-wrapped bundle and unfolded it in the middle of the table, revealing the book, simultaneously filling the entire kitchen with a dank, musty odor they had not noticed earlier. He turned the pages until he reached the symbols he had copied.

Lovecraft reached gingerly into his watch pocket, producing the Artifact with a slight wince of pain. He placed it on top of the of the open page and there, juxtaposed next to the pictogram, the Artifact began to pulse with its sinister glow. It was bright enough to see even in the diffuse sunlight that illuminated the room.

"My God," whispered Glory, involuntarily drawing back.

Smith did the opposite, reaching for the Artifact until his fingers hovered just above it. There, he changed his mind and let his hand rest on the open pages of the book instead. "Tell me, HP, what do you suppose all this means? My impulse is to take this as corroboration of the Cthulhu Mythos—to some significant degree."

"That is what I also fear. And I wish it were not so. What have you gathered from the *Necronomicon*, Clark?"

"I'm afraid my Latin isn't as good as it should be. I should have studied it more intensely instead of branching off into French and Spanish. It's written in some odd Latin cipher, and I've only managed to unravel little bits and pieces." He paused to pour himself some more wine, gesturing to Glory to ask if she wanted her glass refilled also, but then, noticing the disapproving glances from the other men, he sat back. "It's getting rather close in here," he said. "Why don't we retire outside to my study, where we can sit under the sky and breathe some fresh air? It'll be light for a while yet."

"Let's," said Lovecraft. He reached over and retrieved the Artifact. He was surprised at how warm it felt in his hand—the same temperature as human flesh, he thought.

Part Two

KIVA

14

Friday, 23 August, 1935

LOADED WITH THEIR SLEEPING BAGS and other gear, they went out of the back door of the cabin. It was only a few dozen yards to the edge of the property, where a fallen blue oak, still tenaciously alive, marked the boundary between the tree line and Smith's pleasant outdoor compound.

"I work out here most of the time. Until winter," said Smith, gesturing toward the small camp he had set up.

They expected to see the other campers returning any minute to their chairs and their cots. The fire pit was small and cold, but obviously well used, with a coffeepot still perched over the coals. "This is where we'll be sleeping," said Smith. "Unless, of course, it happens to rain."

The camp chairs were quite comfortable, as Lovecraft immediately ascertained for himself. He glanced around at the table, which Smith had placed strategically so it would be in shade for most of the day; it held a few writing supplies and a couple of books held open and weighed down with small stones. Lovecraft found it difficult to imagine this was the spot from which Smith wrote his stories for *Weird Tales*.

Howard put down the sleeping bags. He rattled the box of matches at the rim of the fire pit and poked in the dead coals. "Let's stoke up some coffee and get on with it," he said. "What we need is a nice coupl'a jackrabbits drippin' fat over this. Now that's my idea of a study."

"In true barbarian style, no doubt," said Smith, laughing.

"Not a side of beef or the whole carcass of some wild boar?" asked Glory.

"That would be a tad much for the four of us," Howard replied, not detecting her sarcasm. "Unless you have an appetite like Red Sonja?"

Glory frowned.

"The female counterpart of Conan the barbarian," said Lovecraft. "Bob, if you'd allow me the cot that isn't downwind from the fire. I find the odor of smoke on my clothes to be quite annoying."

"Sure, HP."

Smith put the *Necronomicon* down on the weathered table. "Now if a couple of you will accompany me to the pantry to bring back some supplies, we'll be set up for the night before it's dark."

"Y'all go ahead," said Howard. "I'll keep watch."

"That's hardly—" Smith began out of habit, but he interrupted himself. "We'll only be gone a few minutes."

"Don't worry, Clark, I ain't aimin' to run off nowhere."

As the three headed back toward the cabin, Howard laid his sleeping bag on top of the cot nearest the fire pit. He untied it, rolled it open, and took up the .45 that emerged from its folds. Quickly, like someone being watched, he glanced around before opening the chamber to be sure the bullets were still inside. When he could no longer see the others, he walked the perimeter of the compound, counting his paces for some reason he could not explain to himself. Once, then twice, he quickly spun around to face the tree line as if to surprise someone peeking from behind a tree trunk. He saw nothing, but he could still feel something brooding from the slowly darkening shade in the woods.

Howard stuck the pistol in his waistband and gathered up some wood for the fire. In a few minutes he had a small but cheery flame going, and even in the daylight, it made him feel more secure. "Damn it," he said to himself. "I'm spooked like an old mare."

NOT TEN YARDS from the cabin was a shoulder-high mound of earth with rough planks for a roof. Smith led Glory and Lovecraft over and gestured into the pit inside. "It's our all-purpose pantry," he said. "One of those mine shafts I was telling you about." He took hold of the small ladder that slanted into the hole and took the first steps down. He paused. "Aren't you coming? The ladders don't look like much, but they're sturdy, I assure you."

Lovecraft felt a sudden sense of vertigo wash over him, and he shivered as it passed. It was a powerful *déjà vu* he felt, accompanied by images of fantastic caverns full of gigantic alien shapes. "Clark, why don't you and Glory go on down. I shall remain up here if you don't mind."

"What's the matter, HP?" Glory saw that his complexion had grown even paler than usual, if that was possible.

"It's nothing. I simply have a distaste, at the moment, for dark and conclosed spaces."

" 'Conclosed?' " repeated Smith.

"Did I say that? 'Conclosed.' Hmm. I must have enjambed 'enclosed' and 'confined.' Obviously the workings of my unconscious mood."

"I'll call up if we run into our friend Nyarlathotep," said Smith.

Lovecraft did not look the least bit amused, but he forced a smile.

Glory waited until Smith was down the ladder and below on the other side of the shaft before she followed. Another ladder went down from the small ledge, zagging the other way, and she suddenly found herself in a chamber ventilated by the chilly air of the mines. She rubbed her arms and shivered despite herself.

"It stays remarkably cold through the summer," said Smith. "Here, take some of these." He handed her an egg and pointed to the remainder on the rough-hewn shelf. "We'll need some butter, an onion. Whatever else you think we'll need for omelets in the morning. I'll get the water."

Glory could hear it trickling somewhere, and when her eyes were finally adjusted, she saw the black-surfaced pool. She shivered again. "Does that go all the way down?" she asked.

"Holds quite a bit, but that part there is only thirty or forty feet deep. We diverted the stream, and I only have to fill it once in a long while." Smith dipped two tin pails into the pool and lifted them out, each three-quarters full. "I've already compensated for what gets spilled from the walk back," he said. He found another pail and handed it to Glory.

"More water?"

"No, for the other supplies. You need something in which to carry them."

"Thanks." Glory put the eggs, the butter, the onion, into the pail. She smiled. "Suddenly, I thought of Jack and Jill," she said.

"The nursery rhyme?"

" 'Jack and Jill went up the hill to fetch a pail of water.' "

"Hardly relevant to us," Smith surmised. "I have two pails here. And we've hardly gone up a hill."

"I was thinking of the irony of doing the opposite."

"And what's the ironic opposite of losing one's crown and tumbling after?"

Glory let out an involuntary giggle.

"Hullo?" Lovecraft called from above. "What is transpiring down there?"

"We're trying to imagine the inversion of broken crowns and tumbling," Smith called up. "Help the lady up, why don't you?"

Glory went up the ladder first, holding her pail out for Lovecraft to take. Smith made two trips with the heavier water pails.

"I thought I heard voices other than yours," said Lovecraft, when they were assembled to go back.

"Just the wind, HP."

"That is also my sincerest hope, Clark."

As she started back to the camp, Glory felt compelled to look down into the pit once more. She shivered again before she followed the two men.

• • •

FOR HOWARD THE TEXT was utterly unintelligible, and Lovecraft, though Latin had been one of his best subjects in high school, could do no more than make intelligent guesses at the meaning of the ciphers on the pages. So they hovered over Smith's shoulders like a pair of birds as he ran his fingertips lightly over the text as if to make meaning of it by sensation alone. Watching this procedure from the other side of the table, Glory paced back and forth in boredom until finally she paused to make a suggestion.

"Wouldn't this be easier if we read it out loud and tried to figure out the meaning together?"

"I'm afraid HP and Bob here wouldn't be much help," said Smith.

"That's why we came here in the first place," Howard added.

Glory gave a smile that Howard took to be a smirk. "I haven't been out of college all *that* long," she said. "My Latin's only a bit rusty. Why don't you let me help?"

Howard and Lovecraft exchanged a glance over Smith's head. "Perhaps you could be of service to us by reading the text," Lovecraft offered. "But even if you had the rudiments to offer us the phonics of the text, I doubt you have the depth of learning to make much of its meaning."

"Oh, come on, HP," said Smith. "My Latin isn't much better than a good Catholic high-school boy's. I could use all the help I can get."

At this, Howard and Lovecraft shrugged and moved aside, letting Glory take her place at Smith's side. There was an awkward silence for a moment, and then Howard cleared his throat, and said, "Hey, Smith, ain't you gonna offer the lady your seat?"

"I'm sorry. Where are my manners?" Smith stood up and pulled the chair out for Glory with a flourish, and when she had seated herself, he went to the other side of the camp, where he produced a rough-hewn stool from behind a tree.

Glory began to read: "Nh'we n'it eh! Csu'r oe f'o! Hm-nau tves'ne'ti b'cme oes c'nees yras! F'ro p'noe ple-oe t'dios slvoet'eh p'lta! C'iilo b'ndas ch'hiw ave'hc: non ctede h'tem h'twi t'ran! Hoe dna'to sasu em n'ga om! T'hep r'wo sefo eh'te h'rat t'hes par! Eeta!" And then:

> Y'AI 'NG'NGAH,
> *YOG-SOTHOTH*
> H'EE-L'GEB
> F'AI THRODOG
> *UAAAH*

"This is gibberish," she said. "It's not any kind of Latin I've ever read or heard of."

"It has a certain guttural resonance to my ear," said Lovecraft. "That would be in keeping with the speech apparatus of the Old Ones. A corruption, perhaps?"

Smith perched on the stool, adjusting the uneven three legs. "My guess is that we have anagrams of Latin terms," he said. "The symbols in the margins might serve as a key to how they are to be unscrambled." He read a few lines himself, trying the words in different configurations of letters until he arrived at something familiar.

Glory began to write them down in the order in which they made sense of the individual words. But what they had was still gibberish.

"I recommend you apply the same logic to the words," offered Lovecraft. "Rearrange the words until they appear as sentences?"

"We don't have enough words yet for that," said Glory.

"Then I suggest you proceed."

"HP," said Howard.

"Eh?"

"I suggest we let them get at it. I could use a little leg stretchin' myself. If the two of ya don't mind, me and HP here are gonna go have a look around," said Howard.

"You appear to be getting on just famously without us," said Lovecraft.

Smith gave the men an arched eyebrow, but Glory hardly noticed, her attention transfixed by a small illustration in the text.

"Don't be away too long," said Smith. "And don't stray too far. There are still lots of unmarked and abandoned mineshafts in these hills."

"We ain't kids, Clark."

"Duly noted," said Lovecraft.

The two men walked toward the cabin and then past it on the trail. In the late-afternoon light the oaks looked especially blue, their leaves almost surreal against their dark gray trunks. When they looked back toward the cabin poised there in the dry landscape with the empty Chevy standing in front, the place looked utterly abandoned.

"I have a bad feelin' about all this, HP." Howard hunched his shoulders and kicked at a rock in the dust. "We never shoulda picked her up."

"She seems to have become rather essential to us, in my humble opinion," Lovecraft replied.

"Aren't you suspicious? It's like she was planted there waiting for us. How do we know she ain't the real servant of Cthulhu and the odd men are just following you around to throw us off?"

"That hardly seems likely, given how she has suffered on our account, and given how much of her tragic history we have learned over the past days."

"Would ya put it past your Cthulhu people to fake all of that?"

"In one of our stories, perhaps," Lovecraft said thoughtfully. "If Glory were a character in one of our Weird Tales, then one might expect some machinations in the plot that would expose her as an ally of the Old Ones. But, remember, Bob, this is not one of our tales. This is reality, which is hardly as interesting, and such machinations are unlikely to obtain."

"I'll tell ya what else is unlikely," said Howard. "I'd say Klarkash-Ton finding a real copy of the *Necronomicon* is pretty damn unlikely since you're supposed to have made it up. I wouldn't be usin' our stories as examples for makin' arguments about what's real these days."

Lovecraft paused his steps for a moment. "Touché," he said to Howard's back.

Howard stopped and turned around. He was about to reply when a long swath of the tall grass along the trailside rustled in unison. The motion carried sinuously up the incline behind Lovecraft until it stopped at the base of a large rock.

"It's just the wind," Lovecraft said, noticing Howard's alarm. But there was no wind.

"Clark said there were open mineshafts."

"An exhalation from the netherworld," said Lovecraft.

Howard smiled. They continued down the path, trying to enjoy the quiet, dissipating heat of the day.

GLORY AND SMITH made better progress alone. They were able to unscramble a few strings of words that almost sounded like sentences. But during the pauses while Smith scratched out variations of the anagrams they had discovered, Glory was compelled to page through the book, and what she saw disturbed her in unexpected ways. The book was clearly based on some long-lost original whose pages must have been damaged somehow, perhaps in a fire. Some of the illustrations were only partial, their missing areas left blank because there was no way for a human imagination to predict what might have been there. The bookmakers had made precise woodcuts, but from the way the ink had blotted between the finer lines, Glory could tell the plates must have been old or their edition had been printed late in the run.

She had seen many old books, and so the pages of astronomical charts and symbols were familiar even when the particular figures were not. But she had seen nothing before like those pictures. Hieronymus Bosch came immediately to mind, but his work was clearly derivative of these unholy visions that had come from some entirely alien imagination. The abominations depicted in the woodcuts evoked in her some primitive, instinctive revulsion. She had seen plenty of depictions of Hell and demons in the medieval text collection at Vassar; her imagination was vivid enough to anticipate the extremes of such depictions, the lurid grotesqueries that a mind like de Sade's might have added to such images; but it was not possible to anticipate these protohuman, protoamphibious obscenities. Her response was like the instant nausea and disgust one feels at the sight of spoiled food—it was something that visceral and primitive. And yet these images had some sort of symbolic or ritual meaning—that was abundantly clear by the careful attention paid to their composition and execution, by the way certain configurations would appear again and again like the organic embodiments of some alien alphabet.

Glory turned to another page, this one illustrated by a single small image near the center. "Clark," she said.

Smith looked up, scratching his head.

"Have you seen this?"

He leaned toward her to get a closer look. "There's something wrong with that page," he said. He rubbed his eyes and looked again. "Did it get wet?"

"Wet?" When Glory looked down, she saw what Smith referred to. The image, at first, appeared simply to be another woodcut illustration surrounded by text, but now she could see that it was much more complex, and the text at the borders of the image had begun to bleed—or at least that's how it appeared. When she rubbed her eyes and looked again, the letters seemed to have gotten distorted, stretched out like fibers, and the symbol seemed to have grown larger and more distinct.

"I think our eyes are fatigued," said Smith. "I could swear that image was only half that size when I saw it last. All this staring at letters can distort one's sense of scale."

Glory looked once again at the illustration, then looked away and then quickly back again. She couldn't see any motion, but it seemed to have changed again between glances. It was like comparing sequential frames in a motion picture film to point out the almost invisible differences. "Let's take a break," she said. As she placed a paper marker and closed the book, she saw the image move out of the corner of her eye. One of the tentacles had extended beyond the frame of the woodcut.

She went through with the motion and closed the book, then opened it again, quickly. "Look," she said.

Smith, now standing, peered over her shoulder. "Hideous," he said. "Truly hideous. More repulsive than I recall."

"But Clark!" Glory saw the eye of the squid creature suddenly blink open and stare into hers. She felt the gorge rise in her throat, tasted the acrid bile. She closed her eyes and slammed the book shut.

"Let's rest a while before we become irrational," said Smith. "This book does strange things to the imagination. How about some coffee?"

"That's just what I need," said Glory.

While Smith busied himself with filling the pot, Glory moved to the fire and poked at the wood to feel its warmth. She realized she was cold for some reason, as if the chill of Smith's underground pantry hadn't quite left her bones. She shivered again. She wanted to talk about something other than the book now.

"I feel like I stepped into some sort of dream when I left Texas," Glory said. "HP and Bob are about as queer as they come, but then those men in black and the old Indian medicine man—who would believe all of that? Last week I was living in a hotel and minding my life like anyone else."

"Our lives are hardly ever as mundane as we assume," said Smith, arranging the pot over the flames. "We're always on the threshold of the fantastic, and you've just crossed it for now."

"I'd rather go back. All I wanted was a ride to my sister's place, and now I'm in some sort of mortal danger." Glory lit a cigarette and flicked the match away.

That alarmed Smith. The instant the match hit the dry earth he stepped over and ground it under his heel. "You can never be too careful about the threat of fire this time of year," he said. "Things are easily inflamed this season. Obviously, you haven't been in this part of the country before. Tell me about your home."

"Enough about me," Glory said, somewhat embarrassed at her carelessness. "Let's talk about you."

"Me?" Smith said with mock modesty. "Why, I'm just a self-educated handyman who dabbles in the arts."

"You really underestimate yourself, don't you?"

"There really isn't much to measure. At least not of great consequence."

"Some people have gone as far as to say that you're the American Keats," said Glory.

Smith knew exactly who those people were, but he pretended ignorance. "Sheer flattery," he replied. "I hardly have the adolescent idealism of Keats. Nor do I want to die so young."

"The hottest flame burns most brief?" said Glory.

"But smoldering embers can keep you warm through many a cold night," said Smith. "I've dabbled in lots of forms, but I haven't found my true calling, at least not yet."

"Why are you wasting your time writing for those awful magazines?"

"You have little faith in the power of imagination."

"I'd hardly rank the likes of HP and Bob with Keats and Shelley," said Glory.

"They don't purport to be poets, you know."

"Well . . ."

"And you forget that Bob and HP—and I, for that matter—never enjoyed the education those poets did. We're less beholden to the ghosts of tradition and convention. We're creating our own. And I would dare to say that given another fifty years, it's the stories in *Weird Tales*, if not the names attached to them, that will have the more profound effect on your Everyman. Who even reads the Romantic poets outside the classroom anymore?"

"I do," said Glory.

"So do I."

They laughed.

"I hope this isn't too forward of me, Glory. But I was wondering if you had any attachment to Bob or HP."

"Attachment? You mean romantic attachment? Why, you *are* being forward, aren't you?"

Smith gave a crooked smile.

"The answer is no."

"The reason I ask is because I couldn't help but notice there's a certain tension in Bob's manner when he's around you. Not exactly a possessiveness, but a sort of watchful quality."

"Oh, be frank about it, Clark. He seethes when he's around me, and I'm largely to blame. I confess I made advances at him one night while HP was asleep. I really shouldn't have." Glory smoothed back her hair and noticed the faint disk of the moon in the blue sky. "Bob's the sort of man a girl would love to have as an older brother. He's strong and he's protective. He's kind of thick when it comes to women, though."

"Thick?"

"Oh, you know what I mean. He rebuffed me that night pretending he was morally outraged, but I think it was really because he was scared." She paused momentarily. "Do you think he might be a virgin?"

"Given the deportment of his heroes in his writing, that wouldn't surprise me at all. We really can't hide our true selves even in our most fantastic work."

"You write those sorts of stories, too, don't you?"

"Me?" Smith laughed. "My heroes are suave men of the world compared to Bob's."

"Suave? In what way, exactly?"

Smith approached her and looked down, obliquely, past his nose. "Maybe I should offer an example?" he said, and kissed her.

Glory felt her knees go weak, but she drew back before things got out of hand. "I don't feel right about this," she said. "It feels like I'm betraying their trust."

"I thought—"

"I'd rather know I'm going to be alone with you, without someone barging in."

"They're tired," said Smith. "Let's meet when they've gone to sleep for the night. Would you join me for a moonlight stroll?"

"I bet you say that to all the ladies in Auburn."

"No, just the married ones."

"Scandalous," said Glory.

"I quite agree."

WHEN THEY RETURNED, Howard and Lovecraft found Glory perched on the fallen oak, smoking a cigarette. She waved a mug at them. "Fresh coffee!" she called.

They convened around the table once again, and Smith gave a report of their meager progress. Lovecraft glanced furtively around until Howard pointed out the can of sugar, and then he spooned so much of it into his coffee that Smith's eyes widened in concern.

"I'm not sure what to suggest," said Smith. "The wisest course of action would be to take the book to Berkeley and let the antiquarians and philologists at it. Even so, it could take months or years to translate the text."

"The span of months and years is hardly available to us." Lovecraft added another spoonful of sugar. "Yet I am confident that something will transpire in a timely fashion."

"And why's that?" asked Howard. " 'Cause the crazy old Injun told us his tall tale? I wouldn't be so happy about that, HP, since he told us we was all gonna die."

"That seems rather moot," said Smith. "We *are* all going to die, aren't we? Eventually."

Glory noticed the sun had already set. The horizon stretched purple and maroon across the west and the sky above was a cobalt blue and blue-black; a few wisps of cloud had drawn out like unraveling threads, gray-black on one side, tinted with a miasma of colors on the other. "He gave details," said Glory. "Could we talk about something else?"

"Well, let's have a little something to eat and then retire for the night. Sleeping out here, we'll be up at the crack of dawn." Smith got up and busied himself setting up the kerosene lamps and checking the supply of firewood.

The twilight didn't linger for much longer, and soon, after a small snack and some incidental conversation, they set up their cots and got ready to sleep. Smith offered Glory the option of sleeping in the bedroom in the cabin, but she decided it would be safer for her to camp there with the men. She took the third cot, and Smith made himself a bedroll on the ground.

"I trust we shall have eventful dreams," Lovecraft said by way of good night, "though I myself would much prefer a boring sojourn in the realm of Hypnos. I bid you all pleasant adventures."

"I trust in cold steel and hot lead," Howard mumbled.

"Good night, boys," said Glory.

They continued to exchange quips for a few minutes before they said good night to Smith, who, by then, had silently entered the portals of sleep.

15

HOWARD WOKE UP in the middle of the night with an uncomfortably full bladder. He grumbled and sat up, scratching his head, momentarily disoriented. There were the coals of the fire still glowing, and above the black wall of the nearby tree line, the faint wash of stars behind the face of the moon.

He sat up and disengaged himself from his half-open sleeping bag, then swung his feet over the cot and tapped around for his shoes, which he now regretted taking off. For a moment he thought he had a headache, or perhaps that the coffee had been too strong, but then he realized that the night was vibrating with the sound of crickets—millions of them, it seemed. Recalling the scorpions, he quickly found his flashlight, switched it on, and pointed the beam down into his boots. They were empty.

Now he took his pistol from under his make-do pillow and swept the beam of his light around the campsite, half-expecting to be surrounded by a swarm of insects. There was nothing but the usual debris of camp.

He slipped his boots on and made his way to the tree line, where he paused, and then thought better of it and simply relieved himself there, shivering with the release.

When he turned back toward the camp he thought he could hear something through the shrill droning of the crickets. It was his imagination, he knew, that made it sound like a low whispering chant—"*Cthulhu, Cthulhu, Cthulhu*"—but after recent events he could not be sure. He swept the tree line behind him once again, then turned the beam back to the camp. There was Lovecraft on his cot, safely away from the woodsmoke; there was Smith, oddly languid on the ground in his bedroll; there was his own empty cot near the fire; and there was Glory, bundled under her blankets. But where was her red hair? He walked briskly forward, realizing something was wrong, and just as he got to Glory's cot the whispering abruptly stopped. A loud shriek came from the direction of the cabin, and with it a blast of blinding blue-white light that cut through the darkness like the giant blade of a sword.

"HP! Smith!" Howard called, but they were already up, turning toward the sound. "Glory's missing," Howard said, and not waiting for the others, he immediately ran stumbling toward the cabin, eyes dazzled by purple afterimages.

The back door of the cabin was open, casting a rectangular swatch of light like the negative of a shadow onto the dark ground. Howard drew his pistol and ran in, his boots thundering on the wood floor. The first thing he saw was Glory's silhouette at the table, leaning over the source of the blinding light, whose blue tinge caused her hair to glow an unearthly violet color.

On the table, the pages of the *Necronomicon* fluttered wildly, behaving as if some frantic invisible hand were thumbing back and forth through it looking for a particular passage. Howard watched, bewildered, as the book flattened down, just as abruptly, its tattered pages open to an arcane diagram. Now Glory raised her arms high, the sleeves of her blouse falling to her shoulders, her skin pale blue, and a voice, clearly hers and yet not hers, whispered, "*Cthulhu.*"

"No!"

Instantly, Glory spun in her chair and faced him. Her face was damp, her eyes oddly reddish, her hair tangled. She had opened the buttons of her blouse and pulled the fabric down and back, exposing her breasts and her belly. Howard couldn't help but stare. He tried to hold the pistol steady. "No!" he said again.

Glory smiled a wicked and lascivious smile that distorted the natural beauty of her features. "Put down the gun, Bobby," she said, reaching toward him.

Howard took a step backward and pulled the hammer back. "Miss McKenna," he said, "stop it."

Glory tilted her head back and laughed, then she stared into Howard's eyes and said, "Look at me, Bobby. Look at me." She arched her back and preened for him.

Howard couldn't take his eyes off her body. He thrust the pistol forward, but even to him it no longer felt like a threat. He took a step toward her, pistol still extended, and she reached for the barrel, smiling.

"I'll shoot you, I swear," said Howard.

"Oh, Bobby, you're so brave."

Glory was about to rise from the seat and take the pistol when Smith barged in carrying a lamp, Lovecraft on his heels. "Stop!" cried Smith.

Howard turned his head, momentarily distracted, and in that instant, Glory leaped up and swatted the .45 from his hand, sending it flying into the darkness of the adjoining room. The blow stunned Howard, and he responded with a boxer's instinct, dropping his weight at the knees and swinging. His left hook caught Glory behind the ear, and it might have killed her had he not opened his hand and turned the punch into a mighty slap, which spun her all the way around and left her in a heap on the floor.

Suddenly the light from the table died down into a muted blue glow.

"The Artifact!" cried Lovecraft. "She took it from me!" He did a foolish thing and reached for it, only to burn his fingers on the intense cold that issued from its face on the table.

Smith lifted Glory to her feet and sat her up in a chair, kneeling in front of her to support her. He took her jaw in one hand and turned her head this way and that. "Are you all right, Glory?"

"I'm fine," she said, her eyes still closed. "What's going on?"

"I'm afraid you might be possessed by a demon," said Smith. He pulled her blouse around her and began to button it up. "I hope that doesn't sound as absurd to you as it does to me. A demon."

"Yes, a demon," murmured Lovecraft. "One that haunts one's dreams and hides like an assassin between one and one's sleep. In my dreams I heard its whispering in my brain, and I woke to see the shadow of wings and the eyes of a serpent."

A pall fell over the men in the kitchen. Glory, still in the chair in front of them, made noises of pain and pleasure and what sounded like alien words, and then she laughed loudly, with a guttural edge in her voice.

"A demon is still riding her," said Lovecraft.

Smith silenced him with a gesture, and was about to speak, when Howard said, "My God, she's makin' an animal noise—like a loco coyote. Have we done somethin' to get her mad?"

Lovecraft furrowed his brow in concern. He well knew that after their recent escape from the odd men the Artifact was alerting the servants of Cthulhu of their whereabouts. Smith's deep brown eyes glanced up, and he glared at Howard as if wondering whether to take the question as sarcasm or lack of awareness. Howard began to flush, but the attentive Lovecraft leaned toward his friend and tapped him on his shoulder.

"Look at her!" Lovecraft pointed at Glory, who was laughing even more strangely than a moment before.

The men were drawing away from her apprehensively. She did not look at them, or seem to notice them. She tossed her red hair and her loud laugh resounded in the kitchen. Her pale breasts heaved up and down, her sleeves opened and fell downward again as she raised up her pale arms. Her green eyes shone with a wild spark, her lips twisted with her unnatural sounds.

"The hand of Cthulhu is on her," Lovecraft grumbled uneasily.

"Glory!" Smith called sharply.

The only reply was another burst of manic laughter, but then she cried out, hoarsely, "Gnish'ton nog'na p'sto r'fomem olat f'gni!" Her voice rose into an inhuman pitch, and leaping from her seat, she stood behind the table, a knife in her hand. Lovecraft and Smith cried out and scrambled quickly out of her reach. But it was at Howard that Glory rushed, her pale face a mask of rage. Howard caught her wrist, and even the supernatural strength of her madness was futile against his solid muscles. He flung her from him, down onto the paper-strewn floor, where she lay in a moaning heap, the knife driven into the table as she collapsed again.

THEIR TENUOUS COMPOSURE, which had been so suddenly shattered, resumed again as the men lifted Glory's arms and legs and hoisted her onto the table. Howard disappeared into the other room and, returning with his .45, pushed it in under his belt.

"Calm down," said Smith. "Let's not allow this unexpected complication to discourage us in our work. Spirit possession is common enough."

Howard nodded indecisively. "Ya know, I'm worried about Glory and us. I'm holdin' on to my *pistole*."

"I believe her fit is over," said Smith.

As Lovecraft grumbled in pain and retreated to examine his hand, Glory turned her head and blinked at them, her eyes and expression now quite normal. "What am I doing up here?" she asked.

Smith helped her sit up. "Don't you remember?"

"Remember what? Where are we?"

"In my kitchen," said Smith. "I'm afraid we have some bad news for you."

Glory stood up, feeling her face and looking puzzled. She turned her back to the men to tuck her blouse in, and while they were preoccupied with decorum, she quietly retrieved another large kitchen knife from a countertop knife holder. She matter-of-factly turned back around and stretched her arm over the ancient book with the intention, it seemed, of slashing her wrist.

Howard reacted instantly. He leaped toward Glory and tried to grab the knife before she could harm herself, only to receive a slash across the top of his hand. Part in reflex and partly in desperation, he swatted her across her face again, his blood spraying across the open book and the glowing Artifact. Smith and Lovecraft caught Glory as she staggered, then collapsed into a chair, mumbling in a strange tongue. In a moment she was quiet. Her eyes seemed to clear, and she looked at them as if she had just woken.

Smith was the first to see it. Where the blood from Howard's hand had soaked into the vellumlike surface of the page, a jaundice-colored script was beginning to form in the space between the printed lines. "My God," said Smith. He moved the lamp closer.

Lovecraft and Howard stared in amazement as Smith frantically smeared the blood across the page, revealing more of the formerly invisible text. "Quick!" said Smith. Before Howard knew what was happening, Smith grabbed his injured hand and squeezed, extracting a large gout of blood that splashed across the facing page.

Howard grimaced in pain, momentarily stunned. "What the—!" For a split second it was unclear whether he understood Smith's impulsive act, but then his eyes flashed with a deeper anger that suggested he was reacting with a willful violence. He drew back and slammed his good fist into Smith's jaw.

And now it was Smith's turn to be stunned. He reeled against the desk, then fell to the floor semiconscious. Lovecraft understood the urgency of Smith's act. As he groaned on the kitchen floor, rubbing his sore jaw, Lovecraft quickly stepped forward with a butter knife and proceeded to spread the blood evenly across the surface of the two facing pages. Slowly, numerals began to appear, the jaundice turning into a deep purple color against the dark red that now completely blotted out the original text.

Smith rose unsteadily to his feet. "It's a palimpsest," he explained, massaging his jaw to determine if it was still properly attached. "I'm sorry, Bob, but it had to be done quickly in case there was a limited time for the catalysis."

"What the Sam Hill are ya talkin' about?" Howard nursed his bloody hand. "That hurt like hell."

"Likewise, I'm sure."

"What's a palimpsest?"

"Most commonly a holy text," said Lovecraft. "In the days when paper and parchment were rare, it was customary to write over a pre-existing document. Some, of course, were created on purpose to give symbolic meaning to the layering of text upon text."

"In this case, the surface gives instructions for how to reveal what's underneath," said Smith. "I'm sorry we didn't figure out the meaning of 'iron fluid' until it happened to fall on the page."

"What?" said Howard.

"Iron fluid. Blood. Blood is red because of its high iron content."

"It's a damn shame you eggheads and monkish types don't have anythin' better to do," Howard grumbled, turning to give the text a look.

The numerals had become more defined, filling out a series of what appeared to be coordinates. Hermetic and alchemical symbols, runes, and a hideous, unrecognizable text began to appear, including what appeared to be a webbed letter H and an ominous seven-pointed star that bore the same image as the Artifact.

"These numerical tables look like astronomical charts," said Lovecraft. "Clark, do you have any astrological books in your library?"

"You can take your pick," said Smith.

Lovecraft lifted the book, still open to the same page spread. "Bob, Clark and I will retire into the study to attempt a deciphering of these familiar figures. Would you be averse to guarding Glory during that time?"

"No, I don't mind," said Howard. "But how about givin' me some rope or somethin', Clark? I don't reckon she'll take too kindly to bein' clobbered again."

"No, I wouldn't," said Glory.

"I'm sorry. Terribly sorry. It ain't in my nature to hit a lady."

"I'm hardly a lady, Bob. At least not by your standards."

"At least not when a demon is riding you," said Smith, putting a coiled length of utility rope on the table. "I'm glad I didn't try to take that knife from you." He handed Howard a towel for his bleeding hand. "You might want to dress that wound now. There's water over here. Medical supplies here."

"I can take care of myself," said Howard. "You two go on ahead."

"Call if you require assistance," said Lovecraft.

"Yeah."

Smith and Lovecraft retired into the study with the *Necronomicon*, leaving Howard and Glory alone in the kitchen, illuminated by a single lamp.

"Let me help you with that hand," said Glory. "I'm really sorry, Bob. I don't know what came over me, and I don't remember a thing."

"Well, then you don't recall my hittin' you?"

Glory shook her head. "But I feel like shit, if that helps."

Howard grimaced at her language.

"No, the demon didn't make me say that." She approached him, and while he considered her with suspicion, she washed his hand in a water basin and then painted it with iodine. Howard hissed through his teeth and then whistled a few bars as she applied a salve and dressed the cut with gauze and a clean cloth.

"How do *you* feel?" asked Howard. "A normal person woulda had a busted lip or some bruisin' from how I hit you."

"My face feels a little numb, but I'm all right."

"Musta been the demon protectin' ya."

"Either that, or your right hook isn't what it used to be."

"I'm sorry," said Howard. "I was just reactin', ya understand? Maybe I woulda done different if I thought it through."

"Don't worry about it," said Glory. "It's a good thing I don't remember. I don't have it to hold against you."

"You don't remember nothin'?" Howard said, blushing.

"Nothing."

"Well, that's good then, 'cause I don't reckon Novalyne woulda approved."

"Approved of what? Who's Novalyne?" Glory poured the blood-tinged water out into the rigged sink and placed the iodine back on the shelf.

"Oh, nothin'," Howard said with a laugh. "Novalyne's my girl-friend. Wonderful gal."

"Why, I'm surprised, Bob."

"Huh? You surprised I got a girlfriend?"

"No, it was your tone of voice. You sounded so romantic and wistful."

"Yeah, I suppose." Howard was quiet for a moment. "It's too bad Ma don't approve of her. Can't figure women, you know."

"Maybe she feels threatened."

"Huh? Why would she feel threatened?"

"Oh, you know," said Glory. "Mother is always the central woman in a man's life. You're always her baby, no matter how old you are. It's natural for any mother to feel like her baby's girlfriend is an intruder. After all, who's going to take better care of her baby than she could?"

Howard tried moving his fingers under the dressing. "I hadn't thought of it that way," he said. "These days it's me takin' care of Ma."

"Then your girlfriend is interfering by taking up some of your attention, too."

"Yeah." He mumbled something under his breath. "Hey, how are ya feelin'? Any demons comin' on?"

Glory laughed melodiously. "I'm okay now. Let's make some tea."

IT WAS MORE than an hour before Lovecraft emerged from Smith's study with a satisfied smirk. "I see you haven't had to hog-tie the lady," he said to Howard.

"She's been behavin' ladylike."

"We have succeeded in decoding some coordinates," said Lovecraft. "Come, and we'll show you."

In Smith's study, they had spread a chaotic array of maps and charts all across the large desktop. At each end, under the flickering lamps, there were piles of paper scrawled with figures in pencil. On the floor and in the corners were heaps of crumpled paper.

"We finally figured it out," said Smith. "And here are the coordinates, which seem to indicate a rather remote place in New Mexico."

"I'm tired and out of sorts," said Glory, "but even without any scientific training, I can tell you that's impossible."

"We arrived at the coordinates with a method contrary to what you are assuming," said Lovecraft.

"There couldn't have been geographical coordinates in the book because they didn't exist when it was supposed to have been written," Glory continued. "And, in any case, the New World wasn't even discovered by the Europeans until the end of the Thirteenth Century!"

Lovecraft gave a rather patronizing smile. "Quite observant," he said. "But the numbers in the book were not geographical coordinates. They were numerals designating the ascension of a star called Shub Niggurath in a constellation that looks vaguely like a goat's head. What took us all this time was to work in reverse to determine the spot from which the rising of the star would be visible at the date and time indicated. And thus this disarray of stellar charts and conversion tables."

"Still," Glory insisted, "they couldn't have known that the star would have been visible from the New World. How did the author know there would be land at that spot?"

"Irrelevant," said Lovecraft. "The New World was not known by man, but who is to say that the Old Ones did not know the geography of the entire planet? This text comes down from them the way in which the Bible is said to be the divine word of God."

"I guess I'll accept that." It took only a moment's reflection for her to realize the absurdity of arguing with them after what she had been through. "It's no less believable than any of the other things," she concluded.

Smith touched Glory's shoulder. "There's another odd coincidence," he said. "As you might know by now, HP's *Necronomicon* was modeled on an ancient text called *The Astronomica*."

Glory smiled. "Well, according to some people, the stars *are* the dead, aren't they? It isn't so remarkable a coincidence."

"Touché," said Smith.

Lovecraft frowned. "Well, Miss McKenna, despite what you might see as my derivative nature, I seem to have been an unconscious conduit of information unknowable to me. And since what has transpired in recent days appears to maintain a remarkable closeness to the details in my weird fiction, I suggest we continue to assume such parallels while they are useful.

"According to our calculations, we must now journey back the way we came to the state of New Mexico, to a place near the Carlsbad Caverns. On Klarkash-Ton's map, we found an area labeled 'Shadows Bend.' The name causes me to shudder involuntarily, and I say that not simply out of a tendency toward hyperbole."

"You've proved your point, I think," said Howard.

Glory couldn't help but giggle behind her hand at Lovecraft, but she straightened her face and apologized to him. "I must still be under the influence of the demon," she said.

"Indeed, you must be," Lovecraft replied. He turned to Smith. "Come with us, Klarkash-Ton. There's plenty of room in the car, and God knows what manner of assistance we might require of you."

"I'm sorry." Smith gestured at the cabin around them. "I have all this to take care of, and my parents are both old and infirm, as you know. If I were a bachelor living on my own, I'd like nothing better, but I'm afraid I'll have to bow out of this adventure. I shall send my best thoughts with you all."

"You're doing the right thing," said Glory.

Smith looked at her. "I'm sorry, Glory."

"You're doing the sensible thing, too," she added. "Look what happened to my sister—and she wasn't even involved in this escapade."

Lovecraft and Howard were silent, and neither tried to urge Smith any further.

"I'm hittin' the sack," said Howard. "Somebody's gotta rest up to drive y'all."

. . .

THEY WERE SPOOKED by the house now, or perhaps it was that they were afraid of what the proximity of the *Necronomicon* might do to Glory if they slept inside, as was their first impulse after her possession, but it took only a few moments of debate before they decided to go back out to the compound under the trees. Lovecraft seemed to have no trouble getting back to sleep now that the Artifact was back in his possession, in that now habitual spot in his watch pocket. Howard strode about for a little while until Smith assured him that he would keep watch if necessary.

"Bob, I'm a light sleeper. And I live here, so I'll do the honors of staying awake for a while and keeping an eye on her."

"You didn't sleep so light before."

"I have forewarning now."

"Well, I suppose I gotta do what's sensible, huh?"

"Go on and sleep," said Glory. "I don't feel any demons coming on for a while at least."

Howard gave a sheepish grin that made his face grotesque in the flickering light of the campfire. "Well, good night, y'all."

"Good night."

Howard crawled into the sleeping bag on his cot, tossed and turned a few times, and was still.

"You might as well get some sleep, too," said Glory. "I don't think I'm going to do too well after what just happened."

Smith took a blanket and wrapped it around his shoulders. When he sat in one of the camp chairs, he reminded Glory of the old Indian whose story had moved her so deeply. "One could argue that you're simply trying to get me to sleep because you're still possessed," he said.

"Oh, come on, Clark."

"Well, in any case, I'll keep you company. We can chat until you get tired."

"What I want to do right now is smoke a whole pack of cigarettes, but then when I think about it, it makes me sick to my stomach. I feel like I'm wearing a glove all over my body that's the wrong size, and it's full of cotton or something."

"I've never seen a real case of demonic possession before, Glory, but I must say it's everything I imagined it to be."

"And you say that so casually, like you see it all the time."

"I'm tired."

Glory pulled a chair closer to the fire and sat down, following Smith's example of covering herself with a blanket. She leaned forward until she could feel the heat of the dying flames on her face.

"Throw in more wood if you like."

"No, that's okay. It just makes me feel more solid to feel something against my skin." She heard a rustling sound, a scraping sound, and then Smith was at her side with his chair. He took the blanket from around her shoulders and then enfolded the two of them with a single blanket, his arm around her shoulder. She leaned her head against the side of his neck.

"Does that feel better?" he asked.

"Much."

"Someone like Madame Blavatsky would say that your auric field was disrupted by the possession. Being in the healing presence of my intact auric field will make you feel more secure. I shall think repairing thoughts to activate the appropriate colors of my auric spectrum. And perhaps I should hum also. 'Aum'? Or is it 'Om'?"

"Oh, shut up," said Glory. "It's just nice to be hugged." They laughed quietly, afraid to wake the others.

"Clark?"

"Yes?"

"What do you think I should do?"

"I'm afraid I'm as lost as you are," he said. "For the longest time, I've tried to maintain a Buddhist kind of detachment to the problems of the world, believing everything to be some layer of illusion. But I never would have imagined that imagination and reality would collide like this."

"If you were me, would you go with them?"

"I suppose I'd have little choice. I can predict what would happen if you went to the authorities with a story of what you've been through."

"I've never liked the authorities anyway," said Glory. She closed her eyes for a moment to feel the faint heat of the fire against her eyelids. "Clark, would you mind if I asked you to touch my skin? With your skin?"

Smith was quiet for a moment, and then he moved his other hand up to stroke her cheek. "How's that?"

"Mmm. It feels like my body again where you touch me," she said drowsily. "Touch me all over, Clark."

"Glory?"

"I know what I said."

"We can hardly do that here with Bob and HP."

"How about that moonlight stroll you mentioned earlier?" Glory stood up, leading Smith by the hand. She kept both of them enfolded in the blanket as she walked out of the compound into the clearing, toward the tree line in the east. Away from the fire, their eyes adjusting to the dark, they realized it was later than they had imagined. The sky was already the flat gray of false dawn, and they could see the silhouettes of the trees ahead. Glory took the blanket, folded it in half, and laid it flat on the dew-covered grass. She shivered as she unbuttoned her blouse.

"Glory, are you sure you want to do this?"

"Oh, I'm sure," she said. "I'm possessed, Clark." She laughed sweetly when she saw the look of alarm in his eyes, and she threw her blouse down as she embraced him, to feel the touch of his flesh against hers, to make her feel real again.

Had they been listening attentively, they might have heard a sharp intake of breath, a hard clench of the jaw. From the edge of the compound, Howard crouched behind the trunk of a blue oak, watching them. When he was sure they could not see him, he knelt and crawled to get closer. Birds were already chirping in the still air. Howard drew as close as he dared, and then he parted the blades of grass in front of his eyes and peered through. He was angry, excited, and embarrassed, all in equal measure as he watched their bodies join and unjoin in the cold. He heard the little noises that made him bite his tongue in jealousy.

Their silhouettes were nearly black against the rising sun, and to Howard, still carrying the touch of sleep, Glory's shape above Smith's seemed to transform into a sleek sea creature. As she moved up and down to the increasingly intense rhythm of some invisible ocean, she arched backwards and flung her head, cascading her hair behind her like the shadow of spraying water, and the shape of her breasts, as she moved again, arching farther backward, merged together until they formed a single conical triangle like the dorsal fin of a leaping dolphin. Howard heard the roaring sound of the surf beating against the shore. His breath caught momentarily, and then he suddenly realized it was only the rush of blood behind his own ears. He shook his head to clear himself of this vision and crawled slowly backward in the wet grass until he was sure they couldn't see him. Shivering with cold and emotion, he walked quickly back to camp and bundled himself back into his sleeping bag on the cot, pretending he had never left. It was hard, because he was soaked with the cold dew of morning, and he could not get the images he had just seen to leave his mind.

On the other cot, Lovecraft turned over and closed his own eyes to reenter his own pretense of sleep.

AFTER A HASTY BREAKFAST, Howard loaded up the Chevy with a sense of urgency that caused Lovecraft to make a few sharp noises of annoyance. While the two of them argued about what should go in the trunk and what should remain in the backseat, Glory stepped back to Smith. "Clark," she whispered, "I want to come back. After this is all over and I've seen to my sister, I want to come back."

"I'll be waiting for you," Smith replied. "As ever a poet waited for a nymph."

They only exchanged the briefest of hugs and a lingering friendly kiss, but the air between them held a charge of intense affect. Howard, looking up from the car, did not fail to notice.

"Good-bye," Glory whispered as she walked back to the car under Howard's watchful eye.

"Good-bye and Godspeed!" Smith called. He waved at the sedan as it tumbled down the dusty drive back toward the road. Glory waved back through the rear window which glimmered like clear water in the sunlight, and through the passenger's front window, Lovecraft's arm flapped a few times like a featherless bird's wing as the Chevy traversed the ruts and bumps.

It was a clear day, the sky a milky sort of blue. White puffs of cumulus floated like giant, torn cotton balls above the horizon toward the west. But when Smith looked in the direction his friends would be going, he had a certain premonition of foul weather.

As Smith stepped back in through the front door, remembering Glory all voluptuous in the soft moonlight, he sensed something in his study. He hesitated, wondering if he should run out and try to call back the others, but by then he was at the threshold, and he could see the two dark shapes silhouetted against the window. For a split second, he thought his parents had returned, but then he knew exactly who they were. They were dressed in black, or at least appeared to be on the surface. Their features were indistinct—not obscured in shadow, but shadow itself. To a typical man they might have maintained the illusion of humanness, but to Smith, absorbed in the arcane, they leaked their true and terrible forms: claws, not hands; creased and fleshy wings, not suit lapels. He was struck momentarily by a strong vertigo as he entered their inhuman aura; he expected ill intention, hostility, evil, but what he felt, instead, was an unexpected diplomacy and a distant sense of reverence. It must be the proximity of the book, he thought. They could kill me or do things far worse, and yet they are behaving as if they are in some holy place. He did not know what to do or what to say, so he forced himself to be calm and rational.

"Hello, gentlemen," he said. "I've heard a lot about you."

The figures were silent for a long moment, then the one on the left, the one whose black aura extended farther into the alien dimension, replied: "Hello. Gentle. Man. I. Have. Heard. A. Lot. About. You."

"Really?" said Smith, forcing a smile. Behind him, the door swung shut in a gust of cold wind.

16

WHILE GLORY AND LOVECRAFT DROWSED, Howard drove
without a word down from the foothills of Auburn into Sacramento,
joining Highway 99 southbound through the Central Valley. He tried
to keep his mind focused on the task at hand, a favor that had somehow escalated into an unbelievable quest, but he couldn't help flashing
back, again and again, to the image of Glory and Smith in the meadow.
He had to relax his grip on the wheel periodically when he noticed the
fingertips of his injured hand turning white.

By noon, as they passed through Fresno, the heat of afternoon had
turned the Chevy into a hotbox. Howard blinked away the stinging
sweat that kept trickling into his eyes and stubbornly drove on, awake
only with the strength of his anger and annoyance.

"Bob," said Lovecraft, unfurling his wrinkled handkerchief, "I
myself enjoy this sort of heat, which I imagine is salutory to my cold
blood, but perhaps we should pause for some liquid refreshment?"

Howard only glared at the road ahead. "It'll have to wait."

Glory roused herself from her semiconscious state and lit a cigarette. In a moment the interior of the car was swirling with smoke blown about from the single open window.

"Put your window down, HP," Howard said.

Lovecraft grimaced as if it were the smoke that annoyed him, but the wince he gave as he turned the crank was of a different sort of pain. "The heat is pleasant, but I must complain that the smoke causes me to imagine the Inferno."

"If I can't have something to drink, I might as well smoke myself totally dry," said Glory, blowing another large plume. She was quiet for a few moments before she leaned forward and said over Howard's right shoulder, "I'm guessing you didn't get my hint. I'm about to mess the backseat here, if you know what I mean."

Howard said nothing.

Lovecraft looked at Glory, who merely shrugged her shoulders. He turned his gaze back to Howard. "Bob, I believe Miss McKenna is in dire need of a ladies' room."

Still, Howard failed to respond. He merely adjusted his grip on the steering wheel and clenched his jaw with a bit more force as the scabs under his bandage broke. Just ahead was a Mohawk gas station with the usual placards and a sign that advertised the cleanliness of their bathrooms. Lovecraft glanced at the gas gauge which, from his angle, read just shy of empty.

"Bob, unless you are operating this automobile on some miracle fuel unbeknownst to the rest of us, I believe we are in dire need of gasoline. From the pressure in my bladder, I wager we will attain an equilibrium of fluids as I dispose of the number of gallons we are likely to need."

Without a word, Howard suddenly hit the brakes and twisted the wheel, skidding across a patch of gravel, just missing the Mohawk Indian signpost as they slid into the gas station and stopped in a cloud of dust. They were some fifty feet from the pumps. Howard opened his door and got out.

"Then get some gas, dammit," he said through the open door. He stalked off toward the rest rooms.

Lovecraft slid over into the driver's seat, pulled the door shut, and managed to make it to the pumps after a few alarming grinds from the gearbox. "Hello, there, my fine fellow," he called to the attendant. "Honor us with a full tank, if you please. And do not spare your efforts on the various windows."

"I wasn't kidding. I'm about ready to burst," said Glory. "Excuse me." She stepped out of the car and stretched, brushing her hair back with her fingers, and then she walked in the same direction Howard had taken a few moments earlier.

Lovecraft shut off the ignition and drummed his fingers along the top of the steering wheel. He noticed a dark crust along the top ridge and absentmindedly began to pick at it until he realized it was the blood from the cut on Howard's hand.

"WOULD YOU MIND terribly explaining to me the purpose of this juvenile behavior? Bob?"

Howard finally erupted. "Damn it, HP. She—She . . ." He was so upset his words sputtered before he regained enough composure to continue. "She had—she was with him!"

"With whom? To what are you referring?"

"Smith. She—with—had—was with him last night."

"I see. And for what particular reason does this trouble you so terribly much?"

"Any man worth his salt should be offended by this—this . . . It's immoral!"

"Indeed," said Lovecraft. "Fine words coming from a man who makes his living hawking salacious tales of a thieving barbarian who frequently beds a bevy of women to whom he is hardly betrothed."

"Now that ain't fair, HP! This is the real world we're in."

"Indeed. And is it not in this real world that Miss McKenna's past was known to us? We were well aware of her past . . . indiscretions long before we arrived at Klarkash-Ton's cabin, were we not? And if you were gallant enough to offer her the privilege of our company, knowing her moral character, is it not hypocritical of you to be thus offended when her behavior is merely in keeping with what you assumed of her to begin with?"

Howard frowned. "Now you're soundin' like a damn lawyer," he said, markedly calmer. "But I guess you're right, ain't ya? If she's a whore to begin with, why should I get all fired up if she acts like one with Smith?"

"I can safely venture to say that I find her and Clark's amorous activities even more distasteful than you do, but we have matters far more serious to attend to at present. Agreed?"

Howard had to admit that with all of the incredible happenings they had endured in the past few days, his jealousy was the very least of the problems confronting them. He was suddenly embarrassed by the thought, because, until that moment, it would not have occurred to him to think of himself as jealous of Smith and Glory. It would have been easier to keep his feelings in the realm of anger, but now that the idea had become conscious, he was left with an awkwardness he did not enjoy. "You're right, HP," he said. "I'm sorry."

Lovecraft tapped the inside of the passenger door twice in an odd gesture of triumph. "Good. Then let me welcome you back to the world of the sane. And I assure you, that as far as I am concerned, there is nothing more to be said about this issue." He grinned and pantomimed a parched throat. "Now, I believe we could all do with a round of Dr Pepper."

Howard reached for his wallet but Lovecraft waved his hand, gesturing for him to put it away. "Don't trouble yourself, Bob. If you see to the automobile's refreshment, I shall see to ours."

Howard was at first surprised by his penny-pinching friend's generosity, but then he realized how much more the gas was costing him. As Lovecraft walked over to the ice box full of sodas by the garage, he called after him, "Hey, HP! You sure *you* ain't been possessed?"

Lovecraft looked back in mock indignation as he fished through his trouser pockets for change.

· · ·

WHEN GLORY RETURNED from the rest room and defiantly opened the passenger door to return to her seat, she found Lovecraft and Howard loitering together at the back bumper, enjoying their bottles of Dr Pepper. She sensed that something had passed; the atmosphere was suddenly relaxed once again between the two men. While the attendant was rather ineffectively squeegeeing the dirty windows, she joined them.

"Here, Glory," said Howard, holding an open bottle for her as if it were a peace offering. "We saved you one."

She hesitated, but then decided to take it in good faith. "Why, thank you kindly, Bob."

Howard glanced back and forth between Glory's piercing green eyes and Lovecraft's somewhat smug expression. Lovecraft took it as some sort of signal and walked over to the ice box again to talk to the fat mechanic. It took a moment more for Howard to summon his resolve. "I'm—I want to apologize for my behavior today," he said finally. "I know it ain't my place to pass judgment . . ."

"Well, damned if you aren't right about that."

Howard left his sentence incomplete and paid the attendant.

Lovecraft returned with another round of sodas and passed them out. He sensed the remaining tension between Howard and Glory and decided to divert attention from it. "I'm given to understand from that rather loquacious gentleman in overalls that there is an establishment called Tandy's Diner approximately two miles down the road. He claimed this establishment offers the 'meanest chili east or west of the Pecos,' and from his tone, I took it to be a rather meaningful boast."

Rising immediately to the backhanded slap at his home state as Lovecraft had anticipated, Howard started the car.

"Well, chili was invented where I come from," said Howard. "And I sincerely doubt anybody from California can make a chili meaner than the one I had in San Antonio. I say I'll just have to settle this for myself." He tossed his empty Dr Pepper into a garbage can and opened the driver's side door. "Anyone else hungry?" he asked, almost as an afterthought.

Lovecraft and Glory had been famished for the past several hours during their nonstop drive through the Central Valley. They both answered "Yes" in derisive unison as they got into the Chevy.

BY THE TIME they passed Barstow and rejoined Route 66, with dusk approaching and the sky a bright orange, Howard was suffering silently again; this time it was from the Tandy's chili, which he had stubbornly insisted was not hot by Texas standards. His discomfort helped him stay awake as they crossed into Arizona, but as they turned south on Highway 89 toward Phoenix, he found himself beginning to drift off. He tried breathing more rapidly, blinking his eyes hard to clear the fog, biting the insides of his cheeks, even pinching himself, but as he grew more and more tired even the self-inflicted pain felt as distant as something happening to someone in a movie he was watching through the windshield of the car. By the time they passed Prescott, the faded white lines of the road, barely visible in the headlights, seemed like the flashing trails of arrows shot directly at his eyes, and he began to close them briefly to enjoy the relief.

"Bob?"

Howard eased the wheel slightly to make himself more comfortable. He could hear Lovecraft snoring quietly at his side. It was warm and pleasant.

"Bob?"

He mumbled as that pleasant sense of falling came over him.

"Bob!"

Howard jolted awake and jerked the wheel, just avoiding the deep trench along the shoulder of the road.

"Uh, excuse me, Bob," said Glory, "but did you see the ditch there?"

"Yes."

"Then why the hell were you driving into it!"

Howard jerked his head angrily around to look at Glory, whose eyes grew suddenly wide with fear. Her face lit up with a sudden bright light, which Howard found shocking. For a split second, he thought some demonic force was taking her again, but then he realized the light was coming from outside, and he turned instantly back to face the road, just in time to swerve and miss the oncoming truck.

The loud blare of the horn and the violent jerk of the car jolted Lovecraft out of his sleep.

"That's it!" said Glory. "I don't care what you think about women behind the wheel! Pull over now before you get us all killed!"

Lovecraft blinked himself awake enough to concur with her, though he didn't like the idea of a woman driving any more than Howard did.

"I'm sorry," said Howard. "I'm awake now."

"Yeah, nothing like the threat of instant death to perk you up," said Glory. "Look, you've been nodding for a long time."

"I said I'm awake now."

Lovecraft interjected more for the sake of his own sleep than to be Glory's ally. "Let her take the wheel while the road is good," he said. "I suggest you take over when things are more challenging."

They could nearly hear the sound of Howard seething, but he relented and pulled over. He got out, flooding the interior of the car with cool air, and stalked off into the night for a few moments before he returned and changed seats with Glory.

Soon, with a cigarette in her mouth and singing Billie Holiday's "I Wished on the Moon," Glory was driving. Howard had curled up in the backseat and fallen instantly asleep.

"Thank you," said Lovecraft. "It would have been a shame to meet our doom through sheer carelessness when there are far more noble means of attaining the same goal."

"I was just trying to save my own skin," said Glory.

"You are, no doubt, aware of Bob's intense jealousy regarding your behavior with Clark?"

"Yes."

"Then I shall not trouble you with references to it in the future." Lovecraft hunched back into the most comfortable position he could manage, and for the next half an hour he remained half-awake, warily monitoring Glory at the wheel before once more succumbing to a troubled sleep.

HE DID NOT KNOW how long he had been asleep when he awakened and rubbed his eyes free of grit. He sat up to see the blurred white lines on the desert road drifting beneath the car. He glanced at Glory, who sat confidently behind the wheel, a fresh cigarette between her lips. A loose lock of her red hair obscured her face. He looked back at Howard, who was still sleep in the backseat, fetally curled like a giant prawn, mumbling something that sounded like it might be his mother's name. He removed his watch from his breast pocket and squinted in the darkness to make out the time. Impossible, until the Artifact emitted a faint glow: 1:08. He winced at the pain that followed the Artifact's next pulse of light and then he grimaced as he endured a series of sharp pains in his stomach. He reached into his watch pocket to pluck the Artifact out, to offer himself some relief, but what he drew out was not metal; it was pale and fleshy, and touching it caused a disquieting sensation in his bowels. Still, he pulled on the thing and produced something long and tubelike, like the siphon of a mammoth clam. It was textured like pink flesh and it was smooth. He pulled some more, and now an arm's length stretched from his pocket. It caught for a moment, and then a mass of discolored stuff like rotting meat dangled from the long tube. He realized what he held before him was a length of his own intestine, and the hideous thing at the base was a cancer. He screamed before he could stop himself, shouting at Glory to pull over immediately, but she ignored him. He reached over, agonized by the pain, and tapped her shoulder. She turned, revealing her face to him, and now he realized that the red glow he had taken to be the tip of her cigarette was actually in her eyes. He wanted to say something, but she opened her mouth first, revealing long white teeth that grew longer as her mouth gaped wider. Her teeth were moving, swaying, growing into segmented tentacles that looked like elongated maggots. Lovecraft felt his gorge begin to rise; his voice caught in his throat as he tried to cry out to warn Howard. Glory laughed, a deep guttural laugh, as he recoiled in fear and tried to alert his friend by pounding his hand against the back of the seat. But his arm was all tangled in the coils of his own gut. No avail. They were approaching a sharp right-hand curve. To the sound of her own hideous laughter, Glory spun the wheel, swerving off the road, crashing through a wooden guardrail, straight over a cliff into the black night. Lovecraft opened his mouth to scream again, but he felt himself choking.

WITH A LOUD, coughing gasp, Lovecraft sat bolt upright in his seat, sweat-drenched and trembling. An odd noise issued from his throat, and he flailed his arms in front of himself as if to ward off an imminent collision.

Glory was so startled she impulsively jerked the steering wheel and swerved all the way to the opposite shoulder before unsteadily pulling the Chevy straight. Howard raised his annoyed, sleepy head from the backseat. "What in the Sam Hill—" His voice was cut short by the sight of approaching headlights and the loud blaring of a truck's horn.

For a moment their three heads were all in a line: Glory's, Howard's, and Lovecraft's, all screaming in unison in an unexpectedly harmonious pitch against the background of the truck horn. Their eyes wide in the headlights, their mouths agape, they might have been the trophies of some ghastly headhunt. But Glory regained her senses just in time to swerve back into her lane and the truck whizzed past them, buffeting the side of the car with gravel.

"W-Whereabouts are we?" said Howard. He tried to sound casual, but his voice cracked.

Glory answered with equally feigned casualness. "Just passed through some town called Solomonsville . . ." She gulped air before she finished, ". . . New Mexico?"

"Already?" Wiping his damp brow with his handkerchief, Howard leaned back in his seat and reached under his right arm to unstick his shirt from his armpit. "Makin' good time."

Lovecraft stared ahead blankly, unconsciously licking the sweat on his upper lip.

Howard continued in a feigned nonchalance as he looked out toward the southeast, "Damn shame we ain't got time to pay a visit to Tombstone."

Lovecraft pulled his watch out of his breast pocket. He was still staring blankly into the darkness ahead, and his voice came out in a soft monotone. "Don't fret, Bob. I believe there's an OK Corral of our very own awaiting us."

Now Howard was gazing into the same sea of black just beyond the shivering beams of the headlights. "You're right, HP, but I'd damn well rather shoot it out alone with the whole Clanton Gang than face whatever the hell's waitin' for us at Shadows Bend, that's for sure. What about you, Glory?"

There was no reply.

Lovecraft clicked open his timepiece, and straining his eyes in the darkness to read the time, he was able to make out 1:07. He looked at Glory, sitting rigid behind the wheel, her face oddly frozen in the dim light of the dashboard, and suddenly, the memory of his nightmare flashed in his mind, turning his face white with fear. "Glory," he said. "Glory, stop the car this instant!"

Glory's eyes fluttered.

"NOW!"

Glory shook her head quickly, as if she were trying to stay awake. "What?" she said.

"Just do what I say, woman!" In his panic, Lovecraft leaned over to grab the wheel from her hands.

From the backseat, Howard sat up and put his hand on Lovecraft's shoulder, restraining him. "What the hell's gotten into you, HP?"

Lovecraft jerked away from Howard's hand and lunged across the front seat, trying to wrest control of the vehicle from Glory. He pulled at her rigid hands and put his foot over hers on the brake, but it was too late. With Howard pulling him back, he had failed, and now, in what seemed a single blink, the color in Glory's eyes changed from a bluish green to a glowing red, and a guttural voice echoed from deep in her throat in a barely intelligible whisper. "Iä! Cthulhu! Iä!" Suddenly Lovecraft saw it just ahead, the image from the dream, the right-hand curve in the road, the guardrail, the blackness above the cliff.

"Eh! S'yas!" said Glory. "Eh! K'neros mi a oloruc retwa isnat!" Her lips did not move. The voice came fully formed from inside.

Now Howard realized he had misread Lovecraft's intent. He grabbed Glory by the shoulders from behind and tried to pull her away from the wheel. The car swerved, swerved again, and she did not budge from her frozen posture. "Eh! S'yas inur!" she whispered. "Nad h'net inur f'mor ihm! Nad h'net inur!"

Lovecraft frantically tried to pry Glory's rigid fingers from the wheel. His own strength was amplified with fear, but it was futile against Glory's demonic strength.

"Bob! Help me!"

A low laugh issued from Glory's throat. "Eh! Nidd't eees'm tchwa n'ig!" she said. Her head turned in a bizarrely smooth motion and her eyes glowed brighter. "Eh! P'wi eda r'tea!" With all his might, Howard reached under Glory's armpits and tried to pull her up, but he didn't have enough leverage from his position behind her. It was no use. With Glory petrified like the victim of a Gorgon, the car swerved just as it had in Lovecraft's nightmare.

Glory's mouth opened wider, into a circle. "Gnish'ton nog'na p'sto r'fomem olat f'gni!"

The cliff looming ahead of them, rapidly and relentlessly approaching, Lovecraft and Howard released their grips and slid to the right side of the car. They glanced at each other, then at Glory, their eyes frantic.

"It's too late, HP! Jump for it!"

They opened their doors simultaneously, but just then Glory hit the brakes and the car skidded, fishtailing left and right on the gravelly earth until it came to a rough halt at the very edge of the cliff, stopping with a jolt as the two front wheels left the edge and crashed the car's frame against the rock.

17

A THICK CLOUD of dust swirled around the Chevy. Lovecraft couldn't see it, but he could taste dirt, and he spat to clear his mouth. There was no sound—not even the wind—until Howard heaved a sigh of relief that ended up as a sneeze. And now they could feel the gentle night breeze. It made the open doors swing subtly, and from the back, Howard heard a dry sandy rasp in the hinges.

Suddenly Glory lost her rigid posture all in an instant. She slumped over, unconscious, onto the steering wheel, and the horn blasted so loudly that Lovecraft nearly leaped from the car in sheer reflex. When he cringed involuntarily, then tried to reach out to move Glory, he felt the car shift. The front seemed to be tilting down, then coming back up, but he wasn't sure if it was real motion or simply his disoriented imagination. "Bob?" he said.

Howard couldn't hear him. He grabbed Glory by the shoulders and pulled her head away from the steering wheel. She slumped against the back of the seat, her head flopped backwards, her mouth open, her neck bent at an alarming angle. The horn stopped, just as abruptly, and in the ringing silence, the world moved, gently, up and down, up and down, as if they were bobbing in a boat. Suddenly, there was a jolt, a grating noise, and the nose of the car slipped a bit farther over the edge before it stopped.

"Damn it, HP! Sit still or we're done for!"

"I am not moving, Bob. I was attempting to warn *you* not to make any sudden movements, but you were apparently deafened by the horn." He lay there on the floor with his hands clasped over his chest like a man in a coffin. "My sincerest apologies if I have failed to intervene in time. What do you propose we do next?"

"Let's hope she don't wake up."

"How is she? I can't see from down here."

"Looks like her damn neck's broke, but I don't think it is. Maybe it'd be better if it was."

"How far have are we extended beyond the lip of the precipice?"

"What?"

"To what degree is the car's balance precarious?"

"What the hell are you sayin', HP?"

"How far over the cliff are we?"

"I can't tell, and I sure as hell ain't gonna try movin' to find out. Can ya look out your door without movin' too much?"

"I can't quite determine the degree of our predicament. The front tires are certainly over."

"See if there any rocks on the ground ya can pick up without actually gettin' out of the car," said Howard. From his position, pressed as far as possible against the backseat, he carefully looked behind himself and thought through the possibility of kicking out the back window. It only took him a moment to realize that if he failed in the first attempt, the recoil would drive him toward the front of the car and possibly tip the balance. He was wondering if he could lie sideways and kick with one leg instead of bracing himself against the front seat and kicking with both when he heard Lovecraft's reply.

"Yes, there are many rocks of various sizes within arm's length."

"Good. Hand me the biggest one ya can reach."

Lovecraft strained himself as he contorted his body to reach outside without shifting his body. He picked up a stone about the size of a golf ball and handed it back to Howard.

"Ya got anything a little bigger out there? This is gonna take a while at this rate."

The next stone was a bit larger.

"Bigger!"

The next one was the size of a large grapefruit.

"Bigger, dammit!"

"Bob, how large a stone does it require to—ah! I see. Your plan is to compensate for our weight so that we may exit the vehicle and pull it back to safety. Very clever. Very clever, indeed. Given your pugilistic impulses, I assumed you would smash the rear window and climb out."

"Thanks. I ain't plannin' to wreck my car any more than I need to. How much do ya weigh?"

Lovecraft struggled to pull a large rock in and hand it back. "Oh, I'd venture eleven stone, eleven stone and six."

Howard grabbed the rock impatiently. "That's good, HP. That's good that you can keep your sense of humor at a time like this."

"Bob, I can assure you that I find absolutely nothing about our current predicament the least bit amusing."

"In pounds. How much do you weigh in pounds? You know, the way we weigh things in America."

"I'm sorry if my affinity for things English offends you. Approximately one hundred sixty pounds."

"A middleweight, huh? That's lighter than I thought ya'd be, seein' the set of your jaw and all."

"I'm sorry to hear that my facial disfigurement gives you the wrong impression," Lovecraft replied with no small measure of sarcasm. He continued to bring in as many large rocks as he could with the minimum of bodily motion. It wasn't long before his arm was trembling from exhaustion, the muscle thick and limp.

In the back, Howard mentally weighed each rock before stacking them as far back as possible, jamming as many as he could between the lower and back cushions of the seat.

"I have procured all stones within reasonable reach," said Lovecraft.

"Okay, we're still gonna need more. Reach over to the driver's door and let's see how many ya can get."

Lovecraft dwelt momentarily on the indignity of having to crawl over Glory's lap, but as he laid himself across her thighs, with her warm and softly heaving belly pressed against his shoulder, her breasts slightly touching the top of his back, he found himself wanting to pause in that importunate embrace. He could see himself curling into a semicircle and relaxing into that maternal comfort, into a quiet and restful sleep, but at the moment, he had a task to perform for Howard, and he had no choice but to do as he was instructed.

WHEN THEY HAD finally collected enough stones for Howard to feel safe, Lovecraft slowly crawled out of the car on his belly, getting his already-rumpled clothes covered in dirt and dust. He paused to assess the situation, quickly walking to the other side of the car, stepping back from the cliff's edge to get perspective. It was less precarious than he had imagined from inside, but still quite dangerous all the same. The look on Howard's face made him decide to keep the assessment to himself.

Lovecraft moved to the back of the car and called loudly, "I shall sit on the rear bumper. That should provide adequate counterweight to permit your egress if you are careful."

"What about Glory?"

"Given the fact that she remained unconscious throughout my awkward endeavor to cross her body, I imagine she will remain in that condition for a little while longer."

Lovecraft turned his back to the car and found a solid but uncomfortable perch on the rear bumper. He could feel weight shifting inside as Howard made his way over the seat and out of the passenger side as gingerly as possible.

Howard dusted himself off and immediately opened the trunk to rummage in its black interior. He produced a coil of rope and drew out a length, stepping back for a moment to decide on a place from which to brace himself. "Come on, HP, we gotta do this quick, before she wakes up."

Lovecraft, exhausted from all the rock lifting, wanted to rest a while. "Is it not wise for me to maintain my weight here to counterbalance Glory?"

Howard returned to the car and knelt between Lovecraft's legs to loop the rope around the middle of the bumper, seemingly oblivious of the awkward pose they were striking. "You stay put till I'm ready," he mumbled.

"I beg your pardon?"

"I'm gonna pull here, and when the rope's nice and tight, you jump down and lend a hand."

"I shall apologize in advance for my fatigue."

"Never mind and just help, all right?" Howard got up and walked backwards, playing the rope out until he found a good spot to brace himself for leverage. He pulled the slack tight, planted his feet, and motioned to Lovecraft, who skipped down rather daintily for a man of his size.

While Lovecraft put both hands on the rope and tugged on it, leaning back with his weight, Howard turned his back to the car, braced the rope over his shoulder and, grunting with the effort, pulled as if he were a horse, wincing when he heard the sound of the undercarriage scraping against the rocky ground. Lovecraft was amazed that they were able to move the vehicle at all, and when all four wheels were back on solid ground he called out for Howard to stop before he dragged the car all the way into the middle of the highway.

Howard coiled the rope as he made his way back to the car. Then he reached over Glory's still-unconscious form and set the brake. "You wanna wake her up, be my guest," he said.

Lovecraft pondered the problem for a minute as he dusted his own clothes, cringing at the thought of how he'd look by the light of day. "Let me think out loud for the two of us," he said. "If we were to keep her in this unconscious state and drive on, since our mission is an urgent one, we would obtain a certain advantage. And yet, if she were to wake, once again possessed, with some preternatural strength and aggression she were to expend upon us, then we would certainly suffer a setback. At least. Therefore, the conclusion is only logical. We shall wake her now, ascertain her state of mind, and bind her, if necessary, with the very rope you hold in your hands."

"Go ahead and wake her then," said Howard, looking down at the rope.

Lovecraft leaned over Glory, lifted her head off the seat back with one hand, and lightly slapped her face with the other. He slapped her again, slightly harder, then harder still until her eyes fluttered open and she sat up, disoriented.

"What? What happened? Why are the two of you staring at me like that?"

Lovecraft and Howard looked at each other, temporarily at a loss, and then Lovecraft said, "Miss McKenna, I'm afraid you have once again fallen, albeit briefly, under the influence of the sinister forces which are ever more determined to prevent us from reaching our destination."

Howard could see from Glory's glazed expression that she wasn't fully lucid—at least not enough to understand his friend's ponderous diction. "You got possessed again and just about damn near killed us. That's why we're staring at ya."

"Oh," Glory said, rather matter-of-factly. "Is that all?"

A few minutes later, when Glory had regained her composure and Howard had finished inspecting the car's undercarriage for damage, Lovecraft handed the rope to Howard.

"HP . . ."

"It is the logical thing."

Howard looked at Glory, then at the rope, his expression partially hidden in the darkness. His thoughts were so clear he might as well have pantomimed the dilemma.

"Here," Glory said, offering her wrists. "I want you to tie me up in the backseat until we get to where we're going."

"See here, Glory, I—"

"I don't want any debate on this. It's obvious that whatever it is that's out there has got some kind of hold on me. I don't want to cause any more problems."

"Perhaps an understatement, but she is correct, Bob. It is in our general best interest."

Howard said nothing but ushered Glory into the car and began halfheartedly to bind her hands and feet. Glory glared up at him. "It's not tight enough," she said in a playful tone. "I could slide right out of this without even wrinkling my pretty little forehead."

Howard cinched the knot around her wrist a little tighter. "How's that?"

Now Glory was even more sarcastic. "I thought you Texas boys were all experts with your ropes and guns. Haven't you ever tied any-thing down, Bobby?"

He was trying to be nice to her, but Howard could feel his face grow hot with anger. He gave a flick of the wrist that yanked the knot tight around Glory's wrists. "I ain't ever roped a steer, if that's what ya mean," he said. "But I can tie a knot as good as anyone else. And you ain't hardly no wild animal."

"Oh, I've had more than a few gents tell me different," said Glory. She gave a coy wink that made Howard wonder if she was still possessed.

"BOB?"

An hour had passed since they'd resumed their drive. The desert was dark in an oddly crisp sort of way, the stars particularly bright and hardly twinkling. Howard had eased into a semiconscious state of mind, steering the Chevy as if he were a rigged tiller on a sail-boat.

"Bob?" It was Lovecraft again.

"Yeah?"

Lovecraft unfolded the road map, making a horrible crackling and rustling sound that caused Howard to wince. When he turned on his flashlight, Howard squinted at him and waved a hand in annoyance.

"Bob, I've reason to believe we are presently headed in a northerly direction instead of the preferred easterly course upon which we had embarked."

"Huh? How would ya know? I can't see no landmarks out there."

Lovecraft pointed out the windshield at the night sky.

"Shit—if you're right." Howard pulled over onto the shoulder and stopped the car. He stretched and yawned as the sudden stillness made him feel his tiredness all the more. "I mighta taken the wrong turn back at the junction. Can ya figure what road we're on?"

The silence and lack of motion roused Glory, and she sat up, letting her loose sweater fall off her shoulders. She rested her bound wrists on the back of the front seat between Howard and Lovecraft. "What's the matter, boys? Are we lost or something?"

The three of them regarded the illuminated map together. Lovecraft indicated the compass points, then traced his finger along the road they should have been on. He followed the line back to the last junction and traced their current route. It made no sense. They looked at each other in the dim reflection of the flashlight beam.

"Times like this, ya rely on Texas instinct," Howard declared with false confidence, and he abruptly hit the gas, spitting dirt and gravel from the tires as he pulled a U-turn.

The rhythm of the driving lulled them once again, and soon Glory had fallen back asleep. Howard rubbed his eyes and squinted. "They're even out here," he said incredulously.

"Eh?" Lovecraft shifted in his seat.

"Those damn Burma Shave ads. Even out here in the middle a nowhere."

Lovecraft sat up and watched through the dust of the windshield as they approached the first sign, barely legible in the dim headlights. Involuntarily, they read it together, then the next, and the next, as the rhyme played out with its excruciating slowness.

Every mile

It draws

More near

Lovecraft was about to close his eyes and get some rest when the next sign caught his attention.

The eldritch face

He could feel the car accelerate as Howard's foot grew heavier on the gas pedal. They sped by the next sign and the next without speaking.

The one you fear
IÄ CTHULHU!

Lovecraft was almost relieved by the last sign. He could have drifted off to sleep then and dismissed it all the next morning as his personal hallucination, but Howard was not cooperative.

"You seen what I seen, HP?" he said flatly.

"If you're referring to the fact that we have just passed an advertisement for the Old Ones, then I believe I have."

"Then it ain't just me."

"Clearly not."

"What's goin' on, do ya think?"

"I am too tired to conjecture," said Lovecraft, closing his eyes. "But you may be assured that whether this is real or imagined, it is proof that we are on the right road."

"MAKE SURE SHE'S COVERED," said Howard, easing off on the gas and slowing down to pull into the all-night gas station. "Last thing we want now is someone reportin' us for kidnappin'."

Lovecraft leaned over into the backseat and drew Glory's sweater up to cover her bound wrists. She seemed to be sleeping peacefully, and that provoked in him a quick pang of envy.

Howard pulled up at the pump and got out, stretching his arms above his head and arching backward until he heard the satisfying crunch in his lower back. He shook out his shoulders and drew in a deep breath. From the inside of the gas station, lit by a couple of dangling lightbulbs, the attendant roused himself and emerged rather timidly.

"Fill 'er up," said Howard. "Don't need nothin' else."

"Yessir."

Lovecraft got out, just as stiffly as Howard had, and he rubbed at his sore arm as he limped over to the ice box. "Could you divulge to us our present location?" he asked the attendant, but that only drew a blank look.

"Whereabouts are we?" said Howard.

"Oh, not too far from Deming. Coupl'a miles."

"Thanks," said Howard. "My friend here's from England."

"More the proximity of *New* England," said Lovecraft, fishing for change in his trouser pocket.

The attendant rubbed his hands across the front of his coveralls and walked over to the pump.

Howard leaned over the horizontal ice box and said, in a loud whisper, "Dammit, HP, I was tryin' not to be suspicious."

"Well, now, in addition to my superior diction, our fellow here is wondering if he's seen a foreigner. I'm afraid you've made even a larger impression than would have obtained without your clumsy attempt at anonymity."

"Can't you just talk like an American?"

"I *am* an American. I hardly need to *talk like* one."

Howard shrugged in defeat and looked over his shoulder. The attendant was washing the windows, pulling his squeegee and leaving a line of grimy water that he mopped up with a rag. He seemed to be concentrating especially hard on the rear window.

"Hey!" called Howard.

That startled the man, and he stopped abruptly. "Yessir?"

"I told ya we didn't need nothin' else."

"Your—your windows was so dirty, I thought—"

"Well, you done enough if ya got the front."

"Yessir." The attendant quickly wadded the rag into his back pocket and went back to the side of the car, where he stood nervously over the gas nozzle, nodding to the clicking of the pump.

"Dammit," Howard hissed. He said, loudly, "Hey, you think we should wake her up to use the ladies' room?" He tapped Lovecraft and whispered to him to say no.

Lovecraft hesitated, and then he realized what was up. "Never mind," he said loudly. "We can wait until we reach Deming."

"All right," Howard replied. He walked back and paid the nervous attendant.

When Lovecraft got back in, Howard started the car and quickly pulled out. In the rearview mirror, he could see the attendant walking briskly back to the office, where he quickly closed the door. Howard quickly turned his head to glance at Glory. "God dammit!" he hissed. "You notice if he had a telephone back there, HP?"

Lovecraft looked into the back and saw that Glory's sweater had shifted. Her bound hands would have been clearly visible in the light.

"Can you see what he's doin' back there?"

"I'm afraid we are too far. And the shade is down. But from the presence of the wires leading from the telephone poles toward the station, I would conclude it has a telephone."

"Damn, HP! He saw Glory all hog-tied. I told you to cover her up."

"I'm afraid she must have moved in her sleep. I'm sorry."

"We'd best be on our way, dammit." Howard hit the gas and sped up to return to Highway 70. "Dammit, dammit. Maybe a half hour, maybe forty-five minutes before the state troopers pull us over and lock us up on a kidnapping charge."

"Don't worry yourself," said Lovecraft. "We'll simply untie her and have her tell the officers that the boy was mistaken. Perhaps in his semiconscious state he only imagined her bound."

Howard took a gulp of Coke and winced at the sweetness. He spat a mouthful out of the window, then resigned himself to drinking the next one. "Boy, it's times like this that I really need my Dr Pepper. You better wake her up. Let her know what's going on."

Lovecraft turned and tried to rouse Glory. He tapped her shoulder, then shook her gently, but got no response. "Glory," he said. "Glory." But she was so fast asleep that even his next, rougher, shake of her shoulder was unsuccessful.

"What's wrong?" said Howard.

Lovecraft twisted around and shined the flashlight in Glory's face.

He reached and lifted an eyelid, and there was still no response. "I believe she's in some sort of profound sleep."

"You think she's possessed again?"

"No," said Lovecraft. "Her eyes have not taken on that reddish hue. At least not at the moment."

"Well, we're gonna have to take a chance and untie her."

Lovecraft untied Glory's feet and hands as quickly as he could manage, and then he bundled the rope into a wad and shoved it under his seat to hide it from view.

It was some thirty minutes later that Howard saw the flashing red lights of an approaching state trooper in his rearview mirror. He drove as nonchalantly as he could until the other vehicle drew up dangerously close behind them, and then he finally relented and pulled over. Lovecraft made one last attempt at rousing Glory, but it was to no avail.

The trooper's car maneuvered until its headlights were focused on the Chevy so that when Howard looked at the two approaching silhouettes through the rearview mirror, his eyes were highlighted as if he were some leading man illuminated by a key light. Lovecraft twisted his body around and squinted against the headlights, trying to make out features on the shadows. He was relieved when he could see them dropping their hands down to the obvious lumps of their holsters—that meant they were certainly not the odd men—but then he did a mental double take, realizing that he should perhaps be concerned and not so relieved.

The two troopers walked cautiously forward, their hands on the butts of their weapons. Howard had an uncomfortable feeling, which he hoped was merely his fear of the current predicament, but deep down, he also could not help but associate the black silhouettes with the odd men.

In a moment a flashlight beam lanced through the interior of the Chevy. "Would you boys mind steppin' out of your car?"

Howard and Lovecraft grudgingly got out and stood by their open doors. The trooper closer to them came forward and pointed his flashlight through the rear window, illuminating Glory's unconscious form in the backseat.

"I see her, Joe."

Howard gave Lovecraft a quick glance, hoping he could be seen. "Evenin', Officers. What can we do for you?"

The trooper addressed as Joe wagged his flashlight. "I'd like to see some ID from the both of you."

Howard produced his thick wallet, but Lovecraft paused and looked uncertain. The trooper illuminated them alternately, flicking the beam back and forth until he grew tired of the game. "Both of you—step back to the rear of your car where I can see y'all together."

They took a few steps forward. Lovecraft hesitated.

"What's holdin' you up, buddy?"

"Officer, I'm afraid I carry my documents in a satchel which now happens to be inside the automobile."

"You just stay put for now," said the trooper. He focused his attention on Howard for a moment.

The other trooper had moved over to the passenger-side door, and he leaned in to examine Glory while the trooper named Joe examined the IDs.

Lovecraft had a hunch about what the trooper would discover in the car, so when the other turned to look at Howard's license in the light, Lovecraft took note of his name tag and forced a weak smile. "Officer Vigil, is it? Rather an apt name for a man of the law who keeps such late watch in such a remote locale."

"What's that?" said the trooper. He looked up suspiciously and pointed the beam of his flashlight directly into Lovecraft's squinting eyes as if to dissuade him from making any other idle comments.

There was an awkward silence punctuated by the odd cadence of the two cars' engines not quite in synch. Howard cleared his throat, and said, quickly and loudly, pointing back to the car, "Um, that there's Sonja Kane in the back. She had a couple too many, if you know what I mean."

The trooper at the car brought his head out. "Woman in here looks like she's unconscious in the backseat."

"And what's she doin' in your car?" asked the trooper. "How do you happen to know her?"

"Uh, we wouldn't know her from Adam," said Howard.

"Ahem—Eve," Lovecraft corrected.

Howard shot him an annoyed glance. "She hitched a ride with us back in California. Said she was on her way to Texas."

Trooper Vigil handed their IDs back. "Funny. Most folks these days are skedaddling t'other way 'round."

"Yes, the conditions are rather unfavorable for agriculture in the heart of the nation, are they not? But I believe Miss Mc—Kane's intention is to visit relatives."

"Hey, Joe, come on over here," called the trooper at the car.

"You fellas excuse me a moment. And y'all wait right where you are." Vigil walked over to his partner, gesturing for Lovecraft and Howard to stay put. "What you got, Tommy?"

"You have a look-see yourself, Joe." He directed his partner's attention inside the Chevy and held the flashlight outside the side window to illuminate Glory in her still comatose state. "Look at her wrists and ankles. I'd say we caught ourselves a coupl'a fish."

Vigil could see faint rope marks on both of Glory's wrists in the flashlight beam. He leaned his head in to sniff the air, then hunched in farther to put his nose next to Glory's mouth. "I don't smell nothin'. You smell anythin', Tommy?"

"No."

"City boys said she was drunk."

"Ain't hardly, as far as I can see."

They drew their weapons simultaneously and turned toward Howard and Lovecraft.

"You boys turn around and put your hands behind your backs. Pronto," said Vigil.

Lovecraft gave Howard a quick glance, making the two of them look all the more suspicious, and when he did his best to fake a chuckle, it came out flat and dry. "Why, Officer Vigil, surely you don't mean we are under arrest?"

Vigil's partner waved his pistol as if he were cooling the barrel in the breeze. "That's exactly what he means, city boy."

"What are you arrestin' us for?" asked Howard. "We ain't done nothin' wrong."

Vigil smiled. "How does interstate kidnapping sound to y'all?"

Howard gestured at Lovecraft with his eyes and began to turn around as if to comply with the trooper's order.

Lovecraft ignored the order; he raised an eyebrow as the handcuffs came off the troopers' belts. He held his hands out in front of him and stepped forward. "I can assure the both of you that this is nothing more than a terrible misunderstanding."

"Uh-huh," said the trooper named Tommy, grabbing Lovecraft's wrists to cuff him. "You wouldn't believe how many times I hear that, Mister, though you say it purtier than most folks. Now turn around or I'll spin you eight ways from Sunday."

"I beg your—" Lovecraft spun around with one handcuff attached and one dangling, taking the trooper off guard.

The man lost hold of the cuffs and cursed, just as the trooper named Vigil was taking hold of Howard's wrists. As Vigil glanced to investigate, Howard suddenly jerked his left hand free and, with lightning quickness and agility, pivoted around, slamming his elbow into the man's left ear. With a sickening sound, Vigil flew into his partner, Tommy, and the two of them tumbled down into the dust together.

Howard let out a savage battle cry and leaped onto the two men before they could untangle themselves. They hardly had time to come out of their daze before Howard was pummeling them with his large fists. As they flailed around under him, kicking up a thick dust that obstructed them from view, Howard yanked first one, then the other, up by the collar, giving each man a chance to make a stand. But neither trooper could amount to much under the Texan's berserker strength. They hit him a few times, but he was in such a rage that he hardly felt it. The one-sided fight was over momentarily.

Lovecraft watched intently as the murky dust began to dissipate. Before his amazed eyes, his stocky friend emerged, wild-eyed and alone, his lip bleeding below a wide grin. Howard proudly brandished the troopers' pistols, one in each hand, and backlit by the headlights, the image he created was the epitome of masculine brawn; it was an image that Lovecraft would not soon forget.

Lovecraft pulled out his handkerchief, popped it open with a flourish, and handed it to Howard. "I believe I am looking at the cover illustration to that first tale you sell to *Adventure Magazine*."

Howard ignored the offer. He spat a thick stream of blood from his mouth, as if in contempt, and wiped his lip along his wrist, leaving a red smear. "Those highfalutin' bastards ain't never gonna buy one of my stories," he said. "They hated the first one I sent 'em, and they've never given me a bit of notice since. Face it, HP. We're strictly *Weird Tales* material."

Lovecraft pondered the events of the last few days as he regarded his bizarre surroundings. It didn't take him long to answer. "Yes, perhaps you're right." He helped Howard drag the dazed troopers through the dirt up to the front end of their police car, where they handcuffed both of them to the bumper.

"I really don't wanna be doin' this," said Howard. "But I don't see how we got any other choice."

Lovecraft wiped the sweat from his forehead. "Extreme times require extreme actions," he said. "I only hope we will be equipped to deal later with the consequences of our actions. Are you a man prone to dwelling on past regrets?"

"I ain't got time to think about that right now, HP. Come on." Howard put the troopers' pistols and the keys to their handcuffs in the front seat. He noticed a canteen in back, so he paused to retrieve it before closing the doors and returning to the front.

Howard splashed the troopers with small palmfuls of water until they opened their eyes and squinted up at him. "I'm sorry it's gotta be this way," he said. "Here's your canteen and some jerky. I'm sure someone's gonna be stoppin' before mornin'. Keys to your cuffs are in front. You tell 'em that."

"We'll get you, you son of a bitch," said Vigil. "I ain't forgettin' your ugly faces."

Howard raised a threatening fist, and the trooper shut up. "I said I was sorry," said Howard. "And I ain't plannin' on makin' your acquaintance again." He joined Lovecraft back in the Chevy and didn't even bother to glance in the rearview mirror as he drove off, kicking up dust and gravel that made the troopers wince.

THE GAS IN the troopers' car didn't last for more than another hour, and soon after the engine stopped the headlights began to dim.

"Shoulda filled up tonight, Tommy," said Vigil.

"God damn 'em. You think they coulda done us a favor and shut the headlights off, huh, Joe?"

"Yeah, and fluffed us a pillow or two while they was at it? You stupid son of a bitch."

"Ain't my fault, Joe."

They sat in a sullen silence as the headlights dimmed into amber, then into a faint glow. In a few more minutes they sensed something wrong in the black desert night around them. Their eyes hadn't yet fully adjusted so they saw nothing, but they could hear the sound of something rustling through the nearby sagebrush. A flapping sound came from above.

Vigil felt something land on his back and crawl past his collar, up to the hair on the back of his neck. "What the he—!" He reached with his free hand and jerked the thing off—it was a bat. In what little light remained, he could see the blood dripping from its mouth. With a yelp he closed his fist around the bat's neck until he felt a sick crunch, then he flung the thing into the darkness.

"Joe?"

There was a tug from Tommy. "What?" said Vigil. Now he could hear guttural noises around them, and just as the headlights died, he saw the pointed snouts, the feral teeth, the glowing eyes of the hungry coyotes as they pounced.

The two troopers screamed and writhed helplessly, trying to free themselves from the handcuffs that pinned them like bait against the fender of their dead car.

• • •

AFTER THE ANIMALS had dispersed, before the insects crept in to pick off what little flesh remained on the saliva-covered bones, a pair of headlamps appeared in the lingering darkness. If anyone had been there to witness the approaching vehicle, they would have seen twin beams of light suspended a few feet from the black surface of the road. The lights were angled and positioned like the headlamps of a car, but as they moved, they seemed to be suspended in the darkness with nothing behind them—twin sources of light flying over the road in a precise configuration that mimicked those on the front of a car.

And as the lights came closer, one would have noticed a strange thing about the last vestiges of the night behind them, a sort of thickening or congealing, a coagulation of darkness that solidified into large scabs until the form of a black sedan materialized. The vehicle came to a silent halt in front of the troopers' remains, the beam of its headlights flaring momentarily as it reflected off the white of a single eyeball the animals had somehow overlooked in the socket of a skull.

Two silhouettes emerged from the car, their blackness detaching from its blackness. No door had opened. No sound issued. The black car was utterly silent, and the figures glided over the ground, not leaving footprints. They stopped in front of one of the bloody, tooth-scraped skeletons, and then a sort of rustling sound could be heard as they spoke to each other. There was a sort of hissing noise—perhaps the sound of some alien laughter—then one of the figures leaned down to pick something up. Two blood-spattered strips of beef jerky. The animals, for some reason, had left them. A hand seemed to emerge from the shadow of one of the black figures. It held out a single strip of the beef jerky, and now the other figure took it. More hissing laughter, and then the wet smacking sound of chewing, the sound of teeth sticking in tough meat, the sound of amused shoggoths.

18

EAST ON HIGHWAY 70 to Las Cruces, through the night and the following morning, and then Highway 80 to El Paso. Howard felt good to be back on Texas soil, even if it was only for a hundred-mile drive through. When they reentered New Mexico, they began passing an increasingly annoying array of billboards that advertised the local caverns; they followed the dusty wind into Carlsbad, New Mexico. It was just before four, and Howard pulled up at a diner to eat before the last stretch. Glory was decidedly uncomfortable, bound in the backseat, sweaty and numb and itchy, though out of politeness and concern, she tried not to show it.

"How about it, HP?" said Howard. "She's been nice and ladylike for a while now. I say we untie her so she can get a civilized meal."

Lovecraft looked at Howard, then into the backseat, where Glory sat like a penitent or a convict. She had shifted her ropes as much as the slack would allow, and her skin was red, beginning to chafe from the irritation. "Glory?"

"I suggest you boys park in the shade somewhere where no one will see me. Leave the windows open and bring me back something cool to drink if you can."

"How do you feel?"

"Okay. Like myself, if you know what I mean."

"Will you let us know the moment you feel another attack coming on?"

"I don't want to go in."

"We can't leave you out in the car like a dog," said Howard.

"The consequences."

"I'm willin' to risk them if HP is."

"I vote to be civilized," said Lovecraft. "Civilized but vigilant. And with ropes at the ready."

"You boys sure know how to talk about a lady," Glory said with a smile.

"It's decided," said Howard. With Lovecraft watching for any hints of renewed possession or treachery, Howard leaned into the back and untied her.

Glory rubbed at the red patches on her wrists and ankles, smoothed back her hair, and got out of the car, somewhat unsteadily. "The Crystal Cave," she read. "I would have thought 'The Pegasus' from the picture."

The place had obviously renamed itself to capitalize on the cave traffic—the old sign, still legible despite the peeling paint, had the flying horse of the Phillips 66 logo leaping over the black silhouette of a mesa. The men didn't say anything, but Lovecraft found the image uneasily reminiscent of the story of Perseus and the Gorgon. He hardly needed any reminders of the mythic monster they were on their way to face—the stylized angel on the hood of Howard's Chevy was reminder enough.

Inside the stale-smelling diner, Howard escorted Glory to the ladies' room and posted himself outside while she freshened up. She emerged looking like her old self despite her now permanently disheveled hair.

Lovecraft had already ordered, and his food arrived just as Howard and Glory slid into the booth.

"Well," said Howard, "I see you're a changed man. Is that a ham and egg sandwich I smell?"

"It is customary to indulge a man for his last meal," Lovecraft replied dryly. "I compromise my frugality only out of my own uncertainty."

"Well, we can bring your cans of beans along for the expedition then."

"As you wish." Lovecraft was obviously famished. He had been looking out of the corner of his eye at his sandwich all along.

"Listen," said Glory.

The two men turned their attention to Glory.

She jerked her head quickly to indicate a table where some apparent locals were talking. Everyone else in the diner seemed to be eavesdropping as well, and from what they could gather from the conversation, which was interrupted again and again by long intervals of silence brought on by stuffed mouths, the troopers they had left behind were dead.

"They was handcuffed to their car and murdered in cold blood," one man said. "I shudder ta think of the other possibility, though I hear the county coroner said, and for the record, that it can't rightly be ruled out."

There was a pause. "What can't be ruled out?"

The clatter of silver, a slurp of coffee. "It's possible they was alive and the animals got to 'em. Ain't much meat was left on the bones, but there's marks that say they mighta been tryin' to fight 'em off." Someone at the table coughed, and the others made noises of disbelief. "Swear that's just like I heard it. Talked to a couple police just a half hour ago. If ya don't believe me, wait for the news report."

Glory looked pale, and Howard clenched his fists on the table. From the counter, the portly owner flung down a towel and swore so loudly everyone heard him. "What're you lookin' at?" he said. "I'd just like to get my mitts on those sons a bitches who left those boys out there." The customers turned back to their tables.

"How can you eat after hearing that?" said Glory.

Lovecraft had picked up his sandwich and was nonchalantly chewing a mouthful. He took his time to swallow and wipe his lips. "I would hardly want such an expensive repast to get cold, regardless the circumstances," he said.

Glory turned away in disgust and listened to the weather report: a windstorm warning was in effect—gusts of wind up to seventy miles per hour could last until tomorrow.

"Look," said Howard. "How about we get our food to go? I don't feel like bein' in public at the moment, if ya get my drift."

THEY RETURNED TO the car with their food, Lovecraft having gone to the unusual length of ordering seconds and leaving an adequate tip. "What was the rotund fellow saying?" he asked as Howard pulled out.

"Wanted to know why we was leavin' in such a hurry. I told him we had to beat the storm. Said we were headed toward Santa Fe."

"A good ploy," said Lovecraft. "But might he not notice us driving off in the wrong direction? That might cause suspicion."

"Look, HP, the only suspicious thing in our gang at the moment is you. The way you're dressed, the way you talk, what you talk about, the big production *you* made of leavin' a tip back there—all these folks are gonna remember *you*, not us."

Lovecraft was quiet.

"You boys don't go losing your tempers," said Glory. "We have enough problems ahead of us as it is."

"Sage advice from a woman whose name should be Legion," Lovecraft mumbled under his breath.

They drove a couple of miles down the road before Howard pulled off to tie Glory up once again. They continued the rest of the way dwelling on their own thoughts until they reached the first landmark in the desolate stretch of country in the Guadelupe Mountains. It wasn't much more than five miles from Carlsbad Caverns, but it could have been another time, millions of years earlier, or another world, millions of miles from the earth. For a while after they turned off the main road, there seemed to be absolutely no sign of life, not even the ubiquitous tumbleweeds to which they had grown so accustomed. It was as if the sun had burned everything away in this landscape, sterilizing it so thoroughly that nothing had ever grown back.

As they crested a ridge, Howard jerked his head. "Dust plume behind us," he said.

They were being followed. Lovecraft felt compelled to explain that it was the odd men in their black sedan, but they all knew it now, and he kept silent to spare Howard's mood. He wondered what their true purpose was. Why had they tagged him at such length when they could easily have snuffed him out at the outset in Providence? Their purpose would undoubtedly be revealed soon enough. Perhaps the game would be over then, and he could stop feeling like a dumb sheep being herded by the black dogs of the Great Old Ones.

Now the Artifact in Lovecraft's pocket began a slow, rhythmic pulsing, as if in response to the proximity of their destination. He looked down at his watch pocket and started momentarily, taken aback by the light, so intense it was visible even in the bright daylight. By all reason, the thing should have burned through his clothes right into his flesh, but the light was cool. What he felt instead of heat was a soreness deep within his body, and that pain pulsated in time to the light. "Bob," he whispered.

Howard grunted.

"Bob, I believe we are close by."

"I don't see a damned thing, HP. And I don't think we're gonna be seein' much at all if the weather turns the way it looks."

Indeed, now that they had come over the ridge, they could see the storm front rolling toward them—directly toward them, moving slowly in its boiling motion as if it were searching them out. If they had not been so anxious, they might have stopped to watch the spectacle and its awe-inspiring beauty.

"I feel funny," said Glory.

"So do I," Howard replied, glancing at Lovecraft.

Glory shifted her position to take some pressure off the ropes. "My hair's standing on end, like it does before a thunderstorm."

"We should then be wary of lightning," said Lovecraft. "I believe we are safe in the confines of the car, since it has rubber tires, and its metal body will act much like a Faraday cage." He felt a little more at ease now that he was able to expound upon something, but the fear in his core was growing, just as it was in the others. "Bob, I believe the Artifact is behaving like a homing device and perhaps simultaneously a beacon. It will surely lead us to our destination, but it also seems to be drawing the storm into our proximity. I suggest we continue down-hill."

"Ain't no other way to go now," Howard said sarcastically. Then he sobered. "I think we're headed for that box canyon down there. Road don't have no business goin' anywhere else."

Soon the interior of the car was bitter with the odor of burning brake pads, and they rolled the windows all the way down. Even with the repaired suspension, it was a rough ride. Howard drove as quickly as he could to evade their pursuers even though he realized there was only this single road out here in the Godforsaken badlands. If they didn't catch them going in, they would certainly be waiting for them on the way out. He decided that there would only be one more confrontation between them, and at the risk of driving off the edge, he bent awkwardly down to check his two pistols under his seat.

A mile or so after they reached the base of the mountain, they passed the mouth of the box canyon. Lovecraft called out to turn around when the Artifact suddenly grew dim. Howard backed up and drove off the road onto the windswept surface of scorched reddish earth. The storm-borne wind blasted them with a fine red dust, and they put the windows up again, glad that the weather had dampened the heat.

In a little while, they could no longer see anything behind them. If they were being pursued, now it was the blind chasing the blind. Howard worried that the Chevy would choke in the dust; he tried to drive more reasonably, but then he had no choice but to slow down because of the poor visibility. On the right side of the car, the red dust had begun to cake the windows; drifts of it were forming on the left-hand edge of the windshield.

Without warning, they were all thrown forward and to the right. There was a terrible crunch, and then a muffled thud. Howard braked hard and skidded to a stop, his stomach suddenly hollow with the feeling of doom. If that was the front axle, then they were as good as dead.

Howard parked the car and momentarily rested his sweaty brow against the steering wheel, his eyes closed. He was too tired to curse and too afraid to get out. They were all silent, listening to the roar of the wind and the intermittent misfiring of the Chevy's laboring engine.

"Bob?" said Lovecraft.

"Sometimes, HP, I wish to God I had never written back to you. I should be home takin' care of my Ma and now I'm out in the middle of the God damned desert about to be meat for some coyote. What the hell came over me that night, huh?"

"We have no choice now, Bob. And wasn't it you who wrote first to me?"

Howard looked up and laughed. "We're about to die, and you're sittin' there nitpickin'?"

"The truth is the truth in any circumstance."

There was a thump from the back. Both men turned to look.

"Look outside," said Glory.

Lovecraft's face fell. "I think we're here," he said.

The wind had abated for a moment. Through the windshield they could see an ancient formation of adobe brick. It was impossible to tell how large it was, or how far away, but from photos he had seen of the old pueblos, Lovecraft guessed that they were within a few hundred yards of a massive structure only partially visible to them.

It was a city, or a giant dwelling built halfway into the stone of the cliff that formed the western valley wall. From under the broad stone lip that hung over the stone dwellings, other structures of adobe— walls, embankments, buildings— spread out in half circle formations until they eroded into the barren red clay of the valley floor. A few of the low circular buildings beyond the shadow of the overhang were still standing, the largest of them still imposing though its contours had softened over the centuries.

"Unless y'all want to choke to death out here, we oughta hightail it to one of them houses," said Howard. "Grab whatever you can carry, and let's sit out the storm."

They had to tie wet handkerchiefs around their faces to keep the swirling vermilion dust out of their lungs. Glory also wore a makeshift scarf, which she tied like a pirate's headwrap to keep her hair under control. They gathered up what they could and marked out the direction to the pueblo. The light was waning rapidly under the storm clouds—there wouldn't be much time before it grew too dark to see.

"I'm tempted to say something," said Glory. "That if I could go back to Thalia on the day I met the two of you, I'd accept the ride just the same." She tucked a folded piece of paper into her purse. "But that'd just be me being nice."

Howard grunted something unintelligible.

"There is no turning back now," Lovecraft said. Though he knew he was stating the obvious, the declaration seemed almost a ritual necessity.

Glory smiled, almost wistfully. "Well, here I am, fellas."

"I'm leadin'," said Howard. "We don't want to get separated, so you hold on to my belt here, Glory. And HP, you tie yourself to Glory, too. You take up the rear till we get to the ruins, then ya can lead with the Artifact." He pulled his belt off, then looped it back through the back loop on his pants. He handed the end to Glory.

Lovecraft also took off his belt and pulled it through the back loop of Glory's pants. "I feel like I'm on some mountain-climbing expedition, all roped together," she mumbled.

"Let's go."

It couldn't have been more than a couple of hundred yards to the first ruins, but in the dust that blotted out everything more than a hand's width in front of them, the walk seemed interminable. Lovecraft found himself drifting in and out of a nostalgic reverie, though he knew it was inappropriate. The obscuring dust made the world small and intimate, and though the wind was cold, he was still warm enough in his clothes to feel a sense of misplaced comfort. There was an ordeal to endure ahead—he knew that with certainty—and perhaps he had already begun to withdraw as he was wont to do under stress. He remembered languorous summer days when he never bothered to change out of his pajamas, when he lay in bed into the middle of the afternoon and let his aunts bring him warm milk for the stomach ailment they thought he had. Pleasant days of reading and drowsing between passages, lapsing over the threshold of sleep so that what he had read became immediately real in the world of dreams. Perhaps that was why he was so preoccupied with sleep, and dreaming, with Hypnos and Oneiros, with mythic histories and men gone over into the kingdom of madness. As he squinted his watering eyes and coughed under his wraps, he wondered what would happen if he simply stopped and let the world fade into a dark and comfortable cloud— would he awaken in bed somewhere in some other time, this day but a dream of the future or of the past?

"Ouch!" said Glory.

Lovecraft quickly mumbled an apology and took a step backwards. The wind had died down. They were on the leeward side of an eroded mud-brick wall.

Howard looked back over his shoulder, pulling his mask away from his face. "HP, let's see what your old friend has to say?"

Lovecraft was momentarily confused, but then he came to his senses and produced the Artifact, which was glowing more brightly than ever. Now it threw a halo of light that pulsed brighter along one arc to indicate the direction in which they should continue. "There," he said, indicating one of the pueblos.

"Your turn to lead, HP."

Lovecraft stretched out his hand as if he were taking a reading on a compass. He looked over his shoulder at Glory and Howard, then took a tentative step forward into the wind. It was only a dozen paces to the shelter of the next wall. Lovecraft motioned that they had arrived at what appeared to be their destination—the light from the Artifact began to glow more evenly. Howard took the flashlights from his satchel and distributed them, and then, holding their breaths, they stepped through the jagged opening into the dark pueblo.

The wind abated immediately, but now they had to contend with the eerie moaning through the windows and holes in the adobe walls. They had not been able to tell from the outside, but the inside walls were curved—they were in a low, circular chamber that gave Lovecraft the uneasy feeling of being inside the cylindrical head of a giant Kachina doll. The wall was interrupted at odd intervals by windows and niches whose function he could not determine.

"What is this place?" said Howard. "It's like a bull ring with a roof over it, ain't it?"

"It's a *kiva*," said Glory. "It's a holy building." She shifted the beam of her light and noticed that nothing happened, so she pointed it up at herself to confirm that the bulb was working. "Boys, we might as well save the batteries."

"What?"

"I think the Artifact is brighter than our torches."

The men switched their beams off and discovered that they could see just as well in the cold illumination that seemed to hang in the air like a mist. Lovecraft began to move around the chamber, watching how the Artifact's intensity responded to his position. It seemed brightest toward the center of the room where the top rungs of an ancient ladder jutted out of a black pit.

"Glory is correct," said Lovecraft. "This is a *kiva*, a sacred ceremonial chamber where the Anasazi tribesmen would perform their ancient rites."

"I thought you were going to say 'unholy rites,' " Glory joked.

Lovecraft didn't get the humor. "It is quite likely that they were unholy and primitive," he said. He moved cautiously to the lip of the pit, watching the Artifact glow more brightly, and he pointed silently downward along the ladder.

"I ain't goin' down that thing," said Howard. "Wood must be three hundred years old."

"You should know that wood remains remarkably well preserved in the desert, Bob. Objects in the tomb of Tutankhamen were perfectly preserved over thousands of years."

"Well, why don't you test it then? We'll follow you if it takes your weight."

"But there is no assurance that once I am—"

"Oh, for God's sake," said Glory. Before the men could reply or stop her, she grabbed the ladder with one hand and stepped down into the black pit, pointing the flashlight ahead of her as she moved out of the Artifact's light.

"Glory!" Howard rushed forward and stopped abruptly, afraid of unbalancing the ladder. He could hear the rungs creaking under her weight.

There was a gasp from the pit. Silence.

"It's fine," came Glory's voice. "Just watch the seventh step. It's broken."

"Dammit, Glory! You shoulda let HP go down first!"

"Lower your voice, Bob! It's like a cave down here. You wouldn't want it collapsing, would you?"

Howard sullenly quieted himself. He motioned for Lovecraft to go next. "I'm the heaviest," he said.

"Then you should go next," Lovecraft replied.

"What?"

"Assuming, for argument, that there may be no way out from that nether region, Bob. If your weight should break the ladder, then I would still be up here to go for help. If, on the other hand, I am already down in the pit, then we would all be stranded should the ladder collapse under you."

"Well, maybe we should have Glory come back up and I go down then. That way, both of ya would be safe if I broke the damn ladder."

"I disagree."

"Why?"

"What's taking you two so long?" came Glory's voice.

"Why?" Howard asked again.

"Should you be injured, say with a broken limb, it might be necessary to have someone to nurse you. Glory would be a better candidate for that than would I."

"And what if the person underneath were to catch me, huh?"

"I am taller than you, Bob, but I'm afraid I am too frail to catch a body of your mass. Not all men enjoy the benefits of your constitution."

"Boys? It's getting awful lonely down here."

Howard grunted and descended the ladder, and Lovecraft followed a few moments later to no ill effect.

"What took you two so long?" said Glory. "I thought you boys decided to abandon me down here."

"We were discussing the logistics of this ladder," said Lovecraft. "And while we are on the topic, I recommend we pull it down after us, thereby leaving our pursuers with no mean of following us."

Howard was already pulling the ladder down. "I doubt it's gonna make any difference," he said. "But ya never know."

They were in a smaller, rough-hewn cylindrical pit that had yet another ladder protruding from a dark hole in its center.

"This must be the second level," said Lovecraft. "I would presume four levels in keeping with the Anasazi mythos if we follow the logic of this symbolism to its conclusion." They decided to take the first ladder down with them another level. The masonry diminished with each level until, at the fourth, the circular room wasn't much more than a hole hewn out of the rough stone of bedrock. This was the fourth underworld according to the myth of the Anasazi—this was where they had originated before climbing up onto the surface of the earth.

By the light of the Artifact, now brighter than ever, they looked around the cold stone chamber and found nothing. Just a few shards of pottery and moldering scraps of what looked like coarse fabric. The chamber appeared to be a dead end, and while they bemoaned their luck, they heard sounds from above that were clearly not the windstorm.

19

"IT'S THEM," SAID GLORY. "I can feel it."

Howard drew his .45 and handed his .38 to Lovecraft, who simply held the pistol and stared down at it as if he had never seen a gun before.

"I don't know what the hell those things are, but I don't know of nothin' that's immune to hot lead," said Howard. "If we gotta corner ourselves like this, we go out fightin'."

"I'm afraid these weapons may do little more than fortify our egos," said Lovecraft.

"If you won't use it, HP, give it to Glory."

Lovecraft handed the .38 to Glory and then fumbled in his satchel until he produced a small flint dagger, no larger than a letter opener. Howard rolled his eyes.

Above them, the sounds of the wind grew muffled, then loud again. A trickle of sand fell from one of the levels above them.

"What do we do now?" said Howard.

"I suggest we attempt something with the Artifact. It has led us this far. It only stands to reason that it would not merely strand us in some Godforsaken stone chamber."

Glory stuck the .38 in her waistband and leaned back against the stone wall, feeling its pleasant coldness through her blouse. She pulled out a cigarette and her pack of matches, but the moment she struck the match, a gust of air extinguished it. Frustrated, she turned toward the wall to block the last match she had from being blown out. She lit the cigarette and was about to toss the still-burning match away when she noticed a very faint pictograph of a stone circle on the wall. Above the pictograph was a spiked outcropping of rock that cast a dim shadow from the illuminated Artifact, indicating a small depression in the pattern. "Look!" Glory called. "There's something important here."

Lovecraft arrived first and pointed the beam of his flashlight at the petroglyph. It was badly eroded by time—far older than many of the other carvings on the walls. He thought at first that it was the image of the sun with long curlicue rays extending outward, but then he recognized the stylized splay of curls. They were the limbs of Cthulhu. At that instant Lovecraft felt an intense pain in his side. He doubled over, clutching at his watch pocket. He dropped his flashlight, and yet the light seemed to get brighter.

"HP?"

Lovecraft tried to answer. Suddenly he was blinded by beams of light shooting out of his side—it was the Artifact, glowing so brightly it seemed about to explode. The pulses of light seemed almost sentient; they illuminated the depression at the center of the graven Cthulhu image, and now with their faces partially averted they could all see the shape of that depression. It was the outline of the Artifact, exactly to scale.

"It's the key," said Howard.

Glory helped Lovecraft back to his feet. He seemed unusually light for such a large man, she thought. There was something ephemeral about him, as if half of him did not really exist, as if he were half-gone in the ether.

With unsteady fingers, Lovecraft cautiously removed the blinding Artifact from his watch pocket and placed it against the indentation in the stone. The grit of erosion impeded it, so he leaned forward and blew forcefully, clearing the dust. After a fit of sneezing, he tried again, turning it slightly, and it snapped right in, drawn by a magnetic force. Instantly, the sounds of the howling wind above them halted, and their eardrums popped painfully as if they were suddenly transported, for the most fleeting of instants, into the vacuum of deep space. An absolute, deafening silence enveloped them—the true sound of the grave, Lovecraft thought grimly to himself.

Though Lovecraft held the only source of light perfectly still in his hands the pointed shadow from the outcropping of rock began to tremble. They watched in amazement as it began to stir and then slowly bend, snaking its way across the ceiling over their heads, writhing like a living thing until it finally halted its path near a wall of jagged stone. They had just examined the area minutes before and found nothing, but now, where the shadow rested on the wall, there appeared the mouth of a narrow passageway as if the shadow itself were a hole in the stone.

They did not wait. They stepped into the tight crevasse and squeezed their way between the walls of stone until they emerged on the other side.

It was a stone chamber the likes of which they had never seen. Rising above them was a giant vaulted dome covered in swatches of multicolored stone that looked uncannily like Spanish moss. They were standing at the entrance of what could have been the most magnificent cathedral, but this one was underground and everything in it, each and every thing, was stone. In the light of the Artifact, they could see most of the chamber and the odd formations of stalagmites that stood like clusters of giant red and white mushrooms roughly textured like the side of a sperm whale's head. They were struck silent in their awe, and they began slowly to navigate a path through the stalagmites, following the Artifact's bright pulse.

"How will we get back?" Howard whispered when they got to the far side of the chamber. He pointed in the direction they had come to show that there was no sign of how they had entered.

"The only trick I know is what Theseus used in the Labyrinth," said Glory.

Lovecraft opened his satchel and produced a ball of twine and Howard stifled a laugh. "That won't do us much good, HP. Anyhow, those two odd fellas behind us ain't likely to leave any string on the ground for our convenience. It'll just lead them to us."

"Only a bit of humor," said Lovecraft. "The mention of Theseus bodes well for us, though what we face is hardly the Minotaur. I always wondered how large a ball of string he had."

"You have another idea?"

"We will not need to resort to physical measures," said Lovecraft, putting the twine back. "I will remember the path out, no matter how far in we are likely to go."

"Since when were you a caveman, HP?"

"I cannot explain it now, but I am able to see the cave and our path through it as if I were looking at a map."

"Imanito's sand painting," said Howard.

"Yes. I see it clearly in my mind."

"Well, then let's not wait around," said Glory. "I don't want to meet our friends down here."

Lovecraft moved toward a jagged aperture in the wall of the chamber, and Glory followed.

"Not so fast," said Howard.

"What's the matter?" Glory asked.

"I ain't meanin' no disrespect here, but what if HP don't make it back with us?"

Glory stopped dead in her tracks and gave Howard a cold look. "I can't believe you just said that."

"Well, it's the truth, Glory."

"Don't you trust your best friend? Or is it different for men?"

Howard said nothing, and the tension grew until Lovecraft intervened. "It *is* the truth," he said with a sense of resignation. "I have obviously not devoted my energies to thinking through the various outcomes of our scenarios. What do you suggest, Bob?"

"I'm gonna mark our trail, if ya don't mind."

"And wouldn't that give the odd men something by which to follow us, as you have rightly pointed out yourself?"

"I just thought about it again, and I don't hardly think it makes a difference to them. I'd worry more that they'd erase the markers. We're in their neck of the woods now. Anyhow, the markers wouldn't take them right to us 'cause they'd mark the way back, not forward."

"All right then," said Lovecraft.

Howard found a piece of crystal and scratched a directional arrow onto the wall. "Let's go."

From the vaulted chamber, the narrow passage led steeply downward, its walls coated with what looked precisely like the slime that covered the walls of sewers. It looked smooth, as if it would come off in one's hands, but the slime was petrified, and it was the wrong color. As they descended, the passage became narrower until they had to squeeze through an opening and then climb downward in a giant tube spiked with stalactites the size of broadsword blades.

Lovecraft had once seen the mouth parts of a snail—the circle of teeth not so much chewing as piercing by constriction, and now the image brought on a wash of claustrophobia. He imagined himself crawling down the gullet of a giant, petrified sea snail, and his limbs would no longer obey his brain. He stood there, trembling, in a cold sweat, until Glory put her arms around him and calmed him with soothing words as Howard waited. When Lovecraft's fit passed, they continued; the tunnel leveled out and wound left and right in irregular zigzags until it opened into another chamber.

This one was so large its dimensions were lost in blackness. They wouldn't have been surprised to see stars in the distance. Before them, towering higher than a five-story building, loomed a formation that looked like a gluttonous head wearing a peaked hat; only this head appeared to have been sculpted of layer upon layer of filth, from its corpulent bugging eyes to its flared nostrils to its repulsive overlapping chins. And high above, barely visible even by the ever-brightening glow of the Artifact, dangled tree-sized stalactites like ten thousand swords of Damocles ready to spoil the glutton's feast.

The three of them wound their way among the phallic stalagmites that stood in clusters around the giant head as if they were there in worship. Some of the stone phalluses were seven feet tall, others just forming and startlingly anthropomorphic. Even in the overwhelmingly weird atmosphere, Glory had to stifle her giggles when she inadvertently stepped on some of the smaller ones, breaking them, each time causing Lovecraft or Howard to wince.

The next chamber was less grand, with a flat roof spiked with smaller stalactites that resembled freshly dipped wax candles. Under them, almost surreal, stood pillars with tops that had somehow been sculpted into perfect birdbath shapes. Hundreds of them stretched left and right as if they were pedestals in a stone museum awaiting the treasures to be displayed on their tops. In some places the stalactites extended farther downward, a few so far they grazed the tops of the pedestals like strands of thick rope. Along the far wall, almost lost in the blackness, stretched formations that looked like a forest of trees whose branches had all melded above, but whose trunks were absolutely distinct below. It was a forest the dead color of dried mud.

The next chamber's pure white floor rippled in delicate patterns like windblown dunes seen from high above. As they took their tentative steps they saw stone eggs of varying sizes—the smallest no larger than marbles, the largest the size of a man's head—strewn in random configurations. As they stepped carefully to avoid treading on them, the eggs began to change colors—subtly off-white, then creamy, then yellow—and by the time they reached the far side, more than fifty yards across, the large flattened yellow shapes lay all over the white surface like giant egg yolks.

"I swear one of these things is about to hatch," Glory whispered.

Lovecraft shook his head. "I would rather not witness such an abomination of nature," he said.

Howard said nothing. He was suddenly hungry for a good breakfast of eggs and sausage, hoping his stomach wouldn't rumble audibly.

The wall to the next chamber was translucent in the Artifact's intense light. Inside, the floor remained unchanged, but now the eggs appeared partially submerged, some of them open on top, partially formed, in various stages of completion. In the circular space Lovecraft had the odd feeling that he was in the middle of a giant cauldron of milk that had petrified in the midst of a furious boil, the egg shapes constituting the bubbles. He stepped even more cautiously, not knowing if the surface was a film, like the skim of milk, that they could break with their weight.

The colors changed in the next chamber, and they stood at the lip of a deep pit that stretched downward and coiled to the left. There was no way they could climb down, but along the rim of the pit, only a few feet down, a ledge wound its way to the other side, more than a hundred yards distant, where they could make out a dark aperture. Lovecraft pointed, holding the Artifact out for confirmation. It pulsed even more brightly, hurting their eyes.

"Well," said Howard. "I guess we got some clamberin' to do." He squinted and casually leaped off the rim, aiming for the ledge below.

The sudden splash took them all aback. Howard yelled, Glory screamed, and Lovecraft found himself hunching protectively over the Artifact.

Howard was flailing in water—so absolutely clear it was entirely invisible except where the ripples and splashes distorted the light. The entire chamber was a lake.

"Don't just stand there! Help me out!" said Howard. And now they realized the sound carried differently—the echoes coming far too quickly for a chamber of its apparent size. The sound had that distinct tone of carrying over water.

"I'll be God damned," Howard said when they had pulled him back up. "At least it ain't as cold as you'd expect."

"Look," said Glory.

Now that Howard was out, the water level had become invisible once again. Instead, the ripples made it appear that the submerged rock formations were trembling and swaying. Glory had to remind herself that it was a trick of the light and that everything was underwater.

"How do we get across?" said Howard, emptying a boot. "I ain't the best swimmer. How about y'all?"

Lovecraft looked somber. "I must confess, I cannot swim," he said.

"I was a lifeguard in college at the old Kenyon swimming pool," said Glory. "I suppose I'll just have to tow you boys then."

"That seems neither possible nor desirable to me," said Lovecraft. "Since Imanito drew us the diagram and prophesied our activities here, there must be some other way across."

"Someone musta been down here before us," said Howard. "How else could the Injun know the layout of the cave?" He removed his shirt and did his best to wring it out. "Look, we could go back and get them ladders we pulled down."

"But that would entail a long delay. And perhaps an unwanted confrontation with the odd men."

"You're assuming they followed us down," said Glory.

Howard produced his pistols to dry them, making both Glory and Lovecraft cringe at the thought of what they might do were they to go off. "I know," said Howard. "Wouldn't hardly want to shoot down here, huh? I can just see this whole place comin' down on us. Look, I can go back by myself with a flashlight."

"We may need their full charge on our way out," said Lovecraft.

THEY ARGUED THE VARIOUS MERITS and pitfalls of going back together, or singly, or trying to swim the lake. In the end, after a quick examination of the lake's periphery, they all went back together to fetch one of the ladders. The light of the Artifact diminished sharply as they backtracked, but Howard's markers passed their test of reliability, and they were able to save the flashlight batteries. When they reached the base of the *kiva*, they first checked for signs that they had been followed. There was no evidence of the odd men.

Howard's idea was to break one of the ladders into two pieces, but Lovecraft stopped him.

"How will we get back up?"

Howard's jaw dropped. "I hadn't thought of that."

Glory suggested a practical solution. "Don't break it," she said. "Just take it apart. You could tie it together again later, couldn't you?" She looked at Lovecraft. "With your ball of string?"

"Our hats are off to you," said Lovecraft, producing the twine once again from his satchel. "I knew it would prove useful someday."

Howard disassembled the ladder and the two men lashed the crossbars into three small rafts, which they were able to carry back with ease. When Glory objected that she didn't need one, Howard was quick to point out that she might want something on which to float her shoes and clothes.

"You ain't plannin' to swim all that ways all decked out, are ya?" he said. "Not that your takin' your clothes off is the first thing on my mind or nothin.' " He laughed, and the sound echoed loudly, changing tone and pitch in eerie ways.

"I'm not ashamed of my body, if that's what you're thinking," said Glory. "Men have paid to see me naked."

"Enough talk of nakedness," said Lovecraft. "We have far more important matters upon which to concentrate our attentions."

The swim across might have been pleasant in other circumstances. In the fantastical setting, knowing that they might be the first humans ever to enter the water, feeling the pristine liquid like cool, thick air around them, they might have been enjoying the pure novelty of the situation. But now they could not keep the dark thoughts and anxieties from their minds as they slowly made their way across that span of water that suddenly seemed so utterly wide. What monsters lurked in the wet reaches beyond the power of the Artifact's illumination? What awaited on the other bank? Each of them was lost in thought for those few minutes that seemed to prolong themselves into hours, and finally, they clambered onto the other side and pulled up their makeshift rafts, having had no leisure to consider their nakedness.

Glory had just finished dressing when she heard the sound of splashing. It echoed across the water from the black recesses which they had just navigated for the second time. She glanced at Lovecraft, then at Howard. No one had to say anything. They simply waited to hear the regularity of the noise to confirm that someone—or some *thing*—was following them.

"Come on," said Howard. "We ain't got all day."

They moved on, walking as quickly as possible until Lovecraft interrupted to remove a shoe and pour the water out of it. "Bob, Glory, would you both be so kind as to drain the excess water from your shoes also?" he asked.

"What for?" said Howard, annoyed. Then he turned to see that Lovecraft's pale face bore an expression of barely contained panic. "You okay, HP?"

"It's the wet squishing sounds," said Lovecraft. "I cannot fathom the reason, but for some reason it reminds me of my pursuit by the Night Gaunts in the Providence cemetery. Please, if only to humor me. . . ."

"What we heard back there in the water," said Howard, "it was probably just one of them blind cave lizards or somethin'."

Lovecraft appeared unconvinced, with a pained look of disbelief as the contents of his second shoe splashed onto the stone floor. "I concur with your last hypothesis, Bob. It was indeed *some thing*. Now, if you please?"

Glory and Howard begrudgingly acceded to Lovecraft's request, and they moved on through the next chamber. The diminished squishing offered only a little security as they wound deeper into the stifling blackness of the cathedral-sized cave, a chamber so large the Artifact's light seemed not even to matter. What they could see clearly were the stone walls that appeared on either side of them, carved with the now-familiar symbols from the *Necronomicon*. They said nothing as they stepped cautiously forward toward the place where the walls flared outward. When they reached the spot, the Artifact's light seemed suddenly to diminish, causing their vision to dim momentarily. But then they realized that the light had somehow equalized, and they gaped in awe at what stood before them.

It was a gate of monumental proportions, obviously the product of something other than purely human artifice. Its style was ancient and mysterious. To Lovecraft it looked like some disrespectful or blasphemous hybrid of sacred architecture borrowed from old Egypt and the more ancient Babylon. Its façade bore the earmarks of motifs that had come to florescence among the Hellenics and then in the obscure and secret motifs of the Byzantines, but he knew that what he saw was the most ancient architecture of all—one whose unholy geometries tugged at some instinctive horror and repulsion in man. The inscriptions around the portal itself were familiar now—many of them identical to those in the *Necronomicon*, including the strange H-shaped symbol that seemed almost to haunt him. They were etched into the polished stone surface, not like normal inscriptions chiseled in or cut in relief, but as if they had been branded there, melting the rock.

As they approached closer, they saw something else that shocked them almost as much as the sight of the gate itself. Flanking the hideous architecture, on the natural rock surface, were layers upon layers of petroglyphs—geometric shapes, humanoid forms, even palm prints—obviously put there by humans over the millennia. This place had been visited before—many times.

"My God," exclaimed Lovecraft, "it is no wonder Imanito knew the route so well. His people must have been the protectors of this place since they came to the Americas. I commend you for being right, Bob, though now I am certain he must belong to the lost Anasazi tribe."

Howard grunted at the backhanded compliment.

The decorations around the portal all sprang from a central axis that highlighted a single spot, an indentation designed to receive the Artifact. The patterns that radiated outward from that focal point all shimmered now, all except in one small area that had been defaced, apparently with great effort. A small spot a few palms' width from the Artifact's slot had been manually chiseled into approximately the same size and shape. Around that, someone had labored hard to apply alternate designs to the portal, but over the years the pigments and scratches on the surface of the stone had all worn away, leaving only some subtle discolorations.

But there were other oddities: tripods made of wooden rods bearing glass or crystal bottles filled with colored water; chalked marks on the floor indicating the cardinal directions; strange mechanisms made of wood and stone and bone, wrapped in coils of animal gut and sinew. Now Imanito's story and its accompanying ritual took on new meaning, and yet they still could not understand how they were to play their mythic role. They continued to approach the gate, noticing signs of adjustment, repair, maintenance to the primitive mechanisms.

At a certain point, they seemed to reach a barrier of thick air, almost like suspended water. When they tried to move forward, their bodies grew suddenly weak until they gave up the effort and stepped back.

"The solution to this must be simple," ruminated Lovecraft. "Since the Artifact has brought us this far, it surely serves as the remedy, and therefore I shall apply it, thus." He held the Artifact out in front of him until it touched the thick air.

There was another balancing of the light, and when he blinked, he saw a patch of the air in front of him rippling, as if it were vertical water showing the rings left by a stone cast into its surface. When he pushed at the center of the concentric rings, something gave, and he felt the resistance vanish. A hole of visibly clearer air appeared, and Lovecraft could pull at its edges to make the aperture large enough to step through.

"Hurry," said Lovecraft. "I shall hold the opening and come through after the two of you are safely on the other side."

Howard and Glory followed his directions without argument, and in a moment they were all standing on the other side of the barrier. In front of them the gate loomed even larger than it had appeared before. Behind them, the air had turned into a reflective surface that appeared to be a mirrored wall that stretched all the way across the chamber.

Howard tried to say something, but his voice refused to carry. And then they all simultaneously froze as they felt the power of the gate.

At first, it was like a dull electrical hum in their inner ears. Then, although there was no discernible change in the surrounding temperature, they all shuddered uncontrollably as if they had been blasted by a sudden Arctic chill. Lovecraft had a flash of memory so abrupt it left him with a physical vertigo. He was in Manhattan again, strolling around a corner with his new bride onto Fifty-seventh Street when, from nowhere, he was struck by the severest gust of freezing wind ever to rake his bones. It was a full three days before he could stop the bouts of uncontrollable shivering and chattering of teeth. But this cold seemed a thousand times worse; it seemed to cut somehow past his body and into his very spirit.

The hum grew louder, more intense, and now the three of them struggled to resist the instinctive impulse to flee—it was a visceral sense, a mental cry for self-preservation. As they drew closer to the gate, they found it more and more difficult to move. The gate emanated a palpable, concentrated, pure evil force like some pounding, invisible surf, and now the ever-brighter Artifact pulsed once more to illuminate the massive three-story-tall portal in a nearly blinding light. They instinctively closed their eyes, but it made no difference—there was an equally bright light inside their eyelids, in their brains, and no amount of obstruction, with their hands or their entire forearms, diminished the power of that illumination. One by one, they collapsed to their knees.

Howard thought he must be dying, but he suddenly found himself back at home, standing on the shaded porch. He could feel the day's heat in the breeze and smell the dry bite of sage carried in from the desert. He looked around, trying to get his bearings, knowing, in the back of his head, that this must be a dream. He pinched himself, just to be sure, and winced at the pain. "Ma?" he called. "Poppa?" No answer, but he heard the dry rustle of leaves and the low creak of a loose shutter. Now he turned to the front door, which stood slightly ajar, and as he opened it he heard the sounds coming from his mother's room, sounds of exertion—expulsions of air, grunts and groans, odd sucking noises. His heart sank. It must be his father using the aspirator again, he thought. He's pumping out Ma's congested lungs with that awful thing. Already Howard could imagine the nightmarish scene in the room, and he did not want to go in and interrupt. That would annoy his father because Ma would get all embarrassed even though she was in agony. He didn't want to cause any more pain than what she already had to bear, so he decided just to get a peek; he tiptoed to the doorway and glanced inside. What he saw sickened him at first, but when he realized exactly what his father was doing to his mother he felt such a blind terror and repulsion that his vision went red.

In the scarlet haze, Dr. Howard appeared to be aspirating his wife, draining her lungs. He stood hunched over her, grunting with effort, his body lurching up and down in a pumping motion. Mrs. Howard struggled under him, weakly kicking her feet, her arms spread wide, fingers pathetically curling and uncurling. She gasped and wheezed under his weight, helpless. Scales of dried mucus and blood caked her lips. The disgusting wet noises came from somewhere else. "Poppa? Ma?" Howard said again, his voice high-pitched like a little boy's. His father turned abruptly and faced him guiltily, as if he had been inter-rupted in the middle of a crime. "Bobby," he whispered. "Get out, boy." "But Poppa . . ." Now Dr. Howard moved slightly to the side, revealing his wife's torso.

Long tendrils of coagulated pus and mucus slithered out of her wound; they fell in coils at the foot of the bed, wrapping and unwrap-ping around each other as if they were alive. And then Howard real-ized that what lay at his father's feet was a living, writhing mass of snakes. He shrieked. Mrs. Howard's wound started to gush blood, and the Doctor turned to face the door head-on. From his unbut-toned pants, a gigantic mushroom-headed penis reared up, dripping the same vile gore that issued from his wife's chest, and now as he leered and broke into a loud laugh, tilting his head back, Howard saw the penis move of its own volition and open its serpentine mouth— full of dripping, hooked teeth—into a hideously evil smile. He shrieked again, and he did not care now whether he was dreaming or awake.

Neither Lovecraft nor Glory heard Howard's scream. Their senses were turned inward, occupied to the utmost at the threshold of madness in their personal realms of dream reality.

Lovecraft rolled over from his contorted position and found himself in bed. He looked around, surprised that the cave had vanished, relieved, almost, to think it might all have been one of his nightmares. It took him a moment to realize he was thirteen again, groggily waking up from the afternoon nap his aunts forced him to take for his various maladies. From the pleasant warmth in the room he knew it was early summer. Birds twittered in the trees outside. The rustle of branches almost made him feel the coolness of the breeze, bringing him to full consciousness. He knew what today was—today was the day he would take down the heavy anatomy book and examine the illustrations he had waited so long to see. He slipped on his light robe and opened the door to go downstairs into the library. Quietly, quietly—he didn't want his aunts to hear and come inquiring like the nosey birds they were. He held the doorknob firmly and pulled it slightly as he turned it to the left, and then he drew the door to him in a smooth, single motion until it stood wide-open. A gust of perfumed air. He frowned. And suddenly a woman stood in front of him. Did he know her? It wasn't either of his aunts, and certainly not his mother. "Hello, HP," she said in a coy and melodious voice. "I see you're finally up. Are you ready to do the honors?" "Honors?" said Lovecraft, taking a step backwards. "Carrying me over the threshold couldn't have tired you *that* much," she said, stepping into the room. There was something terribly wrong. Once again, an odd sensation intruded into his consciousness, and he could not decide whether he was dreaming or awake, whether he was an adult dreaming himself as a child or himself—now—with lingering confusion from the dream he had woken from. But who was this woman? And why did he suddenly recognize her as Sonia—his wife? He wouldn't marry until—and then his thoughts broke off and he found himself sitting upright at the foot of his bed, the woman standing in front of him, disrobing. He could not help the excitement that surged through him when he saw her nakedness, the pale gleam of her flesh in the afternoon sun. What he felt reminded him of illness and nausea, but those sensations inverted into something perversely enjoyable. He felt guilt. He felt anxiety that quickly verged on fear as the woman pushed him backwards onto the bed and straddled him, looming over him with the shadows of her pendulous breasts. "What were you going to do today?" she asked. He looked up in confusion. "Where were you going when you opened the door?" He let out a grunt of air before he could say it: "Library." "What were you going to do there when you should have been here, ready for *me*?" "I—I—" He swallowed involuntarily and pressed himself flat against the bed as she reared up, raising her arms to push her hair out of her face. "You were going to look at the anatomy books," she declared. "Is this what you wanted to see?" She moved her hands over her torso, cupping her breasts, and then she hooked her fingers between them and pulled apart. He gasped, and yet he was not surprised when her flesh split and her breasts moved apart, revealing a volume of Quain's *Anatomy*, opened to the page that showed the dissected female body. His face grew flushed, his breathing quickened, and he felt dizzy. Beneath his robe, where she straddled him, he felt wetness and pressure, and then something rigid and painful, pushing upward and simultaneously downward. She leaned down, and the pages turned of their own volition as she pushed herself sinuously and arched upward; the book opened to a diagram of female genitalia, and just as he realized what he was seeing, just as he felt that sick commingling of excitement and revulsion, she pulled her knees up and apart, spreading her legs to show, alive, what he saw on her torso in the diagram. It was a fishy, clamlike thing ringed with hair, and when its two vertical lips parted, it was the color of salmon. He tried to push himself back when it loomed over his face, but he could not move, and when the toothless lips gaped wide, growing slick with a clear mucus, he tried to close his eyes. He could not. The smile widened, and the fluid began to drip on his face. He tried to make a noise, but now all he felt was his paralysis, his revulsion, his fear, and when the first tentacles emerged from that fleshy orifice, all he could do was gurgle, wide-eyed, and enter the depths of insanity.

Glory lay languidly on the cold stone floor as if she were stretched out in the sun. She was in Texas again. In the oil town. She was so tired her body was sore in more places than she could count, and in the evening heat she had fallen momentarily asleep without meaning to. When she awakened, quite suddenly, she had to shake off the oddest nightmare—about being lost in a cave—before she got her bearings. She was in bed, hot and slightly sweaty. A baby was crying in the other room, a thin and congested cry. "Gabriel?" she said. "Baby?" For a split second she felt a profound confusion, thinking that this must be a dream because she remembered he was dead, but then she realized she had been dreaming that awful dream in which he had died—that had been part of the nightmare. She leaped to her feet and rushed to the other room, not even noticing the splinter she caught in her heel. "Gabriel!" she cried, and she reached down into the crib to lift him out. He's been alive all along, she thought, folding the swaddling cloth away from his face. The room was dark, and she could barely see him as she lifted him out of the crib. He made odd, congested mewling sounds, distraught with hunger, and he was wet—all over. "Oh, Baby," Glory whispered, pulling the cloth away from where his face should have been. She saw two large eyes there, but something was terribly wrong. Her baby had no hair. Thick tentacles, like the snakes on a Gorgon's head, grew where his hair should have been. And below those huge, goggly eyes, his body was smooth, streamlined, and sticky with a mucuslike fluid.

Glory realized it was not a baby she held in her arms, but something like an obscene mockery of a squid. In the first wave of utter repulsion, she felt compelled to dash the thing against the wall, but she could not. It was hungry and crying, huge tears welling up in those ghastly round eyes. Its tentacles twitched weakly, and it made that wet mewling sound again. Despite her repulsion, and then to her horror, Glory felt a tingling in her breasts as her milk began to let down; the front of her slip grew wet. The thing in her arms must have smelled the milk, because it mewled with greater urgency, flailing its limbs about, drawing them apart to reveal its tiny mouth—a jaundice-colored beak at the center of the mass of tentacles. She could not help herself. It was an infant in her arms, and whether it was a changeling in Gabriel's place or the thing that her own baby had become, it was hungry, in need of nurture, and she exposed her breast, now beaded with white drops of milk, and pulled the thing to nurse. The tiny beak opened wide and clamped down on her nipple. Glory cried out in pain and gritted her teeth as the creature began its urgent sucking. Tears streamed down her face, obscuring her vision, but still, she held the creature, crying with the unimaginable mixture of loathing, love, and physical agony.

When she opened her eyes, they shone a blank red in the cold light, glittering only momentarily as her tears purged themselves on her cheeks. Glory stood up stiffly, her head swiveling slowly toward her right where, from the periphery of the wall, the figures of the two odd men appeared like shadows materializing into three-dimensional shapes. Even when they had taken full form, there was something about the light that made them seem faceted like the compound eyes of a giant fly.

Howard and Lovecraft lay crumpled in fetal positions on the cold stone floor, their limbs twitching randomly as their minds unhinged in the world of their nightmares. Glory moved stiffly toward Lovecraft, and at the wordless command of the odd men, she reached for the pulsing Artifact clenched in his hand.

As Glory leaned over to pry Lovecraft's fingers apart, her last tear trickled down her cheek and splashed on his upper lip. By some instinct that still moved in him, Lovecraft's tongue slowly emerged and tasted the salty teardrop; his body stopped its random contractions and calmed.

Glory moved slowly and purposefully, the Artifact held out in her hand as if to keep her balance as she walked toward the slot at the center of the gate.

LOVECRAFT OPENED HIS EYES but remained in his posture for a moment as he recovered his bearings. His mind was clear now—

exceptionally clear—and his thoughts raced at an incredible speed. Somehow Glory's tear had snapped him out of the spiraling abyss of dementia into which he had been plunging. What was in that tear? he thought. Was there some alchemical healing property in a droplet of salty water from a human eye? Or was it merely that the tear had triggered a familiar idiosyncrasy that momentarily focused his mind and released it from its unfettered demons? He felt an urgent need to ponder this question, but for the moment Lovecraft quickly assessed the situation and rolled into a crouching position over Howard's gibbering form.

The odd men seemed transfixed for the moment, watching Glory approach the gate, and so Lovecraft shook Howard, then slapped him once, twice, three times to help free him from the nightmares that were nearly visible in his half-open eyes. Lovecraft slapped him again and again, and finally, palms stinging, in desperation at his own weakness, he picked up a fist-sized stone and lifted it above his head. Just as he was about to bring the stone down to strike, a spark seemed to leap across Howard's eyes, and he blinked.

"Whoa!" said Howard, forcefully grabbing Lovecraft's poised wrist. "Whoa there, HP! Ain't no call to brain me with no rock."

"Bob," Lovecraft said in relief. "The odd men. We've got to stop Glory before—"

BUT IT WAS too late.

Glory had already placed the Artifact in its slot. The light changed once again, growing colder and more stable. The Artifact itself dimmed, as if it were expending its energies into the gate that now let out a low, guttural animal-like sound.

Lovecraft and Howard leaped onto their feet only to shudder and nearly fall again as the sound increased in volume until it suddenly was a deafening roar that seemed to issue from everywhere at once. By the time they had raised their hands to cover their ears, the sound had stopped, and they were left with a loud ringing in their heads.

"What in the Sam Hill is happening?" Howard cried out. It was hardly necessary to ask, because the answer was obviously before them. But the mere act of talking offered them a solace—an illusion that they were doing something when in actuality they were all but helpless.

"You've read my stories," said Lovecraft.

"Yeah."

Lovecraft watched with solemn resignation as his fiction turned to fact before his eyes. "That, my good friend, is what is happening."

Howard stared as the great doors cracked open for the first time in thousands of years and exhaled a foul, whistling gust of wet and stagnant air. It was so humid that they could see the brownish vapor beginning to form, and in a moment, as the full force of the exhalation reached them, they grimaced in disgust, engulfed in the fetid and fishy odor.

Glory, her task done, quietly collapsed where she stood, as if her body had suddenly lost all animation. In the same instant, the two odd men became more palpable and solid.

Howard motioned to Lovecraft, and the two of them rushed forward to reach Glory before the odd men decided to move.

"We've got to shut that damned door!" said Howard. "You pull the Artifact out while I help Glory."

"Bob, according to the book, it's too late!"

"We gotta do something!" Howard rushed forward toward Glory.

Just then, the two odd men dematerialized and reappeared standing over Glory. Howard was hardly halfway there.

"*Tekeli-li!*" said the larger shadow.

A puzzled expression crossed Howard's face. He hesitated momentarily.

"*Tekeli-li!*" said the other shadow.

"Oh, my God!" cried Lovecraft. "It's true. It's true!"

"*Tekeli-li!*" the odd men said in unison, and they leaped forward.

No human power could have stopped them, but as they attacked, and Lovecraft's will melted before them, some primitive fury awoke in Howard. His vision went red, and a battle madness came over him, leaving him unrestrained as only those without hope can be. He met the odd men's onslaught head-on, grabbing their shadowy limbs with all his animal strength, ripping at their torsos, digging rigid fingers into their strange papery flesh.

Howard's grip held firm in one odd man, but the other literally tore away from him, leaving pieces of himself dangling in Howard's clenched fist. The nearness of death woke a frenzy in him, and Howard fought like a mortally wounded beast. He had no illusion of winning the fight, but intended only to expend all his fury and hatred—everything hateful he had ever felt for anyone, all the anger and resentment toward the world he had lived with until now—he extinguished on the odd man.

There was little resistance. The odd man's body seemed to absorb all the physical and emotional intensity Howard could produce; it grew thick and heavy, as if it were waterlogged, and then it began to press upon Howard from every direction though it engaged him from the front. Howard struggled with a new fury, but felt his strength beginning to flag. It could not last much longer.

Lovecraft was pressed against a wall of stone by the other odd man's unnatural weight. He felt as if the darkness itself were crushing the breath from his lungs; his vision began to dim. With his last remaining energy and will, he reached into his trouser pocket and, producing his flint dagger, brought it up and around with all his might into the odd man's left eye. Lovecraft collapsed, fully expecting, even in his diminished state, that he was dead, but then, unexpectedly, there came a peculiar sound from above him. The pressure on his chest and lungs relented, and Lovecraft opened his eyes to see the odd man rearing back, clutching at the mangled shadows where once his eye had been. Part of his face seemed to have become smoke, and it was curling away, leaving an eerie, flat black convolution of tissue where the eye socket should have been. Lovecraft quickly grabbed a stone and smashed it into the odd man's head. When the form fell, he lifted another, larger stone and bashed its skull until it did not move again.

Howard concluded his fierce wrestling match by using the last iota of his brute strength to lift his odd man off the ground. He held him crushed to his chest in a bear hug, and when he felt something give in the shadow's torso, he quickly stepped back, and like a weight lifter doing a clean and jerk, he hoisted the odd man up to shoulder level and shoved upward with all his might, impaling him on a low-hanging stalactite. He heard the sickening sound of crunching gristle, but what truly disturbed Howard was the fact that he could feel the vibration of the rock grinding through the odd man's body. He let go and stepped aside, watching the odd man give a few weak twitches before he hung limp and his deadweight pulled him down to the ground, leaving the stalactite dripping his dark blood.

Lovecraft could not help but queasily watch the driblets of blood splash onto the shadowy form. Howard quickly lifted another large rock and brought it down solidly on the skull of the shadowy man. The dull explosive thud startled Lovecraft, bringing him out of his distraction.

Now the men turned their attention to the portal, which was more than half-open. Something was emerging from the other side, something oddly indistinct like the faces of the odd men. To Lovecraft, the thing had the appearance of a giant tentacle, like the monstrous appendage of a prehistoric sea creature oozing primordial slime. To Howard the thing was a gigantic black serpent with glistening scales. Both of them saw it slithering toward Glory's still form.

"Glory! Glory!" Desperately, they called out to her to awaken from her trance, but she could not hear them. They rushed to her and grabbed her from either side, pulling her from the dark serpentine thing, but she was frozen in place. Now the dark tentacle suddenly sprouted other, smaller appendages, and these coiled around the two men, entangling them before they could disengage. In moments, they were gasping, their breaths crushed from their lungs.

The giant tentacle touched Glory's body and then, instead of encircling her, it began to envelop her like a fluid. Had it begun at her head, it might have appeared to be a black oil dripping down her body, but it started at the bottom and crept upward in a spiral, tendrils sprouting the way pseudopodia of water stream out of a droplet blown in a heavy wind.

In a few moments, Glory's entire body had taken on the black sheen of the tentacle. To Howard, she had become a statue covered in gleaming, black serpent's scales. To Lovecraft, she appeared to have become infinitely faceted like the sculpted compound eye of a gigantic insect. The surface moved and pulsed as, inside, Glory somehow began to struggle. As the men watched, helpless, Glory began to squirm and twist inside her black shell; they could not imagine what agony she must be enduring, but her openmouthed scream was clearly visible, though covered in the faceted stuff that killed all sound. Glory's struggle became more and more violent, and then, quite suddenly, the texture and color of her covering changed. The form inside—they could not believe it was Glory—spun at an incredible speed, and then, as if the covering were the final stages of a chrysalis, it exploded away, and what remained of the tentacle drew back in a sudden twitch that was clearly pain.

Glory stood there, covered in a grayish, gelatinous slime. Her eyes opened, and she blinked, still stunned by what had just transpired.

"Glory!" called Howard. "Glory! Wake up!"

She turned toward his voice. Her expression changed into one of recognition and then, unexpectedly, she smiled. It was a smile so out of place that it somehow undid all the terror of the moment, and both Lovecraft and Howard felt themselves suddenly full of hope and energy and life. The pulse of the Artifact behind her seemed to grow dull.

"Now!" cried Lovecraft. "The Artifact! Place it in the other slot!"

Glory looked back in confusion, and then, with a visible act of will, she thrust the Artifact into the rough-hewn slot and violently averted her eyes when it exploded with an entirely different sort of light.

The Artifact's cold light and the light surrounding the portal seemed to come from inside the cavern, but this light, which was warm and full of a living energy, clearly came from outside. It was sunlight—or somehow born of the sun—and it blazed in not from the slot, but through the strange Stone-Age technology that the old Hopi and Anasazi had rigged over the centuries. The containers of fluid on the wooden tripods were aligned so that when the Artifact's cold glow reached them, a beam of blue light shot out into the darkness of the cavern. And then, as if pulled in by the blue beam, a blast of yellow-white light returned like an echo from the sun. It was blinding in an entirely different way: where the Artifact's light was intrusive, their bodies welcomed this light, wanted to open up to it as if they were flowers in a field. As the light leaped from tripod to tripod, amplified each time, it also brought a dull rushing sound with it. When the beam touched the Artifact, the slot turned black and the Artifact fell out, having changed from its cold form into something bright and golden.

Now Glory thrust the new Artifact at the dark tentacle, which was already drawing back from the light, and the creature began to recede whence it came. It was ungainly now, like some appendage too large to carry its own awful weight, and it was too slow to pull back into the portal before the removal of the Artifact caused the doors to close.

Everything was still for a moment, basking in the new light. Fabulous colors shimmered through the cavern. Then, like a worm shriveling in the sun, the giant black tentacle thrashed violently about, snapping stalagmites and stalactites like so much tinder as the doorway grated on its hidden gears, and, deep in the stonework, an ominous rumbling sound began. The vibrations spread throughout the cave, gradually rising in volume as it reached a resonant pitch that shook the very air. Stalactites fell from the darkness of the cave's roof like icicles in spring, some of them impaling the monster's giant tentacle, causing it to thrash even more violently, spewing black ichor that sizzled where it touched stone.

Now that Glory was free and he could breathe once again, Lovecraft started the chant which he knew would seal the portal. The words rushed nearly unbidden from his lips, and the weird sounds, unintended for the human vocal apparatus, resonated through the cavern like animal noises and subhuman utterances, mixing into an insane gibbering noise. The sounds echoed in chamber after chamber as if it were a call being answered in kind, and each echo came accompanied with the noise of collapsing stone. The entire cavern was beginning to collapse.

"HP! We have to get out!" Howard motioned to the falling stone. He pulled Glory by the hand, and when he met resistance, he dragged her. "It's all coming down, dammit!"

Again, the light changed, dimming, growing in intensity, dimming again as the tripods shook and then finally gave way. The cavern was plunged into blackness when the tripods collapsed, breaking the beam of light, and suddenly they were all blind, seeing only the purplish blobs of afterimages. For what seemed the longest time, they groped around until Glory located her flashlight and flicked it on to provide a pathetically weak light.

"Bob!" she called.

Howard appeared at her side. He took her hand for a moment, but didn't know what to say. Before he could articulate anything, Lovecraft was there, shining his own beam at them.

"Do you recall the way back?" He shouted to be heard over all the echoes of the collapsing cavern.

Howard pointed, and the three of them ran toward the lake, splashing into the water as rocks and stalactites fell all around them. Behind them, in the blackness, the gate was buried for all time.

As THE CAVE-IN subsided, a fog of dust settled over the surface of the lake, and Glory, Lovecraft, and Howard swam back, struggling to keep their flashlights above water. They were so exhausted they could barely get their limbs to move through the resistance of the water, which felt icy after their exertions. Lovecraft and Howard clutched their rafts and kicked their feet, moving ever so slowly behind Glory.

"Why did it let you go?" asked Howard.

"I don't know," said Glory. "I don't want to remember what just happened."

"Neither do I," said Howard. "I ain't sleepin' again as long as I live."

"May I suggest we refrain from speaking in order to preserve our energies until we are safe?" said Lovecraft.

Howard grunted. They swam on in a solemn silence, hearing only the wet rippling and splashing of water and the occasional aftershock of the cave-in. Glory, the better swimmer, began to draw ahead.

The flashlight beams, jostling about on the rafts, illuminated eerie swatches of color and bizarre formations of rock, all the stranger because they were glimpses out of context. Glory began to imagine what the things might be: giant convolutions on the inside of a stone womb, the wrinkles at the edges of a mother's aureola, the smooth texture of an infant's belly. She tried to soothe herself as she slowed down and floated, waiting for the men to catch up to her. She wanted desperately to be out of the water, and yet she could not bear the thought of emerging by herself and waiting, all alone, not knowing whether they would ever reach the other shore of the lake.

Suddenly Glory heard a sharp intake of breath—almost a squeak—behind her. She turned her head to see Lovecraft's face go under, then bob back up, mouth agape and gasping wetly. He went down again even before he could cry for help, the water bubbling at the edge of his raft, where Glory could see his pale fingers clutching.

"HP!" cried Howard, flailing at the water. "Help him, Glory!"

He tried to keep Lovecraft in the beam of his light, but it was unnecessary. Glory spun in the water and swam quickly toward Lovecraft's light, which jerked wildly underwater as he struggled with something, the dark *thing* that pulled him from below. Glory could not quite make it out, but in her imagination it seemed to be tattered fragments of blackness that reached upward from below, irregular bubbles of darkness attaching their weight to Lovecraft's already exhausted frame. She dove down just as Lovecraft lost his grip on the raft and sank, trailing a froth of bubbles from his nostrils, his expression a grimace of fear and disbelief.

Kicking through the water with all her might, Glory caught Lovecraft before he was too far down, and she sank with him, struggling with the thing that had wound itself around his legs. She had to scissor her own legs around Lovecraft's waist and contort her body downward to use her hands on the black stuff. It clung like viscous gobs of crude oil; it had an icy texture where she touched it, a debilitating coldness that cut into the flesh of her fingers. She clawed at the stuff, hooking her nails into it until she could feel Lovecraft's skin underneath. A large, gelatinous clump came off in her hands, and she shoved it away as if it were some hideous black afterbirth, ripping and pulling at it, imagining the membrane of an unholy placenta, watching with surprise as it oozed a black blood that puffed into clouds like the inky discharge of a giant squid.

Glory held on as long as she could, until her lungs burned and her vision dimmed, and then she gave a final, desperate double-legged kick at the black mass. She suddenly felt it give, and she let go of Lovecraft to fight her way back up to the surface, where she broke the water with a tortured gasp.

"Glory!"

She heard Howard's voice and squinted as his light caught her in the eyes. She tried to ask about Lovecraft, but was only able to sputter and wheeze until she heard the water break again.

Lovecraft's purple face emerged, eyes red and bulging. He let out a frightening cry and broke into a terrible fit of coughing as the air entered his lungs. For a while there was nothing but the sound of coughing and labored breath echoing through the cavern; Lovecraft was too traumatized to offer his characteristic commentary.

Glory made her way back to her raft to catch her breath; she stayed afloat by bearing her weight on the raft, but when she stopped kicking, her legs sank into the water.

She was poised like someone with chin and arms along the top of a wall, looking over to the other side when she felt her legs grow suddenly heavier. The raft bobbed, and water splashed her face. She gasped in alarm and the sound echoed over the water.

"Glory?" came Howard's voice.

"I—" The weight suddenly yanked her under the water, and as her flashlight tumbled down, spinning its light before it went out, Glory saw the large shadowy form of a multilimbed creature, which she knew now, with an inexplicable certainty, was her death. She knew this calmly, as if were no surprise to her. She knew that it was impossible to fight its grip, which pulled like the force of gravity itself. She knew that her body would never be found. And yet she felt no anxiety at all. Not even the urge to breathe one last time as she glided down in the pristine water.

By the time Howard and Lovecraft had frantically paddled their way forward to respond to Glory's cry, she was receding into the depths, already so far down that it was impossible for them to reach her. All they could do was watch, feeling sick and helpless as they trained the beams of their lights on her.

Glory's wide green eyes looked up at them, and she reached her arms toward them as if to embrace them through the distance of the eerily clear water. But she did not struggle at all as the shadow engulfed her and pulled her down, farther and farther until finally she was lost in the darkness. A flurry of bubbles trailed up for a few moments, then fewer and even fewer, until only a last bubble or two marked her passing.

The water was still. Glory was gone.

Howard's first impulse was to dive after her. He plunged his head in the water and angled himself downward, only to remember, suddenly and sickeningly, that he could not swim. While Lovecraft held on to a ledge of stone jutting into the water, Howard clung to his raft, and the two of them vainly shined their dimming flashlights down into the black shadows beneath them until the terrible futility was too much to endure any longer.

They spoke not a word to each other as they made their way back up to the pueblo and the star-filled night sky that awaited them outside. They had saved the world from an unpredicted Armageddon, but all they could think of was the ultimate sacrifice one woman had made for them.

20

ALL NIGHT THE DUST STORM did not abate. They drove on, south on Highway 285 down into Texas, both of them anxious about what might happen if the Chevy were to overheat and yet unable to make the rational decision to stop. They had to keep moving, to get as far from the caves as they possibly could—as if mere physical distance could somehow mediate the tragedy of what had happened—but as they drove it seemed that the car was simply humming in place, the tires spinning idly as the clouds of red dust whirled by in the dark. Toward dawn—at least it seemed to be dawn—the horizon lightened and they could see the road ahead of them, far enough to make out the boxy shapes of old adobe structures. Nothing stirred among the buildings as they approached, and the sign that read "San Robardo" was only a hundred yards from the first reddish wall.

"I'm stoppin' here," said Howard. "Give the car a rest, dust out the radiator before we go on. Maybe the storm will pass."

"Thank you, Bob. That greatly diminishes my anxiety."

"What is it you're worryin' about? We're alive, ain't we? It's Glory that's dead." There was a touch of anger in Howard's voice.

"Let's not argue," said Lovecraft, wearily. "I am in terrible need of something to drink."

After an uncomfortable silence, Howard pulled over at an adobe building with a single, decrepit gas pump in front. Over the open door of the garage, a Phillips 66 flying-horse sign flapped gently back and forth, squeaking on one remaining hinge. The place seemed deserted.

"Must be some soda-pop," said Howard, getting stiffly out of the car.

Lovecraft opened his door and tried to get out, only to fall back into his seat as a sudden sense of vertigo came over him. He calmed his breath and tried again, swinging his feet out first the way he had seen women exit a taxi, and he was able to rise without the shooting pain in the side that had plagued him the past several days.

With Howard out of his immediate proximity, it seemed he could think more easily about what had happened in the cave. It had all transpired so quickly, he thought. There had been no time to be deliberate or rational, no time to make a decision the way a reasonable man should. Why was it that, at the instant when their doom seemed inevitable, the monster had balked? If Glory had been chosen by the odd men or by Cthulhu himself for vulnerability to possession, then why had she been able to resist at the most critical moment? The memory of his own weakness and what it took to bring him back from his infantile withdrawal left him feeling deeply ashamed, and with that, the burden of guilt for having lost Glory, of having possibly been the cause of her death, weighed heavily on his heart.

Howard emerged from the gas station scratching his head. "It's a ghost town," he said. "Nothin', no people as far as I can tell."

"Bob?"

"Huh?"

"I must confess that I do not understand what happened in those last moments at the portal. But even more seriously, I must confess that in my mind I had grossly misjudged Glory. To say I underestimated her would itself be an understatement."

Howard looked away for a moment, and when he turned back, his expression was hard. "Why can't you just say what the hell ya mean,

HP? Why are ya always hidin' behind your fancy sentences and big talk like a damn coward? I know you feel guilty 'cause ya think you failed. God knows I feel guilty. If I could go back, I'd find ten ways to give up my life for her, ya know that? Now we're alive and cursed rememberin' how we failed the person who saved our hides and probably the whole wide world, too."

"I admit I am prone to circumlocution," said Lovecraft.

"There—you just did it again!" Howard grimaced in frustration and smacked his fist into the palm of his other hand, causing Lovecraft to wince involuntarily. "Admit you feel bad, dammit!"

"Bob, you cannot force me to express myself in a mode—"

Howard grabbed his friend by the lapels and drew his face up close so that they were eye to eye. Lovecraft could feel Howard's breath, the dampness of sweat and the texture of grime on his forehead.

"Say it, HP," Howard hissed, slowly relaxing his grip.

Lovecraft stood up from the hunched posture Howard had yanked him into. He began to nonchalantly straighten his jacket, but then he relented, and said, "I feel bad, Bob. I feel terribly guilty."

Howard gave him a tired smile and patted him on the shoulder.

Suddenly, Howard's expression changed again. At first, Lovecraft believed his failure to respond had provoked another burst of irrational anger, but then he realized Howard was looking at something behind him. He turned around.

It was a young boy—perhaps seven years old from Lovecraft's reckoning, though he knew he was a poor judge of childrens' age, having taken great care to avoid them since his own awkward youth. The boy had the light brown skin of a half-blood, but his eyes were a strange green-and-yellow color, rimmed in blue. He stood halfway in the shadow of the empty garage, regarding them in an attitude that seemed oddly mature.

"Hey there," said Howard with a crooked, wholly unconvincing smile.

The boy did not respond. He took a step forward and paused as if to assess them more fully.

"Hello," said Lovecraft. "Can you tell us where we might purchase some petrol and soda pop . . . preferably of the Dr Pepper variety?"

The boy blinked and said nothing, but then pointed with his left arm.

"And where might that be?"

"Awonawilona," said the boy.

"Well, thank you very much, son," said Howard. He motioned Lovecraft to return to the car. He started the engine as soon as he heard the oddly muffled thud of Lovecraft closing his door, but before he could release the clutch the little boy was suddenly standing directly in front, extending a curious hand toward the silver-tinged figure on the radiator cap. "Don't touch that!" Howard yelled, leaning out of the window. "It's hot!"

The boy gave Howard an annoyed glance and firmly grasped the wings of the figurehead.

"No!" Howard swung his door open and bolted from the car to jerk the boy's hand from the angel, expecting to find his fingers scalded by the heat from the overwrought radiator. "Hell, son! Don't ya understand plain English?" He frantically examined the boy's hand, looking for the telltale signs—redness, blistered skin—but was surprised to find he was perfectly fine. "What the hell . . ." Howard looked up quizzically, holding the boy's hand outstretched so Lovecraft could see. Then he reached over, and with his index finger Howard lightly touched the face of the silver ornament for himself. He jerked his hand back with an involuntary yelp of pain when he felt the stab of heat. "Damn it!" He stuck his finger into his mouth.

"Mama," the boy whispered to himself.

"What did you say?"

"Mama," the boy said again, still looking at the radiator ornament.

"You don't say." Howard scratched his head and looked around at the deserted adobe huts, realizing that neither the boy nor anyone else could possibly live there. "I bet you live in Awanalon—Awanawilona, right? Is that where your mama is?"

The boy, still mesmerized by the shiny silver ornament, did not reply.

"How 'bout you hop in with us and we'll give ya a ride back home?"

"Thank you," said the boy.

"Don't mention it, kid." Howard motioned toward his open door and let the boy climb in first.

The boy sat quietly as Howard turned the ignition and started down the road, but Lovecraft felt rather ill at ease with the boy so close and he sat crushed against the armrest on his door to keep from touching him. There was some sort of aura around him—not altogether unpleasant, but both strange and familiar at the same time, like a word on the tip of the tongue. For Lovecraft it felt like something itching from inside, and he drew away lest the feeling become stronger, even more alien and familiar.

Howard sensed it too, but he tried to hide his mild apprehension at what had just happened by clumsily reaching out his free hand and tousling the boy's dark brown hair as he spun the wheel of the car one-handed. For all appearances he had taken on the attitude of a young father on a Sunday drive with his son—and what did that make Lovecraft but an eccentric uncle.

"Now what's your mama doin' lettin' ya go off so far from home all by yourself in a ghost town?" said Howard. "Ain't you afraid at all?"

"No," was the boy's response. He looked up at Howard as if to check if that was the correct thing to say.

Stealing a look down, Lovecraft noticed the chest pocket on the boy's overalls jutted out. The boy looked up at him in the same instant, and Lovecraft instinctively drew even further back against the passenger door, his complexion going a shade paler than its usual sheet white.

The boy smiled, then reached into his pocket and removed two small wooden figurines. He held one out in each hand, one toward Howard, the other toward Lovecraft.

"Bob," said Lovecraft, his eyes wide.

"Yeah?" Howard kept his eyes on the road as he carefully navigated around a patch of some particularly large potholes.

"Our young passenger has some rather interesting toys you might want to examine."

Howard looked down, and when he saw what the boy held out for him, his foot grew momentarily heavy on the accelerator and the car surged. "What's your mama's name, boy?" Howard asked when he had recovered himself.

"Amma."

"What's her last name?"

Now the boy looked puzzled. "What is a *last* name?"

"Well, I'm Bob *Howard*, and this here is Howard *Lovecraft*. The second name is the last name. That's the name we get from our father."

Now the boy looked even more puzzled. "If Howard is the name you got from your father, then how did it become the first name of your friend? Are you brothers?"

Howard scratched his head, frustrated. "That's just a coincidence," he said. "HP?"

"We are not brothers," said Lovecraft. "Many names are similar, and Mr. Howard's last name happens to be the same as my first name. Perhaps in your culture it is the custom only to have a single name. Is that the case?"

"You injuns just have one name?" said Howard.

"Amma is Amma."

"And what is your name?"

"Gabi."

"Gabi? Is that short for something?"

"Gabi is the name of a great winged spirit who is very brave, like the one on the front of your car," said the boy.

"That's a nice name," said Howard. "No wonder you ain't afraid of bein' in a ghost town, huh?"

The boy looked up at Lovecraft and then looked back at Howard. "You are the only ghosts I have met, but I am not afraid of you," said the boy.

"Well," said Howard, "then I suppose there's nothin' for any of us to be afraid of." He looked over the boy's head at Lovecraft who was clearly not amused. "What's the matter, HP?"

"Just my usual twinge of pain." Lovecraft looked forward, then to the side, trying to make out any landmark in the swirling red dust. It was no longer a storm but something more like a fog—tulle fog as he recalled. The sky above looked perfectly normal, but all around the air was thick and occluded, though there seemed to be no reason for the disturbance.

"Here we are," said Howard as he passed the small sign that read "Awonawilona." "You sure this is the place?"

"Please stop here," said the boy.

"But there ain't nothin' around," Howard replied. "I don't see no house or nothin'."

"You can not see our home from here. The gas station is there." The boy sat up and pointed ahead and to the side.

"All right." Howard opened his door and got out, though that hardly seemed the wise thing to do with such poor visibility on the road.

The boy climbed out, pausing for a moment to look back at Love-craft. Howard reached to shake the boy's hand.

"Here, these are for the two of you," said the boy. He placed both of the figurines in Howard's outstretched palm, and before he could refuse the gesture, the boy was already retreating into the red fog, waving good-bye.

" 'Bye, kid!" Howard watched the boy fade into the dust and then he stepped back into the driver's seat and slammed the door. He sat and contemplated the two wooden figures, holding them up against the steering wheel as Lovecraft looked on silently. "Well, I guess this one belongs to you," Howard said, tossing one of them to Lovecraft.

"Why did you ask the boy what his mother's name was?" Lovecraft turned the figure over and over in his hand. It was a fish carved from a pale wood made whiter with a chalky paint.

Howard carefully wedged his figurine—a bear made black with charcoal—between the windshield and the dashboard directly in front of him. "You know why, Pale Fish Man." He shifted the car into gear and got back onto the road.

In a moment, the dust had cleared. Behind them, the landscape was entirely flat, but there was no sign of the boy. And where the road curved slightly uphill, there was no sign of the town of San Robardo. Lovecraft and Howard both noticed these facts, and yet neither one of them said anything until they had arrived at the gas station in Awanawilona and slaked their thirst on Dr Pepper and Coca-Cola.

AT THE BUS STATION in San Angelo, they made their awkward farewells.

"Now that you ain't carryin' that thing no more," Howard said, reaching out and patting Lovecraft on the watch pocket.

Lovecraft grimaced in pain.

"Sorry, HP. You really oughta get that checked by a doctor. You sure you don't want to come by my place and have my father give you a once-over?"

"Thank you, but no. I must be on my way. And I'm afraid the situation would be much too awkward for me to endure. I had the sense that your father also had his hopes up for the possibility that something good would come of all this for your mother."

"We don't need to talk about that," said Howard. "Look, what we need to figure out is what to tell Glory's sister."

"One or both of us shall have to write her a letter. And her purse— I suppose that should be posted with it."

"I ain't very good at that sort of sensitive thing, HP." Howard reached over into the backseat and brought Glory's purse forward. He put the purse in Lovecraft's lap. "You take it, okay? And you send it to her with a letter?"

"Don't worry. I am soured to writing at the moment because I seem to have lost my pen in the cave, but I shall compose something. It will hardly suffice, I must say, but it will have to do."

"Thanks."

"It is my duty."

"HP," said Howard, "I got a question for you."

"Yes?"

"Back in the cave when you shouted, 'It's true!' What did you mean?"

Lovecraft was silent for a moment. "I had a realization. All my life I believed I was using my own imagination to create my weird tales, but that is not true. It was them all along—the ones I called the Night Gaunts. They were planting the images in my unconscious mind for me to discover and turn into tales to release into the world. I was part of their plan all along without an inkling of suspicion."

"You really think so?"

Lovecraft had no answer now.

"You gonna keep on writin'?"

Lovecraft nodded, his face pinched with a half smile.

"Then I'll be seein' ya, HP." Howard extended his large hand, wiping it first on the leg of his pants. "Here's to better times, then."

"To better times. Farewell, Bob."

Howard got into the Chevy, started the engine, and sat for a moment just listening to the rumble. He did not want to go, and yet he did not want to stay. Something had drained him of all impetus at that moment, and he would have been content to close his eyes and sit there for some indeterminate amount of time until the will to live and move entered him once again. It was with conscious effort that he put the car in gear and glanced in the rearview mirror. Lovecraft was already hunched over his satchel, using it as a portable desk on which he was writing a note; he had opened Glory's purse and was looking into it, taking inventory. A good final image, thought Howard, and he stepped on the gas.

EPILOGUE

Thursday, 11 June, 1936
The Howard House
Cross Plains, Texas

IT WAS JUST after seven in the morning when Robert Ervin Howard left the two packets on the front porch for the mailman and went back into the house to stand at his mother's bedside. It had been another long vigil, and his mother had not stirred from her coma the entire night. Howard had stayed awake, keeping the nurse company, then relieving her, giving her a few hours' respite of sleep since he had long since lost the ability himself.

His mother's wheezing breath was growing weaker—even more shallow than before, if that was possible. The fluid in her lungs had drowned most of the tissue, and she lay there looking pale and blue-lipped like a child just come out of a cold spring lake. Howard wanted to speak to her again, to have her say his name or at least glimpse him through her rheumy eyes and give him a final moment of recognition before passing into the next world. He had been thinking, obsessively, over the past few sleepless days, of what he would do without her, what his life with his father would be, what it would mean to stay here, in this house, silent of her harsh breath after all these years, and face the blank pages of his work. A strange calmness had come over him during the past evening, and now that the nurse had examined her for the morning, he felt the confidence to ask his question bluntly.

"How is she, Mrs. Green? Any chance she'll wake up again?"

The nurse gave a wise and weary smile, and replied gently, "No."

"None?"

Almost imperceptibly, the nurse shook her head.

Without a word, Howard walked to the door, and he stood there for a moment, looking back into the room at his mother breathing on the bed.

"Are you okay, Bobby?" said the nurse.

Howard nodded and walked away to his study, where he sat down at his desk and rolled a fresh sheet of paper into his battered typewriter. He sat there calmly for a while, in silence, as if he were surveying the lay of the land on the blank white page, and then he typed one line, then the next, while the air still shuddered with the sound of the carriage being shoved back for the next line.

He looked at the four lines:

> *All fled, all done,*
> *so lift me on the pyre;*
> *The feast is over*
> *and the lamps expire.*

There was an expression on his face now. It might have been a smile, or just some wistful look as he thought about something. He rolled the paper up a third of the way, clicking the gears of the platen, and then, when he was satisfied with the way the quatrain looked displayed there, as if it were a caption to an exhibit, he left his desk. From his cabinet, he removed the .380 Colt automatic. He checked the action, though he didn't check the chamber, because he had loaded it the night before.

Now, gun in hand, Howard walked outside into what would be a beautiful late-spring morning. He stepped down from the porch to his Chevy and gave it a fond pat on the fender as if it were a horse that had seen him through the adventure of the past year. Casually, as if he were going for a morning drive to enjoy the air, he got into the driver's seat, snapped the door shut, and then put the gun to his temple. He paused only a moment before squeezing the trigger.

For an instant, just before the hammer fell, then while the hammer took its quick course to the firing pin, Howard saw a veil of ocher dust pass before the car. He could see someone out there—no, two people—standing, hand in hand, silently watching him. It was Glory, her red hair billowing in the wind, and at her side the Indian boy he and Lovecraft had taken to Awonawilona. They were standing there, silently watching him through the veil of windswept dust, and they were happy. "They're happy," he thought. "God, I wish HP were here to see them."

The bullet entered his head above his right ear and exited out of the left side of his skull. In the last fleeting instant of consciousness—perhaps the residue of perception—Howard saw himself driving through a storm of powdered clay dust, driving swiftly until the sky cracked with lightning and roared with rain, and when the rain touched the dust it turned thick and red, and Howard's last thought was to wonder why the red rain fell on the *inside* of the windshield.

Monday, 15 March, 1937
The Jane Brown Memorial Hospital
Providence, Rhode Island

Howard Phillips Lovecraft closed the battered cover of his journal and struggled, amidst his sweat-soaked sheets, to sit up in bed. He winced again, out of habit, though such an act hardly did justice to the massive agony he felt in his bowels. It had all been a mystery to the doctors, but he himself knew that the cancer had been brought on by the proximity of the Artifact too long in his watch pocket. That spot under his vest had been the origin of the tumor, they said. How it spread so quickly into his intestines was unknown to them, and they would not have believed his explanations.

The last dose of morphine had worn off more than a day ago, but he had not reminded the nurses though the pain had become nearly unbearable. He had known for a while, even before being admitted to the hospital, that his last days were upon him. All his life, he had languished too long in the refuge of that twilight state between sleep and waking; it was time to move on.

At first he thought the morphine they gave him for the pain would grant him visions of the kind he knew the opium eaters had enjoyed, but in his own waking visions he found little of the beauty he had imagined and longed for. It was not the morphine that helped him—it was the sleep the drug permitted, and in the coils of that sleep, the dreams. He had wandered through enchanted landscapes, in gentle perfumed breezes; he had gazed up at alien constellations breathtakingly beautiful; he had sailed rivers with names like poetry and water the color of the sky. And meanwhile, his times of waking had become less and less endurable because of the specter of pain circumscribed by the dull languor of a drug-induced haze. The days and nights all boring in their gray sameness—if this was waking, then he was ready to enter that dream country of which he had written so often, and once entering, he would not return.

The journal felt heavy in Lovecraft's emaciated grip. The weight of memory and experience, the recollection of his time with Howard and Glory, the news of Howard's death, his visit back to Smith, his final confrontation with his nightmares at the Golden Gate. While he had the strength left he reached across to the night table, shuddering with the effort, and took hold of the matches. He lit one, startling at the sharp hissing explosion and the bitter smell of sulfur, and he put the yellow fire to the lower corner of the journal. He was trembling with the pain. He did not know if he could hold it much longer, and so he leaned to the side and dropped the flaming book into the wastebasket, where it made a single, hollow, metallic thump.

He was ready for his morphine now. He would ask for a larger dose—the pain was worse, after all—and he knew that if he asked in the right tone, with that certain inflection in his voice, that certain hollow and pleading look in his eyes, the doctors would take pity on him to make the passage faster. They were eager for his last days to be peaceful, after all, and they had maintained him—sweet irony—in a state like that of conscious death. The cessation of all feeling with a sense of utter tranquility, perhaps the tranquility that came with the extinction of thought.

They will smell the smoke soon enough and come to investigate, he thought, staring up at the flashes of pain-induced light he saw on the ceiling. He heard a loud rushing sound, like the roar of a waterfall. How odd, he thought, that I would hear the sound of water when I have just lit a fire. He turned his head, very slightly, until he saw the bright red flames fluttering in the corner of his vision. So that was the roaring. The fire, red fire, fire red, fiery red, fluttering like hair, Glory's hair, in the wind. Lovecraft sighed and slumped back against his pillows, the flames filling more of his vision, blurring, clearing into the face of Glory McKenna, and at her side, the small boy he remembered from the town of red dust. They were smiling at him, and Lovecraft smiled back, the corners of his mouth only tentatively upturned, expecting another pang in his bowels, but the pain was gone. His smile beamed brighter, and he said, quietly, "Hello." The word did not seem to come from his mouth. It echoed as if the world were hollow and it came from everywhere at once, and far away, so far he could barely hear, came the sound of voices in alarm. Lovecraft opened his eyes wider, gently, expecting to be consumed by the fire, but instead his vision grew paler—degree by degree—until everything faded into a beautiful, radiant white.

AFTERWORD &
ACKNOWLEDGMENTS

According to L. Sprague de Camp, the biographer of both men, H.P. Lovecraft and Robert E. Howard kept up a lively and voluminous correspondence for many years. They almost met in June of 1932, when Lovecraft traveled to New Orleans, but Howard, who lived in Texas, had no money and was unable to secure bus fare to visit his friend.

As de Camp wrote in *Dark Valley Destiny*, his biography of Robert E. Howard, "Ever since, admirers of Howard and Lovecraft have thought it a pity that these two exceptional men failed to shake each other's hands." Indeed, it was these very words which formed the impetus for me to begin the long, tumultuous route to *Shadows Bend*.

And just as Lovecraft could not have made the journey without Howard, I likewise would not even have attempted so massive an undertaking as this novel without my great friend and collaborator, Richard Raleigh. If not for his unflinching belief and enthusiasm in this story and his brilliant, lyrical prose skills . . . one shudders to think!

I would like to extend special thanks to Kelley Jones for passing along his fascination for all things Lovecraftian, to S.T. Joshi for his recent biographical scholarship and annotations of Lovecraftian texts, and lastly (pun intended) to Larry McMurtry for writing *The Last Picture Show*.

—*David Barbour*

I confess that despite my many careers, my first true ambition was to become a pulp writer. My earliest meaningful readings were the works of C.S. Lewis and J.R.R. Tolkien, but it was not long before I discovered Robert E. Howard and H.P. Lovecraft, whose stories struck chords in me on diametrically opposite ends of the spectrum. Their visions were—respectively—viscerally and metaphysically primal for my adolescent self, and though my opinion of their writing changed many times over the years, their works have an enduring place on the bookshelf of my imagination.

I had only heard hearsay about the friendship of Howard and Lovecraft until David Barbour introduced me to the de Camp biographies and the premise that eventually became this book. Though it required much coaxing and encouragement on my part, I am glad I managed to convince him that it was possible to tell this story as a novel. It is his formidable storytelling skill and his insistence on accuracy that form the infrastructure for my fancy footwork.

To Tori Amos I extend special thanks for lending a layer of meaning that would otherwise be missing from this book. It was by synchronicity that I heard her talk about her miscarriage and her visions of her Pueblo boy; though we had already written a red-haired Glory with a troubled family history and the loss of a half-blood child, it was ruminating on the meaning of the coincidence that made me determined to add certain layers of resonance that would mediate an otherwise male-centered story line. A portion of our royalties will go to R.A.I.N.N., the organization that Amos cofounded for survivors of rape and incest.

And to Leslie Marmon Silko, sincere and belated thanks for the sage advice you offered an aspiring pulp writer when you were Vassar's first Writer-in-Residence. I have taken that advice to heart.

—*Richard Raleigh*

The authors would jointly like to extend their gratitude to the following people: James Merk for providing valuable commentary on the early chapters. Peter Quinones for sharing his knowledge of the life of Clark Ashton Smith. Boyd Pearson for his wonderful Clark Ashton Smith web site all the way in New Zealand. George Haas for invaluable details about the Smith cabin. Ted Naifeh for his early drawing for the *Shadows Bend* proposal. Rick Klaw, for his continuing interest in the project and the veiled threats regarding misrepresentations of Texas, Texians, and Texicans. Joyce Carol Oates for adding literary cachet to the H.P. Lovecraft revival. Arkham House for keeping HPL's memory and works alive. Frank Frazetta, Barry Windsor Smith, and Arnold Schwarzenegger for their representations of Conan the Barbarian. Tracie and Anne for their tolerance and patience (which we know grew thin many times). Susan Allison for the patience that made the quality of this final product possible. Regula Noetzli, for placing the manuscript, though she hardly knew what she was unleashing for the millennium. Meade, for her beautiful Tori Amos web site and for answering the odd late-night queries about Tori's eyes. The Hopi Nation, whose tolerance we beg for the poetic license we've taken with the myth of the four worlds. The illustrious John Dee, whose fragmentary transcriptions of the *Necronomicon* have come to mean so much to those of us who don't read Arabic or Greek. And finally, all you Cthulhuvians out there who keep the mythos alive—*IÄ CTHULHU!*

The title of this book was discovered one night during a dreamquest.

http://www.shadows-bend.com